Checking Out Crime

A BOOKMOBILE CAT MYSTERY

Laurie Cass

$7.99 USA
$10.99 CAN

ISBN 978-0-593-19771-4

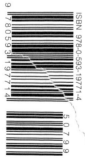

Titles by Laurie Cass

Lending a Paw
Tailing a Tabby
Borrowed Crime
Pouncing on Murder
Cat with a Clue
Wrong Side of the Paw
Booking the Crook
Gone with the Whisker
Checking Out Crime

Checking Out Crime

A BOOKMOBILE CAT MYSTERY

Laurie Cass

BERKLEY PRIME CRIME
New York

BERKLEY PRIME CRIME
Published by Berkley
An imprint of Penguin Random House LLC
penguinrandomhouse.com

ISBN: 9780593197714

First Edition: March 2021

Printed in the United States of America
1 3 5 7 9 10 8 6 4 2

Chapter 1

When we're children, we have all sorts of expectations. We expect to go to school. To learn things. Make friends. Memorize locker combinations. We also expect that someday we'll do things. Maybe great things. That we'll go forth and conquer. Be successful. Marry. Have children. Travel.

For me, the husband and child predictions had been a bit fuzzy, but my career expectations had been specific. At the ripe old age of seven, I decided I wanted to work in a library because then I'd be able to read all day and no one would order me to put my book down and go outside and play because otherwise my eyes were going to get stuck and I'd have to wear progressively stronger glasses the rest of my life.

In due course, I followed through with my decision and was now, at age thirty-five, the happy assistant director of a library in Chilson, Michigan, a lakeshore town in northwest lower Michigan. What I hadn't expected was that I'd be living on a houseboat and driving a bookmobile with a cat as my copilot. But it was an adorable houseboat, running the bookmobile program was tremendously rewarding, and the cat . . . well, he somehow made everything shinier.

Most of the time, anyway.

It was a fresh September morning. Birds were singing, the sun was shining, and I was humming to myself as I tidied up after breakfast, when my feline companion started making troubling noises. "Eddie," I asked, "what are you doing?"

Catlike, he didn't say a thing. Which could have been because he was busy trying to get his nose into the tiny gap at the back of the houseboat's dinette seats. More likely, he didn't feel like responding. And, since he was a cat, whatever he didn't feel like doing, he didn't do.

"There are days," I said, "that I wish I were more like you."

Eddie's yellow eyes flicked in my direction, then away.

For once, reading between the kitty lines was easy. "Yes, I know that anyone with any sense wishes to be a cat in general, and you in particular, but not everyone has sense, now, do they?"

My black-and-white tabby abruptly abandoned his efforts, jumped to the floor, and bumped the top of his head against the back of my leg. Since Eddie is a good-sized cat, this popped my leg forward against the kitchen cabinet.

"Ow!" I tossed the dish towel onto the tiny counter and rubbed my knee. "That's proof. Washing breakfast dishes is hazardous to my health."

"Mrr."

"A bowl of cereal and a glass of orange juice is

the definition of breakfast, my furry friend. At least for all five feet of Minnie Hamilton." I eyeballed myself from toe to shoulder. Other youthful expectations of mine had been that I'd grow taller than my mother and that my freakishly curly black hair would magically straighten. I'd given up on the height thing, but there was always a chance my hair would fix itself someday.

"Ready, Freddie?" I opened the door of the cat carrier. Eddie trotted inside, flopped onto his soft pink blanket, and glared at me.

"Giving me The Look won't get us there any faster," I told him.

"Mrr," he said, and kept on saying that as I carried him into my car, as we pulled out of the marina parking lot and drove past the house where I'd soon be living, and the entire time we drove through downtown Chilson and to the library.

Downtown, with its mix of old and new buildings, some made with wood, some with brick, and a few made with stones hauled years ago from nearby fields, was a complex delight every time I remembered to look around. Today, however, my noticing capacity was limited because Eddie kept distracting me with a running commentary I had no chance of understanding. After we reached the library, he mrr'd as I ran through the preflight bookmobile checks. He mrr'd as I carried him inside and strapped the carrier to the floor of the passenger's side, and he mrr'd at Julia Beaton, my outstanding part-time bookmobile clerk, as she bounded up the stairs.

"And a good 'mrr' to you, too, Mr. Eduardo," she sang out.

I squinted at her. "Do I detect a new accent?"

"My dear assistant library director, there is no such thing as a new accent."

What she'd said sounded familiar, but only sort of. "Did that start as a Mark Twain quote? About ideas?"

"Ideas, accents." She waved a suddenly languid hand. "What's the difference?"

I grinned. It was going to be one of those days, in which the only thing to expect was the unexpected. Julia was in her mid-sixties and had spent years on-stage in New York swooping up suitcases full of awards. When the roles started to dry up, she convinced her husband to move back to her hometown of Chilson, where she grew increasingly bored until my aunt Frances mentioned that I was looking for part-time help. Five minutes after we'd met, I made up my mind to hire her. This decision was confirmed her first day on the job when she started to talk to Eddie just like I did, pretending that he understood every word.

This was important because Eddie was a fixture not only in my life, but also on the bookmobile. He'd stowed away on the vehicle's maiden voyage, and though I'd tried to keep his presence a secret, Eddie wasn't big on secrecy, and even less big on staying in the cabinet I'd tried to hide him in.

Keeping my then boss, Stephen the Stickler-for-Rules, from knowing about Eddie's presence had kept me in anxiety for some time, but it had worked out in the long run and these days I couldn't go anywhere without someone asking how Eddie was doing.

I settled into the driver's seat and glanced over at my furry friend. Two and a half years ago, Eddie had attached himself to me when I'd gone for a walk on an unseasonably warm April day. The fact that this attachment had happened in a cemetery, next to the final resting place of Alonzo Tillotson, born 1847 and died 1926, should have meant that the cat's name would be Alonzo. But Alonzo is a very long name to call a cat, especially since they never come when called, and the name Eddie just fit. He was a very Eddie-like cat.

"Nothing yet?" Julia asked as she buckled herself into the passenger's seat.

"More specifics, please." I started the engine, dropped the transmission into gear, and eased the thirty-one-foot-long vehicle out of the library's back parking lot. "Nothing as in nothing ventured, nothing gained?" I started warming to my theme. "Wasn't it Maya Angelou who said 'Ain't nothin' to it, but to do it'? And don't forget Emily Dickinson's poem that 'Saying nothing sometimes says the most'? Or—"

Julia flung out her long arm and pointed in the direction of my hands. "As in no engagement ring."

I looked at my naked finger. "Oh, that."

"Yes, that."

Fun fact: When a Broadway actress wants her tone to be sarcastic, the sarcasm is so thick it's almost visible.

"How long ago did he propose?" She *tsk*ed at me. "Without a ring, can you trust the man?"

I thought for a moment, then gave a heavy sigh. "That's a good question."

Julia's head whipped around fast enough to send her long strawberry blond braid flying. "It is?" Her mouth dropped open.

"Well, no," I said. "Rafe is the most trustworthy man on the planet. But it was fun to see that shocked look on your face."

"Huh." Julia's feet tapped the top of Eddie's carrier. "Did you hear that, my fine feline friend? Minnie caught me by surprise. Who would have thunk it?"

"Mrr."

The two of them carried on a conversation that didn't include me, so I started thinking about Rafe Niswander, my fiancé. He'd proposed just over a month ago, but we hadn't taken any steps toward the actual wedding since then. This was mostly because Rafe was a middle school principal and right now, at the beginning of the school year, he was busy with zillions of meetings, which left him with little time to think about how and when we wanted to get married.

"See that?" Julia asked, nodding in my direction, but still looking at the carrier. "She's thinking about Rafe."

"Mrr?"

"How can I tell? Soft eyes, goofy smile, warm heart. All of that."

"Mrr."

"I absolutely agree," Julia said. "She's known the man for how long? More than twenty years? And *now* she's suddenly all goo-goo about him? I mean, he's the same guy he was when she got the library job and moved to Chilson permanently. Why the lovefest now, and not then?"

Another good question, and one I'd pondered myself. Rafe, tallish, darkish, and handsome-ish, had indeed not changed a bit since I'd first met him on Chilson's city beach, the first summer I'd been sent north to stay with my aunt Frances. That was the same summer I'd met my best friend, Kristen Jurek, so maybe the two-girls-against-one-boy element had something to do with the delayed love. Or maybe it had taken me this long to recognize that Rafe's annoying habit of pretending to be far dumber than he was would never change and I might as well get used to it.

Or, far more likely, I simply hadn't been ready. Rafe had recently confessed that the gorgeous old house he'd been renovating for three years had been for me all along, and he'd almost given up hope I'd ever come around to loving him.

Every time I thought about that, I shivered. "Timing is everything," I said to Julia.

"Huh." She flopped back against her seat. "Truth in three words. But I still want to see a ring."

So did my mother, sister-in-law, and oldest niece. My dad, brother, nephew, and younger niece were more concerned with making sure we picked a wedding date that didn't interfere with the play-off schedules of multiple sports teams. "What kind of ring would you like me to have?"

Julia perked up. "I get to pick?"

"No. But before you slump, all exaggerated and actor-like, I'd be happy to hear your ideas."

"Nothing normal," she immediately said. "There's nothing average about the two of you, so your rings should reflect non-normality."

I wasn't sure "non-normality" was a word, but I let it go. "You made 'ring' into a plural. How many are we talking about?" I wiggled my empty fingers against the steering wheel. "I'm not used to wearing any." Long ago, I'd had a high school class ring, but that had been lost after my junior year when I'd jumped into Lake Michigan on Memorial Day after being dared to by Kristen. Every part of me had shrunk from the frigid water temperature and my ring had slipped off into the sandy bottom, lost forever to the vagaries of water and wind.

Julia held up her left hand, three fingers extended. "One engagement ring for you. One wedding band for you. One wedding band for Rafe."

"Sounds normal. I thought normal was out."

"You have to maintain some semblance of normalcy to function in society," she said severely. "All three rings need to match, but they can't be overly matchy-matchy. That's cutesy and I can't recommend that in this case. You're too short to do cutesy."

"Or inclined," I said.

"What? Never mind. Doesn't matter. Now, as I was saying, the style of all three rings needs to match."

"Why?"

Julia sighed. "Have you not been paying attention to wedding fashions? No, don't answer that. I'm sure you have not, in spite of both Kristen and your aunt Frances getting married this year, so it's a good thing you have me to help out."

"So lucky," I murmured.

"Yes, you are. Now. The engagement ring is the first step in your forever relationship. This ring symbolizes everything the two of you have done to date and everything that will happen in the future."

Since we'd come to a stop sign, I felt free to raise my hand. "Question. Isn't that a big burden for a hunk of metal and rock?"

"Can't quite hear you over this noisy engine," Julia said, unnecessarily raising her voice. "You might want to have that looked into. But rings are important," she went on more moderately. "Every day for the rest of your life, there they are. Every waking hour you'll notice them on your hand. Make a bad choice, and you'll regret the decision forever."

I glanced over, trying to remember the kind of rings Julia wore. "Voice of experience?"

"You tell me." She pointed at the tiny diamond and narrow wedding band on her left hand. "We were young and poor and bought the cheapest rings in the store. All we could afford, see? We could buy something fancy now, but we like to remember those early years."

I smiled. Julia had a streak of sentimentality in her. Who would have guessed?

"Now," she said, settling back into her seat. "Let's talk rocks. Big ones, because you deserve it."

So we did—or at least she did—the rest of the day. And since it was a very long day, my interest in talking about rings, weddings, receptions, and honeymoons had waned hours before we finally turned toward home. Even Julia's deep well of imagination must have been running dry because her final attempt was weak.

"You could," she said, "have your engagement ring match your wedding. Wait, I have it! An emerald ring and a *Wizard of Oz* theme. Wedding gown like Glinda's dress, put Eddie in a basket like Toto, and the three of you can leave in a balloon."

The idea was ludicrous and I was about to say so, when Eddie did it for me.

"MrrRRR!"

Julia sighed. "Sorry, Edmeister. I know that one was stupid. I'm tired, that's all." She looked over at me. "We're not going to do this kind of day again, are we?"

I hadn't wanted to have such a long day in the

first place, but my boss, Graydon Cain, director of the Chilson District Library, had asked us to try it. Though he was a decent guy, he'd only been director for a few months, and I wasn't sure enough of our relationship to say a flat-out "no" when he asked if the bookmobile would be willing to attend a township board meeting in the farthest-flung corner of Tonedagana County.

"It's a night meeting," he'd said, "but it starts at seven and the township clerk says their meetings hardly ever run more than an hour. The days up here are so long you'll be back before sunset."

He'd been right, but only partly. Though the meeting, which included a tour of the bookmobile by the board members, had indeed lasted less than an hour, the sun was dropping behind the tree line as we pulled out of the parking lot. Twilight lingered long in midsummer, but now that the equinox was approaching, it would be full dark in less than half an hour.

"It was a long day," I said to Julia. "A good one, though, don't you think?"

"Huh." She tapped the cat carrier with her toes. "Did you notice that, Eddie? She didn't swear on a stack of first-edition Angela Thirkell books that we are never, ever, ever going to spend another fifteen-hour day in the bookmobile."

Assuming we didn't get lost on the way back to Chilson, which was unlikely since I'd driven this route through the county's hilly back roads a hundred times in the last two years, her number was an exaggeration by at least four hours. "Ours not to reason why," I said. "And the board members really enjoyed going through the bookmobile."

"Sure, but there's no way we can fit another stop

into our route. We're already starting to turn people away from some stops to get to the next one on time. And soon we'll have to be dealing with snow and our driving times will be a huge question mark."

These were all things I knew. And Julia knew that I knew, because we'd already talked about them ad nauseam.

"It's only September," I said.

"Mid-September." Julia slouched down. "Look out there. The leaves are starting to change."

I squinted through the windshield. Sure, there were a couple of orange- and red-tipped maple leaves in the passing trees, but roughly 99.9 percent of them were still a lush green.

"It's only September," I repeated. "There are weeks to go before we have to start thinking about snow-covered and slippery roads."

"Minnie, how are—"

I cut her off. "We're not going to worry about it."

The unspoken question chewed at both of us. If Graydon wanted more stops on the route, we'd need more bookmobile staff. And that meant . . . well, I wasn't sure what it meant, exactly. But it would certainly mean changes for us and for our patrons, which meant there would be issues to deal with, both foreseen and unforeseen.

The foreseen things we could take care of. It was those sneaky unforeseen things that could throw the whole program into disarray and chaos and start it sliding into a downhill trajectory that ended in a quick sale of the bookmobile to the highest bidder, who I was already envisioning would be a local plumber, and I'd have to spend the next twenty years of my life watching it haul pipe.

"I thought you said we weren't going to worry." Julia was looking at me, doing the one-eyebrow thing. "No saying you weren't, because that little vertical line between your eyebrows is telling the truth."

My right hand went to my face and felt around. Sure enough. I scrubbed at my eyebrows with my palm. "Ta-da! All gone, see?" I turned to show her.

Gasping, she pointed at the windshield.

I whipped around to face front. Though the bookmobile hadn't strayed a millimeter from the center of our lane during my second and a half of inattention, during that brief period of time, an on-coming car had zoomed into view.

Its headlights pierced the dusk and flared bright into my eyes. I immediately did as I'd been trained and looked down and right to watch the white line at the edge of the asphalt. But since we were on a back road there was no white line, so I trained my gaze on the edge of the crumbling asphalt.

From the angle of the approaching vehicle's headlights, I could tell that it was encroaching into our lane. Careful, oh so carefully, I edged the book-mobile as far right as possible. On this road, falling off the pavement could mean a drop into soft soil. With the bookmobile's weight, that could mean a sudden shift in center of gravity and a rollover, something I desperately wanted to avoid.

"He's going to hit us," Julia said in a high voice.

My attention was focused entirely on keeping us on the far edge of the road. "It'll be fine," I said calmly. "I got this."

"He's going to—"

The vehicle zoomed past in a quick *swoosh* and

was already out of view when I glanced in the side mirror.

"Well." I realized there was no air in my lungs, so I pulled in a deep breath and let it out. Wherever the driver was going in such a hurry, I hoped he or she got there without hitting anyone or anything. "That was interesting. Eddie, are you okay?"

"Mrr."

Julia turned to give me a look I felt without seeing. "How can you be so worried about things that haven't actually happened, yet be so cool and collected during an actual scary thing? Do you realize how close we came to getting sideswiped?"

"Well, we're fine, just like I said we would be. And I said we're not going to worry about Graydon wanting more outreach hours, remember?"

She made a scoffing noise that was almost certainly rude. But since I was feeling the aftereffects of an adrenaline rush—sweaty palms, metallic-tasting mouth, et cetera—I didn't have the energy to call her on it.

"That's what you said out loud." Julia made a talking-hand-puppet gesture I could barely see in the glow of the dashboard lights. "However, in spite of your affirmed and reaffirmed vow to be like your aunt Frances and not worry about anything, we all know you do. Constantly."

"Not constantly," I protested.

"Mrr!"

I slid an annoyed glare in my cat's general direction. "No one asked your opinion, buddy of mine."

"Oh, dear." Julia looked through the holes of the cat carrier into its dark interior. "Now you've gone and hurt his feelings. You wouldn't believe the look he's giving you."

I could easily believe it. Though my childhood had been without pets due to an allergy-prone father, I'd lived with Eddie long enough to learn a lot. Specifically that cats were better than any creature on earth for expressions that, if the universe were created in a slightly different manner, would reduce the object of those expressions to smoking rubble. They might feel bad about it afterward, but not for long.

"Mrr!" he said again.

"Sounds like he's trying to tell you something," Julia said. "What do you think it is? Could it be he's hit upon the perfect style of engagement ring? Has he found a solution to Graydon's overly ambitious outreach expansion? Or is he trying to tell us the secret to the universe, life, and everything?"

Smiling at the *Hitchhiker's Guide to the Galaxy* reference, I said, "Or he's telling me it's way past his suppertime. Wonder which scenario is more likely."

"MRRR!"

"Really?" I asked, wincing at the glass-shattering decibel level. "Could you tone it down a little? The bookmobile is big, but it's still an enclosed space and—"

Whatever silly thing I'd been about to say was lost forever, because I was suddenly much too busy driving to think about anything else.

"*Minnie!*" Julia screamed.

This time I didn't say it would be fine. This time I didn't say I had it, because I wasn't sure I did. This time I wasn't doing anything except smashing my foot on the brakes as fast as I could as hard as I could.

Because we'd just come around a curve, and lying in the road, directly in front of us, was a man.

"No, no, no," I murmured as the bookmobile locked into a screeching skid, and it was as much prayer as anything. There were so many things that might go tragically wrong. Maybe we wouldn't stop in time and we'd hit that poor guy. The back end of the bookmobile could start swinging around and I'd lose control. We could—

"No, no, no," I said again, and focused on keeping us straight and solid. A small part of me heard Julia's panicked yells, and another small part of me hoped that Eddie was hanging on tight, but the only thing I saw was the man's legs, bare from mid-thigh down, coming closer and closer.

"Please, no," I whispered. "Please."

I heard shrieking noises and I didn't know if the noise came from the brakes, Eddie, Julia, or myself. We slid, slower and slower and slower . . . and finally, finally came to a stop.

"Call nine-one-one." I punched the four-way flashers, unbuckled myself, and ran to the door.

"What do I say?" Julia called.

I left her to figure that out on her own, because I was already hurtling down the bookmobile stairs and onto the road. We'd managed to stop before hitting the prone figure, but I hadn't seen any movement. That an approaching vehicle, let alone something the size of the bookmobile, hadn't made him even turn his head was a bad sign.

Running, I came around the front, into the beam of our headlights, and saw our large tires stopped two feet away from the prone man wearing a colorful shirt, black shorts, and odd-looking shoes.

I dropped to my knees. "Sir? Do you need help?" I asked, tapping his shoulder gently and looking around for signs of blood or other injuries. It was library policy that all bookmobile staffers be certified in first aid, and I was beyond glad I'd taken a refresher course last summer.

"Sir?" Still no response. I studied his chest.

Julia hurried toward me. "An ambulance is on its way," she said. "Ten minutes out. Fifteen minutes tops. How is he doing?"

I shook my head and started chest compressions. I'd continue doing them until I couldn't do them any longer; then Julia would take over.

But nothing we did would matter, because even with my limited medical knowledge, the signs were there. There was no rise and fall of his chest, no pulse, no eye movement. No movement at all.

He was dead.

Chapter 2

The ambulance lights were circling, making the scene around us turn red, then white, then red, then white. I found myself mesmerized by how the colors moved on the nearby trees. Funny, that green leaves could look so very non-green when lit by a red beam. I frowned, trying to put a name to the temporary coloration. Brown? Amber? Something else? Maybe it was a color without a name. Or maybe—

"Ms. Hamilton?"

I sighed and turned to face the sheriff's deputy, whom I'd never met until now. For a very short while, I'd dated Deputy Ash Wolverson and had known ninety percent of the employees in the sheriff's office. But that had been a year ago, and while Ash and I were still good friends, my insider knowledge of the sheriff's staff had reduced significantly. People retired or left for new opportunities, and those taking their places were unknowns in terms of personalities, habits, and senses of humor. "Sorry. What was the question?"

Deputy Nowlin was looking at me. "Are you all right, ma'am?"

Of course I wasn't. I'd almost run someone over with the weight of twenty-three thousand pounds, done my best to save the life of that still-unknown someone, and failed miserably. My throat ached with the tension of not giving in to tears, my heart was sore, and now my feet were tired from standing around for an hour. Julia had already done the interview thing and was waiting for me inside the bookmobile. The only thing I really wanted to do was go home and snuggle with my fiancé and my cat. And now this young and overly polite law enforcement officer was calling me "ma'am." It wasn't to be borne.

"Minnie," I reminded him. "Please call me Minnie."

"Yes, ma'am," Deputy Nowlin said. "You came upon the victim." He tipped his head, indicating the exact location.

Since we were standing in front of the ambulance, which was in front of the bookmobile, there was no way I'd be able to see the poor man's body, but still I avoided looking.

The deputy was still talking. "After stopping, Ms. Beaton called central dispatch. You checked for signs of life. Seeing none, you performed CPR until the EMTs arrived."

"That's correct." I heard my lapse into report-speak. "I mean, that sounds right."

The deputy nodded and slid his notebook in his shirt pocket. "The victim is wearing bicycling clothing. When you approached him, was he wearing a helmet? Did you take it off to perform first aid?"

"No helmet," I said, trying not to take offense at

the implication that I'd neglected to tell him something so important. "And no bike. I've been wondering how that might have happened, but the only
thing I've come up with is he had a flat tire somewhere and was walking home." Although that scenario didn't answer the question of how he'd ended
up lying in the middle of the road.

"We'll look into it."

He sounded confident in his use of the "we" pro-
noun and I smiled at him fondly. It was obvious the
poor boy had no idea that Detective Hal Inwood
and detective-in-training Deputy Ash Wolverson
would take his report and he'd never again be part
of the investigation.

Then I remembered something I had, in fact, neglected to tell him. "The car." I whirled around to
face the direction it had gone.

"What car, ma'am?"

I gazed into the dark, trying to summon the details from the eternity of an hour earlier. "A few
miles before we . . . found the victim. A car came
toward us around a curve, swinging so wide it almost
hit us. I'm sure he was speeding." Thoughts and theories tumbled around in my head. "There were no
other oncoming vehicles. He had to have seen our
victim. Why didn't he stop? Or did he hit him, and
that's how he died?"

The deputy was already reaching for his notebook. "What can you tell me about the vehicle?"

"It was dark," I said, trying not to sound defensive.
"Or almost. And I was more focused on avoiding a
collision than reading license plates."

"Yes, ma'am. But any information would be helpful. Was it an SUV or a sedan? Were the headlights square? Round? Those bluish ones? Was a headlight aimed high or low?"

I eyed him with an increased measure of respect. The kid was good. Unfortunately, I wasn't. At least not with car stuff. "Sorry, I don't remember. But Julia might."

At that exact moment, Julia's stage voice, the one that had easily carried to the back seats in the top balcony, pierced the night. "Eddie! Stop! Minnie, he's doing it again!"

"Rotten cat," I muttered as I hurried over, visualizing the events. Julia had let Eddie out of his carrier because she felt sorry for him being cooped up. Eddie, who typically stayed inside the bookmobile as long as people were on board, had decided he'd been in there long enough and had trotted outside.

Normally, this meant a short game of Eddie-hide-and-Minnie-seek, but this was different. We were on the side of a road. And it was dark. Really dark. The moon hadn't risen, and the closest streetlight was ten miles away.

"Here, Eddie, Eddie, Eddie!" I should have saved my breath. If he'd wandered off in search of whatever, the last thing he was going to do was reverse his direction to answer my call.

"I am so sorry," Julia said, coming up alongside me.

"Don't worry about it. Did you see what direction he went?" We stood at the bottom of the bookmobile steps. "Left? Right? Straight?" Please not straight. That would be directly north into a thick forest where there was even less light.

"Mrr!"

"That way," Julia said, pointing right, and the two of us jogged in that direction.

"Ms. Hamilton?" Deputy Nowlin called. "Ms. Beaton? Is there a problem?"

"Be right with you," I said over my shoulder. "We have to capture a cat, is all. Shouldn't take a minute."

Julia snorted. "Can't believe you said that and didn't get struck by lightning."

I was a little surprised myself. "Eddie! Where are you?"

"Mrr."

"Did he sound closer?" Julia asked. "I think he did."

I thought she was delusional, but I didn't want to burst her bubble. "Eddie, Eddie, Eddie, come out come out, wherever you are!"

"Mrr!"

Julia, who'd turned on her phone's flashlight app, aimed it in the direction of the feline vocalization. "There! I saw something."

I pulled my phone out of my pocket and thumbed on its light. "I saw something, too, back behind that first line of trees." But it hadn't looked like my black-and-white cat. It had looked metallic.

"Wait here," I told Julia, and jumped across the ditch.

"Mrr." Eddie materialized out of nowhere and thumped the top of his head against my shin.

"Yeah, good to see you, too, buddy." I scooped him up into my arms. "But I want to see what this is about, okay?" We waded through thigh-high grass and then under a canopy of maple trees, where last year's leaves scuffed underfoot. And there, leaning against the back side of a massive tree trunk, was an expensive-looking bicycle with a helmet dangling from the handlebars.

I stood there, staring, then called out, "Deputy? You're going to want to see this."

Later, I was on the houseboat's deck with Eddie, curled up on one of the two lounges, staring at the stars and thinking sadly about this and that, when I heard familiar footsteps on the marina's dock. I smiled into the dark. Soon, everything would be a little bit better.

"Saw your kitchen light was on," Rafe said. "You still awake?"

"Mostly." I scooted over to one side of the lounge. "There's room for all three of us if you don't mind a bit of a squish."

"Squishy is my favorite thing. I thought you knew."

"Last week you said beer was your favorite thing."

"I have lots of favorite things." My beloved rearranged a sleeping Eddie, sat, swung his long legs up onto the lounge, and leaned back. "Good thing you're so short," he said. "This way there's room for me to put my arm around you."

So many responses, so little time. As I tried to choose the best reply, he pulled me close, nestling my head against his shoulder. "How are you doing?" He kissed my forehead and my insides melted a bit. "Your text messages were informative, but only in a factual sense."

I tried to put my skittering thoughts into a semblance of order. "I'm fine. At least I will be."

He hugged me hard. "Good. Because you promised, remember?"

"I did?"

"Sure. You said you'd never become a burden."

That didn't sound like something I'd say. Not that I ever intended to be a burden, of course, but I didn't like to make promises I didn't have complete control to keep. "When did I say that?"

"Let's not get all detaily." He kissed me again. "So we've established that you're not actually fine. You're traumatized in a number of ways, from that car almost hitting the bookmobile, to the bookmobile almost hitting the guy in the road, to not being able to resuscitate him. What are you going to do to heal yourself?"

"I'm not traumatized."

"Are, too," he said. "You're human, aren't you? Hang on, let's check." He tugged lightly on my hair. Pinched my cheek. Wiggled my nose. "Yep. Flesh and blood. And despite your penchant to find dead bodies, there's no way you've become so accustomed to it that you're immune to the trauma of doing so."

"Penchant?" I snuggled into him. "Did someone give you a word-of-the-day calendar?"

Though Rafe often acted as if he'd left his last brain cell in the trunk of his first car, he was actually very intelligent. Accordingly, he ignored my question. "Traumatized," he repeated. "And you know what that means."

I did. It meant my aunt Frances would want to coddle me. That my friend Kristen would berate me. That the library staff, marina staff, marina residents, and everyone else I knew would want details. It also meant one more thing to avoid talking to my parents about.

"Is there any chance," I asked, "that I could be you for a week and you could be me?"

"There's an idea." Rafe smoothed my hair. Unsuccessfully, because the curly stuff coming out of my head resisted all such attempts. His own hair was as black as mine, but shiny and sleek, which went hand in hand with the slightly reddish tone to his skin, both of which were likely inheritances from distant Native American ancestors.

He played with a stray lock of my hair. "How do you feel about one-on-one meetings with parents who are convinced their offspring are being irreversibly damaged by what the school is teaching them?"

"Is that why you were working so late tonight?"

He grinned and even in the dim light I could see the gleam of his white teeth. "The final set of parents and I did eventually adjourn to a different location."

I sniffed loudly. "Do I detect the scent of Hoppe's Brewing?" Chilson's first brewpub, owned by two sisters who rejoiced in the last name of Hoppe, had opened a few weeks ago. But since I wasn't a huge fan of beer, I hadn't made any effort to become a regular patron.

"They're expanding the menu," Rafe said. "You're going to love the gnocchi with tomatoes and mozzarella."

I made a mental note to try it as a take-out lunch. Then I sighed, because the trauma-induced conversation wasn't over. "I didn't text you everything about tonight. We figured out who he was." There'd been a small nylon bag strapped under the bicycle's seat. Deputy Nowlin had unzipped it and found a cell phone and a wallet.

Rafe's arm tightened around my shoulders. "Anyone we know?"

I hadn't, but I hadn't been bred, born, and raised in Chilson like Rafe. I hesitated, not wanting to break bad news. "His name was Brown Bernier."

"Brown?" Rafe's arm went stiff. "You're kidding!"

"Did you know him?"

"Level three, is all. But he's been a three for years."

"A what?"

Rafe sighed. "How can it be that you've never learned the levels of friendship?"

"Surely you're not telling me I don't know how to be a good friend."

"Surely not. What I am telling you is any non-relative can be categorized into one of five different levels of friendship."

"Five," I said, "Why five?"

"Because that's all there are. Level one is someone you meet once and probably never will again. Level two is a nodding acquaintance. Level threes are the ones you'd have a beer with if you ran into them. Level fours are people you make an effort to keep in touch with, and level-five friends are the people who know you inside and out."

It all made sense, in a Rafe-like sort of way. I wondered how it was I'd never heard of his friendship levels before but decided to pursue that some other time. "How did you know Brown?"

"Through Tank."

Tank, whose birth certificate read Cecil, was a high school friend of Rafe's. He'd once been a roofer but now worked for Tonedagana County as maintenance staff. "How did Tank know him?"

"Brown did the city's general maintenance. Nice guy. When Tank was new at the county, Brown helped him out quite a bit and they turned into fishing buddies. He retired just a few months ago. Beginning of the summer, I think it was."

"Was he married? Kids?"

"Pretty sure he was married. I think he had at least a couple of kids. And at his age, probably grandkids, too."

I thought about all the things Brown would be missing, all the things he'd assumed he'd have time to do. Spending more time with his wife. Helping his kids with their home improvement projects. Teaching his grandkids to fish. Watching their soccer games and band concerts.

"You in there?" Rafe tapped my temple. "You're thinking about all the things Brown didn't get to do, aren't you?"

The man knew me well. Level five. "It's so sad," I murmured.

"You did everything you could do. Everything anyone could have done."

"But he's still dead."

Rafe brushed my cheek with the backs of his fingers. "Yes. He is."

For a few minutes, we listened to Eddie's sleepy purrs and watched a half-moon rising above the trees that rimmed Janay Lake. A breeze stirred the lake's surface and came our way, brushing across our skin like a cool, soft sheet. Mid-September was a lovely time of year in the North. The tourist crowds had thinned and the weather was still warm, but there was a hint of chill in the wind that reminded me how close we were to winter. In a few weeks Janay Lake would be frozen and Lake Michigan, just past the western tree line, would be dotted with floating chunks of ice.

"It's getting colder," I said.

Rafe hugged me tight. "Better?"

"Yes, but I was thinking seasonally, not immediately."

"Farmer's almanac says we're in for a mild winter."

"How nice. You do realize that even a mild winter means temperatures below freezing. Within a few weeks."

A stone's throw away was the house Rafe had purchased soon after I'd moved to Chilson. In its one-hundred-years-ago youth, it had been a showpiece of Shingle architecture, but over the years it had been carved up into tiny apartments. Rafe had removed all of that and was slowly restoring it to its original glory. Though he'd been living in it himself for months and was ready to have his fiancée and her cat move in with him, my sinuses didn't like the idea of sleeping in the dust of a construction zone, and paint fumes gave me nasty headaches. Besides, Eddie didn't care for the loud noises of power tools.

"Lots of weeks," Rafe said. "First day it stays below freezing won't be until November."

He spoke with confidence and I believed him. I also didn't care. "You do realize my boat doesn't have central heat. And that I don't have a budget for the repair of frozen pipes."

"Don't worry. It'll be fine. You won't freeze and neither will your pipes."

I trusted this man more than I trusted myself, but even in these final phases of renovation, things could happen to derail the entire Minnie-moves-in-early-October plan. I made a mental note to devise a Plan B. Aunt Frances and new husband, Otto, might be okay with me as a roommate for a few weeks. And there was Cousin Celeste. Or Kristen.

"One of these days," Rafe said, "we'll have to get you a ring. Any thoughts on what you want?"

"Julia designed ten different versions for me today."

"Any that you like?"

"Not a single one." The black diamond she'd described had sounded gorgeous, but then I'd looked it up on my phone and seen how much they could cost. Rafe had to be spending a frightening amount of money on the house and I didn't want my ring to cause him financial pain.

My legs, under the weight of a sleeping Eddie, were themselves going to sleep. I shifted, but slowly, so as not to disturb my furry friend. "I've been thinking. What's the point of paying for an engagement ring? It's not like we're any less engaged without one."

"Male pride," he said. "No way am I going to let Ash Wolverson think he could have done better, ring-wise."

It was a ridiculous statement in a wide variety of ways. But I did believe the kernel of it: that Rafe wanted me to wear his ring. This warmed my heart and, for some reason, almost made me cry.

Which was when I realized how tired I was. A few minutes later, Rafe left and I headed to bed, where Eddie was waiting for me. He'd plopped himself in the middle of the narrow mattress, so I slid him over and wedged myself between the sheets.

Exhaustion had hit when I was brushing my teeth, and I was sure I'd fall sound asleep as soon as I closed my eyes. "Night, Eddie," I murmured, and through the sheets and quilt, I felt the rumbling comfort of his nearly silent nighttime purr.

But as I lay there, waiting for sleep to overtake me, what happened was my mind stirred the evening's events around from one side of my skull to the other. One thing led to another, and soon I was wide awake, with question after question tugging at me.

How had Brown died? There'd been no evidence of injury. A heart attack? Then why had his bicycle, which hadn't seemed to have a thing wrong with it, been hidden behind a tree? And why had he been in the middle of the road?

The next day was a library day. Eddie normally let me know that he didn't approve of library days, since he vastly preferred days that he rode along in the bookmobile. This morning, however, he was snoring hard when my alarm went off, was still sleeping when I finished my short shower, and was still asleep after I ate breakfast and went back to check that he was breathing.

"Yesterday tired you out, didn't it?" Trying not to get any Eddie hairs on my library clothes, I kissed the top of his furry head. He opened his eyes the thinnest of slits, closed them, sighed, and managed to make himself go a teensy bit flatter on the bed.

"Poor little guy," I murmured, patting his hip. "See you tonight, okay?"

He didn't "mrr" in reply, but he did purr, which reassured me that the previous day's events hadn't caused any lasting damage. And which told me that though Rafe was probably right, that I was at least a little traumatized, Eddie probably wasn't. At the door, I blew a kiss to the back of the boat, which my cat ignored. I smiled and went out into the morning.

Dawn had long since broken, and there were signs that my marina neighbor to the west, Eric Apney, was already out and about. His morning newspaper was flopped atop a back deck table, his coffee mug on top of the untidy sections. Eric was a divorced downstate cardiac surgeon in his mid-forties and spent every minute he could Up North. In a couple of weeks his boat would be stowed away for the winter and he'd spend his nonworking weekends on the slopes of Colorado.

My eastward marina neighbors, the retired Louisa and Ted Axford, had already pulled up stakes. In the old days they'd been one of the last boats in the water. Now, however, there were adorable grandkids downstate and I wondered if they'd be selling their boat. The marina's slips were very close to each other—only a few feet apart—and having polite neighbors who were considerate and fun was something to celebrate. If the Axfords sold, something for which the marina rats had already set up a betting pool, who would I get for my new neighbors?

Then I remembered. In a few weeks, just like normal, I'd be moving, but I wouldn't be hauling my belongings up the hill to the boardinghouse. And next summer, I wasn't going to be schlepping my stuff back down the hill to the marina. In a few weeks, I'd be living in Rafe's house. *Our* house.

I walked past my future home, looking for signs of renovation progress. There weren't any, of course, because Rafe had been at my place until nearly eleven the night before, and he routinely arrived at the middle school an hour before classes started. Still, I looked. My imaginary X-ray vision saw the upstairs master bathroom as I'd seen it last. Unfin-

ished drywall, unfinished flooring. No sink, no toilet, no tub, no cabinets,

Though going downstairs to use the bathroom
wasn't a real problem, I was concerned that if I ac-
cepted the unfinished status before moving in, the
house would never be completed. One of these days,
it was going to get done, I was sure of it. But I vastly
preferred that day to be before our tenth wedding
anniversary.

"Or our first," I said to the seagull who was
squawking at me, and waved it off. "Nothing for you
today. Or ever, to tell you the truth."

"Making new friends, are you?"

I turned to see a white-haired man walking toward me, smiling and waving his cane in a friendly
fashion. "Good morning, Mr. Goodwin," I said,
smiling back. "How is my favorite library patron?"

"Let me guess," he said. "That's what you tell everyone who walks into the library."

"You think we'd give kitchen privileges to just
anyone?"

"Yes."

He was right, of course. But we'd only opened up
the staff break room to all library patrons after we'd
learned of Mr. Goodwin's near addiction to caffeine.
"Are you coming in today?" I asked. "We haven't
seen you much this summer. We've missed you."

"And I've missed you, but the grandchildren kept
us remarkably busy. Took me two weeks to recover.
These old bones, you know."

I didn't believe a word of it. I'd long ago learned
that the cane he carried was more hiking stick than
elderly assistance. Mr. Goodwin's morning walk
was a five-mile loop that included hills steep enough

to make a car downshift two gears. More likely he and his wife just needed some peace and quiet after school started. Then again, Mr. Goodwin had to be close to eighty years old. I peered at him, trying not to look like I was giving him a visual physical. "Your bones look the same as they did in June."

"Only on the outside, my dear. Only on the outside." He smiled and headed on his way, and I continued on mine.

Library days were often walk-to-work days for me. Coward that I was, rain would push me to drive, as would freezing rain and howling blizzards, but in every other kind of weather I walked up the hill from the marina to the heart of Chilson. Normally in mid-September, the summer crowds had already tailed off, but a recent article in a popular national magazine aimed at retirees seemed to be bringing more folks to town than usual. Though northwest lower Michigan had been a popular location for retirees for decades, the article was catching a lot of interest and there was some grumbling that you could have too much of a good thing. But I decided not to think about that and focused on enjoying the blue sky up above and the sun on my face.

"Morning, Minnie," Tom Abinaw said as he swept away a leaf that had had the temerity to fall in front of his store.

Tom, known throughout the land as Cookie Tom, was the skinniest baker I'd ever met. How he managed to cook such amazing pastries yet stay so thin was a great mystery of life. "Morning, Tom. Bookmobile day tomorrow."

He nodded. "I'll have a bag waiting."

Tom had my eternal gratitude for giving me a reduced rate on the cookies I bought for bookmobile
patrons. Even better, in summer, he let me come in
the back door to avoid the long line that snaked
through the store.

"You're the best!" I called over my shoulder.

"How nice of you to say so," said a voice from the
other side of the street. "But what is it I'm best at
doing?"

I grinned at the fiftyish dark-haired woman sitting on the front step of a retail store. "Pretty much
anything you feel like," I said.

And I meant that from the bottom of my heart.
Pam Fazio had spent most of her life in Ohio and in
her old life she'd spent decades working graphic design and marketing for a corporate conglomerate.
One morning she'd woken up, realized she was unhappy, and cast about for something new to do.

Thanks to a random website search, she'd seen a
picture of Chilson's downtown and instantly decided to become a part of it. Thus, Pam now owned
and ran the very successful Older Than Dirt. Its ec-
centric collection of old and new fit into Chilson's
retail landscape like a hand in a glove and I was beyond pleased that we were friends.

"Got an extra, if you want one." Pam nodded at
her steaming mug of coffee and patted the seat next
to her.

Upon her departure from corporation-land, Pam
had vowed that every morning the rest of her life
she'd drink her first cup of coffee outside in the
fresh air, and as far as I knew, she'd kept that promise. Well, if you counted the glassed-in front porch

of her house as outside, which I did when there was active precipitation or any temperature below forty-five degrees.

"Thanks, but I can't. I need to get up to the library ahead of Kelsey."

"There's a distinct line," Pam said darkly, "between need and want." But she said it with a smile and toasted me with her mug as I hurried off.

Pam was right. We often said "need" when we meant "want." This pertained to new cars, food choices, and the type of countertops ordered for a kitchen. Coffee, though, was different. Drink the wrong kind in the morning, and it could instigate a bad mood that permeated the rest of the day.

I hurried through the rest of downtown, up the hill, and into the library, giving scant attention to the glorious building around me. Most days I made a point to appreciate the former school, renovated a few years ago into a library so stunning it was a regular stop for architecture buffs. Wide oak doors opened to a flagstone-floored lobby. To the left was the former gymnasium, now the main stacks, lit by Arts and Crafts chandeliers above and similarly themed lights on individual desks. To the right were the checkout desk, children and young adult sections, restrooms, and offices. Upstairs was the slightly scary boardroom, the director's office, the computer lab, and the Friends of the Library book-sale room.

Oak trim was everywhere, metallic tile surrounded drinking fountains and doorways, and on the far side of the checkout desk was my favorite part of the entire building: the reading room, with its window seat and working gas fireplace. The reading room was the hangout spot for people from ages ten to a hundred and ten, and it was the heart of the library.

Yes, on most days I appreciated it all, and especially appreciated the generosity of Chilson's taxpayers, who had approved a special millage, but this morning I was on a mission.

Without even bothering to drop my backpack in my office, I zoomed into the break room, which was . . . empty. Perfect. I smiled and opened the cabinet to begin the coffee-making task. Three seconds after I'd put the filter into the basket, I heard footsteps and turned. There, in the doorway, was my coffee nemesis, the person in the library who made coffee strong enough you had to stir it with a stick. For me, caffeine was the staff of life, but I didn't need—or want—hair to grow on my chest.

"Hah!" I held the coffee scoop high, brandishing it like the trophy it was. "You snooze, you lose."

"Well, dang." Kelsey Lyons, one of our part-time clerks, made a face. "And I was so sure you'd be late today, what with your accident last night."

I felt my insides crumple. For a few minutes, the coffee race had pushed Brown's death out of my head, but now the memories came rushing back.

"She doesn't want to talk about it." Holly Terpening, a full-time clerk, took the coffee from my hand and nudged me into a chair. "Look," she said. "I got up early and made brownies."

"Brownies? Cool!" Josh Hadden, our in-house IT guy, came into the room.

Holly slapped his reaching hand. "Minnie gets first pick."

I shook my head, smiling. Holly and Josh acted more like sister and brother than many brothers and

sisters did. And, since Holly's brownies were legendary and there was the off chance that they might
still be warm, I opened the container and felt no
compunction about taking the first one. "Thanks,
Holly. You're right, I don't want to talk about it. But
I will answer one question each."

Kelsey, Holly, Josh, and I were all about the same
age. I got along well with the entire library staff, but
the four of us had a bit more in common with one
another than with the seventy-something ultrafit
Donna, or Gareth, our fiftyish maintenance guy, or
even the just-past-forty library director, Graydon.
The other part-time clerks were either in the early
twenties range or retirement age. All of us worked
together swimmingly, but mutual age is a bond that
can't be denied.

"Was it anyone we know?" Holly asked.

Via morning text messages to Ash, I'd confirmed
that the name was now public knowledge. "I won't
count that as a question. He was the city's maintenance guy. Brown Bernier."

Though all three knew the name, none of them
knew him personally.

"I was in high school with one of his sons," Kelsey
said. "But he was a senior when I was a sophomore,
so we didn't mix much."

"Was he really wearing a bright pink shirt?" Holly
asked.

Josh rolled his eyes. "That's your question? Seriously?"

She shrugged, making her long, straight brown
hair flip forward over her shoulders. "That's what I
heard. And who else is going to tell me?"

To keep them from starting a regional conflict, I

said, "His shirt was multicolored. There was some pink in it, but not much."

"Good morning." Graydon poked his head in the doorway. "Kelsey, Holly. Do you two have a minute? I'd like some help with rearranging the boardroom. Got a call that the chamber of commerce meeting room had a water leak and they need an emergency location."

They went off. I took a bite of brownie and set the remainder on a napkin. The baking had been a kind gesture of Holly's, but for some reason, one bite was enough.

"Can I ask a question?" Josh sat next to me.

"Sure, it's your turn."

"Not about last night." He took a brownie. "It's about Mia."

Uh-oh. Mia was Josh's girlfriend. As far as I knew, they'd been getting along like peanut butter and jelly. "What did you do?"

Josh rolled his eyes almost up into his wavy dark hair. "You sound like Holly. Why do you assume I did something wrong?"

"Precedent. If you didn't do something, what's the matter? I thought things were good with the two of you." Mia was adorable and her career was also in IT. Which was all I knew about her profession. Every time I asked her about it, she told me, and I walked away with no real idea of what she actually did.

"Things are good. It's, well . . ." He toyed with the brownie, sending crumbled bits of it to the table. "I asked her to move in with me. At first she was on board for it, but now she's backing off."

"It's a big step," I said. "A little fear is understandable."

"Sure. I get that." Josh frowned. "But it's not like her to go back on a decision."

"Did she say she was going to move in?"

"Well, not those exact words."

"Then there you go. She hasn't reached a decision yet, is all. Give her time."

Josh's face cleared. "You know what? You're right. Thanks, Minnie!" He jumped from his chair, grabbed both his brownie and mine, and sauntered off, grinning at me over his shoulder.

"Funny," I said to no one, but it kind of was.

My smile only lasted for a moment. Because I was suddenly back in the bookmobile, driving, barreling through the darkness, straight toward a man lying in the road.

Traumatized, Rafe had said. Maybe he was right.

I pulled in a breath and let it out. Traumatized or not, I had a job to do.

So I stood, poured myself a cup of coffee, and went to start doing it.

Chapter 3

A couple of days later, after a night of nearly trauma-free dreams, I gave Eddie a gentle pat and headed out with the full intention of walking to work. Three steps onto the dock, lightning flashed, thunder crashed, rain poured down, and I ran pell-mell for the shelter of my car.

I'd parked facing the water, and through the windshield, across the wide sidewalk rimming the marina, I could make out the unmistakable shape of Eddie's face smushed up against the houseboat's rear window. This meant he was standing on top of my small nightstand, having scattered everything on it, which ranged from a stack of to-be-read books to my alarm clock to a box of tissues.

"Down!" I mouthed loudly, and pointed at him with a threatening index finger.

His mouth opened and closed in what was, from here, a silent "mrr"; then he did what he would have done if we'd been in the same room, which was ignore me.

"Horrible cat." I started the car and headed to

the library, but I was smiling. Seeing his furry face behind the lace curtain had been pretty funny. Why he'd decided to climb up there, when he'd never been interested in that particular climb before, was another unanswerable Eddie question to add to the list.

I mentally added to the list throughout the day and was still adding to it when I walked through the front door of Lakeview Medical Care Facility.

"Why," I asked Heather, one of the many outstanding certified nursing assistants at the facility, "do his hairs end up in places he's never been, up to and including the library's freezer and the couch at my parents' house in Dearborn?"

"You're talking about your cat, not your fiancé, right?"

"This time, yes."

"Do you really want to know?"

I laughed. "Probably not. What's the book of the month?"

The two of us were in a comfortable living room–type space. Couches and armchairs abounded, with plenty of space for wheelchairs. A couple of years ago, I'd begun stopping at Lakeview to visit a friend of mine in rehab after a stroke. During that time I'd developed a friendship with the fortyish Heather and we'd concocted a Book of the Month read-aloud program. Residents voted on the book they wanted to hear, and volunteers dropped in to do the reading. We now had so many volunteer readers that the books were almost being read quickly enough to change the program's title to Book of the Week.

"*Snow Falling on Cedars*." Heather handed me a

bookmarked copy. "They're up to chapter fifteen, and don't let him tell you any different."

"Him who?" Although I had a good idea who she was talking about.

"Me!" said a proud voice. "Maxwell Compton at your service." Max, skinny, severely arthritic, and at least eighty-five years old, thumped his narrow chest.

"Interesting." I rubbed my chin. "And here I always figured your name was short for Maximilian. Or maybe Maximus."

"Wouldn't that have been fun?" He sounded wistful. "But back to the critical point our Heather just made, I'm quite sure we're only starting chapter fourteen."

Heather laughed. "Try telling that to Mrs. Bryant. You know she barely tolerated that chapter the first time, let alone a second."

"Please?" Max wheedled, clasping his hands. "Her memory is worse than mine. She'll never know the difference."

I deeply wanted to open the book up to the fourteenth chapter to see what it was that Max wanted to hear again. And just as deeply, I didn't want to see. How my brain could have two ideas at the same time that were in total conflict with each other, I did not know. I only knew it was true.

"Sorry, Max," I said. "No way am I going against Heather."

He banged his fist on the arm of his wheelchair. "You women stick together, don't you?"

Heather slung her arm around my shoulders and I wrapped my arm around her sturdy waist. "You bet," she said. "We're like Laverne and Shirley."

"Cagney and Lacey," I said.

"Betty and Wilma. We could do a show ourselves, I bet. Minnie and Me."

"Minnie Hamilton?"

I turned.

The couple standing in the doorway looked sort of, but not quite, familiar. "Yes? May I help you?"

"Don't you remember?" the man asked. He was of a size that meant a lot of shopping at the big-and-tall store, and his wife wasn't much smaller. They were both sixtyish, wearing shorts and comfy-looking walking shoes. His shirt was bright yellow and had the logo of the Los Angeles Lakers across the front; her shirt was a more sedate light pink polo. "Out past Dooley, a few weeks ago?"

The light bulb went on. "Will!" I said, smiling and hurrying forward. "And Iris! How are you? How is . . ." I faltered, because I realized, two words too late, that I should have kept that question entirely to myself.

Iris patted my arm. "Yes, he passed away. But don't worry, honey, we made it there in time, thanks to your wonderful bookmobile."

Both Heather and Max were looking a little too interested in this conversation. Max, of course, was the one who opened his mouth. "Sounds like story time to me." He rubbed his palms together. "You've been holding out on us, Minnie."

"There isn't much to tell." I shifted, wanting to change the subject, but not sure how to do it without hustling Will and Iris out of the room.

"Not much to tell? Hah!" Will slapped me on the back. I managed to keep my balance, but it wasn't easy. "This little one came to our rescue when no one else would. Cars passed us by, left and right, but she's the only one who stopped."

"Someone would have," I murmured.

"And it would have been too late." Will thumped me on the shoulder. "There we were, Iris and me, stranded on that stretch of county road east of Mitchell State Forest. You know, the one everyone takes as a shortcut to get to Dooley?"

Heather was eating this up. "Sure. There's no cell phone reception for miles."

"Bingo," Will pointed at her. "We're in a hurry to get to the hospital because my old man's on his way out for the final time and—"

"God rest his soul," Iris said.

"Sure, you bet." Will squeezed my shoulder, which made an odd *pop*ping sound under his grip. Though I tried to keep my wince invisible, I was pretty sure Max noticed, because he gave me a sly wink. "Anyway," Will went on, "Dad and me hadn't talked in years. The stubborn old coot thought I was nuts to buy that time-share condo down in South Carolina—"

"Which we still have. We go every year," Iris cut in.

"Yeah, we love that place. Anyway, one big family Thanksgiving dinner at the old house, Dad kept going on and on about it. I told him to stop, but of course he wouldn't. Finally, I stood up said, 'Iris, we're leaving and not coming back until he apologizes.' We walked out the door and didn't look back."

"Never did get a bite of turkey that year," Iris said, sounding regretful.

The scene was easy to imagine. A table crowded with family, the patriarch at the end, looking over his offspring and their families, and, in this case, passing judgment. Classic stuff, really.

"Must have been hard on your mom," Heather said.

Will shook his head. "Mom passed the year before all this. He was a cranky old bugger before she died, but turned a lot worse after she was gone. Anyway, that was twenty years ago—"

"Seventeen," Iris said.

"Right, almost twenty years back. And Dad and me haven't said a word to each other since. But then my baby brother calls and says Dad's at the Petoskey hospital, had a bad heart attack, and isn't supposed to last much longer. Well, my Iris here said we had to go. So we jumped in the car, took that shortcut, and wouldn't you know it, the transmission went out and we were dead on the road. Popped the hood, but no one stopped, not until this little girl in that great big bookmobile stopped for us."

"Took us all the way to the highway," Iris said. "Miles from where she wanted to go."

"That's right." Will beamed down at me. "Drove us to that gas station, where we could get cell phone reception and call a friend who could get us to Petoskey."

"We are so grateful, Minnie," Iris said. "If we'd spent any longer stranded, I doubt we would have made it in time to say good-bye."

I smiled but was uncomfortable with the effusive praise. Julia had been more helpful than I'd been with talking to them and figuring the logistics. All I'd done was drive. "Glad we could help."

Will gave my shoulder what I hoped was one last pat. "Timing is everything, right? We were on our way out after seeing a neighbor and heard your name. Can't be that many Minnies around here. Especially ones this short." He laughed. "You're a mini Minnie! Get it?"

Smiling as much as I could at a joke I'd heard ten thousand times, I said, "Happy to hear everything worked out."

Max watched the pair as they walked away. "Minnie, my dear one, do you recall their last name?"

I tried but couldn't get there. "Started with an A, I think. Maybe an H? I remember thinking it sounded like a Greek name."

"Hallenius?"

"Sounds right. Do you know them? Why didn't you say?"

"Because that stubborn old coot they were talking about was a friend of mine."

"Oh, Max. I'm so sorry."

His thin shoulders went up and down. "Well, he was old. And he really was a cranky bugger. I didn't connect the dots right away, because Fred always called his son Willy. And I never knew the wife's name. He called her 'That Woman Who Ruined My Son's Life.'"

"Sounds like a great guy." Heather rolled her eyes and walked over to finish setting up the room for Reading Hour. "Forgive me for speaking ill of the dead, how was it that you and a man like that were friends?"

"Worked together," Max said. "Not a speck of charm in him. Never had anything good to say about anyone. The kind of person who left half a cup of coffee in the pot so he wouldn't have to make new."

But even though he was doing nothing but bad-mouth Fred Hallenius, there was an expression on his face that gave me the feeling he was more upset about Fred's death than he was letting on.

Gently, I put my hand on his shoulder and again said, "I'm so sorry."

"You're a good girl, Minnie." He patted my hand. "Get to my age and there's not many of us left. You know what the moral of the story is?"

"What's that?"

"Make young friends," he said, winking at me. "Now, back to chapter fourteen, yes?"

Rain had been falling intermittently all day long, and it seemed to be falling the heaviest whenever I needed to venture out into it. I stood in the shelter of Lakeview's big entrance awning and peered through the deluge at my car, which was in the far corner of the parking lot. An hour and a half ago, I'd intentionally parked there because I'd been virtuously leaving the closer spots for folks who might not be as hale and hearty as myself. But the parking lot was mostly empty and the gesture I'd proudly added to my mental list of good deeds now looked stupidly unnecessary.

Deeply regretting that I'd left my umbrella in the car, I sighed and took a step toward what was going to be an instant drenching, when I felt my cell phone vibrate in the pocket of my raincoat.

I pulled it out and took the call. "Hey, Ash. What's up?"

"Can you stop by the sheriff's office?"

"Sure. When?"

"Right now would be good."

I looked balefully at the sky. Just when you thought it couldn't rain any harder, it did. If I went out there now, I'd inevitably end up with wet socks. I hated wet socks.

"It's about Brown Bernier," Ash said. "There's something you need to know."

"Be there in five minutes." I thumbed off the phone and ran into the rain.

Four and a half minutes later, I squelched my way into the lobby of the sheriff's office. Behind the bulletproof glass, a woman in civilian clothes looked up from her computer and came to the window. "Are you Minnie Hamilton?"

She looked about my age, give or take a couple of years, and had enviable straight brown hair cut into wavy layers that looked as if they did exactly what she wanted them to. I wanted to dislike her, but her friendly smile made it impossible.

"That's me." I peeled my raincoat from my skin and shook as many drops as I could onto the absorbent mat. "Sorry about the mess, but it's ark-building rain out there."

"No worries. Deputy Wolverson said to tell you he's waiting in your regular room."

I smiled. In the past two and a half years I'd spent so much time in the sheriff's office I'd been thinking of asking if I could have a plaque installed with my name on it, but I couldn't decide between "Minnie's Annex" and "The Hamilton Room." "Have you worked here long?" I asked. "I don't think we've met."

"Chelsea Stille, the new office manager. I've been here almost two weeks."

I'd heard Sheriff Kit Richardson was finally getting around to replacing her longtime office manager, who had retired a few months ago, but I hadn't heard the deed had been done. "How do you like it so far?"

"So far, so good," she said cheerfully. She buzzed the door open, we gave the "been nice to meet you" greetings that people do, and I headed down the hallway to my room.

Inside, the too-handsome-for-his-own-good Ash Wolverson was already sitting at the chipped laminate table that should have been retired out to pasture a decade ago. He was flipping through a small pile of papers and frowning.

"Hey." I hung my still-dripping coat on the back of the chair opposite him and sat down. "What's the deal?"

Ash flipped the folder shut. "We have to wait for Hal."

Two things were suddenly making me uneasy. One, having to wait for Hal, which meant the conversation was going to take a far more serious tone than I'd been mentally prepared for. Two, that Ash wouldn't look at me directly. He only did that when he knew I wouldn't like what was about to happen.

"I'm getting a bad feeling about this." I tucked my hair behind my ears. Rather, I tried to. My way-too-curly hair was unmanageable at the best of times, and now that I'd been out in the rain, it bounced right back out from where I'd put it. "Do you think Hal will be long?"

"He's with the sheriff." Ash glanced at the door. "Sorry to make you wait. She called him into her office just as we were heading in here."

"Uh-oh." I laughed. "Is Hal in trouble?"

It was hard to imagine. Detective Hal Inwood

had retired Up North after a career as a detective in greater Detroit. The story went that after three months of retirement, he and his wife had so little to talk about that he came into the sheriff's office begging for a job. The second part of the story was the sheriff didn't hire him at first, saying she didn't want any bad downstate habits in her people, and that she didn't hire him until he passed some sort of test.

I wasn't sure I believed any of that, especially the part about the test. If there had been a test, the entire office would have known about it, because men talk just as much as women do when it comes to something like that. And since no one could tell me what the test had been—and I'd done my best to find out, once I'd heard the rumor—I'd decided it was complete fiction.

"Hal is not in trouble," the detective himself said, coming into the room. He sat his tall self next to Ash. "Good afternoon, Ms. Hamilton. Or evening, I suppose it is now."

The small room, with Hal in it, suddenly seemed to be twice as crowded. I swallowed down a faint feeling of claustrophobia. "What's in that?" I pointed at the closed folder. "Ash said there's something I need to know."

"Yes." Hal, whose long face could look mournful on the sunniest summer day, sighed. "That contains the preliminary findings for Brown Bernier's death. Though the autopsy has been performed, the full report won't be available for some days."

That was all standard information. They wouldn't have dragged me in here to tell me things I already knew.

So I waited.

"Mr. Bernier was sixty-six years old." Hal pulled the file toward him but didn't open it. "The cause of death was from a blow to the head."

I frowned. "That doesn't make any sense. We found a helmet next to his bike, so it only follows that he wore it when riding. And his bike was behind a tree. How could he have fallen from his bike and hit his head?"

"He didn't fall." Hal laid his hands flat on the folder. "The findings clearly indicate skull fractures that could not have been caused by a fall. In addition, there were no other injuries consistent with a fall. No scrapes or abrasions of any kind, no dirt on the knees, hips, palms, or elbows."

My mind was blank. There was a conclusion right in front of me, but I didn't want to make the jump.

Ash glanced at Hal and received a small nod. "Minnie," Ash said gently, "Brown Bernier didn't have a bicycling accident. He was murdered."

Chapter 4

My first reaction was textbook. "No," I said, denying reality. "That can't be right. There are all sorts of ways he could have died. Tell your pathologist to look again."

"Minnie—"

I ran over whatever Ash was trying to say. "How can you be sure that doctor checked for everything? It's only been a few days. I'm no doctor and I can think of a whole bunch of ways he could have died. Heart attack, for one. Did your doctor look for that? Or a stroke. You don't have to be elderly to have a stroke, people get them at every age. You can even have them before you're born! Or an aneurysm. There are lots of kinds of those. In your brain, or in your heart. And I've read you can get aneurysms anywhere you have arteries, so I bet those are tricky to pin down. And . . . and . . ."

All through my soliloquy, Ash and Hal kept looking at me with calm compassion. When I ran out of possibilities, which didn't take too long because my medical knowledge was limited, silence filled the room.

Death came in many guises. A calm death at the end of a long life, like Fred Hallenius, was one. Though you might always grieve when an elderly friend or relative passed, it was the natural order of things. And though accidental deaths and early deaths from disease were awful, they were also part of the human experience. But murder? Murder was an intentional snuffing out of a life. A violation of every value system I knew. An assault against all that was right and good in the world.

My breaths were going in and out as fast as if I'd just finished a hard run. I crossed my arms and shifted rapidly into grief's second stage: anger.

"Why are you telling me this?" I demanded. "All I did was come up to him after he was already dead. What are you going to do, arrest me for not finding him early enough to save his life?" I made fists of my hands and stuck them out. "Slap the cuffs on me, Officer, it was me. I did it."

Ash laid a hand across my wrists and pushed them softly to the table. "Minnie, we knew this was going to be hard on you. That's why we asked you to come in. We wanted to tell you this in person, not over the phone."

Detective Inwood stirred. "There was nothing you could have done, Ms. Hamilton. There's an extremely high certainty that Mr. Bernier's death occurred moments after he sustained the injury."

I pulled my hands out from underneath Ash's, put them on my lap, and stared at the table, trying to wrap my mind around the two big things that had just happened. One, learning that Brown Bernier

was a murder victim. Two, that Hal Inwood was trying to be nice to me. Number one was tragic and far
more important, of course, but that shouldn't completely eclipse the significance of number two.

"Thanks," I said. "I appreciate you saying so."

Since I hadn't known Brown Bernier before his
death, I wasn't sure I was going to move through the
bargaining stage of grief, and Hal's assurance might
keep me from sliding into the depression part. Ac-
ceptance was next, and though my dreams the next
few nights might be dark, I could already feel myself
accepting the truth of what I'd been told.

"So." I sighed and looked up. "He was murdered."

The two men nodded. "The pathologist," Hal
said, "is taking the case very seriously. She is ana-
lyzing the skull fragments in hopes of learning more
about the object that caused the injury."

I shied away from thinking about that. Let the
forensics people do their jobs; I had no desire to
think about angles and trajectories and force and
mass. Too much math, for one thing. For another, it
would provide my dreams with more detail than I
wanted them to have.

"That night, afterward," I said, "I talked to Rafe
about what happened. He said Brown worked for
the city."

Hal said, "Correct. Mr. Bernier recently retired
from the city's employ. He'd worked in the maintenance department for thirty-three years and been
the department's director for eleven years. Preliminary reports are that he was well liked by his subor-
dinates and trusted by his superiors."

"The kind of guy," Ash said, "that people say
doesn't have an enemy in the world."

Detective Inwood slid Ash a glance that was easy to interpret. Everybody has enemies, it said. And I was inclined to agree. Even if you were the mildest-mannered person ever, you could unknowingly make enemies. You could have bought a property coveted by another, for instance. Or you could have married the woman someone else loved. Enemies were all about us; it was just that most of them never made the leap to murder.

"What about Brown's wife?" I asked.

Without having to open the file, Hal said, "He'd been married for forty-one years, to Lindy Bernier. Her maiden name isn't yet part of the investigative record."

"Kids? Grandkids?"

"Yes, and yes." He rattled off their names and ages. Two sons and a daughter, all married, all with young children of their own. "The three families live downstate, within a few miles of each other, and have for a number of years."

It sounded nice. If you couldn't find a way to make a living Up North, at least they had each other to rely on. My sole sibling was my brother, Matt, and he and his family lived in Florida. The distance wasn't conducive to close relationships. My oldest niece had spent last summer with me, but that wasn't the same as watching the kids grow up day by day, or being able to drop off a casserole when everyone was sick. Not that I knew how to make a casserole, but I was pretty sure takeout would be okay.

Ash glanced at Hal and said, "Now that we know it's murder, we wanted to ask you to tell us all over again what happened. We'll ask Julia, too," he hastened to add, "but we wanted to talk to you first."

So, once again, I had to relive the entire episode. I told them about the moment I saw Brown lying in the road, about those long-drawn-out-horrifying eternal seconds when I thought I might hit him, about the arrival of the EMTs and Deputy Nowlin, Eddie's escape, and the finding of the bicycle.

When I finished, I shook my head. "But knowing he was murdered doesn't change any of that. Or change how I perceived anything."

"No?" Hal asked, and I could have sworn there was a smile lurking somewhere behind his typically bland expression.

"Not a single thing?" Ash leaned forward.

"Well, now I'm wondering even more about the fact that his bike was stashed behind a tree. It just seemed weird, and . . ." The two men shared a look. "What?"

"You're seeing the forest," Ash said, "but not the most usual explanation for someone stopping by the side of the road in the middle of nowhere."

I frowned at him, feeling stupid. "No idea what you're talking about."

"Um, maybe it's more of a guy thing."

The light bulb suddenly went on. "Oh," I said, feeling even more stupid. The most likely explanation for the hidden bike was that Brown had needed to make a short pit stop, something that was physiologically and socially easier for boys than for girls.

"The location of Mr. Bernier's bicycle was noted carefully and we are now considering it a crime scene." Hal eyed me and, in addition to feeling dumb, I was suddenly feeling he was disappointed in me for not catching on to . . . something. And then I had it.

"That car!"

The one that had been speeding so fast it had taken a wide swing around a curve and almost side-swiped us. The one I'd forgotten about in the wake of coming across Brown. There had been no other roads or driveways in those last couple of miles; the car must have seen Brown. Or . . .

"Do you think . . ." My voice was coming out high and tight. I stopped, coughed, and tried again. "Do you think whoever was driving that car is the killer?"

"We don't know," Ash said. "But the driver must have seen Brown in the roadway, and we definitely want to find him. Or her."

I thought about it for a moment. "It just stands to reason that the driver killed Brown. Otherwise why would he—or she—be speeding like that?"

Ash started spouting a number of theories ranging from a suspended driver's license to a general fear of getting involved. Midway through his recitation, I started shaking my head but caught Hal's gaze. He half smiled and nodded at me.

I settled back down into my chair and listened to Ash ramble on.

Let him spin out as many theories as he wanted. It didn't matter. Because Hal and I agreed. The car's driver was almost certainly the killer.

Now all we had to do was find him.

Or her.

"Hail, Minerva, well met!" The bearlike Trock Farrand enveloped me in a hug so vast I thought I might disappear forever into his front side, which was currently a cooking apron smelling like whatever it was he and Kristen Jurek, my best friend other than Rafe, had been cooking the last few hours.

Through a tiny gap between Trock's elbow and ribs, I could see Kristen look up from the pot she was stirring. "Trock, you're squishing her. I'm not sure she can breathe."

"Nonsense," he bellowed over the top of my head. But he released me. "Minnie, dear heart, it has been far too long since I've seen you." He leaned down and kissed my cheek with a smack. "What have you been doing with yourself all these long lonely months I've been without you?"

I counted in my head. It had barely been four months since Kristen and Trock's son, Scruffy Gronkowski, had been wedded in holy matrimony. "Looks like you've done okay without me," I said heartlessly, poking his stomach with my forefinger.

He gave a Pillsbury Doughboy giggle, which amused a total of no one in the room.

"Minnie, my sweet, my gorgeous, my favorite bookmobile driver ever," he began, but I was having none of it.

"Trock, after the wedding you promised you'd stop sneaking out to eat fried food. You promised you'd start losing weight, and you promised you'd make a doctor's appointment. Have you done any of that?" I demanded. "At all?"

Trock Farrand (not his real name) was a celebrity chef, current host of the very popular *Trock's Troubles*. Son Scruffy (not his real first name) produced the show, which in addition to the dishes Trock made in whatever kitchen the show was using, also highlighted different restaurants around the country.

Three Seasons, Kristen's restaurant, had been featured on the show last year, and her Chilson-based business had been booming ever since. Not that things had been slow before, but it was now so successful she was interviewing for a full-time manager so she could pull back from the day-to-day work and spend more time touring the country with the show. I had full confidence that it wouldn't be long before we saw Kristen cohosting on *Trock's Troubles*, and Rafe and I had recently made a five-dollar bet on what date that would happen.

Why, exactly, both Scruffy and Trock were in Chilson for a few days, I didn't know, but then I'd never understood the show's filming schedule. And I was not about to turn down a dinner cooked by Trock and Kristen, even if Rafe wasn't sure he'd be able to make it until the dessert course. What I also didn't know was if this Friday night dinner would cancel out the Sunday night crème brûlée that Kristen, almost without fail, made for the two of us at her restaurant. I hoped not, because I looked forward to that evening all week, especially considering that Kristen would be closing the aptly named Three Seasons soon and hightailing it to Key West, where she relaxed and tended bar in the warm sunshine for five months.

"There was," Trock said, rubbing his chin, "one day I ordered a salad instead of French fries."

I started to congratulate him but stopped in time. "And what did you have on the salad? Cheese? Croutons? Double salad dressing? More cheese?"

"You think so little of me?" He gave me a sad, sad look.

"When it comes to eating foods that are horrible

for you? Yes. Absolutely." Not that I was much better, but we were talking about him, not me.

"Give it up, Minnie," Scruffy said over his shoulder. He was in the corner, sharpening knives. "The last person who could get him to do anything was my mother, and in the ten years since she died, no one has stepped up to take up the slack."

I turned to Kristen. "Don't look at me," she said. "I'm a newlywed. You think I'm going to tackle my father-in-law's lifelong habits?"

Clearly, it was up to me.

But before I could marshal my arguments, there was a dinner to be had. We were in the kitchen of Trock's summer home. Though the house was spacious, it wasn't extremely so. The kitchen, however, was the stuff of happy dreams for those inclined toward chef-ness. Me? Not so much. At some level, I knew the intended function of all the implements of destruction in the kitchen, but knowing what they did and knowing how to use them, let alone wanting to use them, were three very different things.

In an effort to get out of the way of the chopping and stirring, I started to settle on a stool as far out of the way as possible. Before I got fully situated, Trock appeared in front of me, arms akimbo, face frowning. And when a man as big as Trock frowns, it is a sight to behold.

"What did I do this time?" I asked, putting my hands in my lap and crossing my ankles tidily, like a good little girl.

"That!" he roared, pointing at my hands. "You have become an engaged person! Without first talking to me to warn you of What Men Can Be Like!"

He spoke the last few words in capital letters,

which amused me almost as much as his histrionics. Trock, like pretty much everyone else in Chilson, had known Rafe for years, and he couldn't possibly have a single opposition to our eventual marriage.

"Would it help," I asked, "if I told you that Rafe asked Eddie for my hand?"

Trock tipped his head back and shouted with laughter. "Delightful! When the young man arrives, I'll have to congratulate his creativity."

"And feel free to warn me now. What are men like?"

"Depends on the man, of course." Trock assumed a thoughtful stance. "Rafe Niswander, though, let me think."

"Still hasn't bought her a ring," Scruffy said.

"Yes, I see that." Trock sighed. "Not an omen of good fortune. Not at all."

I was getting a little tired of so many people giving Rafe a hard time about the stupid ring. "It's not him, it's me. I haven't decided what kind of ring I want." I glared at Trock. "I'm not even sure I want one. What's the point, anyway? To spend a lot of money?"

"Societal conventions," Trock said promptly. "Buck them, and you'll grow exhausted with explaining yourself forever."

Now my back was up. "You don't recommend individuality? You're saying I shouldn't stay true to who I am as a person? That I should just roll over and do whatever it is that social norms say I should do? Is that what Boudicca did? And Elizabeth Cady Stanton? And what about Amelia Earhart?"

Trock blinked. "Um, dear one, I was merely—"

"Speaking of rolling over," Scruffy said. "What's this about the bookmobile running over someone?"

I looked at him, but he was still focused on the knives, so his facial expression didn't tell me anything about the level of knowledge he may or may not have had about recent events at the sheriff's office. "Yeah, about that."

Kristen cursed.

Uh-oh. Cautiously, I turned to look at her.

"Not you," she said. "This sauce. It tastes like carp."

"Don't you mean crap?"

"No, I do not. It tastes like it belongs on fish. And since it's going over fish, that's not the taste I want."

That made no sense to me, but Trock nodded and suggested adding an herb I'd never heard of.

Kristen brightened. "Perfect! I'm so glad I married your son."

Scruffy and I exchanged indulgent glances. "Anyway," I said, "like I told Kristen on the phone the other night, we didn't run over Brown Bernier." It had been frighteningly close, of course, but I wasn't going to dwell on that. "And anyway, he was dead before we got there."

"Do they know how he died?" Scruffy eyed his shoulder, picked off an invisible piece of whatever, and deposited it into a nearby wastebasket.

"Well, yes. They do. Ash asked me to stop by because Hal Inwood wanted to tell me in person."

Scruffy and Trock continued to look mildly interested in the tale. Kristen, however, had been down this road before. "Inwood's the tall guy, right?" she asked. "That detective?" Her gaze fastened on me. "What would Detective Inwood need to tell you that Ash couldn't?"

I shifted under the weight of her gaze. "Because, um . . . well . . ."

When I couldn't manage to eke out a complete sentence, Kristen shook her head, which flicked her long blond ponytail from side to side, and spread her arms wide, including all the world in her gesture. "This, my friends, is the proud possessor of a high school diploma, and bachelor's and master's degrees in library and information science. All that schooling, yet she cannot form an answer to a simple question."

"It's formed in my head just fine," I said. "It's the speaking-it-out-loud part I'm having a hard time with."

"And now she's ending a sentence with a preposition." Trock *tsk*ed at me.

"Is something the matter, Minnie?" Scruffy was wiping down a long, very-sharp-looking chef's knife. "You look a little pale."

"She's fine," Kristen said. "She always looks like that when she's holding out on me. Spill, Minnie Hamilton. What is it you're not saying?"

I sighed. "Brown Bernier. We were assuming he had a heart attack, but that wasn't it. He was murdered."

Kristen sat down hard on a nearby stool. "Murdered? But that . . . that can't be right. He's the kind of guy who opened windows to let flies out."

"I didn't know you knew him." Scruffy came to his bride's side and gave her a hug.

"He and my dad played poker together, back in the day," she said. "They were in the same high school class, along with their other poker cronies."

I made a mental note to ask her about the other poker players. "Hal and I figure the car that almost hit the bookmobile was the killer speeding away."

"Hark!" Trock put one hand to his ear. "Do I hear the sounds of a unified front with the sheriff's office? That would be so unlike you, Minnie."

"The only unusual thing," I said, "is that Hal and I are on one side and Ash is on the other. He's being weirdly stubborn about it, saying that lots of people speed on that stretch of road and spending a lot of time hunting down the driver isn't the best use of resources."

"You think he's wrong?" Kristen pulled out of Scruffy's embrace and faced me.

"Well, yes. I do." Cars did speed on that road, but the odds of a random speeder, coinciding with the bookmobile, combined with a murder victim, all at roughly the same place and time, had to be far beyond what anyone could realistically calculate.

"Then," Kristen said, looking at me hard, "you have two choices. Run your own side investigation. Or stop complaining about Ash."

My mouth opened, then closed. Because she was right. Ash didn't deserve my whining. And her late father had been a friend of Brown's, which made the decision even easier.

"You're right," I said. "The side investigation starts tomorrow."

Chapter 5

Saturday dawned bright and breezy, with big puffy clouds doing that scudding thing across the sky.

"Look at that," I said to Eddie, nodding through the bedroom window. "I counted, and it took less than three seconds for that cloud, you know, the one that looks like a baby bunny, to get from one side of the window to the next. Wonder how long the next one will take."

Eddie purred but didn't lift his head to see, or even guess at the time frame for the next cloud movement. However, he did purr, which made me snuggle down under the comforter a little deeper, which kept me nice and toasty warm, something that wouldn't have happened if I'd actually climbed out of bed, because that bright and breezy wind was from the north and it had brought remarkably chilly air along with it.

"Chilly for mid-September," I reminded Eddie, who was paying zero attention to me. "Not cold at all for November, let alone December through April."

The knowledge of the upcoming plunging temperatures made me slide a little deeper into the covers. Where would I be in November? By that time the houseboat would be out of the water and in storage. Would I be staying temporarily with Aunt Frances and Otto? Cousin Celeste, the new owner of my aunt's boardinghouse, hadn't offered me a winter home as Aunt Frances had done for years, but then Celeste was new to town and didn't know about my possible housing needs due to Rafe's tendency to drop his own renovation tasks to give friends a lending hand.

"And he has a lot of friends," I said, sighing. That was a good thing, of course, but the whole moving-in date kept getting pushed further and further back in the calendar because of it.

"Mrr." Eddie put one paw over his eyes. "Mrr," he said again, purring.

"You're right." I patted him from under the blanket, which didn't work out very well, but if I'd put my hand outside the covers, I'd realize how cold it was, and I wasn't ready to confront environmental reality. "Of course you're right. Not sure what you're right about, but that doesn't matter, does it?"

"Mrr!"

Eddie sat up, gave me a Look, and in one smooth motion, jumped off the bed and onto the floor.

If, as Julia seemed to think, Eddie and I could communicate in a manner far exceeding the typical Eddie tendency to ignore the "No!" command and the typical Minnie tendency to think everything Eddie said meant he wanted a cat treat, that last "Mrr" would have meant something.

But it didn't. And since my cat was clearly refusing to accompany me in my desire to stay in bed until the outside temperature increased by twenty degrees, I took a deep breath, flung back the covers, and got up to face the morning.

And it wasn't one I was looking forward to. At all.

An hour and a half later, I'd showered, dressed, met Rafe for breakfast at the Round Table, confirmed the location of my morning destination via a couple of Google searches, and driven to the part of the county where Brown Bernier and his wife, Lindy, had lived for years and years.

When my phone's GPS lady told me I was within five hundred feet of my destination, I turned her off and slowed the car to a crawl.

Brown and Lindy's house was a 1970s-era split-level ranch, one of those houses that meant you'd always be in good physical shape because every time you wanted something from a different room, you'd be going up and down stairs.

The lawn was lushly green, the bushes in front were tidy, and the house's light gray paint, trimmed with white, appeared new. Window boxes filled with brightly colored annual flowers made the house look cheerful and happy, a feeling that had to be in direct opposition to the emotions going on inside.

Three cars were in the driveway, but I had no way of knowing if the Berniers were the kind of people who filled up their garage with stuff and left their cars in the drive, or if they were people who always kept their cars in the garage and the ones in front of me were family's and friends'.

"You're stalling," I said out loud. When I'd texted

Ash if he thought it would be okay if I gave my condolences to Brown's wife in person, he'd checked with Lindy and told me that Saturday morning, about ten, would be a good time to stop by.

Cowardly Minnie had hoped that his answer would be different. I'd hoped he would say, Don't be ridiculous, you're the last person she wants to see. There's going to be a memorial service in October. Talk to her then.

But he hadn't, so now I was stuck.

"The investigation starts now," I murmured, echoing what I'd told Kristen last night, though I wasn't sure I was starting anything. My only intention was to introduce myself to Lindy and tell her how sorry I was for her loss.

I inched the car closer and closer, and since even a very slow pace gets you where you want to go if you stick with it long enough, before long I was parked behind a dusty SUV, walking up to the house, and ringing the doorbell.

The man who answered the door was tall and thin and had a thick shock of hair a color that wasn't exactly blond but wasn't exactly white, either. "Hello?"

His single-syllable question was polite but brusque. Understandable, given the circumstances, so I decided not to read anything into it. "Hi, I'm Minnie Hamilton. I talked to the sheriff's office about stopping by, and—"

"Bob?" a female voice called. "Is that the bookmobile lady?"

Bob's eyebrows went up. I nodded.

"Yeah, it's her."

"Well, let her in, for goodness' sake! Don't let her

stand out there on the doorstep for everybody to see."

I wasn't sure who'd be paying any attention to their doorstep since the Berniers' nearest neighbor was a quarter mile away. Then again, I'd been eyeing their front door for ten minutes, summoning my courage, and I couldn't be the only one who did that.

Bob stepped back and opened the door wide, letting me into the entryway.

To the right was the living room, where a woman in her mid-sixties sat on a couch, pushing aside photo albums that had been on her lap. "Minnie, I'm so glad to meet you!" She jumped to her feet and hurried across the room, arms stretched wide.

"Oh, um—" That was all I got out before I was enveloped in the biggest hug I've ever received from an adult shorter than I was.

"Thank you, thank you, thank you," Lindy murmured over and over again. When she released me, she said it again. "Thank you so, so much."

She turned to face the man who'd let me inside. "Bob, this is the woman who found Brown. She's the one who tried to save him. She and that actor, Julia what's her name, called nine-one-one and did CPR until they got there. She parked the bookmobile so no one would—" Her voice caught.

"You're very welcome." I gave her another hug. "I only wish I could have done more."

"You did plenty." Lindy patted my shoulder. "Now. Come sit with me a minute. The kids all went to town and won't be back for hours, so we won't be interrupted."

I let myself be pulled to the couch and helped her

move photo albums. Bob stood nearby, watching with an expression that hovered between fondness and exasperation. "Lindy," he said, "are you sure you—"

"Bob," she cut in, "why don't you get us something to drink. Tea? Water? Coffee?"

I blinked. "Um, coffee would be okay."

"Our guest wants coffee, Bob." Lindy picked up a photo album and opened it. "I'd appreciate it if you brewed a pot. You know where everything is."

Bob hesitated. I sent him what I hoped was a sympathetic smile. Lindy continued to ignore him, and eventually up the short flight of stairs he went.

"Now," Lindy said comfortably. "Tell me about the bookmobile. I was a sales rep and was on the road a lot for a few years, and I don't keep up with the newspapers, but I've seen it on the road a few times and think the whole thing is just marvelous!"

So I talked about getting a commercial driver's license, about choosing the books, about the non-book items we carried, about our outreach efforts to nursing homes and child development centers, and about the drop-off books we supplied to shut-ins. I could have talked about Graydon's direction to expand the bookmobile hours and how I had no idea how that was going to work, but in spite of the coffee Bob had supplied, my voice was getting hoarse, and I suspected she wasn't really interested in the topic, anyway.

"Would you mind?" I asked, nodding at the photo albums. "If it's okay with you, I'd like to see some pictures of Brown."

"I was hoping you'd ask." Lindy's smile dimpled. "The first couple of days I couldn't bear to look, but now I think I'm ready, right, Bob?"

Bob had settled into the armchair across from us. He eyed Lindy. "Up to you," he said shortly.

Since I'd missed the window for politely asking what role Bob played in Lindy's life, I'd had to come up with my own explanation and decided he must be Lindy's brother. There was a tension in the air that felt like sibling stress. In my experience, there was no other stress quite like it.

"Well, then." Lindy picked up the top album and opened it. "These are the most recent pictures. Here's Brown with his new friends. I took this one myself at the beginning of the summer." The photo was of a group of bicyclists, all smiling and waving at the camera. "There he is, two in from the right."

I studied the picture and saw a happy man. A man who had no idea he'd be dead within months. "This is a local bike group?"

"From what Brown said, they're not a formal group. Just a bunch of people that meet up at different spots to ride together. He was so happy to find a group like that. He was hoping to get fit enough to do some really long rides. We were talking about a cross-country trip. I was going to drive the car and while he was riding I'd tour the museums he didn't care about anyway . . ." Her voice trailed off.

She touched the photo, then closed the album. "I think I'll look at this one later," she said, putting it aside and picking up another. "My mother-in-law gave me all sorts of photos before she passed. Aren't they just adorable?" She pointed to two boys mugging for the camera. The slightly taller one was dressed as a soldier; the other boy was decked out in full firefighter regalia.

Lindy smiled at the photo. "When he was grown,

Brown became a volunteer firefighter. I was so proud of him. And Bob here, well, he ended up having a career in the air force."

Bob, who was turning into a man of few words, nodded and didn't say anything.

I smiled, but my mind was working furiously.

So. Not brother, but brother-in-law. And there was clearly tension between the two. How very interesting. Plus, Brown had been riding with a group of bicyclists and each one of them might have useful information.

The investigation was underway.

It wasn't quite noon when I left Lindy and her brother-in-law. In the time I'd been inside, the clouds had multiplied and thickened and the wind speed had gone up a notch. I fast-walked to the car, which was where I'd left my jacket, started the engine, and flicked the heater to high.

September, in the land of Up North, was a mixed bag of weather. Some years it was nicer in September than it had been in August, but sometimes September felt more like November. You just never knew, and if you were sensible you prepared for a wide range of temperatures every time you walked out the door.

I backed out of Lindy's driveway, wondering where I fell on the Sensible Scale. And also, where did I want to fall?

I thought about it all the way back to Chilson, and was still thinking about it as I snuck undetected through the library's side door and tried to tiptoe into my office without being seen.

"Hey, Minnie!"

I looked at my office door, a mere five steps away. So close, yet so far. I turned. "Hey, Josh. What's up?"

"Didn't know you were scheduled to work today."

"I'm not. I just needed to, um, pick up a book I wanted to read this weekend." This was true. But I also wanted to use the library's Internet access, which was far faster than the marina's. The Internet at the house was almost as fast, but Rafe's Saturday plans had a lot to do with noisy tools I wasn't good at using, and which tended to interfere with the Wi-Fi connection. "Why are you here?"

"Stopped to check on an error message from one of the network switches." He shrugged and shoved his hands in the pockets of his cargo pants. "Rebooted and it was fine."

"And we pay you how much for that?"

He gave his stock response. "Not enough. It's not the rebooting, it's—"

"Knowing what to reboot. I know." Having an in-house IT guy was expensive, but to my mind it was worth every penny in these days of increasing and ever-changing technologies. "How's it going with Mia?"

"That's what I wanted to talk to you about."

"She's still undecided about moving in with you?"

He blew out a huge sigh. "Like I said before, she's waffling on the whole thing. She was all excited at first, but now not so much. She doesn't even want to talk about it any more."

"Let's see. What did I say the other day? That it's a big step and a little fear is understandable?"

"Well, yeah, but—"

I ran over what was sure to be a silly objection. "And, as I recall, she never actually agreed to move in."

"No, but—"

"And what was my very wise recommendation? To give her time?" I quickly counted on my fingers. "And that was all of what, four days ago? Josh, four days is not a long time to think over a life change." I held up my hand, forestalling his next objection. "Yes, I'm sure the total time she's been thinking about is more than four days, but let's use four days ago as the start of a new clock. And what's the rush? You love her, right? Then you should be happy to wait until she's ready."

Josh had the grace to look abashed. "You're right. It's just . . . I'm worried there's something else going on with her I don't know about."

Probably lots of things, I thought, but didn't say out loud. Mia was a complex person. So far, Josh had seemed fine with taking the time to gently unwrap each layer of her, and I hoped he would find the patience to work through this wrinkle in their relationship.

"Talk to her," I said.

"That's all I've been doing," he muttered. "She just changes the subject." He looked at me. "You know Mia. You're good friends with her sister. Can you talk to her? Ask what's going on?"

I was not about to talk to either Mia or Leese, technically her half sister, about Mia's living arrangements. "Sorry, Josh. It's none of my business, and Mia would have every right to be furious with both of us if I interfered. You're going to have to wait."

"Had a feeling you were going to say that." He

twisted his mouth around in a grimace. "You're right, but I don't have to like it, do I?"

I smiled. "Not a bit."

"Why is it," he said, sighing, "that doing the right thing is so hard?"

But for that, I didn't have an answer.

Saturday's cold front blew through fast and furious, and Rafe and I spent the much warmer Sunday morning writing up a punch list of things that needed to be done before Minnie's Move-In date. We'd intended to do a walk-through of the entire house, but the list got so depressingly long by the time we finished the first floor that neither of us had the heart to go upstairs. So we abandoned the chore and headed up to the Headlands, a lovely park in Emmet County, and spent the afternoon wandering the trails and skipping stones on the unusually flat Lake Michigan.

Back in Chilson, Rafe abandoned me in favor of watching football with friends, and I went to spend my Sunday evening in the normal way, by hanging out in Kristen's office at Three Seasons, having crème brûlée served to us by Harvey, her loyal sous-chef.

Kristen, who had been oddly cranky all Friday evening, seemed to have recovered her normal good spirits. "Harvey!" she shouted into the phone. "Where are they?"

"Right here, milady." Harvey swept into the small room, a tray balanced on one upturned hand, carrying a tray stand in the other, a white linen towel draped over his upraised arm.

Over the years, Harvey's crème brûlée presentation had evolved to be a *Downton Abbey* version of dessert, and tonight he'd upped his game, having changed from his normal white jacket and black-and-white-checked pants into black pants, black cutaway jacket, striped vest, white shirt, and black bow tie.

Where he'd come up with the costume I did not know, but the fit was so good it could have been custom ordered. Well, other than the pants being a bit short, but I mentally gave him a score of ten for the effort.

Kristen, much like the Dowager Countess, didn't bat an eye as Harvey set up the stand, placed the tray, and delivered the desserts. "Thank you, Harvey," she said. "If we need anything else, I'll ring."

"Yes, milady." He bowed and swept out, closing the door behind him so softly it made no sound.

I tapped the crystallized sugar with the back of my spoon, enjoying the dull thud, and tipped my head toward the door. "I think he's maxed out. What can he do to top this?"

Kristen laughed. "Can't wait to find out. What he wants is for me to break, and you know I won't do that."

"You won't want to, anyway." I plunged my spoon through the sugar layer and into the delectable custard. "One of these days he'll come up with something that'll crack that stone face of yours."

"Not a chance." She eyed the dessert as critically as only a restaurateur can and picked up her own spoon. "But what I really want to know is if you've done anything about finding Brown's killer."

I frowned. "If I recall correctly, not so very long

ago, you were telling me to stay out of murder investigations. That we have law enforcement officers for a reason, and that they're highly trained whereas I am not."

"Did I say that?" Kristen squinted at the ceiling. "If I did, it was before and not now. This is different. Brown was a friend of my dad's. Besides, you know you want to prove Ash wrong."

Since I didn't want to explore that unfortunate, petty side of my character, I told her what I'd learned from Lindy. And that my Saturday afternoon online research into local bike groups hadn't been productive, at least not in terms of figuring out what group Brown had joined.

"Okay," she said. "What's next?"

I blinked. "Um, well, I know some people who are into bicycling. I figured I'd talk to them, trying to find Brown's group. But I don't know how to find out more about the relationship between Lindy and Bob. Do you have any ideas?"

"You're missing something obvious," she said, snapping her fingers. "Where do people spend most of their waking hours?"

"Depends on the person."

She rolled her eyes. "Okay, let's talk about you. Where do you spend more hours than are reasonable?"

"The library," I said tartly, "but you're one to talk. You—" And that's when the light bulb went on. "The city. I wasn't thinking about it because he was retired. But Brown worked there for years. Somebody is bound to have been friends with him."

"Exactly." Kristen toasted me with a custard-laden spoon. "City offices open at eight. Plenty of time to stop in before you have to be at the library. And don't you know Bax Tously? He still works for the city, doesn't he?"

I looked at her. "You're being awfully bossy about this. You could help, you know."

She snorted. "As if. Imagine me, tiptoeing around asking questions. What are the odds that any stranger anywhere would confide in me about anything?"

That was true. Kristen was many wonderful things, but her default demeanor of "bull in a china shop" wasn't likely to be a helpful attitude during an amateur investigation.

"Besides," she went on. "I have . . ." She paused. "Um, well . . ."

I laughed. "You have no excuses whatsoever. As long as you keep me in Sunday desserts the rest of my life, I'm happy to do this for you."

"Done," Kristen said, and we finished the custard in perfect accord.

Monday morning, Kristen's investigative advice seemed as sound as it had over dessert. Accordingly, I patted a sleeping Eddie on the head and left the houseboat a few minutes earlier than normal, the change in my routine affecting my fuzzy friend not at all.

As I walked up to the city offices, I wondered, as I often did, what was really going on in Eddie's feline brain. Sometimes he shocked me with his level of intelligence. For example, he would jump on the houseboat's dashboard to paw at the front door handle. But sometimes he shocked me with how stupid he could be. For example, when I gently nudged him aside to keep him from slipping out a door I was opening, he routinely tried to get out through the hinge side.

Then again, I could do smart things and stupid things, too, so maybe he was thinking the same thing about me.

The thought amused me, so I was smiling when I entered the offices of the city of Chilson.

"Good morning." The woman returning my smile was fiftyish, with smooth shoulder-length black hair. "What can I do for you?"

I'd meant to prepare a good story on the walk over, but my musing about Eddie's brain had occupied me fully. I had nothing, so I did the only thing I could think of and defaulted to the truth.

"I'm Minnie Hamilton. I drive the bookmobile, and—"

"Oh!" The woman jumped to her feet. "You're the one who tried to save Brown!" She hurried around her desk to give me a big hug. "Thank you so much. It must have been hard, but we're all so glad you were there to . . . to do what you did. Let me get Isaac in here. He worked with Brown forever. I'm sure he'll want to thank you, too. Hang on."

And so, two minutes later, I was talking to the exact man I'd been hoping to find, which only reinforced my bad habit of inadequate preparation.

Isaac was in his mid-fifties, and the word "round" was the best descriptor possible. Round body, round face; even his voice managed to be round. He towered over me, and thankfully he wasn't of the hugging inclination. Instead, he offered a meaty hand and shook with gentle firmness.

"So good to meet you, Minnie. My wife spends a lot of time at the library and she speaks well of you."

"Oh? What's your last name?"

"Finter."

I beamed. "Susan is your wife? She's great. Tell her I said hello."

"Will do. Now, I want to thank you for what you did for Brown. And don't say you did nothing, because that would minimize our feelings and you don't want to do that, do you?"

"Wouldn't dream of it. Cathy here"—I nodded at the pleasant black-haired woman, pleased that I'd noticed the name plate on her desk—"said you worked with him for a long time?"

"Almost thirty years." Isaac nodded. "He was maintenance, I'm in planning, but doesn't that matter when you both work in the same place for so long." He paused. "You heard that Brown was murdered?"

"I was told a couple of days ago."

"It's horrible." Cathy shook her head. "It was hard enough when we were thinking he'd had a heart attack, but murder is just . . . awful."

"I'm sure the sheriff's office will talk to you soon," I said. "Asking if any city residents complained about him."

"That just never happened," Cathy said. "First off, he was too nice to get complaints, but second, he was maintenance for all the city buildings. Mr. Fix-it and Mr. Cleanup. All internal, really. He didn't have much contact with the general public, other than to sometimes chat with people as he shoveled snow off the walks."

"Hard to shovel wrong enough that someone would want to commit murder over it," Isaac said.

I hesitated. As Kristen had suggested, I'd contacted Bax Tousely. He was out of town on vacation, so we didn't talk face-to-face, but his text messages all indicated that Brown had been a great guy, everyone liked him, et cetera, et cetera.

I continued to hesitate, because I was talking to two city employees, and even if my first impression of them was compassion and kindness, who knew what lurked in their hearts? But opportunity was presenting itself, so I went ahead. "What about the people who work here? Did anyone have a grudge against him for any reason?"

Isaac frowned. "Can't think of anyone."

"Ariella Tice," Cathy said. "Remember?"

Isaac's frown turned into a full-on grimace. "Thanks. I'd tried to forget."

Cathy looked at me. "She was hired a couple of years ago, right out of college, but she was fired in, oh, let me think. Late April. She was assistant to the finance director, but it wasn't working out, so the city manager let her go." She glanced at a closed door. "You could talk to him, but he's busy prepping for the first budget workshop."

She stopped, but there was clearly a story coming, so I waited.

"Brown retired in early May," Cathy said. "And the day, the very day, he was leaving, Ariella stomped in here, barged straight back to his office, and yelled at him that no one her age would ever get the kind of pension he was getting, that it wasn't fair, that all the city cared about was taking care of the older employees, and that people in her generation were on their own and it was all because of people like him."

Isaac shifted. "There is some truth in that."

"Sure," Cathy said, "but why take it out on poor Brown? He couldn't help when he was born."

Though we chatted a few minutes longer, they couldn't come up with anyone else at the City who had ever spoken a harsh word to Brown. They thanked me again, and I did my best to accept their thanks.

All the way up to the library, I wondered if what I'd just learned about Ariella Tice could have been twisted into a reason to kill someone. I didn't see it, but as Detective Hal Inwood had told me many times, almost anything could become a motive for murder.

Chapter 6

Just about the time I was wondering what Rafe and I were going to do for dinner, my phone dinged with a text message from one person to three others.

Aunt Frances: *Do you two have plans to cook tonight?*

Minnie (after laughing out loud hard enough to startle a passing patron): *Nope. You?*

Aunt Frances: *I want to try a new coleslaw recipe and I bought too many mixed greens at the farmers' market.*

Otto: *And I want to try a new grilled chicken rub.*

Minnie: *Glad to be your guinea pigs. What time?*

Rafe: *Don't I get a vote?*

Minnie: *Nope.*

Aunt Frances: *No.*

Otto: *I can't believe you asked that question.*

And so it was that, at six thirty on the dot, Rafe and I were scheduled to meet on the sidewalk outside of the house where my aunt now lived. Across the street was the rambling old boardinghouse, where she'd lived for decade upon decade. It was there that I'd been sent to spend my youthful summers with my dad's sister, and it was there that I'd returned when I'd landed my job with the Chilson District Library.

For years I'd lived with my loving aunt through the cold northern months. May through September, though, I cheerfully abandoned her in favor of the houseboat while she took in summer boarders who paid far more a month than I could afford on a librarian's salary.

But a few short months ago, Aunt Frances and Otto got married. And my aunt, who also taught woodworking classes at the local community college during the school year, sold the boardinghouse to our cousin Celeste.

"Minnie!"

I'd been about to walk up the steps to my aunt's house, but that clear, high voice stopped me in my tracks. "Celeste, how are you doing?"

Cousin-wise, Celeste was in the second-cousin-twice-removed kind of category. The exact relationship had been explained to me more than once, but that kind of thing didn't seem to stick in my head. What mattered to me was that Celeste, in her mid-fifties, with long gray hair most often braided, or rolled up into a bun, or both, was cheerful and was running the boardinghouse almost exactly as my aunt had.

The fact that she was only a teensy bit taller than my own efficient five feet wasn't a Thing, not really, but it was nice to have a relative who fully understood what it meant to have to ask for help to get items from the top shelves of grocery stores.

"I never knew house cleaning could be so much fun!" She tossed a brightly colored throw rug over the porch railing and started thumping with a broom. "Take that, dust!" she shouted, grinning.

Grinning myself, I asked, "What are you going to do this winter, have you decided?"

"Not yet." She paused her thumping efforts. "Say, is Rafe going to have the house finished before the snow flies? Are you going to need a place to stay? Because if you do . . ." She looked over her shoulder at the boardinghouse.

"He promises it'll be finished before cold sets in." I listened to my own voice and felt confident it wasn't expressing the doubt I felt inside about Rafe's timetable.

"Oh, honey." Celeste gave me a sympathetic smile. "It's going to be all different for you, isn't it?"

Apparently she'd heard something else entirely, something I'd tried to hide even from myself. "It will," I said honestly. "Some things, a lot of things, will be better. But spending winters with Aunt Frances was great, too."

"Everything comes to an end," Celeste said kindly. "But those winters helped develop a wonderful relationship between you and Frances that will last forever."

Before I could decide whether or not to point out how contradictory her statements were, Celeste smiled. "And there's your sweetheart. You two have a nice night, now."

Rafe, who was indeed striding toward me, gave Celeste a wave and swept me into a big hug. "Hey," he murmured into my hair.

"Hey, back," I said, loving him, but a tiny part of

my brain was thinking about Celeste and Aunt Frances. There'd been a few rough patches for the two women. After so many years running the boardinghouse, it had been hard for my aunt to watch it survive, and thrive, under someone else's care. Thanks to Otto's help and understanding, though, she came through the rough days and was now as perky and sunshiny as I'd ever seen her.

"Well, there you are." My perky aunt opened the front door and glared. "Late. Are you ever going to be on time to anything?"

I broke away from Rafe's embrace and mercilessly tossed him under the bus. "His fault. I would have been on time except he needed a hug."

"True fact," Rafe said, nodding.

"True fact?" She snorted. "What a ridiculous phrase. Redundancy at its finest."

My aunt's dry tone made me grin. If Aunt Frances was being snarky, all was right with the world. We walked up the front steps and I handed her a plastic container filled with a thick, reddish liquid. "Kristen says hey."

"Is this her new cider vinaigrette dressing? Thank you, dear heart." She patted me on the head, something I permitted from only two people in the world, and right then they were standing within five feet of each other.

In short order, the four of us were in the backyard, drinks in hand, waiting for the chicken to cook. "That's new, isn't it?" I asked, nodding at a stone birdbath tucked between two lilac bushes.

Otto nodded. "We bought that on our latest trip. Fits nicely there, doesn't it?"

"If we buy something that big every trip we take,"

Aunt Frances said, "we're going to need a bigger house."

I looked at the two of them. Otto, tall and elegant in a Paul Newman sort of way, and my aunt, sharp angled and elegant in a Katharine Hepburn sort of way. If there was anything that fit nicely, it was those two. Well, other than Rafe and me. I smiled at my beloved, but he was too busy following up on my aunt's comment to notice.

"Every trip?" he asked. "The last few months you hit every town in the northern lower and in the Upper Peninsula. What's next?"

The two elder statespeople in the group grinned and bumped knuckles. "We've become infected," Otto said.

I sat up straight, wide-eyed. "Are you okay? What's the matter? Have you been to a doctor?"

"We've been bitten," my aunt calmly said, "with the traveling bug."

"How does—" I stopped short. Tried to look like a doctor conferring a second opinion. "Most reports indicate that's a horrible thing to get out of your system. And if both of you are coming down with it?" I *tsk*ed and shook my head.

Rafe nodded. "From what I hear, there's no real cure. The best you can do is learn to live with it."

"And that's what we intend to do." Otto started listing all the places in downstate Michigan they wanted to visit, then launched out into the rest of the Great Lakes states.

Aunt Frances leaned across the table and beckoned me forward. "He'll go on like that for hours, if we let him, which gives me time to ask about your latest bookmobile escapade."

Though I'd texted her the bare details, I hadn't taken the time to talk to her in person. "Sorry," I said. "I should have stopped by earlier."

She waved away my apology. "What I want to know is whether or not the rumor is true. Was Brown Bernier murdered?"

I suddenly realized Aunt Frances and Brown were about the same age. Though she hadn't grown up in Chilson, she'd spent more than forty years in this town after marrying Everett Pixley, my uncle by marriage who'd passed away so long ago. She and Rafe were my go-to people for town history, and here the opportunity was, presenting itself in front of my silly nose.

"Yes, I'm afraid so." I waited for her to absorb the sad news, then asked, "Did you know him?"

"Not directly. His wife worked in the college admissions office for a few years, so what I mostly know is through Lindy. I only met him face-to-face a couple of times."

"What were your impressions?"

She was silent for a moment. "A nice man," she finally said. "Just a nice, nice man. It's horribly wrong that someone killed him." She gave me a fierce look. "Are you helping Ash and Hal Inwood on this?"

I squirmed the teensiest bit. My aunt was not always pleased to have me poking into police matters. "Well . . ."

"They need you," she said, her voice low and penetrating. "You notice things no one else does. Even if they won't admit it, they need your help."

A wave of sorrow went through me, grief for a man I'd never met, grief for all the people he'd left behind, and a bit of grief for myself, that I'd never had the opportunity to meet Brown.

"I'll do what I can," I said quietly. "I promise."

The next day was a bookmobile day. Eddie, who had a secret cat sense for detecting the days he'd be riding with us, was already sitting on his carrier when I trod up the few steps from the bedroom and bath part of the houseboat to the kitchen and dining area.

"Mrr." He pawed the top of the carrier.

"Yes, it is indeed a bookmobile day. See? I'm showered and dressed in appropriate clothing." I held out my arms and turned in a circle. My library wear was dress pants, knit shirt, and loose jacket. Bookmobile wear was the same on top, but dressy jeans on the bottom. "And now, my fine furry friend, I'm going to eat breakfast and make a peanut butter and jelly sandwich, at which point we'll go on our merry way to spread joy and books across the land."

"Mrr!"

"Well, yes, the two things are synonymous. It was a test to see if . . . well, rats." I was staring at the inside of a refrigerator that had no milk and no jam, because I'd intended to get both yesterday and had completely forgotten.

It took me roughly half a second to come up with an alternate plan. "In you go, pal." I ushered Eddie into his carrier. "Hope you don't mind spending a bit of solo time in the car. You'll be fine. It's not hot, it's not cold. It's baby-bear temperature out there."

Two minutes later, I was parking in the Round Table's parking lot, sliding into a spot that was nicely shaded by a tall maple tree. "Be back as soon as I can, okay?" Eddie didn't seem to be concerned about his pending abandonment. He yawned, settled his chin on his paws, and yawned again.

"Silly kitty," I said, and found myself yawning as I crossed the lot and went in the front door and into a restaurant surprisingly crowded for a Tuesday morning in mid-September.

My yawn caught the attention of Sabrina, the diner's forever waitress. "Don't you dare," she said, but it was too late. She yawned. "How could you?" she asked, glaring.

"Sorry." Laughing, I slid into the last open booth. "Eddie started it. He's in the car."

Sabrina pulled a pencil out of her hair, a graying bun. "That's different. Cat yawns are more contagious than anyone else's. If he's waiting, we'd better make this fast. How about oatmeal and a biscuit, with coffee to go?"

"Perfect. But in addition to the milk I forgot to buy last night, I also forgot jam. Any chance Cookie could make me PB&J?"

"Consider it done." Sabrina tapped her pad. "But you need more lunch than that. You're going to get an apple, sliced and drizzled with lemon to keep it from getting all brown, a snack bag of crackers, and some slices of cheese. Don't bother changing the order, because that's what you're going to get."

Meekly, I raised my hand. "Can I get strawberry jam on the sandwich?"

She heaved a huge sigh and made a crossing-out motion on the pad. "Raspberry out, strawberry in. Anything else, princess?"

"No, ma'am."

Sabrina winked. I smiled. I loved Sabrina and couldn't imagine the Round Table without her.

"How's he doing?" I asked, tipping my head to the back corner, where a man was typing on his laptop, magically making oodles of money doing something mysterious with stocks. Or bonds. Or something. Bill D'Arcy, after driving into the outside wall of the restaurant, had admitted to Sabrina that he had macular degeneration, at which time they'd publicly confessed their love for each other and married soon after.

"Right now his eyesight is stable," she said. "So fingers crossed. I'll be back in a jiff with your coffee."

She bustled off and before the kitchen door swung shut, I could hear her shouting to the cook to get off his heinie and start Miss Minnie's breakfast.

The front door opened and closed, and I heard a woman say, "Let's sit in a booth, Hal."

"None open," said a familiar voice.

I turned. Yes, it was indeed Detective Hal Inwood. Excellent. I waved. "You can sit with me. I'm by myself today."

Hal looked at me, looked at the woman I assumed to be his wife, and hesitated.

"Goodness, Hal," she said, "let's sit with the young woman. I'm sure she won't bite."

I told myself not to take his hesitation personally, and smiled. "Not today, anyway. I've already ordered breakfast. And a peanut butter sandwich to go."

Hal frowned as they sat across from me. "That's not on the menu."

"Nope." I smiled beatifically.

His wife glanced from Hal to me. "Why do I get the feeling you two know each other?"

"Minnie Hamilton." I reached out to shake her hand. "Assistant director at the library, and bookmobile librarian. Nice to meet you."

"You're Minnie!" She looked, I was pleased to see, delighted. "How is it I've never met you?"

"Believe me, it took a lot of effort on my part," Hal said. "Tabitha, this is Minnie. Minnie, this is my wife, Tabitha."

Tabitha's hair was a silky and bouncing white and her eyes were the bluest I've even seen. She had an open face that looked designed to be happy, and I found myself smiling at her just because she was smiling.

"How long have you been married?" I asked, trying not to sound amazed. Maybe opposites attract, but picturing the morose Hal and the sweet Tabitha as lifelong companions required more imagination that I had in me.

"Forty-three years," Tabitha said, smiling and patting Hal's hand fondly. "More than four decades of marital stress, discord, and strife. At least for me. Him, who knows? It's not as if he ever talks to me about his feelings. But that works out, because I get to make my own assumptions about what he thinks and can act accordingly."

I decided I liked Hal's wife very much.

Hal himself was paying no attention to the two of us, because he was pulling out a vibrating cell phone. "Good morning, Sheriff," he said, and got up to take the call outside.

"And now with him out of the way," Tabitha said comfortably, "we can have a nice talk."

I laughed. "Did you engineer that call?"

"Not this time," she said. "But I know what will

happen. He'll talk to Kit for thirty seconds, come back in here, and say he has to go, then he'll ask if I can make my own way home. He'll barely listen to my response, because I can always get home, and he'll hurry away, and I will never know why."

"Sorry about that." Hal was standing over us. "I have to go. Can you get a ride home?"

"Of course, dear," Tabitha said, but he was already gone.

The two of us watched him cross the room and bang out the front door. I turned to face Tabitha. "You were wrong. That was only twenty seconds."

We laughed so hard the other patrons turned their heads, including Bill D'Arcy, who famously didn't even notice the stir in the restaurant last summer when the decade's hottest movie star had stopped in for a cinnamon roll.

"Hal has told me a lot about you," Tabitha said, wiping her eyes with a napkin. "But he never once said you were funny."

"Didn't want me to upstage him, probably."

For some reason, this sent Tabitha into another gale of laughter. When she finally subsided, she said, "Do you realize how much he likes you? No, let those eyebrows drop down into their normal position. He likes and respects you and he appreciates the help you've provided."

My eyebrows went up again.

"Okay," she admitted. "Maybe 'appreciates' was a little strong, but he definitely thinks you bring a fresh point of view to the cases you're worked on."

That, I could more easily believe. "Has he mentioned the latest murder?"

"Brown Bernier." She nodded. "So sad. He sounds

like a very nice man. Hal didn't say much about it. He won't, not during an active investigation. But he did say you were the one to find Mr. Bernier."

Sabrina, who had already dropped off my coffee, put a plate of breakfast in front of me and looked at Tabitha. "What can I get for you, hon?"

"I'll have what she's having," Tabitha said. "Thanks, sweetie."

I'd heard the often-acerbic Sabrina called many things, but "sweetie" was not one of them. I pushed away the thought and said, "It's been a week since Brown was killed. And unless things have changed dramatically since forty-five minutes ago, which was the last time I texted Ash and asked, they don't have any suspects."

"Not even the spouse?"

"Well." I tried to picture Lindy as a killer and couldn't do it. Still, you never knew. "I'm sure they'll check."

Tabitha gave me a long look. "Do you know what I did before I retired?"

"Until today, I didn't even know your name." I picked up my spoon and dug in.

"Men." She made a rude noise in the back of her throat. "For years and years, I worked for a non-profit organization. I did deep research of state legislative policies. Property taxation was my specialty, but I also worked with planning and zoning issues."

I closed my mouth, which had been opening all on its own. "For some reason I thought you were a retired teacher."

"Don't let the white curls fool you." Tabitha fluffed her hair. "Underneath this mass of stuff lies a brain that likes to be used. The first couple of years of retirement were fine. I rested and read and did fun craft projects. But I've learned that without more mental stimulation I'm going to turn into a harping shrew."

While I found that hard to believe, I did have an inkling what she meant. And I also had an idea. "My fiancé sometimes helps me with research when I'm poking around into things that may or may not be none of my business. But he's a school principal and busy with beginning-of-the-year stuff. What do you think about helping me? I don't want to cause any trouble between you and your husband," I said quickly. "But maybe this—"

"Would be perfect." Tabitha gave me a sharp nod. "Just what I need. If Hal doesn't like it, well, that's just too bad, isn't it?" She smiled. "Tell me what happened that night, if it's not too upsetting for you. Maybe one more retelling will jog something loose."

Though it would upset me, it had to be done.

"It started with a meeting that went late . . ."

I apologized to Eddie when I got back to my car after the far-longer-than-expected breakfast. But all he did was blink one eye and put his head back down on the fluffy pink blanket that had been a gift from a boarder of my aunt's.

Aboard the bookmobile, Julia eyed the bright blue paper bag Cookie had unearthed and stuffed my Sabrina-dictated meal into. "Nice lunch sack," she said. "Don't tell me you've turned over a new leaf, started doing some real-live cooking, and upgraded its transportation."

As if. "Choose a far more likely explanation."

Without a pause, she asked, "Who's doing take-out in bags that color?"

I grinned and told her about my morning. "Do you know Tabitha Inwood?"

"Haven't had the pleasure. But it sounds like I need to amend that situation sooner rather than later."

The two would get along swimmingly, and I said so. "You know what else we need to amend?"

"Absolutely," she said. "The US Constitution. It's well past the time we should have an amendment to—"

Since the last thing I wanted to do was bring politics onto the bookmobile, I cut her off. "We need to amend the bookmobile's schedule. Every time I see Graydon, he asks how many new stops I have lined up for the rest of September."

Julia tapped Eddie's carrier with the toes of her sneakers, which today were in an adorable crowded bookshelves pattern. "Do you have any planned?"

We were at a four-way stop. To our right, a car had arrived just before us, and I was waiting for it to move. But the driver was waving at us to go first. I smiled, waved back, Julia did the same thing, and we puttered through the intersection.

"Most people are pretty darn nice, aren't they?" Julia said, still smiling. "Except for Graydon. I'm beginning to wonder about him. Is the man trying to work me into exhaustion?"

"You? What about me?"

She flapped her hand. "You are young. Full of vim and vigor. Working oodles of hours per week is good for someone your age. Teaches you many things about yourself."

Later, we had the unusual experience of a book-mobile stop with no patrons. Instead of chatting with Julia, playing with Eddie, or tidying, I hunkered over my laptop, working on a spreadsheet, trying to fit more hours into the day.

"It's possible," I murmured. Just barely, but it was possible.

That evening, Rafe stared at me. "That's not possible," he said in disbelief.

"Hey, you can't talk to Minnie that way." Keith Tanaka, one of the older teachers who worked in Rafe's middle school, aimed the pointy end of his pizza slice at my beloved. "She's your fiancée. Be more respectful."

I grinned around the big bite of pizza I'd just put into my mouth. In many situations it would have been inappropriate for an employee to help his boss install light fixtures in his house, but this was Chilson, and here all things were possible. And while there were many reasons I liked Keith—how he truly listened to each and every one of his students, how he had the worst-ever fake English accent, how he could pull off a bow tie—the way he talked back to Rafe was one of my favorites.

"Okay," Rafe said. "Minnie, my sweet, love of my life, light of my heart, what on earth makes you think you should schedule yourself to work that many hours in a week? Are you nuts?"

I chewed and swallowed. "I have it on good authority that I am full of vim and vigor."

"Not if you schedule yourself for that many hours a week. Because I know you. Schedule for fifty, and you'll work more like sixty. Or seventy. You do remember you're salary, right? You don't get paid overtime."

Annoyance crept in. "And how many hours did you put in last week? You were at the school by seven every morning, and did you get back before eight any evening? You did not. Hang on, let me do that math. That's, um . . ." Once again, I realized I did not have a Math Brain.

"Sixty-five," Keith whispered to me.

"That's sixty-five hours a week! You think you can do it but I can't?"

With the flats of his hands, Keith did a drumroll on the card table we were using as a dining table. "Gotcha! Your turn, boss," he said.

Rafe eyed him. "Isn't it about time you retired? I know you said in a couple of years, but what do you think about this coming June?"

"Questions like that make me want to keep working forever," Keith said. "And where are you going to find another math teacher with my background and experience?"

"That's right." I pushed the pizza box in Keith's direction. "Not many math teachers spend their summers helping their electrician sons with their contracting business. It's very handy for us."

"Just another of my many careers." Keith picked up a piece of sausage and onion. "Want to hear about the summer jobs I had through college?"

"No," Rafe said.

"Absolutely," I said.

Keith smiled. "One year I had two, and they were the best- and worst-ever summer jobs."

As he launched into tales of shredding bulk bank statements and working for a roofing company, I inched my hand over to Rafe's, palm up. He reached out and covered my hand with his, squeezing gently.

I smiled. Even if we were both working long hours, it wouldn't be forever. We'd figure things out.

It would be okay.

That night, as I was getting ready for bed, I was doing what I normally did at that time, which was talk to Eddie.

"All those stories Keith had of awful summer jobs," I said through the brushing of my teeth, "makes me feel like I missed out. Mr. Herrington was the nicest boss ever."

"Mrr?"

"Oh, sure. You never knew him, did you? Mr. Herrington was director of the Dearborn library. I practically haunted the place as a kid and started working there as soon as I was old enough."

"Mrr?"

"You thought I spent my summers in Chilson? I did. Mom and Dad sent me up here starting the summer I turned twelve, and I kept coming for years and years. But as I got older, I had to work more and had less time to spend up here."

A thought scampered through my brain, that working meant less time with family and friends, that there was a line between doing a job thoroughly and sliding into professional burnout, and that I'd best figure out how to stay on the safe side of that line.

"You know one thing about the summers I spent up here?" I asked after rinsing my mouth. "It's something I got to do, but Matt didn't." My brother was nine years older than me, so much older that I'd often felt like I had not two parents, but three. "And I have no idea why."

Eddie, who'd long ago stopped paying any attention to me, suddenly felt the need to run as fast as he could to the back of the houseboat. Since that wasn't far, he jumped onto the bed, ran the length of it, jumped down, whirled around, and hurtled forward.

I poked my head out of the tiny bathroom. "What are you doing?"

In one long jump he cleared the three stairs and landed on the smooth floor of the upper deck. At that point he had two choices: one, keep running, or two, try to stop.

Since he was Eddie, he opted for door number two and ended up looking like a cartoon cat on ice, his tail lashing and his paws scrabbling for a grip that wasn't possible.

I watched, shaking my head. "Do you enjoy that? Because you seem to do it on a regular basis. I mean, I appreciate the humor and all, but—hey! Cut that out!"

My cat had already recovered his balance. He'd also abandoned his pell-mell pelting and was, instead, crouching in front of my backpack, which was in its regular home, on the floor next to the front door. Eddie was doing that pre-leap thing, wiggling his back half from side to side, which did not bode well for my backpack.

"That's not a cat toy, okay? And it's open. There are books and papers and—hey! Get out of there!" I trotted up front. "Will you quit already!" I leaned down to pull the backpack away from him, but he'd managed to magically slide his front half inside. "How on earth did you do that?" I sat on the floor and started to detangle pack from cat and cat from pack. "Oh, quit purring. Or not. That could be the only thing that keeps you in treats."

I extracted Eddie from the pack, but he was clutching something tight to his furry chest with his front paws and rabbit-kicking me with his back paws. "Let go of that, whatever it is. It's not a cat toy, and—"

"Mrr!"

"Fine." Because now I could see what he had, and what was a cat going to do with a cell phone? "Have it your way."

He stopped, rolled one yellow eye in my direction, and bolted toward the bedroom.

"You are so weird," I called.

"Mrr!"

"Am not," I muttered, and reached for my phone, which had somehow ended up under the dining table. When I picked it up, I saw that Eddie had managed to turn it on and open up my Favorites list. Josh was always yelling at me to use two-factor authentication to protect my phone, and I finally understood why.

I started to shut it down but saw my brother's name and pushed the Call button instead.

"Hey," he said. "What's up, sis?"

"Remember all those summers I got sent to stay with Aunt Frances when I was a kid?" I asked. "Why didn't you ever get sent north?"

He laughed. "You want to know this now? Twenty-some years later?"

"Yep."

"Sorry, but you'll have to ask Mom and Dad," he said. "I have no idea."

"Really?"

"Really. My guess is they just never thought about it."

That was not the answer I'd expected. "Were you mad?"

"At the time, a little. Didn't seem fair that you got to spend all that time up there and I didn't. But I got over it."

"Would it help if I apologized?"

"Nope," he said cheerfully. "And now please tell me you're doing something about getting an engagement ring, because otherwise Jennifer might come up there and buy you one herself."

"What was that? Sorry, losing the connection. Better go now, bye!"

I thumbed off the phone but continued to sit on the floor, staring at it. "I wonder . . ."

Quickly, I scrolled through my text messages and found where Ash had sent me Lindy Bernier's address, and did it . . . yes! It also had her phone number.

"Lindy? This is Minnie Hamilton, from the bookmobile. Sorry to call so late."

"You're fine," Lindy said, but there was a question mark in her voice.

Once again, I'd jumped into action without thinking through all the steps. Or any of the steps, other than pushing buttons on the phone. "Um, I just wanted to say again how sorry I am about Brown."

"Oh. Well, thank you. It's going to take time, but I have friends and family to help me through this."

And there was my opening. "Must be good to have the support of Brown's brother. From those pictures you were showing me, they looked like they were close."

"When they were young, yes," Lindy said. "But to tell you the truth, they haven't talked since I can't think when." Her sigh gusted into the phone. "All those years. Makes me so sad. You always think there will be time to fix things, and then suddenly there isn't."

I asked softly, "Is it something you want to talk about?"

"Not much to tell. And it was all so silly. My in-laws died years back, and we needed to make a decision about their house. It had been in the family for a hundred years, but the medical bills had taken priority over maintenance, and it needed, oh, just so much work."

"I can imagine," I said feelingly.

"The only sensible thing to do," Lindy said, "was to sell it. Neither of them had the money to fix it, and it would have taken thousands and thousands of dollars. Brown didn't want to sell, but Bob did. And, since Bob was the executor of the estate, he . . . well, he just went ahead and did it."

"Brown must have been furious."

She half laughed. "My husband rarely got angry, but when he did, everyone within a five-mile radius knew it. He . . . oh, Minnie, I'm sorry, but I'm going to start crying so I'll say good night."

"Good-bye," I started to say, but she was already gone.

Eddie bumped the bottom of my shoe. "Mrr?"

I lightly tapped the top of his head with the corner of the phone. "Not. A. Cat. Toy."

"Mrr," he said, reaching up for it.

I pulled him into my lap and held him tight. He struggled for a moment, then melted into my hug and started purring.

So the Bernier brothers had been estranged for years. Could something have happened recently to flame those angry embers into murder? And if so, what?

Chapter 7

The revelation that Brown and his brother hadn't spoken in ages had, at night, seemed to be proof of revenge for motive. The next morning, the connection felt tenuous at best and ridiculous at worst.

"Ash already thinks the car didn't have anything to do with Brown's murder," I said to Eddie as I spooned up the last of my cereal. "If I tell him this, without anything to back it up, he's going to laugh in my face."

Since the sky was clear and the air warm, we were out on the deck, me on one lounge, Eddie on the other. Normally he sat with me, but today he was focused on the ducks paddling around in the water next to the boat, and that lounge was three feet closer to the ducks and therefore far better.

"I know the waterfowl are more interesting than I am, but a little opinion here would be helpful."

Eddie gave me a quick glance over his shoulder and went back to his ducks.

"They're not your ducks," I said, trying not to sound sullen. "And if you're going to ignore me about this, I'll talk to someone else." Not Rafe. He was far too busy these days. Aunt Frances had, once upon a time, listened to me babble, but she was still in the newlywed stage and I didn't want to distract her. Kristen? Also a newlywed, and busy with the restaurant. Who else could I . . .

"I'm so stupid."

"Mrr."

"You didn't have to agree so fast." I picked up my phone and started texting.

Minnie: *When would you have a minute to talk about the investigation? I learned something last night.*

Tabitha: *No time like the present.*

Almost before I finished reading the message, my phone rang. "Hal can't get over his old downstate shift schedule," Tabitha said. "He's up by five thirty every morning and if I'm going to criticize him all day like he claims I do, I have to get up at the same time. What did you learn?"

"It's about Brown's brother." I told her everything I knew, then said, "I'm not sure there's enough in that to talk to Ash or Hal."

"Agreed. So what's the next step?"

Excellent question, and one I hadn't thought about because I'd been too busy ruminating on brotherly motives. In addition to the speeding car I'd described to her, I'd also filled her in on everything else I'd learned, from visiting the city offices to Brown's bike club, and I was ready for a direction. "Not sure. What do you think?"

"Ariella Tice," she said promptly. "That young woman who used to work at the city, the one who thinks life is so unfair."

I felt obliged to defend someone I'd never met. "Well, it is."

"Of course it is, and it should be part of everyone's mission to make life more fair, but getting angry doesn't solve anything and gives you lines in your face before your time. Now. Yesterday I called the city to ask about dear Ariella, a young lady I wanted to thank for helping me with a problem on my water bill last winter, and was told she'd left. I worked up some tears and was finally told she now works at the Chilson State Bank. Next step is to talk to her."

I stood and, not for the first time, wished for an extra hand. Two was not enough to talk on the phone and carry both cereal bowl and cat inside. "And ask her what? Hello, nice to meet you, were you out on Ledwich Road last Tuesday speeding? And by the way, did you kill Brown Bernier?"

"You could try that approach," Tabitha said. "But I don't recommend it."

I laughed. "That was a joke. Honest. I'm open for suggestions."

"You know," Tabitha said slowly, "I have an idea."

A few hours later, at lunchtime, Tabitha and I met a block away from the Chilson State Bank. We'd texted back and forth a few times during the morning, fleshing out her plan, which I thought was brilliant.

"We all set?" I asked.

Tabitha, who had looked serene and confident the day before, and who had sounded just as serene and confident that morning, suddenly looked pensive and uncertain. "I don't know, Minnie. Aren't we going to be lying? Isn't that wrong?"

"Yes," I said. "It is. But along with the life-being-unfair thing, we also have to recognize that to accomplish our goals, we might have to do things we're not comfortable doing."

Her blue eyes gave me a long look. "Ends justify the means?"

"Not what I meant." That way could lead to deep, dark places I didn't want to peek into. "It's more like, um, a compromise."

She smiled. "You've thought about this a lot, have you?"

Almost every day. "Are we ready?"

"Possibly not, but here we come!"

The bank was one street back from the core of downtown. It was a relatively new building, all white pillars and reddish brick, and sent out an aura of solidity and permanence. I held one of the two glass doors open for Tabitha, and she marched inside, holding her purse tight in front of her with both hands.

She marched across the lobby's tile floor, where I popped ahead and held a second interior glass door, and kept marching forward until she reached the closest open teller.

"Hi," the young woman said. "Can I help you?"

"Perhaps," Tabitha said. "I want to talk to Ariella Tice. They said she works here."

The teller, whose name tag read KYLAH, nodded and looked at us a bit warily. "She does. Is there a problem? Do you want to talk to the manager?"

Interesting that the default reaction to an inquiry about Ariella was to assume trouble.

"No problem," Tabitha said. "Quite the opposite, in fact. I would like to talk to her if she's available."

The unspoken subtext of "I want to talk to her

even if she's not available" was quite clear to Kylah. She glanced around. "Um, she's on lunch, actually. Mara?" she called to the teller working the drive-through window. "Did Ariella go out to lunch?"

Over her shoulder, Mara said, "She's out back. You know."

I slid over to stand behind Tabitha. Mara had been on the bookmobile. At the time she'd worked at a different bank, but there was probably a fair amount of turnover in teller jobs, just like most places. And it wasn't that I was trying to hide; it was more that it would be better if I wasn't recognized.

Kylah turned back. From behind, I couldn't see Tabitha's face, but I assumed she was looking at Kylah beseechingly, with hope and expectation. In other words, Tabitha was using that kindly expression that contained a foundation of steely resolve.

"Okay," Kylah said, capitulating under the Grandmother Gaze. "Like I said, Ariella's on lunch, but since it's nice, I'm sure she's out back at the picnic table."

"Thank you, my dear," Tabitha said.

Kylah smiled, blushing a little. "Happy to help."

Back outside, Tabitha and I walked around the building and saw a twenty-something woman with long and straight dark hair sitting at a picnic table, cell phone in one hand, and an empty Fat Boys pizza box in front of her.

"Ariella Tice?" I asked, shifting straight into the script.

"I'm on lunch." She didn't look up from her phone. "If you need something, you'll have to go into the bank."

Tabitha and I exchanged a quick glance. Our

script was suddenly far less believable, but I plunged ahead. "You used to work for the city, didn't you? Doing utility billing? My aunt here"—I patted the arm of my newly honorary aunt—"wants to thank you for what you did for her last winter."

"That's right," Tabitha said, using a slightly shaky voice. "I was in Florida for a couple of months. When I was gone, one of the toilets started running on something fierce, using oh, just so much water!" Her eyes went wide. "So expensive! But you called me and told me all about the high use and I was able to call my niece here"—she patted my hand—"and she went over to the house and figured out what was going on."

Ariella looked, as might be expected, very confused. "Uh, sorry, but I don't remember."

"That's all right, honey." Tabitha smiled. "I just wanted to thank you in person. I'm sure you talked to so many people in that position you just plumb forgot. I stopped at the city offices yesterday, and they said you'd moved on. I was sorry to hear that. It seemed like such a good job for you."

Ariella put her phone down and glared. "Those idiots. I was set, working there. The finance director was going to retire in two years, and I would have taken over."

"You poor dear," Tabitha crooned. "I'm sure they're recognizing their mistake already."

"I wouldn't go back there if they came begging. Not after what they did to me." She harrumphed. "Give me a story about having to let me go because of budget cuts, and then what do they do? Buy a whole bunch of new stuff for the sewer department."

I'd spent enough time reading newspapers and

working on budgets to know that funding sources for general city operations and sewer operations were completely different. And, since she'd worked in the Finance Department, Ariella should have known that, too. Either she didn't know as much as she thought she did, or she didn't care about the facts.

"That sounds awful," Tabitha said.

"Yeah. They were out to get me, I know it. They just used any old excuse to get me out of there. They said I didn't have any customer service skills. I mean, seriously, what did they want, me to be sticky-sweet fake nice to everybody? You just can't. Especially when that someone—" She suddenly stopped. "Well," she said, getting to her feet. "I have to go back to work."

And she left, without saying good-bye, and leaving the empty pizza box on the picnic table.

I looked at Tabitha. "'Plumb forgot'? Seriously?"

Tabitha smiled contentedly. "Maybe a tad excessive, but it worked. We learned a lot, didn't we?"

We had indeed. That Ariella was one of those people who would dig for the prize at the bottom of the cereal box without bothering to eat any of the cereal. That she was nursing a grudge against the city of Chilson for her termination. And that she'd almost named someone who'd sounded like an enemy.

Had it been a city employee? Had it been Brown? And if so, had there been enough ill will between them to incite murder?

I needed to get back to the library, so Tabitha and I agreed to talk strategy at a time and place to be arranged later.

"Soon!" I called, waving at her and walking backward down the sidewalk. "Tomorrow at the latest!"

"Yes, but—"

"Text you later, okay!" I said, still walking.

"Minnie, you're—"

"Stop!" thundered a male voice.

I jumped straight out of my skin. Then, lungs heaving, I felt myself assemble again. I stared up at the library's IT guy. "Josh Hadden," I said severely, trying and failing not to pant like a frightened rabbit. "Promise you won't ever scare me like that again!"

He shrugged. "Okay. But it's not like it was my fault. You were the one not looking where you were going."

"True, but why didn't you say anything before I got a foot away?"

"Did. You didn't hear me."

This conversation was clearly going nowhere, so I diverted. "What are you doing in the great outdoors, anyway? I thought IT guys had to stay inside to keep their eyes from adjusting to bright light."

On a normal day, that type of friendly insult would have been met with an insult at a slightly higher level, and gone up from there until one of us missed a turn and victory would have been declared. This time, however, it seemed that things were going to be different.

"What?" Josh looked left and right but didn't focus on anything going on around us.

"Never mind. Were you out for lunch?"

Once upon a time, Josh had eaten many of his meals out of the library's vending machine, and any other food he ingested had come from restaurants. But when he'd bought a house, he'd arrived at the stark realization that his disposable income had been reduced significantly, adjusted his eating habits, and even become interested in cooking. He'd also lost some weight in the process, though he never wanted to talk about that.

"Yeah. Lunch."

We started walking back to the library. I couldn't think of a time that Josh had ever, in the history of our coworkership, talked to me outside the building during working hours. After work, sure, when a group of library staffers would gather together for some occasion, but not one-on-one. Clearly, he wanted to say something, and just as clearly he was uncomfortable and unhappy.

Which could mean only one thing.

Darn it.

"So how's Mia?" I asked.

"What?" His head whipped around. "What makes you think there's anything wrong? She had lunch with me, so we're good, right? That's what that means. She wouldn't go out to lunch with me if she was about to break up, would she?"

I tried to remember exactly how my relationships had ended. Had I hemmed and hawed while still going out with whomever? My memories were thankfully foggy. But anyway, I wasn't Mia, and Mia wasn't me, so my experiences didn't count. "Has she said anything about breaking up?"

"Well, no, but—"

This was starting to feel familiar. "Are you pressuring her to decide about moving in with you?"

"I asked her weeks ago!"

"Josh," I said, "this is what, Wednesday? Didn't you say less than a week ago that you'd give her time? That you'd give her all the time she needs to make such a big decision? That you'd be patient and not bug her?"

He hung his head. "It's just hard," he muttered. "I mean, she keeps saying she loves me. But if she really did, wouldn't she want us to be together all the time? I don't get it."

An idea struck me. "You should talk to Rafe," I said. "Ask him how long he waited for me to make up my mind."

"Niswander?" Josh glanced in the direction of the middle school, which from here you couldn't see because of hills, trees, buildings, and sheer distance. "He might be able to help me?"

Probably not. "Just ask," I said. "You never know, right?"

"Just ask," I said out loud as I stared at the computer screen. When I'd said those same words to Josh ten minutes earlier, I'd felt confident and secure that asking was an easy thing to do. People were, in a broad and very general sense, happy to help. People liked to feel their knowledge and experience were useful. People liked to share.

So why was I dawdling about calling someone who might have information that could lead us to Brown's killer?

"Quit being such a scaredy-cat," I told myself. After all, what was the worst that could happen?

Possible answers to that question simultaneously gave me confidence and terrified me. Nonetheless, I picked up my cell phone and called the contact phone number on the website for the proposed non-motorized trail connecting Chilson to Petoskey.

"Hello," said a pleasant-sounding female. "Toned-agana Connection, this is Honey."

"Hi, Honey. I don't know if you remember me, but this is Minnie Hamilton."

"Minnie! Of course! How could anyone forget the bookmobile librarian? How are you?"

We chatted briefly about things of no consequence; then I took a deep breath and launched into the spiel I'd spent all of ten seconds preparing. "You're the only person I know around here who's seriously into bicycling, and I heard about an informal weeknight group?"

I intentionally made it a question, to make it easy for her to respond. Maybe Brown had told Lindy that his group was informal, but what he'd really meant was that it was just some friends getting together, and it wasn't really a *group* group at all. Maybe trying to contact these people was a wild-goose chase and I'd be able to cross this off the list and—

"You must mean the Wednesday night ride," Honey said, laughing. "Because the Tuesday group is hard-core. Nothing informal about them."

"Do you know where they meet?"

"Hang on, let me check. I keep a hard copy of that stuff handy, in case people ask." Papers rustled. "Here it is! Let's see. I was told they're meeting this week out toward Chancellor. Should be a good ride, lots of hill work for interval training. If you're looking to get into biking, this is a great group for getting your feet wet. Most of them are summer people, but they're really friendly and won't make fun of your equipment even if you bought it at a big-box store."

I had no idea that bike snobbery was a thing. I'd

obtained my current bike through Ash, who had bought it at a sheriff's sale of seized property for next to nothing. Its original provenance was a question mark. "Um," I said, but didn't get any further.

"Tell you what. The weather today couldn't be better for a ride, and there won't be many days like this left. I'll text the group's coordinator and tell them to expect you."

And there it was. The worst thing had just happened.

"Um—"

"I'm so glad you called. Before you know it, you'll be helping out with the new trail." Honey laughed.

"Wait, I didn't, I don't . . ."

But she was already gone.

And so it was that, six hours later, I found myself in the middle of the county, in the tiny burg of Chancellor, pulling into a church parking lot partially filled with vehicles, every one of which had a bike rack.

I came to a stop a little distance away from everyone else and got out of my car slowly, counting ten people of various ages wandering about the lot in various flavors of biking gear. Some were in colorful nylon and shiny black shorts, some in T-shirts and baggy shorts. I looked down at the biking shorts Ash had basically made me purchase and the T-shirt I'd purchased from the middle school band boosters and figured I'd be fine.

"You must be Minnie." A sixtyish man walked toward me, smiling. "Honey texted me you might be coming. Good to have you with us!" We shook hands, and he introduced himself as Terry Ridenour, recently retired Grand Rapids dentist.

"Want some help with that?" He gestured at my car's trunk, which I'd popped open.

"Sure, thanks." Between the two of us, we leveraged my bike out and onto the ground, and he held it upright while I reached back into the trunk for the front wheel.

"Honey said there's going to be a lot of hills tonight?"

Terry laughed. "Don't worry. Take a look at us. We're not fast riders. And you have enough gears"— he nodded at my bike—"to get you up the steepest grades. And even if you can't, we don't make fun if you have to get off and walk. Happens to all of us."

I suddenly wondered if that was why Brown had been off his bike. Not that he'd been on a big hill, but at the end of a long ride, I'd bet even a small hill could seem mountainous.

"Thanks." I rotated the quick-release lever into place and pushed it down firmly. "Are all these folks regulars?"

Terry stepped back and looked around. "It's a fluid group. Most of us are summer people, and you know what we're like."

He laughed and I smiled. Summer people had a reputation for being undependable for group activities, from chili cook-offs to fund-raising concerts. I'd come to the conclusion that the reputation could be just as easily applied to locals, but so far I'd managed to keep that opinion to myself.

"Didn't Brown Bernier ride with this group?" I asked. "So sad about him."

Terry's shoulders slumped and he looked away. "Yeah. It is," he said quietly. "We'll miss him. He was a good guy. Did you know him?"

"I know his wife better." Which was the absolute truth. "She was asking if anyone in this group might be interested in attending the memorial service. It's not scheduled yet," I said quickly. "But when it is, do you think people would want to go?"

"Some of us. Most, probably." Terry surveyed his fellow bikers. "Let Honey know. She'll get the info to me and I'll get it out to everyone else."

I hesitated, searching for the right words. "Did everyone get along with Brown? Because I wouldn't want to invite anyone who would upset Lindy or the rest of the family."

"Not getting along with Brown," Terry said, half smiling, "would be like not getting along with Santa Claus. I can't think of a single person who—" He stopped abruptly.

I let the space hang for a moment. "You've remembered something? Someone?"

"There was this guy," Terry said, frowning. "When he showed up a few weeks ago, Brown was surprised to see him and not happy about it. Brown obviously knew him, but never said how."

My pulse quickened. "Is he here tonight?" But Terry was shaking his head. "Do you remember his name? What he looked like? Anything?"

Terry didn't, other than that he'd been in the fortyish age range. "Sorry. Like I said, we're a pretty casual group, and people come and go. I collect phone numbers for people who want to get the updates on where we're going to meet, but I put that on Facebook, too." He studied me. "I can see this is important to you. Let's ask everyone else if they remember anything." He looked around. "Rosalind? How about you?"

"Sure," said a nearby young woman who might have been fifteen. "He came with us on that ride around Dooley. Was he the one with that yellow bike? His name was . . . oh, darn. I thought I knew it. Started with an A, maybe? I think? Or a D? No, I'm probably thinking D because we went to Dooley." She shrugged. "Sorry."

And no one else, not at the beginning of the ride, or throughout the entire length of the ten-mile ride, could remember anything else.

The only thing that saved me from collapsing into a small pile of sweaty Minnie on our return to the parking lot was the happy fact that the sun was down at seven thirty, and it wasn't safe for bicyclists to be out on the road, so the ride was miles and miles shorter than summer rides.

Rosalind, my new young friend, helped me get my bike back into my car and slammed the trunk lid down for me. "See you next week?" she asked.

"I might have a meeting," I said. Which could be true. There was undoubtedly a meeting somewhere I could find to attend. Chamber of commerce. Historical society. Fantasy football. Anything.

"Only a few more weeks of this." She tugged at the hem of her shirt and grinned. "Then it's time to do things steep and snowy. Do you ride? Or ski?"

Snowboards and I weren't compatible, but I did ski. However, I had a feeling this energetic youngster wouldn't consider my easy cruising down the intermediate slopes as true skiing. Still, I didn't want to come across like the old fuddy-duddy I suddenly felt myself to be, so I smiled, waved, and said, "See you on the slopes!"

I dropped into my driver's seat and collapsed. "Just out of shape, that's all," I muttered. No way was I old. I was only thirty-five. Not even all the way to middle age. But I was old enough to know I was probably going to hurt the next day.

Sighing, I put my car key into the ignition, but instead of starting the engine, I opened the baby backpack I'd stuffed my cell phone into and checked for text messages. No texts, but there was a voice mail from a number I didn't recognize.

"Minnie? This is Heather. From Lakeview. It's Max and . . ." She stopped, and started again. "Sorry, but this isn't something I want to leave a message about. Would you have time to stop by? Tonight?"

Sooner than any law enforcement officer would have considered legal, I was back in Chilson and fast-walking through Lakeview's front door. All sorts of horrible things might have happened to Max. He'd had a heart attack. He'd had a stroke. He'd fallen and broken his hip. He'd managed, despite not having traveled beyond the borders of Tonedagana County in the last three years, to contract dengue fever.

Out of breath and worried sick, I poked my head into the first nurse's station I came to. "Sorry to bother you, but does anyone know where Heather is?"

A nurse with red hair as curly as mine gestured down the hall to the left. "Saw her headed that way a few minutes ago. She might still be down there."

I thanked him and hurried off, hoping to catch sight of Heather. But this wasn't the hall where Max lived. Maybe I should go there instead? My mind shied away from that, because what if his bed was empty? What if all the bedding was gone; what if his belongings had already been packed away? What if—

My mind was so busy creating fearful possibilities that I almost walked right into the lap of an elderly man in a wheelchair.

"It's about time," he said, crossing his arms and giving me a hard stare. "What took you so long?"

"Max!" I put my hands to my mouth, trying to quiet my shriek of happiness at finding him alive. "What are you doing?"

"Looking for you. Yes, I know this isn't my hall, but I have my reasons. Come along, now. We have things to discuss."

I blinked. We did?

Heather poked her head out of a nearby room. "Minnie, there you are—" Then she spied Max. "Well, darn. I'm too late."

"For what?" I asked.

"Never you mind, missy." Max wheeled himself away. "There's no time to lose. Are you coming or what?"

"I recommend the 'or what,'" Heather murmured.

"What's going on?" I edged toward Max but kept my focus on his CNA. "Is he okay?"

"Physically, he's as good as he's been in months. Mentally he's fine. Emotionally?" She shook her head. "He just heard that another friend of his passed away and he's got a bee in his bonnet that—"

"Mi-NER-va!" Max bellowed.

"I'll see what he wants," I said. "Catch up with you later, okay?" I trotted down to where Max was opening the door of a small parlor-type room designed for families to meet with residents in a homelike atmosphere.

Max wheeled himself up to a table and pointed. "Sit there. Do you have paper and pencil in that purse of yours?"

"Sure, but—"

"We have work to do," he said, and for the first time I could remember, he didn't have even a glint of humor in his voice or on his face.

"Um, what kind of work?" I sat where directed and rummaged through my backpack for a memo pad and pen.

"Two of my friends have died in the last few weeks. They shouldn't have. Something's going on. Something monstrous and vile."

And now I knew what Heather had meant. "Sorry to hear that," I said slowly. "How old were they?"

"Eighty-six and seventy-nine."

I put my pen down. "Max . . ."

"Don't you start," he snapped in a very un-Max-like way. "They were both hale and hearty. No reason they shouldn't have lived another ten years."

"You think someone killed them?" I tried to keep the disbelief out of my voice, but wasn't sure I achieved my goal.

"Something's going on," he repeated, glaring at me. "Find out what it is."

I looked at Max. My friend. The man who had become almost a grandfather to me, if I'd wanted to adopt a wheedling, cheerful, manipulative grandfather with a twisted sense of humor. "Okay," I said. "Who are they?"

"Fred Hallenius. David Olivarez. You can find their obituaries online. That will get you started."

I wrote the names on the pad, recognizing Fred

as the father of Will and father-in-law of Iris Hallenius, who'd hitched a ride on the bookmobile. The
other name I wasn't familiar with.

"With you on the job," Max said, rubbing his
palms together, "it's as good as done."

Though I was glad he was so confident in my abilities, I was more concerned with how I was going to
tell him that his friends were not, in fact, victims of
any crime, but had simply passed away from natural
causes.

"I'll do my best," I promised.

"You're a good girl, Minnie Hamilton." Max
winked and gave me a thumbs-up.

I gave him a wan smile and hoped he'd continue
to think so.

But I wasn't at all sure he would.

By the time I got back to the houseboat, my legs had
stiffened, a sad indicator that I was in for a couple of
days of pain and misery.

"Tomorrow," I told Eddie, "I am going to be doing the Grandpa Shuffle all day long."

"Mrr."

"What's the Grandpa Shuffle, you ask?" To demonstrate, I scuffed across the kitchen, not lifting my shoes
off the floor. "It's how people who have lots of joint,
back, or muscle pain sometimes end up walking."

Eddie, who was flopped across the dashboard,
watched my feet intently.

"Oh, I get it." I slid onto the bench seat and picked
up my phone. "You're okay with this style of walking
because it means your tail is far less likely to get
stepped on. Well, you know what my response to

that is going to be. Pay a little more attention to where my feet are and you wouldn't have a problem."

"Mrr!"

I ignored him—rarely a wise thing to do—and called Tabitha. "Hi, it's Minnie. It's not too late to call, is it?"

"Good heavens, no," Tabitha said. "No sleep for me until I watch the news and get all sorts of bad images in my head to ruin my dreams. Let's talk suspects. Compare notes. Assess possibilities. Do whatever it is that the formal law enforcement does, but backward and in high heels."

I smiled at the Ginger Rogers–Fred Astaire reference and once again made a mental note to make sure my aunt and Tabitha met. "Are you a list maker?"

"From way back." Tabitha laughed. "I used to . . . no, never mind. You don't care about what I did forty years ago, before you were born, when I was fresh out of college and making my way in the world."

I sort of cared, particularly if it was funny, but for efficiency's sake, I said, "Shall we each do a list, or should we use one master?"

"Young lady, the two of us are going to get along just fine."

"Master it is," I said happily. "I'll take notes now, put it into the computer tomorrow, and then we can figure out if we want to e-mail it back and forth or use a shared file."

"Perfect. First on the list is our unhappy and entitled little friend Ariella Tice."

"Alphabetical by first name?" I pulled paper and pen from my backpack and starting writing.

"Hmm. I was thinking more in terms of who popped into my head first, but your slant is better."

My laugh turned into a sigh. "She wasn't a very happy person, was she?"

"The poor thing," Tabitha said. "But what we need to determine is motive. And see if we can tie her to the car that almost hit our precious bookmobile."

As always when I heard someone I barely knew refer to "our" bookmobile, my heart swelled with pleasure and pride. "Ideas on that?"

"Not yet. Let's move on to other suspects." She paused. "Bob Bernier. He and his brother hadn't talked in years, and then he's calling on Lindy right after Brown died? Seems more than a little suspicious."

I hesitated. Thinking that someone might be a killer was harder than I'd thought it would be. But temporarily thinking the worst of someone had to be better than letting a murderer go free. "When I stopped to talk to Lindy, Brown's wife, his brother was there with her and . . . cut that out!"

"Excuse me?"

"Sorry. My cat burrowed himself into my backpack and is . . . no, my wallet is not a cat toy, so quit already, will you?"

Eddie squirreled out of my grasp and glared at me. "Mrr!" he said, and jumped to the floor.

Cats.

"Anyway," I said. "It wasn't anything specific, just some weirdness. Bob didn't say much. Neither of them introduced him to me; I only figured out by accident who he was. But there was just an odd feeling in the room."

"Hmm," Tabitha said. "People are most often killed by someone they know."

I half smiled. She'd sounded just like her husband. "Yes. I'll add him to the list."

"Anyone else? Because right now we're pretty limited, suspect-wise."

"Maybe." I told her about the bike ride and how there'd been a new guy a few weeks back that Brown hadn't been happy to see. "I asked around but didn't get any consistent answer about what he looked like. Or even his name, other than that it might have started with an A."

"Not much to go on," Tabitha said, again sounding a lot like Hal.

Speaking of which, a question needed to be asked. "Are you going to talk to your husband about any of this?"

"Next question, please."

I stifled a sudden concern for the state of the Inwood marriage. But they'd been married for decades, after all, and its internal machinations were none of my business. "How about developing a plan?"

"Let's sleep on how to get more information about Ariella and where she might have been the night Brown was killed. Same thing with learning the identity of the mystery bicyclist."

Serial yawns were threatening to unhinge my jaw. "Works for me."

"So our very next step," Tabitha said, "is to learn more about Brother Bob."

"Agreed."

And I knew exactly how to go about doing that very thing.

Well, at least sort of.

Chapter 8

The next day was another marathon bookmobile day. We were out on the road at first light and still on the road when the sun dropped below the other horizon. My initial post–bike ride morning stiffness rated a solid six on the one-to-ten pain scale, and Julia's first greeting was "What on earth did you do to yourself? Are you sure you can drive?"

But I could, and did. Plus, one of the many benefits of being on the bookmobile was that, during stops, I was able to move around and loosen up. By the end of the long day, I'd almost forgotten I'd been sore.

Julia's parting comment, back in Chilson, was a cheerful, "You only feel better because you're young. Don't expect to be able to feel the same way in a few more years."

"Not me," I called to her departing back. "I'm going to be the exception."

She responded with a peal of laughter, and since her laugh was among the most contagious ever, I laughed, too. At some root level in my brain, I recognized that she was right. But I didn't have to acknowledge that now, or even think about it, so I put Eddie's carrier into the car and asked what he did to deal with muscle aches and pains.

"Do you have some secret remedy? Because I've never seen you limping around after a day of chasing after, but never catching, seagulls."

Eddie blinked at me, then looked away.

"Okay, I get it. You can't break the Cat Code."

All the way back to the houseboat, I lectured Eddie about the benefits of cross-species ideas, how the world would improve if we all just talked to each other, and how the effort should start with the two of us.

Outside of one very loud "Mrr!" he ignored me, and by the time he was in the houseboat and I was out of work clothes, he was snoring. And since it had been a long day for me, too, I finished the day as it had begun, with a bowl of cold cereal, and went to bed with a book.

All this meant I didn't have time to poke around about Bob Bernier until the next morning. I was thinking about a plan before my alarm went off, and when I slid out from underneath a purring Eddie, I was pleased to feel only the slightest twinge of pain from my legs.

"Looks like I'm in better shape than I thought," I said. Eddie opened his eyes to teeny-tiny slits, then closed them. "You, of course, have the entire day to rest and recuperate. I have to get out and fetch the bacon. Metaphorical bacon," I hastened to add. "Me cooking bacon is bad for my frying pan and hard on the smoke detector."

It occurred to me that Rafe and I hadn't talked about cooking duties after I moved to the house. This lapse wasn't really surprising, since cooking and its subsequent cleanup were my least favorite household chores, but you'd have thought it would come up at some point.

"Something to worry about later," I told Eddie. "What I need to do now is head downtown. Yes, I know it's early, but I'm not headed to work, I'm—"

Eddie's snore, always loud, was suddenly loud enough to drown out my voice.

"Fine," I said, tossing my nose in the air and walking into the bathroom. "Since you're super not interested in my day, I'll stop talking to you about it."

I could have sworn I heard a faint "Mrr" but decided I must have been mistaken.

Not very many minutes later, I was standing at the front door of the *Chilson Gazette*, waiting for internal signs of life. Camille Pomeranz, who bore the title of editor but had been known to scribble *aka Jack of all Trades* at the bottom of her business card, was usually in early, and usually started a pot of coffee going first thing after walking in the door.

I had my hands cupped to the door's glass when I felt a tap on my shoulder. I jumped, and when I came back down to earth and could breathe normally, I looked at the tapper.

"Waiting for someone?" Camille handed me a mug of steaming coffee. "That lock is broken. Didn't you see the sign?" She pointed to a homemade sign just above my head that clearly read DOOR DOESN'T OPEN. USE BACK ENTRANCE.

"If you want people five foot tall and under to notice it," I said, taking the coffee, "you might want to consider a relocation."

"When it's so much fun watching you peek in?" Camille, a fiftyish African American downstate transplant, laughed. "Come around back and tell me why you're haunting my doorstep at seven thirty in the morning. If you want fifty newspaper subscriptions, or if you want to place a recurring full-page advertisement for three months straight, I'm all yours."

"Sorry, I'm after the usual."

"Information?" Camille held the door open for me. "What do you think I am, a newspaper?"

"Pretty sure that's what it says on your sign, so yes."

Camille swiveled her head around to look at the front window, where, from the back, the words CHIL-SON GAZETTE looked more like ETTEZAG NOSLIHC. "Hmm. Seems like you're right. Ask away, dear librarian."

"I need anything you have on Bob Bernier."

She frowned. "Bernier? That's the last name of the guy you and the bookmobile found out on Ledwich Road."

"How did—never mind. Yes, same last name, same parents. Bob is his older brother."

Camille eyed me, then went around the counter to the nearest computer. "May I ask why you're asking?"

"You can."

"And will you answer me fully and truthfully?"

"Probably not. At least not right away."

"Promise to answer all questions at some point?" she asked, typing. "A nod will suffice, that's good.

Okay, we have all articles back to 1947 scanned and indexed. That should cover everything. Robert, I assume? I'll add Bob into the search string, too, and . . ." She paused. "That's odd."

"What?"

"Hang on." She tapped the keyboard a few more times. "Yep, that's it. Born in 1952 in Petoskey. Played football, basketball, baseball, and was on the honor roll. Went to Central Michigan for a degree in business. Went into the air force right after that. Rose up through the ranks, and retired as a lieutenant colonel."

"That sounds more interesting than odd."

"It's not what's there; it's what is missing."

I tried to see over the counter and onto the computer screen, but I lacked the vertical capacity. "What?"

"No wedding notice."

"That's odd?"

"For a town this size, especially back then? You bet. Even kids who got married across the country would have notices in the paper. The parents would do it, just to get the word out about their kids."

I wasn't convinced, but now that I had his age, I knew who to talk to next. "Thanks, Camille." Laying my hand on my heart, I said, "This is my vow to give you whatever scoop there is as soon as I can."

Soon after that, I was in the library, working at my computer. As soon as I heard footsteps, indicating the presence of a coworker, I jumped out of my chair and hurried to the door. "Donna, do you have a second?"

The slim, gray-haired woman didn't pause on her way into the break room. "Kelsey just got here. Be with you in three minutes." And, true to her word, three minutes later she was in my office with two mugs of coffee.

"You are a kindness," I said, gratefully accepting caffeine for the second time that morning. "I have a nonlibrary question. Do you know Bob Bernier? Brown's older brother? He's a few years younger than you."

"Bob." She smiled fondly. "Now, that name takes me back. Yes, three years behind me, just far enough to make him a child to me. One of those boys who was good at everything. Was a big success in the air force, if I recall correctly."

"Do you remember if he ever married?"

Donna thought a moment. "You know, I don't think he did. Might be hard to find a wife, if you're career military. All that moving around has to be difficult."

But I was thinking in a different direction. Why would someone who graduated with a degree in business suddenly go into the air force? Could he have gone into the military in the first place to get away from a marriage—the one between his brother and Lindy? Had he been in love with his brother's wife back then? And was he still?

Saturday dawned, although the term "dawn" didn't seem to be an accurate description of the muted light fuzzed with a drizzle of rain and accompanied by a biting wind. I stepped outside the houseboat and immediately stepped back inside to change coats from light windbreaker to a lined shell with a hood.

"Winter is coming," I said to Eddie, picking up his carrier for a second time. "Good thing you're already wearing a fur coat."

All the way to the library and throughout the bookmobile drive time, I wondered how cats and dogs and birds and cows and basically all living creatures outside of humans managed to stay warm in winter and cool in summer.

"They're made differently," Julia said, yawning. "Google it. You'll get a million answers."

"But we're librarians. We're supposed to have the right answer."

"Not without researching, we aren't."

Which reminded me. "New topic. Did you know either of the Bernier brothers in high school?"

"Nope. Bob graduated before I got there, and Brown was, what, a senior when I was a freshman? We didn't cross paths much. Wouldn't have even if we'd been in the same class. They were both sports guys, I was theater, and you know how well those two things mix."

"Even in a school the size of Chilson?" My graduating class, down in Dearborn, had been over six hundred. If Chilson's was over one hundred, it was a big class. I felt Julia give me a pitying look and I glanced over to make sure I was getting the feeling correctly. "What?"

"Just when I think you've gotten the hang of small-town life," she said, "you say something so patently ridiculous that I wonder what you've gotten yourself into."

"You just used the word 'gotten' twice in one sentence."

There was a short silence. "I did, didn't I?" She sighed, and after a long pause she said, "Minnie, there's something I need to tell you."

All the life and fun were gone from her voice, and in the space of a single breath, my mind raced through a hundred frightening possibilities. Julia had been diagnosed with some awful disease. Her husband had cancer. While on vacation in some tropical land, a sibling had wound up with one of those creepy parasites people on hospital television shows are always getting.

No. If something that serious were going on, she wouldn't have told me while I was driving. "Tell me what?"

Julia being Julia, she went at it obliquely. "For years, I've kept up. Exercise. Healthy eating. Drinking lots of water. Everything we're supposed to do."

I slid her a look. "Healthy? Is that what your potato chips and ham-and-cheese sandwiches are called these days?"

"Very little fried food," she said, waving me off. "I've kept off the weight, more or less. Stayed out of the sun, mostly."

Her voice had shifted into a serious tone and I suddenly realized this conversation was headed somewhere specific. By now I'd pulled into a gas station parking lot for the first stop of the day. Two cars I recognized were already on the far side of the lot, waiting for us. I shut down the engine and turned to face Julia across the console.

"What's wrong?" I asked. "Because something clearly is and I'm not opening that door until you tell me."

Julia fiddled with her seat belt. "I'm so sorry, but I can't keep doing this."

My breath caught somewhere in the middle of my throat. I swallowed it, where it settled in my stomach like a rock. "It'll be okay," I said. "But, just to be sure I know what we're talking about, what is it you can't keep doing?"

She laughed. "Tell me it'll work out and *then* ask me specifics? Shouldn't it be the other way around?"

"For someone who isn't as good at problem solving as we are, maybe. The two of us, though? Sorry, Eddie, the three of us? There's nothing we can't do. Now. Details, please."

"It's the new schedule," Julia said, looking at her hands twisting together in her lap. "I can't keep this pace. I'm tired. Plus my husband is getting cranky, and—"

I held out a hand in the manner of a traffic cop stopping traffic. "Say no more. One last question before I let the hordes in. Are you okay with the old schedule, or do you need to leave the bookmobile altogether?"

"What? No! I mean, yes!" She sent me a look of horror that was, in many ways, rewarding. "Of course I want to stay! I just can't work so many hours."

"Then we'll figure it out," I said, and got up to let in the first patrons of the day. But how, exactly, we'd figure it out was the big question, and Julia knew this as well as I did.

The board and my then boss, along with the library's attorney, had long ago decreed that no volunteers would ride on the bookmobile. I'd never been convinced the presence of volunteers would increase the library's liability in any real way, but my vote didn't count, and so I couldn't ask any Friends of the Library to help out.

"Did you hear?" Abe Begley, a regular bookmobiler, came up the steps, his long gray hair bouncing off his shoulders. Abe and his wife spent winters in their studio blowing glass of surpassing beauty and spent their summers selling their wares across the Midwest, and were expanding into online sales. "Well, good morning, Mr. Eduardo."

Eddie had perched himself on the console and was giving Abe a hard stare.

"Put it there, pal," Abe said, holding out his hand.

I laughed. "He's a cat, not a dog. He's never going to—"

"Mrr," Eddie said, and patted Abe's hand with his paw.

"You were saying?" He grinned.

"Just when you think you know a cat," I said. "But what have we heard?"

"Or not heard," Julia murmured.

"Which is far more likely," I agreed, "because I can't think of any big news."

Abe pointed to the open doorway. "Out there," he said, "in Mitchell State Forest. Early this morning, a couple of hikers found a woman."

Julia sat down suddenly on the carpeted step that ran the length of the bookmobile. I gripped my upper arms, holding myself tight. "You mean . . ."

He nodded. "A dead body. No identification, which is kind of strange. And you want to know what's even stranger? The hikers were on a footpath, but right next to her, they found a bicycle."

The rest of that day and all of Sunday, I thought about the poor woman who'd died out in the state forest. From the limited information Abe had given us—which of course was questionable since it was at least secondhand, and maybe third or fourth—it sounded as if the hikers had first seen the bike propped up against a tree, and the woman next to it, her back to the tree trunk, eyes closed as if she were sleeping.

"Like she'd reached her limit," he'd said, "sat down to rest, and never got up again."

It sounded a little Rip Van Winkle–ish, but with a worse ending. Abe had also said the hikers had guessed the woman's age as around sixty, so everyone's assumption was a heart attack.

"Women get heart attacks, too," I told Eddie on Monday morning. "They're harder to detect, though, from what I've read."

Eddie looked remarkably unconcerned about my health. He was perched atop his carrier and glaring at me. "Mrr!"

"Sorry, buddy. Yes, it's a bookmobile day, but only for the morning. I have to be in the library this afternoon and I won't have time to drop you off down here."

"Mrr!"

"I know, I'm the worst Cat Mom ever and I'm not your real mom anyway, am I, and I have no doubt you'll make me pay for abandoning you like this, but I'll do my best to make it up to you."

Babbling away, I slipped out the door before Eddie made his move. It was a small victory and a hollow one, because as I walked down the dock, I saw Eddie jump on the kitchen counter, where he knew he wasn't allowed, and continue his glaring.

I stopped, opened my mouth to scold him, but gave up the effort before I started. I'd lived with Eddie long enough to know that The Cat Always Wins, especially if that cat was Eddie.

Four hours later, my new helper was stumbling out of the bookmobile and into the library's parking lot, white-faced and groaning, her hands held to her tummy. "How do you do it?" Holly moaned. "Day after day, riding around in that thing, I can't believe you're still alive." She sat on a handy rock and leaned forward, putting her head in her hands.

I crouched next to her. "Holly, I am so sorry. Can I get you anything? Water? Crackers?"

Her head went back and forth in a super-slow-motion version of "No." "I'll be fine in a few minutes. I just need to sit on something that isn't bouncing every cell in my body."

Patting her knee, I said again, "I am so sorry. No one else has had motion sickness at all. I never once thought about the possibility." As a small child, I'd had problems myself, but since I'd never had any troubles on the bookmobile, I figured no one would.

"Seasickness and I are good friends," she said into her hands. "But it's been years since I had any troubles in a car. I was fine, though, until we got on Kolb Road."

Kolb was one of those classic Up North roads, full of curves and hills and curves and valleys and more curves. And lots and lots of potholes.

"I'm sorry, Minnie." Holly took a deep breath. "But I don't think this is going to work out."

It was a conclusion I'd come to three hours and fifty-nine minutes earlier. "Don't worry about it. I'll figure out another way." What exactly that might be I wasn't sure, but there had to be options. After all, there were other employees at the library, right? Who wouldn't jump at the chance to work on the bookmobile?

After escorting Holly to the break room and making sure she had water and something mild to eat, I headed out to shift books from vehicle to building and back.

"You want some help?" called a male voice.

I turned. "Hey, Josh. If you don't mind, sure." And since I was pretty sure that behind the highly unusual offer—as in it had never happened before ever—lurked a predictable conversation, I cut to the chase. "Did you talk to Rafe? About how long he waited for me?"

Josh shook his head. "Never would have thought Niswander had that much patience."

I'd often thought the same thing. "Three years is a long time."

"Three?" Josh's eyebrows drew together. "He told me he waited more than twenty."

"A nice story," I said, "but I don't believe it. No one meets a skinny twelve-year-old with scabs on her knees and falls so much in love with her that he patiently waits until she's thirty-five to propose."

"Kind of what I figured." Josh picked up the book-filled crate I'd pointed to. "And I love Mia a lot, but I don't want to wait until I'm fifty to marry her."

"How long would you?" I asked. "Wait, I mean?"

Halfway down the steps, he paused. And kept pausing long enough that I was starting to wonder if I'd have time to eat my peanut butter sandwich before I was due to meet with the Friends of the Library about the winter lecture series schedule.

"Well," he finally said in a quiet, low tone I'd never heard before, "I'm pretty sure that as long as there's hope, I'd wait forever."

It was the catch in his voice, right at the end of the sentence, that changed my mind about the whole thing. Josh was not an emotional guy. He was the kind of guy who, during father-daughter wedding dances, took the opportunity to go to the bar for another beer. He didn't see the point to musical theater and could barely be bothered to buy Christmas presents, let alone Mother's Day cards or flowers. If he was willing to let his emotions for Mia show, then he was deeper in love than I'd realized. And since Josh was my friend, I needed to do what I could to help.

Ten seconds after telling Josh I'd talk to Mia for him, I desperately wanted to run after him, to tell him I'd changed my mind, to say I'd temporarily lost all impulse control and could we forget that I'd ever volunteered to intervene in his love life?

But instead of any of that, I sighed and went into my office to eat my sandwich and small bag of potato chips as I prepared for the Friends' meeting. For a change, the meeting went smoothly and even finished on time, primarily because the long-running Friends' president, Denise Slade, was out of town. I commended the vice president on a well-run meeting and headed down the stairs and back to my office with the full intent of magically figuring out a way to staff the bookmobile's expanded schedule.

"There you are." Tabitha popped out of the reading room. "They said you were upstairs, so I've been lying in wait for you."

I looked left and right and saw no one. Still, I kept my voice quiet as I said, "Camille did a search on Bob Bernier."

"And?" Tabitha asked. "Don't leave me hanging, missy."

"Right. From what she found, he had a great military career. Lots of promotions, lots of moving around. But here's the thing; he's never been married."

"Never?" Tabitha squinted at me, frowning. "Not married young and divorced?"

I shook my head. "Doesn't seem like it. No engagement or wedding announcements in the paper. And my local source for that age group doesn't remember him getting married, either."

"Interesting." Tabitha tapped her chin. "And curious. But I wonder what percentage of career military never get married, and how that differs from the general population." She looked thoughtful. "I have a friend who works for Veterans Affairs. I'll ask him if there are statistics we can get."

Clearly, Tabitha was going into the research mode she'd used during her professional life. "That would be interesting," I agreed, because it would be. "More specifically, I'm wondering if Bob loved his sister-in-law from afar for years, and if he has, whether or not he killed his brother."

"To clear the field?" Tabitha nodded, her soft white curls nodding a fraction of a second later. "A definite possibility. So how do we find out if Bob has, in fact, been yearning for Lindy all this time?"

"No idea," I said. "But I'm sure we can come up with something."

Tabitha beamed. "My thoughts exactly. What time do you get off work today? Because I have an idea on how we can learn more about Ariella."

And so it was that at five minutes past four that afternoon, I met up with Tabitha outside the city of Chilson offices.

"Do you really think this is going to work?" I asked. "It was only a week ago I was in here talking about Brown. They're bound to remember me, and they're the ones who told me about Ariella in the first place."

"What do we have to lose?" Tabitha approached the front door and I hurried to hold it open for her. "And what's the worst that could happen, they say no, we can't talk to the city manager? My experience is that public officials are happy to talk to any member of the public who isn't complaining about something."

Cathy, at the front desk, looked up as we entered. "Good afternoon, what can I—Oh, hello, Minnie." She smiled. "How are you doing?"

I slid Tabitha a quick glance, which she ignored. Cathy and I exchanged pleasantries; then I plunged into the vague script Tabitha and I had developed out on the sidewalk. "Is there any chance we can talk to the city manager? Sorry for the short notice, but my aunt here is in town today"—not too much of a stretch because who doesn't have a non-related aunt, and Tabitha was in town today because she lived here—"and we're really hoping to talk to him about something personal."

"Oh." Cathy glanced over her shoulder. "Um, sure. Let me check. I'll be right back." She got up and disappeared down the same hall that Isaac had appeared from a week ago. Before I had a chance to get anxious about developing a Plan B, Cathy returned. "Come on back," she said, waving us forward.

And then Tabitha and I were walking into the corner office of Drew Parnell, Chilson's city manager. Light filled and spacious, the walls that weren't windows were hung with various city maps and sepia-toned photos of Chilson in years gone by.

Behind the large and imposing desk was a man in the fortyish age range. He stood when we entered, revealing himself to be of average height with a mild middle-aged spread. His close-cropped hair was light brown and getting patchy in places that he probably didn't want to talk about.

"What can I do for you ladies?" he asked affably, and gestured to the chairs in front of his desk.

I made sure Tabitha was settled down before sitting myself, and when I looked at Drew, I found myself feeling even shorter than usual. The chair's height didn't quite fit the desk and I found myself looking straight across a vast expanse of wood. I spent a brief second of envy for a desk that could stay so clean of paperwork, then opened my mouth to start talking. But Tabitha got there half a beat earlier.

"Mr. Parnell," she said a little breathlessly. "I want to take advantage of the time I have left in this world to spread the good news about people who have helped me on my way along this path we call life."

Though I was pretty sure my mouth hadn't dropped open far enough for adult flies to zip into my throat, a younger and smaller one might have. Up until now, I'd had no idea the woman sitting next to me could change personalities at the drop of a hat. All she and Julia needed for a hugely successful two-woman show was a script.

"That's right," I said, belatedly jumping into the conversation. "My aunt had a good turn done to her by a young woman who used to work here, and she was hoping to return the favor."

"Oh?" Drew leaned back and steepled his index fingers. "Can you tell me what happened?"

"Yes, sir, I certainly can." Tabitha spun out her tale of being down south for the winter, having her water bill run high, and having that nice young Ariella contact her.

"These days," Tabitha said, "you hear so much about the younger generation having poor work habits. I wanted to make sure you knew what an asset Ariella was to the city." She looked at Drew straight on, clearly doing her best to look old and weak but also charming. Though she didn't technically bat her eyes, she might as well have. "I hear that my young friend doesn't work for you any longer, that she's working as a bank teller for a lot less money. I want to know if I can convince you to hire her back."

Drew laughed out loud. "You have got to be—" He stopped himself, shook his head, and started again. "I'm sorry, ma'am, but Ms. Tice was let go from the city for reasons I can't talk about."

"But you could reconsider." Tabitha actually clasped her hands. "She did such a good turn for me, I'd like to be able to return the favor. Now that you know how helpful she was, surely there's nothing to keep you from hiring her back?"

And that was the whole point of the conversation. To gather more details about Ariella. Had she been terminated because of budget cuts? Had she threatened Brown? Our short conversation with her and her former coworkers indicated "yes" answers to both questions, but the question we most wanted answered was whether or not she was the type who might lash out in angry vengeance for actions either real or perceived. And who better to get that type of information from than her former boss?

Drew gave a faint smile. "To tell you the truth, there are a lot of reasons."

"But maybe not very good ones?" Tabitha asked. "Time has passed, and now you're reconsidering?"

He was shaking his head. "Like I said, I can't give any specifics, but maybe I'll ask you a question. Let's say your neighbor came over to your house and yelled at you for having a nice lawn and threatened to rip your lawn up with his lawn mower. What would you do?"

Tabitha pursed her lips. "I'd try to be kind to the poor soul, because he obviously needs more love in his life. Everyone deserves a second chance."

"How about a third chance?" Drew held up the requisite number of fingers. "Or a fourth. Even a fifth? And what happens when that neighbor disappoints you every time? Incident by incident, the situation escalates until you become certain that someone is going to get hurt. Is that when you call the police?" He paused. "Or do you decide it's easier to just move?"

I wasn't sure about the aptness of his analogy, but I was certain of one thing. He was drawing a very close connection between Ariella and violence.

Chapter 9

The next morning, Julia tapped her toes on Eddie's carrier. "So Holly and the bookmobile didn't get along?"

"More like Holly didn't get along with the bookmobile than the bookmobile didn't along with Holly." An image of Holly's pasty skin color and contorted face came and, thankfully, went. "Let's just say it isn't going to work out."

"I wish I could help more."

"Don't worry about it," I said. "This isn't your problem; it's mine." And if I couldn't figure out a way to staff the expanded outreach schedule Graydon wanted, I'd have to tell him it couldn't be done. But since disappointing my boss was something I truly didn't want to do, I was going to work extremely hard to find something that worked.

"Don't worry about it," I said again, which earned me a surprised look from Julia.

"About what?" she asked.

I blinked and looked around. More than ten miles had rolled under our tires since the last time we'd spoken. Julia had probably zipped through three dozen different topics in her head. "About anything," I said, laughing. "That's what Aunt Frances would say."

"Quite right." Julia's voice suddenly took on an upper-crust English accent. "There is no value to it. Worry brings no solutions and can only exacerbate problems."

I gave her an admiring look. "Kudos for use of a big college word."

"Four syllables, yes. I commend myself."

"Mrr!"

"And so does Eddie," I said. "Although if he wanted to play, he could beat both of us with just one long multisyllabic 'mrr.'"

"Easily," Julia agreed.

A few miles later, we crested a hill and were treated to a stunning view of the Mitchell River valley. I pulled in a deep breath of satisfaction at the sight. The maple leaves were just beginning their shift to the glorious reds, oranges, and yellows that would soon fill the valley with colors so intense you could almost see them in full darkness.

The leaves would fall, and then there'd be Halloween, and Thanksgiving, and Christmas, and New Year's . . . and where would I be? In the house, headachey and cranky from the paint fumes of final projects? No, far better to be in temporary quarters. Once again.

I tried to reconcile myself to my pending future, telling myself that it would be for two or three months at most. But as the days were growing shorter and colder, the more I found myself wanting to be done with moving twice a year. Though relocating from boardinghouse to houseboat and back had been fun, I was ready for a permanent home. One with Rafe. Because what I wanted was to wake up next to him every morning and to fall sleep by his side every night. To make fun of his clothing choices and to have him make fun of my cooking. To be married. Forever and ever.

"All we need is a house," I muttered.

"Did you say something?" Julia asked.

Not really. "Have you heard anything about the woman those hikers found in the state forest?" Due to my work with Tabitha, I'd been staying away from the sheriff's office, because I was quite sure I wouldn't be able to keep my mouth shut about what we'd learned.

"Only that they're still trying to figure out who she is. They didn't find any identification on her or her bicycle."

Which seemed a bit odd, but I supposed there were reasonable explanations for that. She could have lost it on the trail. Or had it carried away by a critter. Or maybe she hadn't carried any with her, something I'd done myself in the past—at least until my mother had found out and forced a vow that I'd always, always, *always* have ID on my person.

But what seemed even more odd was that no one had come looking for her, and I said as much to Julia.

"I've been thinking the same thing," she said. "And since it sounds as if she was about my age, more than a little disconcerting."

I didn't see why. "Your husband would send out a posse if you were more than ten minutes late to anything."

"Yes, but that's not the point."

"It's not?"

"No. The point is that this is happening at all. Every person should be missed. No one should be able to vanish for a week and not have a hue and cry raised."

"Okay," I said, and she was right. Everyone should be valued, and the loss of any person should leave a hole somewhere. "But there are reasons why a person could be gone and not be missed right away."

"Like what?"

Rats. I should have known she was going to call me on that. "Well, for one, a solo vacation. People do that, even happily married people. They leave everything behind for a week, no electronics, no nothing, and just get away."

Julia's sniff indicated that she wasn't on board with my theory. "Any other ideas?"

"Look at that!" I said, a little too brightly. "We're at the first stop, and there's so much to do!"

There were opportunities to think about other possibilities, but by the end of the day, I'd only come up with one. By this time we were in another corner of the county, leaving our last stop, a kindergarten-through-eighth-grade charter school that focused on arts of all kinds. It was a wonderful stop—the kids were engaged and enthusiastic—but after shutting the door behind them, we always took a moment to breathe in the quiet peace.

"One other idea," I said, starting the engine.

Julia checked the strap on Eddie's carrier and fastened her own seat belt. "Excellent. An idea for what?"

"For how a well-loved person could be missing for a week and no one would notice."

"You're still on that?" Julia laughed. "Dog on a bone, aren't you? Sorry, Eddie."

"Maybe the person's loved one is the one who's gone. On a trip with a group of friends. Or maybe at a conference. Or at a retreat. No communication expected, and that's why no red flags went up."

"Possible," Julia said. "Not very likely, though."

"Well, no, but I wasn't asked to assess likelihood. Just realistic possibilities, and—"

"And what?"

We were coming up to the intersection of the road that went to Brown and Lindy Bernier's house, a road that narrowed to a seasonal road not too far past their house and ended completely not much farther after that.

There was a familiar-looking truck waiting at the stop sign. I was sort of sure it was the same truck that had been in the driveway when I'd stopped to talk to Lindy the first time. And as we drove past, I took a hard look at the driver.

Bob. Bob Bernier.

Once again, Bob was spending time with the newly widowed Lindy. Was he just being a good brother-in-law, trying to help? Or was he trying to worm his way into her affections? And if so, had he killed his own brother to clear the way?

I didn't want to think so, but the possibility seemed to be getting more and more real.

Kristen eyed our foursome with a grim countenance. "I suppose you want to look at menus."

"Wouldn't think of it," Aunt Frances said.

Otto smiled. "Can't think why we'd bother."

"Haven't done in years," I said.

We all looked at Rafe, who actually opened his mouth.

"Can I—"

"No," Kristen snapped, "you can't. You'll eat what I order and you'll like it."

"But—"

She whipped around and stalked off.

"Huh." Rafe watched her go. "Is it just me, or does The Tall Blonde seem more irritable than usual?"

I'd been wondering the same thing. "She wasn't cranky during Sunday dessert. Maybe it's just you."

"I get that a lot," he said, nodding.

He absolutely did not. Rafe had to be on the top ten list of Easy to Work With. Kristen and I were pretty much the only two people who found him occasionally annoying, and that was because the three of us had been friends for so long, which created special circumstances.

"Not sure what I did this time," he said.

Aunt Frances smiled. "Your mistake is thinking that you did something. It could just as easily be something you didn't do."

"Or something you didn't do quite right," Otto added.

Kristen, though she'd originally waited on us, was now sending the wine steward in our direction. As I was immune to the intricacies of wine-food pairing, I quickly tuned out the sommelier and, instead of paying attention to her descriptions, surreptitiously looked around to take in the restaurant that my best friend had created.

Three Seasons was the former summer residence of a long-gone wealthy family. It had been a bed-

and-breakfast when Kristen had snapped up the five-thousand-square-foot building and converted it into what it was today. Kristen had championed the farm-to-table movement before it had been given a name, and she'd stayed true to her original vision. The result was more than a restaurant; it was a destination. It was a sort of community. It was becoming intertwined with the identity of Chilson, and I was so proud of Kristen that I could get all sniffly thinking about it.

An elbow to my upper arm brought me back to the present. "You in there?" my beloved asked. "Because you looked kind of fuzzy for a second."

"Fine," I said automatically, and looked across the table. "Are you two making any plans for trips?"

My aunt and Otto smiled simultaneously, smiles that looked identical in their relaxed ease. Aunt Frances laughed. "We're working on where we can go during the fall break. Maybe driving to Toronto. Only a seven-hour drive if the weather holds."

"But the break over Christmas and New Year's is almost three weeks long," Otto said. "We can get some good mileage in."

"And then there's spring break." My aunt looked thoughtful. "If I take an extra day at both ends, that's almost two weeks. I've read if you're willing to fly standby, you can get some tremendous deals."

Rafe, Otto, and my aunt all started to tell stories of travel savings they'd heard about, some that ended happily and some that didn't. As a humble assistant library director with an associated humble salary that was still paying off student loans, I tended not to pay attention to insider travel tips.

Someday, I told myself, I'd get to all the places I'd read about. Meanwhile, I'd go on being happy that my aunt was finally able to stretch her legs, both literally and metaphorically.

Right in the middle of a sentence about the timing of buying plane tickets, Rafe reached for my hand and gave it a nice, firm squeeze. My heart instantly went all mushy. Rafe understood. He knew how badly I was trying to get out from under the weight of my loans. Not badly enough to give up the occasional meal out, of course, but enough to keep driving an already elderly car, enough to buy most of my clothes from a local consignment shop, and enough to wonder how on earth I was going to be able to pay my half of whatever Rafe was paying for the house.

"Right over here, gentlemen." The hostess led a group of three men past our table. While I didn't recognize two of them, the third was Drew Parnell.

Hmm.

After a moment, I eased my hand out from underneath Rafe's, murmured something about the restroom, and wandered in that direction, which just happened to be in the direction of the table where Drew and his companions were getting the recitation of the day's specials, something we hadn't heard because of Kristen's high-handedness.

By the time I drew near, the three men were deep in conversation about tax-exemption certificates and, if I'd heard correctly, rehabilitation districts, whatever those were.

I mentally crossed my eyes—doing my income taxes was second only to dental checkups on my

Least Favorite Things To Do list—and went around the corner and into an alcove that led to the restroom. When I came out, I paused just inside the alcove, keeping myself out of view of the three men but within earshot of their conversation, because why not take advantage of the opportunity offered?

"Drew," one of the men said, "all these plans for economic development are interesting, but how do they help our budget in the short term?"

"And the rest of the city council will want to know the same thing," said the other man.

"I'm glad you asked," Drew said, in a very different voice from the one he'd used with Tabitha and me. He'd been calm and very patient with the slightly daffy old lady and her helpful niece. Now, he was talking fast and bright, almost as if he was trying to sell something.

"When you hired me," he said, "I promised to get the city's finances out of the red and into the black inside of two years. I'm closing in on that deadline, but let me tell you about what I'm implementing and how soon we can expect to get our budget balanced."

Eavesdropping, I decided, was not all I'd hoped it would be. I'd thought I might hear stories about Brown, who had been a longtime city employee. Or even Ariella, a recently fired city employee. Instead, I was overhearing conversations that sounded a lot like what I heard at library board meetings.

I headed back to the table and slid into my chair, where the conversation had shifted to predictions about the upcoming winter, a favorite topic for Up North folks. Rafe squeezed my hand again, and I squeezed back.

But instead of joining in to guess average temperatures and total seasonal snowfall, I was instead thinking about Ariella. And Brown. And Bob.

And bicycles.

My bike-ward thoughts didn't distract me for long, because our food came soon and Kristen's choice of cider-glazed pork tenderloin with garlic mashed potatoes accompanied by roasted Brussels sprouts drizzled with maple glaze diverted me—and my dinner companions—totally and completely and we ate as if we weren't likely to get another meal for months.

When I said as much out loud, Aunt Frances looked up from her plate. "In some ways that's true. It's the end of September. Kristen isn't going to stay open more than two or three weeks."

"Sooner," Rafe said, "if we get early snow. If she sees any little snowflake images on her phone's weather app, I bet she starts packing her bags."

This pained me for two reasons. First off, it was always hard when Kristen left for the winter. She was my best friend, and even though the older we got, the less time we were able to spend together, she was still my rock, my confidante, and the only person who knew how stupid I could be at times. Maybe someday I'd tell Rafe about the unfortunate mix-up with the milk and coffee and breakfast cereal, but since I hadn't yet, maybe I never would.

Second, the closing of Three Seasons meant cold, and since I was still on the houseboat, the thought of snow, sleet, and below-freezing temperatures was not a welcome one.

After Rafe had walked me back to the marina

and given me a hug and a chaste kiss ("Sorry, but I have to be at the school early tomorrow, and I'd like to give that handrail another coat of polyurethane tonight"), I changed my bed's sheets from percale to cozy flannel and slid in with a book in my hand and an Eddie tucked into the crook of my elbow.

I woke in the morning with dream fragments wisping in and out of my thoughts.

"Everything was so weird," I said to Eddie as I toweled my hair as dry as I could get it. "But I already can't remember if they were a lot of different dreams or all one long bizzaro one."

There had been bicycles. Lots of bicycles. Big ones and small ones. Fat-tire bikes. Sleek racing bikes. Mountain bikes. There'd even been a speedy tricycle ridden by a miniature version of Rafe, although his face had looked his current age. Ariella had been in a dream sequence, too, shouting at Bob Bernier for taking everything she'd ever wanted, which made absolutely no sense.

"But that's dreams for you, right?" I asked, shrugging. Eddie, who was still on the bed, didn't lift his head or even open his eyes.

How he knew it wasn't a bookmobile day I had no idea. When I'd mentioned Eddie's tendency to sit on the cat carrier as I ate my breakfast on days he went with me, Julia had given a stage smile and said something about cats and bonds and love that knew no bounds.

I'd been pretty sure she was misquoting somebody, but not sure enough to call her on it. Julia, when she felt the occasion warranted, could make the most mundane sentence sound like a pronouncement from the heavens. I had to be able to cite the source document to get her to recant, and if I could do that one out of five times, I considered myself lucky.

Eddie dropped deeper into sleep and was snoring when I quietly let myself out of the houseboat and started my walk across downtown and up to the library. The morning was chilly, and I was watching the high clouds scoot from north to south, thinking about the cold weather a north wind tended to bring, when I heard my name.

"Minnie, do you have a minute?"

Deputy Ash Wolverson was half in and half out of the sheriff's office front entry.

I looked up the street to check the time on the giant Victorian-style four-faced clock. Oodles of time to get to the library ahead of Kelsey. "Sure. What's up?" I asked cheerfully. But as I got closer, the expression on his face had me ask another and completely different question. "Ash, what's wrong?"

As soon as I got back to the houseboat that evening, dodging fat raindrops all the way, I called Tabitha to give her Ash's news.

"Remember a few days ago, some hikers found a woman's body in the state forest? Well, they've identified her. Her name was Emily Acosta. She's from downstate, and moved north this summer after she retired."

"The poor soul," Tabitha murmured. "Do they know what happened?"

I sighed a sad breath. "Yes. She was murdered."

There was nothing on the other end of the phone for a long minute. Finally, Tabitha asked, "What else did Ash tell you that my husband could have told me but has chosen not to?"

Uh-oh. "They just heard this morning," I said. "Maybe he's going to tell you tonight."

"Minnie, it's sweet that you're defending him, but Hal has never once talked to me about his work and I don't see him starting now, just because I happen to be tangentially involved. So. Tell me everything."

An odd sliding noise went from one side of my bedroom floor to the other. Still talking to Tabitha, I walked to the top of the stairs and looked down to see my cat batting around his new toy. A nickel. Where he'd found it, I had no idea, but I was pleased he'd found it during the day and not at three in the morning, which was when he most typically found new toys.

I pocketed the coin, earning myself a dirty cat look, and relayed the rest of Ash's information. "The cause of death was strangulation." I shivered and went on. "Her husband still lives downstate; he has a couple of years to go until retirement. He was on a hunting trip out west with his brothers and hadn't expected to hear from her until he got back, which was why no one reported her missing." I sighed, thinking about the years together that Emily and her husband would never have.

After a moment, Tabitha spoke. "Not that I want to borrow trouble," she said thoughtfully, "but there is a common element between Brown's murder and poor Emily's."

My recent dreams came back to me in full color. "Bicycles," I agreed.

And we started making plans.

Chapter 10

Tabitha and I discussed investigative tactics and in an efficient few minutes came up with tasks for both of us. "Let's talk again tomorrow," she said. I agreed, saying I'd call about the same time.

I put my phone on the kitchen counter. "Eddie?"

My cat, who wasn't a small version of his breed, seemed to have disappeared. This meant one of two things. Either he'd found a way to escape the houseboat, which would be very bad, or he was lying on the small pile of shoes in my tiny closet.

I pushed open the narrow door and looked down. He wasn't on top of my shoes; he was lying next to them, as he'd managed to push every single piece of footwear aside and was curled up on the bare floor. "Why?" I asked.

Eddie stared at me and opened his mouth in a silent "Mrr."

"Right. Well, if you don't want to tell me, just say so."

This got me another silent "Mrr," which I probably deserved. I reached down and patted him on the head. "Just don't put teeth marks in my flip-flops, okay? And I'm headed over to the house."

Not that I would be there long. Rafe was headed to Gaylord for a meeting the purpose of which I couldn't remember, and the two of us were having a short, quick dinner that would be tasty but undeniably unhealthy.

Accordingly, we were soon in the kitchen, opening the pizza box. "See?" Rafe pointed. "Onions on the whole thing. We're eating vegetables."

"Works for me," I said, digging in, because although I wasn't completely sure that nutritional experts classified onions as a vegetable, I didn't see what else they could be.

After a couple of bites of sausage and onion, Rafe said, "Remember when Keith was over the other day, and I was ragging him about retiring? Looks like he's going to be a former teacher sooner rather than later. He's moved his retirement up from the end of next school year to the end of this calendar year."

"Is he okay?" Because the only reason I could think of for such a thing was an unexpected illness.

"Not after I gave him a hard time for quitting on me early." Rafe grinned. "I think it was this last round of parent-teacher conferences that tipped him over the edge. Plus he said his investments are doing better than expected."

"Good for him," I said, and made a mental note to start investing in something. Then I asked the question that was pulsing in my head so bright and loud I was surprised Rafe couldn't see it. "How much longer until this place is construction-free enough for me to move in? Because I don't know if you noticed, but it's getting cold out there."

Rafe nodded as he chewed and waited until he'd swallowed and taken a drink of water before saying, "Yeah, about that."

"No." I spoke the single-syllable word calmly and precisely. "You are not going to say we're out of top-coat paint and that it's out of stock and has to be special ordered and will take six weeks to show up. You're not going to say the upstairs carpet that should have been installed in August has been damaged in a warehouse fire. And you are most definitely not going to tell me the electrical inspector found some faulty wiring and yanked our occupancy permit until it's all replaced, and since that particular wire runs through the whole house, we have to redo everything, everywhere, and it's going to take months and months."

Rafe had resumed eating during my soliloquy. When I finished, he stared at me with wide eyes. "How did you know?"

Abject fear chilled my entire body. "You have got to be kidding."

"Of course I am." He stood and kissed the top of my head. "Love of my life, I'm sorry but I have to get going or risk professional ostracism if I show up to this meeting late," he said, pulling on his coat and yanking papers out of his briefcase. "We could continue this entertaining conversation while I'm driving, but I told my Charlevoix counterpart I'd give him a ride."

I looked at the pizza and decided the short walk to the library and back had been enough exercise to justify another piece. "Drive carefully."

"Since you said so, I suppose I have to." He opened the back door. "Say, remember my buddy from college, Dave? He's up this weekend, so I probably won't get much work done on the house. And there's really nothing you can do by yourself, but since you're busy all weekend anyway, that's okay, right?"

"Wait, what do you mean—"

"Love you!"

And he was gone.

"I love that man to the depths of my soul," I said, "but sometimes he's more irritating than you are." I waited for a "Mrr" of agreement, then remembered Eddie was in the houseboat next to my shoes.

"Bad enough talking to cats," I muttered. "Now I'm talking to a cat that isn't even here."

Which reminded me of my promise to Josh, that I'd talk to Mia. I'd sent her numerous text messages and had even left voice mails, but she was ghosting me completely. I pulled my phone out and tapped out yet another text.

Minnie: *Lunch tomorrow at Shomin's? I'll buy!*
Mia:

Nothing came back from Mia. Not as I finished eating, not when I wrapped up the leftovers, not after I tossed the pizza box into the garbage, and not by the time I got back to the houseboat, not even the telltale dots of a canceled text.

"Maybe she's just working on a big project," I said to Eddie, this time for real. "She's so into whatever she's working on that the world around her doesn't exist."

Though this was possible, Josh had mentioned that Mia was between projects and was doing the kind of cleanup tasks we all tend to put off as long as we can.

I looked at my phone one last time and sighed.

Next step was to stalk the poor girl. "In a nice way, of course," I said.

Eddie, still in the closet, didn't reply.

I sat on the edge of my bed and thought about how it might feel to be stalked. To be followed by someone who meant to hurt you. To know someone wished you ill. To hear footsteps approaching, coming faster than you could run.

A tendril of fear started at the base of my neck and spread out across my back. I jumped to my feet, hurried to the door, and locked it. Outside, the wind was up and I sat in the cockpit, elbows on the steering wheel, chin in my hands, and watched the waves curl and crash, thinking and wondering.

Had Emily been stalked, out there on a lonely trail? Had Brown?

Why had the lives of Brown and Emily been cut short? What could they have done to get in the way of a murderer? Who had taken the awful, irrevocable step of ending the lives of two people?

And then my thoughts took a new, and even more frightening, turn.

Was there going to be a third murder?

Or even more?

The next day, the rain let up enough that I didn't get drenched when I walked to Shomin's Deli for lunch, on the off chance that though Mia hadn't responded to my text, she might show up anyway.

I waited by the counter a few minutes before ordering, then gave up and asked for the turkey and provolone with basil mayonnaise, my new favorite, and slid into a wood-seated booth to wait for my food to arrive.

I'd just had time to pull out my phone to check for e-mails when there was a heavy thump on the opposite seat.

"Going out for lunch all by yourself?" Kristen asked. "What, you don't have a best friend anymore?" She put her arms on the table and glared at me.

"Since you haven't had time to go out for lunch in four years, how was I to know today was going to be different?" I put my phone away. "And I sort of got stood up, so thanks for keeping me from looking like a social outcast."

Kristen rolled her eyes. "Going out to eat by yourself doesn't mean you don't have friends. It just means you're eating by yourself, something people do every freaking day in their houses, so why is it different to do it in a restaurant?"

I didn't know, but it was. I also didn't feel like arguing with her. "I was looking at the weather. It looks nice for the next few days, but it's almost October, so that's bound to change in a heartbeat. How many more crème brûlée Sundays do we have left? Two? Three, tops? Um, what's the matter?"

Because Kristen had an odd expression on her face. One that looked a lot like the one I'd seen on my own face after a long-ago picnic when I'd eaten deviled eggs that had sat out in the sun too long.

"Are you okay?" I asked, because she wasn't saying anything.

"Fine. It's just . . ." She stopped and looked at me with what looked like, but couldn't possibly have been, embarrassment. Kristen didn't embarrass. The last time she'd blushed about anything had been never. "It's just . . . well . . . is it okay if we have something else? Because I don't think I'm up to cooking crème brûlée, is all."

Not up to it? That made no sense whatsoever. "Of course it's okay," I said. "We only got stuck on crème brûlée because—" But I couldn't remember why. "Of course it's okay," I said again. "Anything you want."

"Okay. Great." She sighed with what looked like relief. Which was also strange, because if she'd really thought I'd be angry about a change in the dessert menu, there was something truly wrong.

"Kristen," I started, but she glanced at the wall clock and leapt to her feet.

"Sorry, I need to get going. We'll catch up Sunday, right? Right."

Rushing out, she almost barreled right into a woman a few years older than myself, who waved at me and said, "Hey, Minnie!"

It took me a beat to recognize Heather, because she was wearing jeans and a fleece sweatshirt and not the pastel-colored scrubs she wore at Lakeview. "Are you eating in? Come sit with me."

She nodded and in short order she was sitting in the spot Kristen had vacated, trying to get her hands all the way around a tall stack of corned beef on rye.

"Not working today?" I asked.

"Thanks to the scheduling gods," she said, "I have three days off in a row. And what am I doing with my time? Running errands for my husband and children, who are old enough to take care of themselves. Why do I do this?"

I laughed. "Every woman in the history of womankind has asked themselves that question, I think."

"Speaking of questions," Heather said, using one of the small pile of napkins she'd brought to the table to wipe her mouth. "Max was asking if I'd seen you . . . and from that look on your face, I'm guessing something's wrong. What's the matter?"

"Nothing. Not really," I said, stricken. "It's just I completely forgot to do something."

Heather looked at me over the top of her sandwich. "Doesn't sound like you."

"You need to get to know me better. I've been known to pull out my phone to look up my own phone number."

"Everybody does that," Heather said, which I didn't believe, but it was nice of her to say so. "What is it Max wants you to do? Please don't tell me it has to do with single-malt Scotch, because that interferes with his medications something fierce."

"No, nothing to do with whiskey. Or any alcohol." I hesitated, then remembered that she knew all about Max's request. "It's about those friends of his. I sort of promised I'd look into all that."

Heather shook her head. "He's just upset about their deaths."

"Sure, but . . ." I sighed. "But it's Max, so I'll do it."

Heather laughed. "You're so not alone. I'm embarrassed to tell you what that man has talked me into dressing up as on Halloween. So embarrassed that I'm not going to tell you. You'll have to come see."

My imagination flashed. Little Bo Peep? Wonder Woman? Glinda the Good Witch? Smiling, I asked about the next books the residents had chosen for reading aloud.

"They're trying to decide between *The Full Cupboard of Life* and *Rebecca*."

"Go with the Alexander McCall Smith," I said confidently. "*Rebecca* is an amazing book, but it creeped me out for weeks after I read it. Besides, happy endings are better than sad ones. And speaking of sad endings, I really have to go. See you soon, okay?"

I deposited my wrappings in the waste can and headed outside. But instead of turning left and heading back up to the library, I turned right.

Ash waited until I was done talking, then pushed his notepad and pen away and said, "Let me make sure I have this right." He leaned back in his chair and gave the ceiling a thoughtful look. "Max Compton, your octogenarian friend, recently had two friends die. Both of these men were, as far as we know, approximately the same age as Mr. Compton. For reasons unknown, Mr. Compton is convinced that one or both of his friends died under suspicious circumstances, specifically murder. Mr. Compton is so certain of his convictions that he has reached out to you, asking you to contact us to make sure justice is done."

Laid out like that in one long thought, it sounded as ridiculous as it had in my head. But Max was my friend, and I owed it to him to make as strong a case as I could.

"Both deaths were relatively unexpected," I said. "Yes, they were on the elderly side"—I ignored Ash's raised eyebrows—"but what are the odds of a man having two friends die in such a short time frame?"

"You're calling a heart attack for a man who'd

already had heart attacks 'relatively unexpected'?" Ash asked, and his calm, reasonable voice made me cringe on the inside.

For Max, I told myself. Though I didn't believe either death had been due to anything other than natural causes, for Max's sake I had to try. "And, yes, Fred Hallenius died of heart failure, but he hadn't had anything else wrong with him." Especially if you discounted the facts that he was in his eighties, and, according to Max, had smoked like a chimney for years and had high cholesterol.

Ash picked up his pen and started tapping the edge of the table with it. Since I was asking a huge favor, I made a solemn vow to not find it annoying. But since that was close to impossible, I started trying to make up words to fit the rhythm.

Rat-a-tat-tat, this is for Max. Rat-a-tat-tat, Ash needs to think. Rat-a-tat-tat, do not interrupt. Rat-a-tat-tat, this will work out.

"Tell you what." Ash stopped tapping and I sent up a silent prayer of relief. "I'll have the medical examiner take a closer look at the investigation reports."

"Thank you," I said, smiling gratefully.

"Can't promise it'll be soon," he cautioned. "And we both know what she'll almost certainly find."

Nothing, was what she was going to find, but still. "Anything is possible." I started to stand, then sat back down. Because this was a perfect time to shift into the task Tabitha and I had assigned to me. "Speaking of which, thanks for telling me about Emily Acosta."

He looked up from the notes he was making on a notepad. "I knew you'd hear eventually and I didn't want you to get any misinformation."

Otherwise known as gossip and rumors. "Thanks. But Tabi—" I caught myself. "But I've been thinking about Brown's murder, and I was wondering if you've come across the same information I have."

The pen tapping started again. I held my hands together to keep from reaching across the table and snatching it from him.

"You know I can't talk about an active investigation," he said.

Of course I knew. I'd heard nothing but that from Detective Hal Inwood for years. "How about this. I tell you what I've found out, and you look interested?"

Ash laughed. "I'll do my best."

So I talked about Brown's brother Bob, and how they hadn't spoken in years. How Bob had been spending what seemed to be a lot of time at Lindy's house. And how Bob had never married, not even once. I also mentioned the bike club ride, and the nameless and somewhat shadowy figure Brown had stayed away from.

As I talked, I detected a flicker or two of interest in Ash's face, so I figured there was some momentum, which had to be a good thing. "And then there's Ariella Tice."

"Who?" Ash asked, frowning.

Hah! Two points for the Tabitha-Minnie team! "A former coworker of Brown's. She was let go from the city just before he retired, and she seems to hold a huge grudge against him."

"Hmm." Ash made some notes. "Anything else?"

I took a breath. This was the big thing. "Doesn't it seem odd to you that we had two murders in the county within two weeks, and that both murder victims were out bicycling?"

"Odd?" Ash squinted. "Let's say outside of the normal bell curve of statistical probability."

Which was another way of saying odd. "So you agree there's a connection between Brown and Emily. With the bicycles."

"No, I didn't say that at all." Ash slipped his notebook into his shirt pocket and dropped the pen next to it. "I agree it's unusual, but correlation is not causation, and there are lots of things we need to investigate. We can't focus on that one thing and neglect everything else."

"Of course not," I said. "But because it's so unusual, it seems like a good place to start."

Ash nodded. "It does seem that way. And no, I'm not doing that mansplaining thing you hate so much, so lay those hackles back down. Murder investigations have procedures and processes, and we have to follow them if we want to get the evidence that's necessary for a solid conviction."

I sighed. "Makes sense." I didn't like it, but it made sense. On the other hand, Tabitha and I were not constrained by procedures or processes, and I said as much that evening on the phone.

"Exactly," she said. "Now, let me tell you what I learned today about Emily."

Tabitha's task for the day had been Internet research, which had felt odd to assign to her since I was the librarian in the group. But since she didn't have a full-time job, it only made sense.

"Turns out our Emily was influential in the display-fixture industry," Tabitha said.

"The what?"

"You heard me. Every shelving unit in every store has to come from somewhere, and that somewhere is the display-fixture industry. Emily apparently developed a type of universal unit that let stores adapt fixtures multiple ways."

"Sounds . . . interesting?"

Tabitha laughed. "For some people, I'm sure. But I don't see how any of that could lead to murder. And I didn't find anything that connected Emily to Brown."

"Except for the bicycles," I said.

There was a long silence that ended when Tabitha gently said, "You know what you need to do."

I did. But what I didn't know was if I could actually do it.

The rain, wind, and gray skies of the past two days blew out in time for Friday to turn clear and almost summer warm. At noon, I looked at the bike club's Facebook page and saw that Terry had rescheduled Wednesday night's ride for that evening and all were welcome.

After examining my current level of fortitude, I texted Tabitha my intention to go, and in return received a thumbs-up emoji and a tiny moving GIF of a bike-racing crash on cobblestones.

"With friends like this . . ." I sighed and resigned myself to my fate.

A few hours later I was out in the fresh air with a dozen other bicyclists, doing my best to keep up.

"Aren't we lucky?" Rosalind, on the bike next to me, gave a peal of laughter so infectious that, if I'd been able, I would have laughed out loud, too. As it was, I eked out a smile and said, "Looks like," though what I heard through my pants was more like "Ook. Ike."

I'd taken Rosalind for a fifteen-year-old on the previous ride, but I'd learned in the parking lot tonight that she was an eighteen-year-old college freshman going to North Central Michigan College in Petoskey. While Rosalind had listened to me describe my job driving Chilson's bookmobile with marginal interest, when I said my aunt taught woodshop at the college, her demeanor changed completely.

"Mrs. Pixley is your aunt? I mean, Mrs. Bingham? She's super great, isn't she?" Rosalind had beamed. "You're so lucky to be related to her."

I knew I'd been exceedingly lucky in the aunt lottery, but I wasn't so sure about the luck of getting in one more evening bike club ride.

"After tonight," Rosalind now said, downshifting to compensate for an increased incline that was doing its best to kill me, "we'll be riding weekends only. Not enough light in the day to get in any decent mileage."

Thank heavens for small favors, I thought. "How. Late. Do. You. Ride?"

"Until there's snow. But enough of us have fat-tire bikes now that we might do weekend rides all winter."

She sounded excited about the possibility, but I gave her a look of doubt. I liked snow and all, but winter was for skiing and sledding and skating, not more bicycling.

"You should try it," she said. "Doing fat tire is super fun!"

We crested the hill and I made a noise that wasn't agreement, but wasn't exactly disagreement, either.

Rosalind grinned. "You sound just like I used to. When it snows, come on out and I'll show you how much fun it is. We can . . . oh, wow, we're at the halfway point already," she said, nodding at a small road-side park now populated with bikes and brightly dressed people. "You want to stop? We don't have to."

Of course I wanted to. Rosalind and I braked near everyone else, and Terry, the dentist, promptly offered us water and protein bars.

"How did that go for you?" he asked.

I gulped down half a bottle of water, then said, "Ask me in a couple of days and I'll give you a better answer."

He laughed. "Like they say, what doesn't kill us makes us stronger, right?"

I half smiled but didn't have the heart to do any more than that.

The laughter fell off his face. "Sorry, that was in poor taste. With Brown dead, and now Emily, too."

And there was the opportunity I'd been hoping to find. "Emily rode with you folks, too?"

Terry nodded. "Most of the summer, I'd say. Not every week, because like I said we're not one of those die-hard groups that goes out no matter what."

"She was funny," Rosalind said. "Ms. Acosta. She had lots of stories about how dumb . . . um . . ." The young woman darted a glance at Terry.

"About how dumb men can be," he said affably. "Emily had been in a business dominated by males. She had stories about stupid men that would knock your socks off."

Rosalind quirked a smile at me. "This one time? She drove all the way to Chicago to look at a fixture that wasn't lighting. And you know what the problem was? It wasn't plugged in."

I laughed. "Let me guess. She found the problem in five minutes, and they weren't happy about it."

"Not at all." Rosalind shook her head. "Ms. Acosta said that had happened a long time ago, and now she would have known to take a little longer to tell them what was wrong."

"Ten minutes?" I suggested, which made Terry laugh out loud.

"Something funny?" asked a thirtyish man with a soft middle and a receding hairline. He'd been standing with another small group and had turned at the laughter.

"Just telling one of Emily's stories." Terry clasped Rosalind's shoulder. "Turns out my granddaughter has been collecting them."

Granddaughter? Had I known that little fact and forgotten it? Or had I never known? And did it matter at all?

"Emily." The man made what sounded suspiciously like a snort. "Not to speak ill of the dead and all, but I won't be attending her funeral."

"Well, Warren," Terry said affably, "not sure anyone asked you to go. Now." He clapped his hands. "We need to get going to make sure we're back before dark. Tallyho!"

There was a general move bike-ward, but I hung back and inched toward Warren. "You didn't like Emily?" I asked.

"Barely knew her." He grabbed his bike's handlebars and slung one leg over the crossbar. "But some people you don't have to know well, if you know what I mean."

"Like sometimes you meet someone and you instantly know you could be good friends, only the opposite?"

"Sure. I guess." He put one foot on a pedal.

"What about Brown?" I asked quickly. "I hear the family has scheduled his memorial service. Will you be going to that?"

He frowned. "Look, are you trying to ask me out? Sorry, but I'm not interested."

"What? No!" Heat flushed over my face, undoubtedly turning it bright red. "No, I was just wondering about Brown. He seemed like a nice guy."

Warren shrugged. "To some, I guess. I won't be putting on a dark suit for him, either." He leaned forward and rolled off, leaving me standing there with my mouth half open.

Eventually I closed it, but went on thinking.

And increased the suspect list by one.

Chapter 11

That night my sleep was broken into numerous little bits, mainly because Eddie kept yelling at me.

The third time he did it, at 2:23 a.m., I sat bolt upright and yelled back. "What is your problem?"

"Mrr!"

"Really? Do you hear me mrr'ing at you when you're trying to get some sleep?"

"Mrr!"

I opened my mouth, but shut it. Because there'd been numerous times in our life together that I had, in fact, woken him up from a sound sleep and felt not the least amount of guilt. "In my defense," I said, "you get, what, fifteen hours of sleep a day and I get seven or eight. This makes my sleep more valuable than yours. Besides, I'm the one with the pay check, so—"

"Mrr!"

"Of course monetary value isn't the only kind of value," I said, a little snappishly. "But it's two thirty in the morning and I'm talking to a cat. What do you want from me?"

I'd fully expected a "Mrr" of increased volume in return for my outburst. There was nothing. I leaned over the side of the bed and, in the dim light, saw Eddie looking down at his feet.

Guilt flooded through me. He was a cat, a semi-nocturnal creature, and here I was yelling at him for doing what came naturally. Apologizing profusely, I scooped him off the floor and snuggled him tight, murmuring promises of undying love and adoration.

His purrs came fast and strong. So fast and strong, in fact, that if I'd been completely awake, I would have suspected that I'd been manipulated into giving him more room on the left side of the bed, but since I was still mostly asleep, I didn't think about it until hours later, as I was opening the cat carrier door for an Eddie who looked remarkably well rested.

When we were all on the bookmobile, I posed the question to Julia, who thought it was entirely possible, and even if it wasn't, that it should be because of the humor value.

Even Doreen Ives, one of our newest bookmobile patrons, laughed out loud at the story. "With cats," she said, "you never know. Maybe he was trying to tell you something and was frustrated that you don't speak cat."

We all looked at Eddie, who was flopped across the dashboard, soaking up the weak sunlight. He managed to sense our attention and responded by shifting, rotating so that his back end faced us.

"Nice," I said, and said it again just after lunch when I deposited him back at the houseboat. I'd opened the cat carrier door and he lay inside, not moving, and glaring at me with the Look That Should Kill.

"You realize what's going to happen?" I asked. "If I walk out and leave this door unlatched, at some point you'll get out, swinging the door open as wide as it'll go, and when I come home I'll forget it's open and bash into it with my shin."

Eddie didn't move. Either he didn't think the scenario was realistic, or he didn't care, or he was a cat and didn't understand a word I was saying.

I blew him a kiss and walked downtown to meet Tabitha. We'd made plans to meet at the local bike and kayak shop around one, and just as the city's big clock was striking the hour, I spotted her white curls bobbing toward me. We met at the next intersection, turned down a side street, and three storefronts down, walked into Paddles & Pedals, jingling a cheery set of bells.

The shop's ceiling hung low over us, but that first feeling of slight claustrophobia was quickly offset by the bright lights that shone on what had to be a hundred bicycles, bouncing sparkling rays of starlight across the walls, the floor, and us. I brushed at the bits of white dancing on my front and was slightly disappointed that I couldn't feel them.

"Hey." The sole human in the place, a man about my age standing behind the counter and poking at a computer, nodded at us. "How's it going?"

Tabitha glanced around and said, as she often did, exactly what she was thinking. "I thought this place would be busy on a Saturday."

We'd actually hoped for that. Our plan had been to ease into what we'd assumed would be a crowded retail space, split up, eavesdrop on multiple conversations, and, in a friendly manner, ask questions that were pointed but not overly intrusive. It had been an excellent plan, but now we had to go to Plan B. Which we hadn't developed at all.

Before Tabitha could make the situation even more awkward, I jumped in with introductions that were true, though incomplete. "Minnie Hamilton," I said, holding out my hand. "I work at the library. And this is Tabitha. My aunt."

"Cody Sisk," he said, as we shook hands over the counter. "Owner, mechanic, sales, janitor, bookkeeper, and HR director of Paddles & Pedals."

Tabitha laughed. "A man of many hats."

He glanced at a nearby rack of helmets. "Some fit better than others, but yeah."

There was nothing like an on-the-fly metaphor to incline me toward instant friendship. I beamed at Cody, who, if my life's path had sent me in his direction a few years ago, I might well have considered dating. His smile was natural and his expression of genial interest was appealing. He was also slim and fit and had the weathered look of someone who spent a fair amount of time outside, which made sense for the owner of a bike shop.

All in all, I was already feeling guilty about asking him questions that might not be in his best interest. But I forced myself to think about the greater good and the reality that two people had been murdered. And that the killer was still out there, somewhere.

"My aunt here," I said, tipping my head at Tabitha, "has been thinking about getting into biking, but with what's been going on, now she's not so sure."

Cody frowned. "'What's been going on'? Not sure what you mean."

"Oh, you must have heard!" Tabitha clasped her hands together, gripping her fingers tight enough to leave white marks in her skin. "Those people, dying like that. It makes me scared to think about getting on a bike! What if I'm next?"

I gave Cody an apologetic glance that I'd brought my slightly wacky, overly emotional aunt into his store. "We heard about the murders of Brown Bernier and Emily Acosta. And that they were both into bicycling. It's understandable"—sort of—"that my aunt is a little concerned."

"Sure, I get it." Cody nodded. "It's horrible how both of them were killed. And my recommendation is to always bike with at least one other person. The buddy system, like in scuba diving."

Tabitha's eyes went wide. "That's so smart!" she gushed. "If only Mr. Bernier and Ms. Acosta had heard you say that. Maybe they'd still be alive."

"That's not the only thing I wanted to tell them," Cody muttered.

I shared a quick glanced with Tabitha. "Oh?" I tried to infuse the single syllable with enough interest to get him to answer but not enough to scare him off. "They were both customers of yours?"

"Do you call someone who buys an expensive bike on an installment plan but doesn't make the payments promptly a customer?"

"Oh, dear." Tabitha gave Cody a grandmotherly look of sympathy. "Did both of them do that? That's awful. And now who's going to make those payments?"

"Exactly." Cody sighed. "Makes me wonder why I ever dreamed up the idea of installment plans in the first place. I thought it would attract customers, and maybe it did, but the paperwork is a nightmare."

"Maybe their spouses will just return the bikes," I said.

He gave a listless shrug. "I'd never recover my costs. Bikes are kind of like cars; they depreciate as soon as you roll them out the door. I told Brown I really needed to get those payments on time, and he kept apologizing, saying he'd get right on it."

"But he didn't, did he?" I asked gently.

"No. And neither did Emily. I sent e-mail after e-mail and nothing ever changed." A flicker of something came and went on Cody's face.

There was a quiet moment; then he smiled and shook his head. "But you don't need to hear about all that. You came in to look at bikes, and bikes are fun." He gave Tabitha an appraising glance, taking in her white hair, perky dotted jacket, and fashionable-but-not-trendy jeans. "And I have one you might fall in love with. Let's take a look."

He came out from behind the counter and led us to a cluster of nearby bikes. "First question is where do you think you'll be riding? Road, trails, or a mix of both?"

Tabitha entered into the conversation with enthusiasm. But as I watched her charm Cody into the possibility of price cuts and discounts on accessories, I thought about the expression that had come and gone so quickly.

Because, just for the briefest moment, I'd seen raw, naked fear.

Tabitha and I walked out of the bike shop, waving good-bye to Cody and promising to stop in again soon. When we were safely away, I said, "For a while there, I thought I was going to have to explain to Hal why there was a brand-new bike in his garage."

"I like to think of it as *our* garage, thank you very much." Tabitha said, tossing her nose into the air vigorously.

"Point taken," I said, laughing. "Have you had lunch? Because if you haven't, I could buy you a late one to make up for my regrettable assumption of traditional gender roles." I'd eaten my peanut butter and jelly hours ago, and there was no reason I couldn't eat a little something.

Tabitha looked at her wristwatch. "I had lunch at noon, but I wouldn't mind a little snack."

"Where have you been all my life?" I asked. "Okay, that was kind of a joke, but honestly, why haven't we met until now?"

"Because while my husband is many things, he isn't stupid. He knows the two of us would double-team him and ruin his life."

I was pretty sure she was joking. At least I hoped she was joking. "Um, speaking of Hal," I said. "The other day when I stopped in to talk to Ash about all this, I got the feeling that he was doing most of this investigation on his own. Is your husband working on something else?"

She laughed, but not in a way that sounded like she thought anything was actually funny. "You're asking the wrong person, Minnie, remember? He does not talk to me about his work. At all."

"I suppose," I said slowly, trying to understand, "that he wants to leave all the violence and trouble and darkness behind him when he walks out of the office. That talking to you about it would bring it home. That making a kind of mental wall between home and work is his way to keep the two worlds from merging."

"That's one way to look at it." Tabitha nodded toward Corner Coffee, a new place in town, which served an amazing coffee/muffin combination, and we headed in that direction. "The other way is he has created a barrier between us. An impermeable wall that might have come down when we moved to Chilson, but instead has grown higher, wider, and stronger."

Finally I understood what was going on. When the Inwoods had moved north after Hal had retired from his big-city detective job, Tabitha had hoped for a change in their relationship, a change that hadn't happened.

I suddenly wondered how much Hal and Tabitha had discussed his potential employment with the Tonedagana County Sheriff's Office before he'd sent in his application. And, just as suddenly, I decided I would never ask.

"Say, isn't that Drew what's his name?" Tabitha asked, looking through the glass door of the coffee shop.

I was reaching in front of her for the door handle and paused to peer inside. Chilson's city manager was indeed sitting at a table. He was in the far corner, frowning fiercely at a laptop computer and drumming his fingers on the table.

"Opportunity is presenting itself," Tabitha said.

"It is indeed. But we should have a plan."

"Planning is for sissies." Tabitha smiled broadly.

"Um . . ." I said, but my companion had already made her move, sailing inside with an obvious intent.

"Good afternoon!" she said cheerily.

Drew lifted his head, blinking, and registered Tabitha's approach. "Oh. Um, hello. You're . . . ah . . ."

"I'm the one," Tabitha said in a rush, "who was really hoping you'd reconsider your decision not to rehire Ariella Tice. Now, I know you said she had some problems, but don't we all?"

"Ma'am, I'm sorry, but this isn't something I'm prepared to discuss right now. I can give you my card, though, and you can call my office to make an appointment."

"But surely you could—"

"Aunt Tabitha?" I interrupted. "Could you go get us some of those luscious-looking cherry chocolate chip muffins?"

"Oh!" Tabitha's attention was diverted. "That is what we came in for, isn't it? I'll go do that right now."

As she wandered off, I pulled out a chair and sat on the edge of its seat. "Sorry about that," I said, doing my best to sound like a niece who was accustomed to cleaning up her aunt's social mishaps. Sort of like the good cop/bad cop routine, only different. "Sometimes she gets focused on things and it takes forever to divert her away from them."

Drew smiled. "No apology necessary. We can't choose our relatives, right?"

"Right." I returned the smile. "Thanks for understanding. And I'm sure your decision to fire that young woman my aunt was going on about was a good one."

He leaned forward a little. "Terminations are usually hard, but I have to tell you, we really dodged the bullet on that one. She was trouble, and a lot of things that have happened around here since then make me thank my lucky stars I got rid of her when I did."

"Timing is everything," I agreed, hitching my chair forward. "Like they say, serendipity can be a real thing." I wasn't sure if anyone had actually said that, but if not, someone should have. "But what do you mean, things have happened?"

"Well, Brown Bernier's death, for one thing."

I blinked. "You think Ariella had something to do with his murder?"

Drew hesitated. "I'm just saying there was bad blood between the two of them. And that woman who was found in the state forest? Emily something? She and Ariella . . ." He paused and pursed his lips. "Well, what I can say is the interaction between them was the final thing I needed to justify Ariella's termination."

"You should talk to the sheriff's office," I said.

"No, no." He shook his head. "The last thing I want is to get the city pulled into a murder investigation. This is all just guesswork, anyway. I don't have proof of anything."

And even though I did my best to persuade him, he didn't budge from that position.

The summers I'd spent in Chilson as a youngster had led me to consider the boardinghouse as the one place where things didn't change. It wasn't true, of course, and I had to keep telling myself that. The place had seen oodles of changes over its hundred-odd-year life; it was just that they were made when I wasn't looking.

My aunt had come into its ownership after her first husband, Everett, had passed away, and it had come into his hands because he'd been the only person in the Pixley family who'd had any interest in owning the behemoth. "Rip it down" had been the general feeling at the time, but Uncle Everett and his young wife had felt differently.

Renovating the aging structure had been a labor of love for Aunt Frances and Uncle Everett, and the skills my aunt had gained during those efforts had led to her career as a teacher of woodworking.

The walls themselves were soaked with the memories of generations, all the way down through the plaster to the lath and studs made from virgin timber cut from Michigan's vast and now vanished pine forests. The floor was unfinished oak, grown from an acorn in . . . well, where had it come from? I closed my eyes, trying to recall what I'd once learned. There were oak trees here, but had they ever been commercially lumbered? Of course, someone could have logged off a local oak grove and sold that, so—

"Are you okay?"

My eyes flew open. Cousin Celeste was standing in front of me, her arms piled so high with boxes that she was peering around them to make eye contact. I scrambled off the attic floor, got to my feet, and dusted the seat of my pants. "Sorry, I was just thinking about where the floor's wood might have come from."

"A tree, is my guess."

I grinned. Celeste was one of the most pragmatic people I'd met in my life. "By golly, I bet you're right."

She laughed. "Let me guess. You were thinking deep thoughts about history and culture and local economies and I ruined it all by wanting to clean out the attic."

"Well, that is why I'm here." I looked around. As a kid, I'd found the boardinghouse attic beyond creepy and had done my best to stay out of it. As an adult, I still found the space a little creepy, but that was now offset by the fascination I felt for its contents.

Trunks with labels from faraway places. Antlers from deer and what I thought was an elk. Perfectly good chairs, tables, and bookcases that someone had managed to haul up the tiny attic stairs. Boxes and boxes, some full, some not, some labeled, most not. And then there was my favorite, the magazines. Stacks of them, piled hither and yon over the decades, all full of advertisements for products that were sort of familiar, but not quite.

And now Celeste was cleaning it all out, thinking to convert the attic into usable space. Space for what, she hadn't decided, but she wasn't about to let that small fact stop her. Celeste had cautiously approached Aunt Frances about the idea, and my aunt had laughed, saying she'd thought about doing that exact thing years ago but had never gotten around to it.

"What's next?" I asked, putting my hands on my hips.

"Are you sure Frances doesn't want anything

from up here?" Celeste looked around. "I mean, sure sure-sure?"

"That's what she said." I averted my eyes from the stuffed owl Celeste was bobbing up and down. Way too lifelike for an attic environment. "That big pile of boxes in that dark corner is mine, and I promise I'll get those out of here soon. But Aunt Frances said if she'd wanted any of this crap, she would have taken it with her. It's all yours."

"And yours." Celeste put the owl down and patted its head, releasing a small cloud of dust. "It's your history, too."

I appreciated the sentiment, but the attic at the house was already half full with castoff objects, some from former owners, some from Rafe, and some from my own self because the dining room bookcases hadn't been installed. Still . . . "I wouldn't mind some of the magazines."

"Perfect." She pushed an empty box my way. "Fill 'er up."

Um.

Celeste noted my hesitation. "No time like the present," she said briskly. "If not now, when?"

That was a good point, so I sat down next to a heaping stack and started sorting into piles of Want and Don't Want. Car, truck, and fishing magazines went into the Don't Want pile, along with knitting, needlecraft, and sewing magazines. All very interesting for someone, but that someone wasn't in the attic doing the sorting.

After a few minutes, I realized the Want pile was ten times higher than the Don't Want pile. This shouldn't have been a surprise—I was a librarian, after all—but there was no way I was going to haul more than one box of these things into the house.

"One of each," I murmured to myself. Because this was for the sake of nostalgia, and did I really need more than one copy of a 1953 *Popular Mechanics*? Or all of the *Seventeen* magazines from 1968?

I pulled out a random copy of *Seventeen* from the pile, hesitated, then pulled out another one and put them both into the box, firmly telling myself that when it was full, there would be no second box.

This decision simultaneously made me feel better and more stressed, but I took a deep breath and leaned forward, reaching for whatever was next on the unreviewed pile.

"Oh, wow," I breathed. It was a December 1964 copy of *Life* magazine, with a photo of a gorgeous, tousled-hair Elizabeth Taylor in full-blown color, accompanied by the teaser headline of ELIZABETH TAYLOR TALKS ABOUT HERSELF.

Since I'd had a fascination with the actor ever since I was nine and I'd watched *National Velvet* during a nasty episode of strep throat, I started flipping through the pages to find the article.

Halfway there, I stopped, thinking about the article's title.

Elizabeth Taylor had talked about herself, and that was something Brown and Emily would never be able to do again. Their voices were forever silenced, cut off before they'd had a chance to finish talking.

What I really needed to do was find a way to listen to their voices.

* * *

"Hello, hello, hello, Minnie!" A wide-smiled Lindy opened her front door wide and let me in. "I'm so glad you called. It's been a quiet day and I was starting to wonder what I was going to do with myself."

She put my coat into the front closet and led me into the dining room. "I wasn't sure if you'd be hungry, and I wasn't sure what you liked."

As soon as I entered the room, it became all too clear what she'd done in the time between my phone call and my arrival on the Bernier doorstep. The table was crowded with snacks of all shapes and sizes. Cheese and crackers. Grapes, strawberries, and melon. Tortilla chips and salsa. Spiraled rolls of ham and cream cheese. Chocolate chip cookies, brownies, and even a cake. How had she assembled all this in three hours?

Lindy looked at the spread on the dining table, looked at me, then back at the table. "I might have gone a little overboard," she said uncertainly.

I stood there, staring at an amount of food that would feed thirty people, and tried to think of something to say that wouldn't make Lindy feel stupid. As I floundered for words, I heard a small sniffing and looked over to see tears streaming down her cheeks.

Without saying a thing, I went to her and gave her a long hug, rubbing her back and letting her cry and cry and cry.

When her sobs ran down and she pulled away to blow her nose, I asked, "How about this? Let's go into the living room and just have a nice chat. Here on the sofa? That looks like a great spot to sit and read. You get comfortable, and I'll fill up a plate for us, okay? Do you have a favorite?"

She asked for roll-ups, so I made sure the plate had a few of those, along with a scattering of the table's options, both sweet and savory. I also fetched two glasses of water from the kitchen and made sure Lindy ate and drank it all down.

"You know," she said, staring at the empty glass, "I don't think I've had a glass of water since . . . then."

"Don't move," I said, jumping to my feet and hurrying to the kitchen. I found a pitcher, rinsed it out, and filled it with ice and water. Back in the living room, I refilled Lindy's glass and topped mine off, too, before setting the pitcher on a napkin.

"There." I plopped down on the upholstered chair opposite Lindy. "Now we can properly rehydrate ourselves."

Though I hadn't been trying to be funny, Lindy smiled anyway. "You're a sweetie to let me cry all over you like that. I barely know you, and now you're taking care of me?" She shook her head. "You're too good to be real."

I laughed. "Call my brother. He'll be happy to tell you all my flaws."

"There's nothing like a brother, is there?" Lindy glanced at a photo on a side table. From where I was sitting it was a stretch for me to identify the faces, but with a little bit of squinting, I made out Lindy flanked by Bob and Brown.

"Did you have that picture out before?" I asked, because I couldn't remember seeing it.

"No." Lindy touched the corner of the frame. "I'd never seen it myself until Bob brought it by the other day. It's from last year. We were all out taking a walk after Thanksgiving dinner, and Bob handed his phone to our oldest and asked her take a picture."

Since I now had social license to look closer, I hitched forward. Lindy's arms were around the waists of both Bernier brothers, who each had an arm across her shoulders.

"You look happy," I said. "But didn't you say that Bob and Brown hadn't talked for years? Because of their mom and dad's house?"

"Oh, they got over that a while back. Took some mediation on my part, but it worked out." Lindy studied the photo. "It was a good Thanksgiving."

What she wasn't saying was that it had also been the last Thanksgiving with her husband of many years. All the traditions the family had developed and grown into were now part of a history that could never be revisited.

"But you know what?" Lindy asked. "I will never again have to make that horrible rutabaga casserole. Every year, Brown wanted me to cook it, saying it wouldn't be Thanksgiving without it, and every year no one eats a single bite."

"Um, if Brown didn't eat any, why did he want it on the table?"

"No idea," she said. "I think it had something to do with his grandmother, but he could never really explain it."

She touched the photo again, half smiling, and I got the sneaking suspicion that the rutabaga casserole would be making an appearance in late November.

"You know that cute Deputy Wolverson, don't you?" Lindy asked. "Last time he stopped by I happened to mention your name and the look on his face me think there was some history between you two."

Um. I really didn't want to go into all that, but I didn't want to be rude, either, so I came up with a short synopsis. "We're friends. A while back we used to date, but I'm engaged to someone else now."

Lindy glanced at my still-naked left hand. "So you and Ash talk?"

"On a regular basis. He's friends with my fiancé, too."

"Well, there's something . . ." She sat back, shaking her head. "Never mind. It's too stupid."

The hairs on the back of my neck tingled. "If it's anything with the least possibility of having something to do with your husband's death, just tell me. I can pass it on to Ash, and if he laughs and thinks it's stupid—which he wouldn't, because he's way too nice—but if he did, I'm the only one who'll know."

Lindy bit her lips, considering. "All right," she said. "Brown had turned serious about bicycling, but I barely know the difference between a road bike and a mountain bike."

I nodded. I'd been the same way not long ago.

"For a few weeks before . . . Brown died, I saw someone I didn't recognize ride past the house." She nodded toward the road. "It happened probably half a dozen times, at different times of the day. Morning. Noon. Evening. It was odd, because this road isn't on the way to anything."

After a short hesitation, I asked, "How do you know for sure it was the same person?"

She smiled. "Because the bike was the brightest

yellow you've ever seen. I've never seen another one like it."

"This isn't stupid at all," I said. "I'll tell Ash right away."

That's what I said out loud, but on the inside I was making small whimpering noises.

Because, once again, I needed to go riding with the bike club.

Chapter 12

That night, after a dessert of apple dumplings and ice cream with Kristen, I managed to schedule breakfast the following morning with both Ash and Rafe. This seemingly simple transition took, thanks to the wonders of modern communication, a surprising amount of effort, though that could have been due to the nature of my fellow texters, and not the technological medium itself.

Minnie: *Hey, you two. How about breakfast tomorrow morning? Round Table at 7 am?*

Rafe: *On a school day???*

Ash: *A Monday, no less. What is she thinking?*

Rafe: *Too late for beauty sleep to help you.*

Ash: *Don't need help, I'm already pretty.*

Minnie (rolling her eyes): *None of that answers my question.*

Rafe: *Don't remember what it was.*

Ash: *Memory is the first thing to go, old man.*

Minnie (shaking her head): *See you at 7 am.*

As I was getting ready for bed, Rafe texted me the not-so-stunning news that since he'd been hanging with his buddy Dave all weekend, he hadn't had time to work on the house, and that he was glad I hadn't spent any time over there, either, but not to worry because things were going to be okay.

That was my interpretation of his text message anyway, which was laden with questionable abbreviations and emojis that made no sense.

Eyeing the garbled message, I strongly suspected that Dave was still in town and that the two of them were hanging out at a local establishment that sold nothing but adult beverages. But I also knew that, deep down where he kept it hidden from the world, Rafe was a solidly responsible human being who wouldn't drive while intoxicated, wouldn't let his friend drive intoxicated, and would be in bed at an hour appropriate for a Sunday night.

I blew a kiss in the direction of the house and snuggled up with a purring Eddie to read *Old Baggage* by Lissa Evans until I fell asleep. The next morning was so mild that, even though Eddie looked at it longingly, I didn't bother to plug in and turn on the space heater.

"You have a fur coat," I said, while I was toweling my hair, post-shower. "You're the last one on this boat that truly needs the extra heat."

I got a sudden image of Rafe and me on the couch in front of the fireplace, curled up under a cozy blanket, wind howling and snow blasting outside. And Eddie was on the hearth, belly turned toward the heat, head tipped upside down so he would see me, one eye winking.

It was an image so real I could almost feel the blanket's fleece, an image so real that when it wisped out of my thoughts, I felt a sense of loss so intense that tears pricked at my eyes. Which was ridiculous, because the vision wasn't a mirage; it was something that would eventually come true, even if it wasn't coming true as soon as I'd hoped.

A stray thought seared my brain. What if Rafe was being so slow with the house because he'd fallen out of love with me? What if he was getting tired of waiting for me to get the hint? What if—

"Don't be stupid," I said out loud as I left the houseboat and walked up to the restaurant. Rafe loved me and I loved him and the delays all had reasonable explanations. We were fine. It would work out. All I had to do was be patient.

"Here." Rafe, who'd already claimed Round Table's prime booth, pushed a steaming mug of coffee at me. "Don't say I never gave you anything."

I slid in next to him and leaned over for a morning kiss. "You give me all sorts of things."

"Colds, flus, sore throats." Ash sat across from us. "Viruses. Headaches. Hangovers."

Rafe grinned. "Not my fault if you can't keep up with the big dogs."

Why was it that every time males came in contact with each other, it turned into a contest? Was it the testosterone zipping around in their bodies? Was it a learned behavior? Likely both, but was there a way to unlearn it? Then again, if we eliminated male competition, there would likely be unintended consequences.

"Hello? Are you in there?"

I blinked, because Rafe's fingers were in front of my face, snapping away. "Sorry. I was just—"

"Thinking," Rafe and Ash said simultaneously. Then they nodded at each other and did a knuckle bump.

"What's the occasion?" Ash gestured at the mostly empty restaurant.

"Two birds with one stone," I said. "Rafe was busy with his buddy Dave all weekend and I didn't see hide nor hair of him, and I wanted to ask if you'd learned anything about Max's friends."

At the beginning of my sentence, Ash's expression had been one of puzzlement, but by the time I got to the part about Max, it had smoothed out into comprehension and a teensy bit of reluctance.

"Right. About that." He paused. "Hang on, here's Sabrina to take our order."

I twisted around. Sabrina was in the back, talking to her husband, Bill. Untwisting, I said, "Quit with the delaying tactics. She's five minutes away from our table, and anyway, when was the last time you got to put in your own order?"

"Last March," Ash said. "When did she start ordering for us, anyway?"

The three of us pondered. It hadn't always been this way. Once upon a time, we'd been able to walk into the Round Table and order anything we wanted.

"Summer before last I ordered a ham and cheese on rye," Rafe said. "No way would she let me have that now."

Ash started to say something, but I pointed my index finger at him and cut him off. "Later. I want to know about Max's friends."

He looked at me, but it was a sideways kind of look, and I suddenly knew exactly what he was going to say.

"Fred Hallenius," Ash said, "had a long history of heart disease and died of congestive heart failure. The medical examiner had no questions about the cause of death and there was no autopsy." Before I could say anything, he went on. "David Olivarez had a number of health issues, many of them respiratory, and he had an underlying kidney disease. Pneumonia was the stated cause of death, and again the medical examiner had no cause-of-death questions and there was no autopsy."

It was pretty much what I'd expected. I squinted at Ash. "Why did you not want to tell me that?" An awkward phrasing, but he seemed to catch my point, because he shrugged.

Annoyance flashed. "You think I *wanted* them to be murder victims? Do you think I imagine killers are lurking behind every tree in the county? Do you think—"

"Here." Sabrina plopped three plates of breakfast on the table. "Eat. Then yell at him. No doubt he deserves it, but it can wait until after you get food in you."

In silence, we started on the fried eggs, hash browns, and sausage patties (Rafe and Ash) and cinnamon pancakes with bacon (Minnie). Ash polished off all his eggs and half the sausage and said, "It wasn't you, Minnie; it was your friend Max. I know you have to tell him all this and I know it won't be easy for you or him. So I'm sorry."

My mild anger had deflated three bites into the bacon. "It's okay. I jumped to a conclusion I shouldn't have. So I'm sorry, too."

Rafe reached for the Tabasco sauce. "It's got to be hard for Max," he said, adding a disturbing amount of hot sauce to his hash browns, which he'd already doused with the stuff. "Having two friends die so close to each other can't be the easiest thing to deal with, no matter how old you are."

"Fred wasn't a friend friend," I said. "He and Max were coworkers. They both worked for the road commission."

Ash took the Tabasco bottle from Rafe. "David Olivarez worked there, too. Hallenius was a driver and Olivarez was an engineer."

I was touched that Ash had spent so much time on what was essentially a favor for me. "Thanks for looking into this. I really do appreciate it."

"No problem." He picked up his fork. "Do you want me to help you tell Max?"

Yes, absolutely. "No," I said, trying not to sigh and doing a poor job of it. "Thanks, but Max is my friend. He should hear this from me."

Ash nodded. "Okay, but if you change your mind, let me know."

"I can go with you," Rafe said.

My heart swelled with love and affection for these men. How did I get so lucky?

"But it would have to be early because of Monday night football."

"Going to be a good game," Ash said. "Tank said we're welcome to watch at his place. He bought a new flat-screen. Eighty-six-inch, I think he said."

My mushy smile faded as I remembered that I didn't have a completed house to move into. And was it my imagination, or was Ash starting to take on some of Hal Inwood's least-appealing characteristics?

As Rafe and Ash argued good-naturedly over

whose turn it was to bring the beer that night, I decided to put a hold on telling Ash what Lindy had told me about the bicyclist. It could wait a few days.

"What was that?" Ash asked.

"Didn't say a word," I said.

"No, but your face was speaking in complete sentences."

I made a mental note to start taking my poker-face practice more seriously. "It's getting late, is all," I said. "Who's paying?"

Outside the restaurant, I exchanged a hug and a kiss with Rafe; then he got in his car to head up to the middle school and I hurried back to the marina for Eddie, because it was a bookmobile day and if Eddie wasn't riding along, I'd never hear the end of it.

"You're late." Donna, who was sitting on a rock and soaking in the morning sun, pointed at her wristwatch.

I picked up Eddie's carrier and shut my car's passenger door. "Would you believe that I'm a minute and a half late on purpose so you could get more time in the sunshine?"

"No, but it is a nice byproduct. Hello, little friend."

The greeting was for Eddie, who mrr'd in return.

"He said hello to me!" Donna smiled in delight.

"Sure he did." I unlocked the bookmobile door and *oomph*ed Eddie's carrier up the stairs. "Because cats are so well-known for their social conversation skills."

"Maybe not all cats, but certainly Eddie." Donna came up behind me and looked around. "You know, I forget how wonderful this place is."

I beamed. "Comments like that will get you the choice chores of the day."

Her look was cautious. "Such as?"

My smile went wider. "You'll just have to wait and see."

Donna's wary expression grew even warier, but she needn't have worried, because all the bookmobile chores were fun. Setting up for each stop, tidying afterward, wrestling with the occasional technology issue, chatting with patrons, taking their requests for special orders, finding the exact book they wanted—it was what we were here to do, and it fulfilled me like nothing else.

"So what do you think?" I asked at the end of the day as we pulled into the library parking lot. "Isn't this the best job ever?"

"Mrr!"

"Thanks, Eddie, but I wasn't asking you. I was talking to Donna."

"Donna is all talked out." She patted Eddie's carrier. "Thanks for helping me out with all the twins, by the way."

I laughed. Donna had endured the ultimate bookmobile visit. The Engstrom twins had descended upon us today in full force. After more than two years, I finally had the names of all three sets of twins stuck in my head. Rose and Trevor, Emma and Patrick, Cara and Ethan. Ages fourteen, eleven, and eight, respectively, although I wouldn't have sworn to it. Their father, Chad, a designer of educational video games, worked out of their house and also homeschooled the entire group.

It had been young Ethan who, on the bookmobile's first trip, had outed the stowaway Eddie. Literally outed, because I'd been freaked out by my cat's unexpected presence and had been putting him in the vehicle's biggest cabinet when patrons were aboard.

All six were good kids, but they could become rambunctious at times, something Eddie wouldn't tolerate for more than a few minutes. And apparently, neither did Donna.

"You're lucky you have a carrier to escape into," she told Eddie as I hefted him down the bookmobile steps. "Maybe we could come up with something like that for adults."

It was an interesting idea, and as we ferried the crates of returned books into the library, I wondered out loud if hobbies were the equivalent of a hideaway.

"Golf is, for sure," Donna said.

"Maybe anything outside," I mused. "All those things you do, snowshoeing, running, they can be meditative, right?"

"Sometimes." She shrugged. "Sometimes it's just plain hard work and you wonder why you're out there, but other times, maybe even most times, it's a mental vacation."

I was still thinking about Donna's comment after I'd returned Eddie to the houseboat and driven to Lakeview. "Bicycling," I said out loud. Bicycling could also fall into the category of a hobby that was a mental vacation. And if I'd been on vacation this week, I could have delayed giving Max this news.

"Minnie!" Max zipped over before I'd walked ten feet into the lobby. He rolled to a stop inches from my toes and peered up at me. "You are the one person I wanted to see. Come into my office."

Office? "Um . . ."

But he was already wheeling away, so I trailed after him around the corner, down a hall, and into a small conference space that bore a strong resemblance to the interview room in the sheriff's office.

I looked around. "Is it okay that we're here?"

Max snorted. "What are they going to do, kick me out? Sit, sit, sit. I have something to tell you."

"Okay, but first I need to tell you something." I folded my hands on the table and started talking to them, because I didn't want to watch Max's face. "Your friends, your former coworkers, Fred Hallenius and David Olivarez? I talked to my deputy friend at the sheriff's office, and he talked to the medical examiner. There was no evidence of anything but death from natural causes. None at all."

"Yep."

Wait, what? That was not the reaction I'd expected. I looked up to see Max nodding. "But . . . before . . ."

"Ah." He waved his knobby hands. "I was having a bad day. It happens when you get this old. David and Fred, you know how old they were? In their eighties, for crying out loud, or almost. Of course they died of natural causes. Who would bother killing someone who's about to die anyway?"

I winced. "Max, that's a little . . ."

He reached across the table to pat my hands. "Inappropriate jokes are one of the privileges of old age, Minnie my sweet."

"Old age?" I eyed him. "So you're telling me you haven't made inappropriate jokes your entire life?"

He grinned. "How, exactly, are you going to prove me wrong? And that's another privilege of old age: There's no one around to mess up my stories."

It was something I'd never thought about. I pictured Rafe, Ash, and myself at the Round Table, decades hence, gray-haired and creaky, the two of them arguing about whose turn it was to buy the beer, and all three of us bickering about whose turn it was to pick up the check.

The image made me smile. I was still smiling when I got back to the houseboat, but that stopped as soon as I walked in the door.

"Eddie! What have you done?"

My cat was nowhere to be seen. He had, however, managed to scatter my entire pile of take-out menus all over the floor, and to shred at least one of them to small scraps.

I put my coat away and muttered as I cleaned up his mess. "Okay, I guess it's clear what you've done, but the big question is why did you do it in the first place?"

Though I heard a distant "Mrr," there was no sign of Eddie prancing out to greet me. He knew he was in trouble.

"That's what I figured." I picked up the Fat Boys menu, which I hadn't actually looked at in two years because I ordered one of three things every time. "You don't know why you did it, do you? Maybe you should think about things before you do them."

I picked up intact menus for Shomin's and the local Chinese restaurant, and realized that the scattered scraps were all from Three Seasons. "And now I have to tell Kristen that hers is the only menu you shredded. Do you realize how that's going to make her feel? Do you?"

The trill of an incoming phone call interrupted my monologue, which was starting to sound a lot like the parental lectures I'd received as a child. I dug my cell out of my coat pocket. "Hey, Tabitha. What's up?"

"Isn't tonight the night we were going to talk?"

"Probably. I just got in, though."

"You haven't had supper? Get something to eat and give me a call afterward."

"No, I ate already." And I wasn't just saying that. Max had almost force-fed me some of his secret snacks in unnecessary apology for sending me on a wild-goose chase. The second red velvet cupcake had been way more than enough, but then he'd offered chocolate chip cookies that his youngest granddaughter had baked. Lots of calories and not much substance, but it had all tasted extremely good going down and was sticking to my ribs enough that my dinner plans for the evening included nothing except a bowl of cold cereal.

"All right, then," Tabitha said. "Let's get our ducks in a row. The suspect list now includes the brother, the former coworker, the bully from the bike club, and the hipster from the bike shop."

I named them in her order. "Bob Bernier, Ariella Tice, Warren Jorgenson, and Cody Sisk." I'd found Warren's last name on the bike club's Facebook page, feeling a little sneaky about it, although I wasn't quite sure why.

"Exactly," she said. "We know quite a bit about brother Bob and a fair amount about Ariella. We have some slight knowledge about Cody and essentially none on Warren Jorgenson."

"Yes, and—"

A *thump-thump* noise in the bathroom alerted

me to a feline undertaking that was almost certainly one of destruction.

"Hang on, I have to check on my cat. He's in a real mood tonight. You should have seen the mess he made with . . . Oh, Eddie, seriously?"

He looked up at me with the classic deer-in-the-headlights cast to his furry face. He was standing on his hind legs, his front legs stretched high, with his front claws sinking deep into a fresh roll of toilet paper.

"Mrr!" He jumped to the top of the small sink, swatted my small rubber duck to the floor, jumped to the floor alongside the duck, and hurtled out of the room.

Rolling my eyes, I bent down for the bright yellow duck. Yellow . . .

"There's one more suspect." I told her about the bicyclist Lindy had mentioned.

"All right," Tabitha said briskly. "If there's a Saturday ride, you'll go out with the bike club and cautiously but cleverly find out what there is to learn about our friend Warren and the rider of the yellow bike. You'll be fine. You're young and slim and fit and an exhilarating ride is just the ticket."

Easy for her to say. She wasn't the one who was going to have to tackle hills that would turn into mountains the second I started to climb the buggers. And she wasn't the one who was going to wake up Sunday morning with legs so sore that getting up from a chair would be a struggle. Sure, the last time I'd gone out I hadn't been very sore, but I was certain that wasn't going to last.

"But it's only Monday night," she was saying, "so

there are four days for investigating between then and now. Do you have any suggestions?"

And, as it turned out, I did.

Just before noon the next day, I was at my desk working on capital requests for the next year's library budget ("No time like the present," Graydon had said with an over-the-top cheery attitude; my instinctive facial expression had been so negative that I'd been very glad he'd called and not asked in person) when my phone pinged with a text message.

Tabitha: *She's moving. Destination looks like Fat Boys.*

Minnie (while grabbing her coat): *Be at the corner in five.*

My suggestion from the night before had been something about which I now felt a trifle guilty. I'd suggested following Ariella in order to talk to her again, but I didn't have time to do any of the following and it would have to be my fellow investigator.

When I caught up with Tabitha half a block away from Fat Boys, she was bouncing on her toes, her energy level so high I could almost see sparks shooting out of her skin. Clearly, my guilt that I was asking too much from her was misplaced.

Ever since the two of us had started this venture, I'd wondered if she'd missed her calling, that she should have gone into law enforcement, that she and her husband would have made an amazing team. But looking at her now, I recognized something—this was how I looked when I was deep in Research Librarian Mode. And I suddenly had the complete conviction that during her career of legislative research, when her writing was moving fast and furious, she'd looked just like she did now.

"Ariella just sat down," Tabitha said. "She's by herself. I think a window of opportunity is presenting itself."

It was indeed, and we moved into the second phase of our plan. I went to the counter and ordered two lunches, and Tabitha, in what came across as an entirely aimless way, wandered over to the table where Ariella was sitting.

"Why, hello there!" Tabitha cried out. "It's you, isn't it? Miss Ariella from the bank?"

Ariella looked up from her phone. "Uh, yeah?" Then she narrowed her eyes. "You and your niece talked to me the other day. About your water bill from last winter."

A smiling Tabitha took the acknowledgment as an invitation and pulled out a chair for herself. "That's right. How clever you are to remember all that! I'm lucky if I can remember my own phone number and I've had it for years. Look, honey," she said, waving me over. "Look who I found! It's Miss Ariella."

I gave Ariella an apologetic look. "Um, seems like my aunt is settled in here. Now that it's noon, she's probably getting tired, so is it okay if we eat with you? Were you expecting anyone?"

Tabitha smiled and managed to look old, weak, and winsome.

"Well, no," Ariella said.

"Great. Thanks." I sat down before she could say anything else. "They'll bring our food out," I said to Tabitha. "Should only take a few minutes."

"They bring it right to our table?" Her eyes went wide. "Oh my goodness, I hope you give them a big tip."

I shot her a "ramp it down a little" glance. She, of course, completely ignored my warning, almost certainly to pay me back for the "getting tired" comment.

"How are things going at the bank?" Tabitha asked. "I bet they're grooming you for assistant manager."

Ariella, who was scrolling through her phone, shrugged and made a face. "Not really. Anyway, I'm not sure how much longer I'll stay there. It doesn't seem to be a good fit."

"Then you should move on," Tabitha said. "Doesn't do anyone any good to stay in a place where you're not happy. Not good for the organization and not good for you."

Sound advice, but Ariella bristled. "What do you mean, it's not good for them? I work my hours. I work harder than any of them, but no one sees it."

"Exactly," Tabitha said, nodding briskly. "You're showing them up, see? That makes people unhappy. Unhappy people can't provide good customer service, and that's where you shine."

"Oh, I get it." Ariella smiled, a simple act that transformed her from a sullen millennial into a friendly young woman.

"But you can't make everyone happy, can you?" Tabitha oozed sympathy. "No matter what, there's going to be someone who refuses to be pleased."

"Well, yeah." Ariella put her phone down. "There's always someone. They could be old or young or a guy or a girl. There's no way to predict, you know?"

Tabitha was leaning forward. "No way at all. Like

that poor woman they found in the state forest. Emily, her name was? Sad she was killed, naturally, but I heard she was really hard to please."

Ariella's smile vanished. "Whoever you heard that from was right. She was a . . . She was awful."

"You poor dear." Tabitha reached across the table to pat her hand. "Do you want to tell us about it?"

"No," she said shortly. "I don't. I tried to help her, and she complained to the city manager about me. Can you believe it?"

I could, actually, because my guess was that Ariella's customer service had been more the stone-faced-stubborn kind than the kindly "let's figure out a way to make this work" variety.

"You poor dear," Tabitha said again. "Do you think that's why the city let you go? Because of her complaint?"

Ariella's face went red. "I'd bet on it. I'd bet a lot."

Chapter 13

Rafe had said he had another regional meeting to attend that night, so I texted my aunt about inviting myself over.

Minnie: *Any chance I can mooch dinner tonight?*

Aunt Frances: *Rafe coming, too?*

Minnie: *He has a meeting.*

Aunt Frances: *Another one? Does he usually have this many?*

Minnie (after thinking a minute): *No, but it sounds like all these meetings are because of changes at the state. Plus he's always busy at the start of the school year.*

Aunt Frances: *Any chance you'll do the dishes?*

Minnie: *100%*

Aunt Frances: *6 pm. You are my favorite niece.*

Minnie: *I'd say you are my favorite aunt, but I just acquired a new one.*

I shut down my phone before she asked questions and tucked my knees under her dining table precisely at six o'clock. "This looks amazing," I said, admiring the interesting texture and colors of the arrangement of chicken, tomatoes, and squash.

Otto quirked an eyebrow as he filled my wineglass. "Don't tell me you're getting interested in cooking."

"Not a chance," I said cheerfully. "Eating, yes. Cooking, no."

Aunt Frances pointed her fork at me. "Enough with the chitchat. Where did you get a new aunt?"

I ignored Otto's startled glance. "She's adorable," I said dreamily. "Like an aunt from Hollywood's central casting. White-haired. Round-faced. Perky. Bubbly."

Frowning, my aunt put her fork down. "Brains of a pea?"

"Oh, no. She's very smart. Retired from a career of legislative policy research for a downstate non-profit. We're working together on . . . on a project."

"What kind of project?" Otto asked at the same time my aunt asked, "Where did you meet her?"

"At the Round Table"—which was perfectly true, though somewhat misleading—"and we're . . . uh . . ." I half laughed. "Okay, I'll come clean if you promise not to tell Mom and Dad."

Aunt Frances eyed me. "Then I can guess what you're doing with your new aunt. Looking into those murders. Brown and that woman they found in the state forest."

"Emily Acosta," I murmured.

"Right. But who's this other aunt?"

Otto smiled at his wife. "If I didn't know better, I'd say you're showing signs of jealousy."

"Of course I'm jealous," Aunt Frances said. "For thirty-five years I've had no competition in the aunt category and now I have to share Minnie's nieceness with a stranger?" She blinked and rubbed her eyes, as if there were tears forming.

She was kidding, of course, but all the same I felt a twinge of guilt. "We were just pretending," I said. "I was acting the concerned niece and Tabitha was being the slightly addled elderly aunt."

"Tabitha?" My aunt's ears practically swiveled toward me. "Are we talking about Tabitha Inwood?"

"Well, yeah. You know her?"

She smiled and her attention went back to her food. "Any and all objections to sharing you have been withdrawn. Tabitha is a gem. Carry on."

Otto looked at her. "Is there something going on here that I don't know about?"

"Not really," Aunt Frances said. "Tabitha sat in on a woodcraft lecture I gave a few weeks ago at the senior center. We chatted afterward and as soon as we can set a date, we're going to have her and Hal over to dinner."

I dearly hoped I'd learn that date ahead of time so I could sneak into the house and listen in. Because if, in a social situation, Detective Hal Inwood turned into a real human being with actual conversational skills, I wanted to witness the occasion.

"Always good to meet new people." Otto handed around a bowl of fresh rolls. "So, Minnie. Tell us about your investigation. Maybe talking about it will open up a new line of thinking."

Excellent. I hadn't wanted to plunge into all of that without an invitation. "Well, since you asked . . ."

And so I told them everything, from my first visit with Lindy, to how I'd met Tabitha and Hal at the diner, to how we'd teamed up, to our belief that the two deaths were connected through bicycling, to our suspect list of Bob, Ariella, Cody, Warren, and the yellow bicycle guy.

Otto lifted his hand, then let it drop to the table.

"What?" I asked.

He shook his head. "Give me a minute."

Aunt Frances and I looked at each other as he left the room and went into the kitchen. "Do you know what's going on?" I whispered.

"No idea." She glanced toward the kitchen, half stood, then dropped down. "He said needed a minute, and that's what I'll give him," she said, looking at her watch. What was surely a precise sixty seconds later, she said loudly, "Your time is up. Are you coming out, or do I have to come in after you?"

"Not to worry, my dear." Otto returned, sliding smoothly back into his chair. "I just needed to a little time to work through an ethical question."

I squirmed. "Otto, please don't tell me anything that makes you feel uncomfortable. Compromised. Whatever."

"Your concern is appreciated," he said, "but I know where the line is, and I will not cross it."

"As long as you're sure."

"Very." He smiled. "Now. Thanks to your gentle push, late last year I gave a couple of library lectures to senior citizens on managing their finances. That was so popular I started showing up every couple of weeks to help any individual or small-business owner who wants some general financial coaching."

Aunt Frances and I nodded. "Yes," I said, "and the feedback has been extremely positive. Thanks so much for doing that."

"You're welcome." He paused. "If I thought the

city of Chilson would take my advice, I could help them, too, but I don't see much chance of that happening. Anyway, with the library a public entity, it only follows that the fact of a certain small-business owner meeting with me multiple times can be considered public knowledge."

"Um, I suppose so."

"And," Otto went on, "one might easily conclude a few things from these multiple meetings."

He looked at me expectantly and my brain chunked into gear, because he was obviously expecting me to connect the dots.

"Cody Sisk," I said. "He's a small-business owner."

"And?"

"The shop must be in financial trouble," Aunt Frances said. "Because if he was doing well, he'd have the money to pay for an accountant."

I tried to dredge the few things I knew about Paddles & Pedals up out of my memory. "Up until this summer, the store was in a different location," I remembered out loud. "This new place is way bigger and a lot closer to downtown."

"Bound to be more expensive," my aunt said. "He expanded too fast, didn't he?"

Otto reached for his wine. "Next time we use this recipe, I think we should pair it with a bottle of Late Harvest Riesling."

Clearly, he'd said all he was going to say about Cody Sisk. But it was enough to start me thinking in a completely new direction.

If Cody's business had expanded too fast, he was almost certainly having cash-flow problems. If he was having cash-flow problems, the fact that Brown and Emily had been late with their bike payments could have been a serious financial hardship. And if Cody was under financial stress, anger could easily have surfaced. And if he was angry, could he have been angry enough to kill?

After dinner, I told my aunt and Otto to stay put and finish the wine and I went to take care of the dishes. Two minutes later, they wandered into the kitchen and sat in the window seat so we could all discuss the latest escapades of my niece Kate, oldest daughter of my brother and his wife. Kate had spent much of the previous summer with me. It hadn't started well, but by August I was confident we'd established a lifelong bond.

"Kate said she's dyed her hair purple," I said.

My aunt approved. "A good color for her."

"Not sure her parents agree."

Otto poured the last of the wine into my aunt's glass. "Isn't that the basic role for parents?"

He'd asked the question with a laugh, but I thought about it seriously as I put a large sauté pan into the sink and ran hot water into it. Was that what parents were supposed to do? Scowl and lay down rules and regulations? Probably, but couldn't they also be fun loving and happy? Maybe, but those things were polar opposites, and how on earth could you do both?

I sighed. Rafe and I, as an engaged couple, should be talking about these things, especially now that I was a smidgen closer to forty years old than thirty. But, like a number of other serious issues, we hadn't discussed it at all.

"Note to self," I murmured to the soapsuds. "Start discussing the big things."

"What was that, Minnie?" my aunt asked. "Don't talk to the sink if you want us to hear."

Smiling, I flicked a dollop of suds in her direction. "Is that any way to talk to your favorite niece? After all, I have another aunt now, and—" I broke off because my pants pocket was buzzing with an incoming text.

Tabitha: *Found Warren Jorgenson. Bowling alley in ten?*

Minnie (after trying to text with wet fingers, failing, then drying her hands like she should have in the first place): *Make it fifteen.*

"Who was that?" Aunt Frances asked.

I grinned. "Your competition."

Fourteen minutes later, I found Tabitha, wearing a snappy navy blue beret, in the parking lot outside of Chilson's only bowling alley. While I wasn't a bowler, I had been inside the echoing building, most recently last year when it had been the location of the world's most amicable breakup. That Ash and I hadn't clicked romantically still didn't make much sense, but I'd stopped thinking about it ages ago. Rafe and I fit together like popcorn and butter, even if it had taken me years to acknowledge the truth of it.

The sun was down, darkness had fallen all around, and the parking lot's single light seemed to be casting more shadow than anything else. A breeze gusted down my neck and I zipped my coat up to the collar, trying to put out of my mind what my weather app had predicted for a low temperature that night. And, anyway, forty-nine degrees was almost the same as fifty, and how could any native Michigander think fifty degrees was cold?

I pushed out of my mind the knowledge that fifty degrees outside was significantly different from fifty degrees inside, and waved at a waiting Tabitha. "How did you find him?"

"You young people never cease to amaze me." She shook her head. "The information you put out there for all the world to see is astonishing. Don't you have any interest in privacy?"

By this, I concluded that she'd determined Warren's whereabouts via social media. My own personal tendency was to share very little publicly, and I didn't think Rafe even had a Facebook account, but I had friends who felt differently. "Aren't you glad?" I asked. "Makes this job a lot easier."

"True enough." Tabitha adjusted her beret to a rakish angle. "Ready?"

"As I'll ever be. By the way," I said, holding the door open for her, "do we have a plan?"

"Plans are for sissies, remember?" She sailed up the concrete steps, opened the glass door, and went inside.

Shaking my head, I went after her. Inside, the noise was shattering. Pins clashing, balls rolling, people shouting . . . the din was a shock to my eardrums and I remembered once again how little bowling alleys and libraries had in common.

Tabitha elbowed me. "There he is. Wearing a black and royal blue shirt."

Warren, along with his bowling teammates, was indeed wearing the colors that represented a local insurance agency. Three of them were cheering the fourth, who'd just flung his ball down the lane and toppled ten pins at once.

Hand slaps went all around, and, glancing up at the scores on the screen, I suddenly knew what to do.

"They just finished a game," I said. "Someone will head to the bar. Come on."

Sure enough, as soon as the cheering was done, Warren and one of his teammates approached the bar, where Tabitha and I were sitting on stools.

"Two pitchers of PBR," Warren's teammate said. "This guy's paying."

"PBR?" Tabitha asked brightly. "That was the first beer I ever drank. Loved it then, love it now."

"Stuff of dreams," the teammate said, not quite paying attention to her.

"It's Warren, right?" I asked, trying to sound tentative and unsure.

"Yeah." He turned and brushed back his thinning hair. "Um . . ." He blinked, clearly not remembering me.

"We met at the bike club the other night," I said.

"Oh, sure. You were asking about Brown and what's her name."

Emily, I wanted to say, but restrained myself. The man was prickly and annoying, but we wanted information and antagonizing him probably wasn't the best way to go about it.

"This is my aunt," I said.

"Oh, you were friends with Brown? And that . . . Emily?" Tabitha's voice dripped with disdain.

"Not friends." Warren extracted some cash from his wallet and handed it to the bartender. "Don't know why you'd say that. Be right there," he said to his teammate, who'd picked up the pitchers. Then he faced Tabitha square on. "Doesn't sound like they were friends of yours, either."

"Don't want to speak ill of the dead, but . . ." She shrugged.

Warren leaned in. "Yeah, I get it. It's good to talk to someone who doesn't think they should both be made saints or something."

Tabitha smirked. "Different strokes for different folks."

How that fit this conversation, I didn't know, but Warren nodded. "Right. That's what burns me, that no one can see what those two were really like. I mean, there I was, finally getting the recognition I deserve by getting to be vice president of the bike club. But when I stood up to make a speech, they laughed. Out-and-out laughed at me!"

His face turned a curious shade of purple. "They made me look stupid in front of the entire club. So, no, I'm not going to their funerals or memorial services, and I'm not sending flowers or cards. Far as I'm concerned, they got what was coming to them."

Warren's angry pronouncement disturbed us to the extent that we felt the need to adjourn to a nearby adult beverage establishment to calm ourselves and talk over the incident.

Tabitha looked at me over the rim of a shiny hammered-copper mug. "The man has issues."

I nodded and sipped my wine. Everyone had issues; I was old enough to know that. But some people's were more obvious, and some people's were more serious. "He scared me," I admitted. "Not for my own personal safety. More a general adding-more-anger-to-the-universe type of fear."

"Mmm." Tabitha didn't sound convinced. And for good reason, because I wasn't sure myself that Warren's barely stifled fury wouldn't creep into my dreams that night. Eddie would help, though. Cat purrs did wonders to soothe the soul, and it had always seemed to me that Eddie purrs had a level of comfort beyond any normal cat's capacity.

Tabitha and I agreed that we needed to learn more about Mr. Jorgenson and by common consent agreed to develop a plan later. We talked about this and that—I learned about her and Hal's grandchildren, she learned about my housing arrangements and clucked at my naked ring finger—and I rolled into my bed so tired that Eddie barely had time to get his purr going before I was sound asleep.

The next morning was indeed chilly. My little space heater ran enough to keep my teeth from chattering, but it wasn't what you'd call warm. I texted Rafe emojis of a Popsicle, a snowman, a house, and a question mark. His return text, a photo taken last winter of Eddie jumping over a snowbank, made me laugh but didn't actually answer my question.

Since the temperature was supposed to inch up over sixty, I opted for my light coat and thin gloves for the walk to work, but thanks to a brisk wind, found that I couldn't walk fast enough to keep from shivering.

When I got to the library, I went straight to the break room and fumbled through the coffee-making procedure. I waited until the coffee drizzled into the pot, then wrapped my hands around my Association of Bookmobile and Outreach Services mug and huddled around its warmth until I stopped shivering.

Mug in hand, I wandered down the still-empty hall—because it was half an hour before anyone else would arrive—and got to work on e-mail and budget spreadsheets. After I'd cleaned out my inbox and grown frustrated with the numbers, I pushed back from my desk. Because if I had another cup of coffee, maybe everything would start to make sense. And if it didn't, at least I'd have another cup of coffee in me, and how could that be bad?

Smiling, because half a plan is far better than no plan at all, I picked up my mug and sallied forth.

"Here she is," Holly said.

I slowed as I entered the room, because it was so full with library staff it was going to take a carefully planned route to get to the coffeepot. "'Here she is'?" I repeated, sliding between Josh and Gareth. "That sounds ominous."

"Minnie, there's something we need to talk about," Donna said.

"And that sounded serious." When my mug had been refilled, I turned and took stock of the room. "Holly, why are you here? You're not scheduled to work today." Neither was Shilah, our newest part-time clerk. "What's up?"

"Told you she wouldn't get it," Josh said. "She doesn't watch enough TV."

He made it sound like a criticism, not a compliment. "Wouldn't get what?"

Donna pulled out a chair. "Minnie, please sit down."

I half laughed, but sat. "This is starting to feel like an intervention."

"And I told you she would get it," Holly said smugly.

Josh rolled his eyes. "Not right away. Doesn't count."

"Children," Donna said sharply. "Not the time or place. Now. Minnie." She sat in a chair opposite me. "You have spent the last three and a half years getting our wonderful bookmobile up and running and fully operational. It is a runaway success, far more than most people would have dreamed."

"Including me," I murmured.

"Right," Holly said. "You planned for every situation except one."

Gareth nodded. "A fast expansion. It's the downfall of many companies. You spend so much time figuring the start-up that you don't have enough time to give thought to managing growth."

I sighed. He was right. They were all right. I'd never expected to spend as much time in the bookmobile as I did in the library, and I was struggling to make it all work.

"And there's something you need to know," Donna said gently.

Kelsey topped off my coffee. "Here. You're going to want this."

"There's brownies for after," Holly said. "We just need to get through this first."

Frowning, I put my mug down. "Get through what?"

Donna put a hand on my shoulder. "Minnie. As much as we love the bookmobile and what it's done for outreach and bringing joy to all, there's one little problem."

I waited. No one said a word. "What's the problem?" I finally asked.

There was a shuffling of feet while everyone looked at each other. Finally, Holly said bluntly, "None of us like being on it."

"You . . . what?" I stared at them, not comprehending. "What do you mean?"

"The bookmobile is great," Josh said. "But of all the people that went with you the last few weeks, a total of none of them liked it."

"But . . . but . . ." My mouth hung open.

"Minnie, I'm sorry." Gareth's gentle voice was soothing. "It turns out that riding on the bookmobile is a special skill set and we don't have it."

"But . . ." But after that one word, I didn't know what else to say.

"I know Graydon wants extra trips and visits," Holly said. "And I don't know how you're going to figure that all out, because none of us are going to volunteer to go along."

"Sorry, Minnie," Donna said. "I really am. It's just that being in a vehicle for so many hours, even one as big as the bookmobile, fires up my claustrophobia."

One by one, they gave different reasons for bailing on me. And they were all good reasons, ranging from a proclivity to kidney stones to motion sickness.

"No, I get it." I sighed and tried not to slump under the pressure of this new knowledge. "Thanks for letting me know."

"You'll find a solution," Holly said reassuringly. "You always do."

"Thanks," I said, trying to smile. "You're probably right."

But I wasn't at all sure that she was.

The weather forecast for Saturday was sunny with high temperatures in the mid-sixties, warm for early October. I made a face at my phone's weather app. "Where's a good thunderstorm when you need it?" I asked, but it didn't respond. Which was lucky, because I was already feeling guilty about wishing for bad weather, especially on a weekend.

"Sorry, didn't mean that," I muttered to my phone, and shut it down as I left the library and headed downtown, slowing, then literally dragging my feet as I walked into Paddles & Pedals, Cody Sisk's store. With weather out as an excuse not to go on the next bike club ride, I needed to be responsible and pick up my own spare inner tube, repair kit, and set of tire irons. Not that I expected to have a flat, of course. But who ever did?

Thanks to the magic of Internet video instructions, I knew in theory how to fix a bicycle's flat tire, but my previous online fix-it situation regarding a small plumbing situation hadn't ended well. At Paddles & Pedals, I was hoping to pick up the needed equipment and also get some hands-on instruction geared for people who weren't mechanically inclined. And if I could gather additional information about Cody, Emily, or Brown, well, that would be an added bonus.

The jingling of the front door's bells alerted the people inside, and three faces turned toward me. One was Cody and the other two were men about his own age, and so also about mine. I didn't recognize either of them, and they had the look of down-staters. What that look was, exactly, I'd never been able to pin down. All I knew was downstaters were like that quote about art: I knew them when I saw them.

"Hey there," Cody said. "You were in here with your aunt the other day, right? On Saturday?"

I nodded, giving him two points for a good memory, but taking away a point for making his second sentence lift up in an unnecessary question. "She still hasn't decided on a bike."

"Oh." His shoulders drooped slightly. "Well, if she has any questions, I'd be glad to answer them."

"You bet. That's not why I'm here, though." I gestured at the glass counter, the inside of which was festooned with mechanical bits that undoubtedly had something to do with bicycles, but whose specific purposes were unknown to me. "I decided to ride with that bike club on Saturday, and I really need to buy my own stuff for fixing a flat tire."

It would be a teeny-tiny sale compared to the multi-hundred-dollar sale of a new bicycle, but he said, "Absolutely."

I glanced at the other two customers. "Um, I can wait until you finish up here."

Cody grinned. "These two will never be finished. They're my riding buddies. Been riding Glacial Hills in Bellaire the last two days and came up to give me a hard time."

He introduced them as Tyler and Rob—I never did learn their last names—and I introduced myself. We shook hands all around, and Cody said, "You'll want a new tube, a repair kit, and tire irons. What size tire?"

"Oh. Um . . . well, I have no idea. I know what make and model it is, though." And what color, but I was smart enough to keep that to myself.

I gave him the information I had, and he started typing into the computer. "Got it." He peered through the glass and slid open the door. "Do you want one or two?"

Since I figured they couldn't be that expensive, and I felt guilty for leading him astray with Tabitha's nonpurchase, I asked for two.

"Just getting into biking?" Rob asked.

"Nothing like it." Tyler laughed. "Wind in your face, sweat in your eyes, blisters on your—"

Rob elbowed him. "Don't scare her off. We need more women in this sport."

I smiled, and saw a way to switch the topic. "As of a couple of weeks ago, there's one less woman. And one less man, too."

The two men frowned. "What do you mean?" Tyler asked. "Someone have an accident?"

"Not like you think. A local bike club guy was murdered three weeks ago. And just a little after that, so was Emily Acosta. She was in the bike club, too."

"Whoa." Rob reared back. "That's just too weird. Cody, did you know them? Hey, dude, are you okay? You look like—" He glanced at me. "You look sick, all of a sudden."

Cody put a hand to his forehead and backed away. "I'm fine. I just need a second to get . . . to get some aspirin or something."

He hurried off and, frowning, I watched him go. He'd seemed perfectly healthy until thirty seconds ago, when I'd started talking about Emily and Brown.

Why had he suddenly turned so pale? Had it simply reminded him of the money owed him? Or was he suffering from a guilty conscience? Could he be the killer?

As soon as I exited Paddles & Pedals, I texted Tabitha about how oddly Cody had acted when I'd mentioned Emily and Brown.

Tabitha: *Interesting, but do you want to learn more about Warren?*

Minnie (after being miffed for half a second that her insider dirt on Cody had been dismissed so readily): *Of course! What do you have in mind?*

And so, ten minutes later, I found myself walking through the front door of a local fitness center, an establishment that, heretofore, I'd never once entered. Every New Year's Day, like most everyone else, I thought about getting a membership, but the thought always passed quickly. I sated my guilt by telling myself I was young, I walked a lot, and anyway, I wasn't *that* overweight.

Tabitha thrust a piece of paper at me as soon as I walked into the small lobby. "We both have guest passes for this visit. Free to me special because I have these." She smiled and pointed at her dimples.

"Should get myself some of those," I said, accepting the pass. "Um, we don't actually have to *use* these, do we?"

"Now, Minnie," she said severely. "Where is your sense of adventure? How can you be the brave and intrepid bookmobile librarian who rights wrongs if you don't put yourself out there?"

I scrambled for an excuse that would keep me from looking like an idiot in front of everyone in the gym. I didn't mind being laughed at, in a general sort of way, but I needed time to mentally prepare for public humiliation. "How about tomorrow? Because I don't have the right shoes."

We looked at my footwear. My office desk had a drawer full of dress shoes and I walked back and forth in ancient sneakers I'd worn in college.

Tabitha eyed them. "Those don't look suitable for anything, but I'll admit that you're not dressed properly. How about this? We'll use the passes to look around. Chat with people. Because a further look into Mr. Jorgenson's Facebook page gave me the distinct impression that he spends a lot of time here."

I looked around, slightly alarmed. "He's here now?"

"No, no. I'm sure he's not." She tipped her head, considering. "Well, almost sure."

"Tabitha," I protested, "we saw him last night at the bowling alley. What's he going to think if we run into him two nights in a row?"

"That this is a small town in northern lower Michigan and that you run into the same people over and over October through May. Now. Are you coming in or aren't you?" She pulled the interior door open and stood there, waiting.

Since she was right about the small-town thing, and since we were there, I shrugged and went inside. A twenty-something receptionist with polo shirt-sleeves tight around his biceps took our passes and waved us in the direction of the women's locker room.

"Weight room is over there," he said, pointing. "Treadmills, ellipticals, stationary bikes, and the rowing machines are on the other side. There's an exercise classroom in the back. Yoga, aerobics, stretching, that kind of thing. There's a schedule on the door. On our website, too." He handed us flyers. "If you have any questions, just let me know."

I gave him a slightly overwhelmed and intimidated thank-you nod and Tabitha said, "Well, aren't you the most helpful young man ever. My grandson could take lessons from you." She beamed and the guy colored prettily.

"You weren't at the table when the shyness cards were dealt, were you?" I asked as we walked away. "Wish I could be more like that."

"Oh, you will be," Tabitha said. "I can tell. I was far quieter, not so long ago. Exquisitely capable, but not a hundred percent confident. All you need is a few more years and some white hair, and the knowledge that none of this matters will come your way. When you understand that down to your bones . . . well . . ." She grinned. "Anything is possible."

"That's what I'm afraid of," I muttered.

"Sorry?"

"That sounds like a plan." I looked left and right through the glass doors that led into the other rooms. "Let's look at that posted schedule first. If people are waiting for a class to start, they'll be easy for us to talk to."

But when we looked at the list, classes were done for the day. We moved on to the treadmill room and quickly learned that casual chatter was not a part of that environment.

"They all looked so serious," Tabitha observed as we wandered back out. "Why do you think that is?"

"Because it takes focus to run on a treadmill and not fall off."

Tabitha laughed. "Is that the voice of experience talking?"

I changed the subject. "I think we'll have better luck in the weight room."

"Mmm." Tabitha gave me an appraising glance. "Which one of us will get more attention? You, being young and cute? Or me, being elderly and cute?"

"Depends on who's in there," I said, and pushed the door open.

Inside, men—and one woman—labored at machines whose purpose I didn't understand. Weights clanked, pulleys whirled, and metal cables sang tunes that I didn't recognize. This was a world I'd never ventured into, and I hesitated in the doorway.

Tabitha, of course, had no such compunctions.

"Hello," she said brightly to a bald man who might have been fifty, or seventy. "My niece and I are here to take a look around. Is there anything we should know about this place? Warren Jorgenson recommended it."

The man, who'd been sitting on a bench wiping his face with a towel, stopped short. "You're friends with Warren?"

"Not to say friends," Tabitha said slowly. "More like acquaintances."

Bald Guy finished wiping his face, then said, "You two look like nice women. If I were your brother or dad, I'd tell you to stay away from Jorgenson."

The hairs on the back of my neck stirred. "Okay, thanks," I said. "Um, do you mind telling us why? I'm not asking you to break a confidence or anything, it's just . . ." I stopped because I wasn't sure where to go next.

Tabitha picked it up. "It's just that when you're two women, living without a man, you need to be careful."

I slid her a sideways glance. Okay, she hadn't outright lied, but she'd certainly led him in a direction that wasn't the truth. Which was what I'd done multiple times when trying to learn more about suspects, so I certainly wasn't going to throw stones. It was just odd, hearing it from someone else.

"Yeah, I get it." Bald Guy tossed the towel into a waiting bin. "Okay," he said, looking around. "Here's what I know for sure. Jorgenson had a girlfriend, and when she broke up with him a couple of months ago, he turned nasty. She ended up filing a PPO against him."

The acronym was almost, but not quite, familiar. "A what?"

"Personal protection order," Tabitha said softly.

"That's right," Bald Guy said. "He's not supposed to come anywhere near her."

"Do you know why?" I asked.

Bald Guy sort of nodded. "She's my neighbor. I heard more than one fight. And called the cops when I heard . . . well, when I heard something that sounded like the cops should get involved." He gave us a long look. "If I were you, I'd stay away. Far, far away."

Chapter 14

After Mr. Bald Guy's revelation, Tabitha and I unanimously decided that another trip to the adult beverage establishment was in order. By the time our glasses were empty, we'd come to the conclusion that it was time to talk to our friends in law enforcement about all we'd discovered.

"Fine, but what do we do, just hand over everything we've learned?" Tabitha asked.

I looked at my glass, which had formerly held wine, thought about having a second, but decided against it. School night, and all. "Yes. They're the professionals and we're not. It's not like we're going to arrest anyone ourselves."

She sighed. "I suppose. But if we want Hal to be there, we're going to have to wait until Friday, because he's downstate at a training and won't be back until then."

We discussed the pros and cons of talking only to Ash and decided, in the end, that it would be better to have the senior officer in the room. "Ash isn't a full detective yet," I said. "And your husband has so much experience. It might make a difference."

Tabitha laughed. "A good or a bad one? No, never mind, your point is well taken. Friday it is."

I texted Ash with a request for a Friday morning appointment. He suggested half past seven, I agreed, and I shut off my phone before I saw any questions about the point of the meeting.

Since it was raining, Tabitha dropped me off at the marina and gazed approvingly at the house where I would, I hoped, soon be living. "Lovely," she said. "The Shingle style is one of my favorites. Looks just right in this location."

What it looked to me was dark, which meant that, once again, Rafe wasn't there doing any work. And since he'd told me to stay away, nothing was getting done.

Once inside the houseboat, I muttered to Eddie about it, but he yawned in my face.

"Nice," I said. "You do realize that the roof of your mouth is one of your least attractive features. Did you ever think about covering your mouth when you yawn?"

He yawned again, not covering, and I averted my eyes. "You're going to spoil my dinner."

Dinner was a marginally healthy frozen meal of chicken, broccoli, and pasta, and I was just finishing up when my phone pinged with an incoming text. I picked it up in a Pavlovian reaction before my brain could connect with my hand and tell it to stop because I didn't feel like answering any of Ash's questions. But it wasn't Ash.

Josh: *Have you talked to Mia yet?*

Minnie (after freaking out a bit because she'd completely forgotten about Josh's romance issues): *Working on it. Will let you know.*

I scrolled through my contact list and found Leese Lacombe, Mia's half sister.

Minnie: *Need some help re: Josh and Mia. Can you bring her to breakfast at the Round Table tomorrow morning?*

Leese (after a pause): *Sure thing. Anything in particular?*

Minnie: *Josh asked her to move in and she's backing away.*

Leese: *You sure you want to get involved?*

Minnie: *I absolutely do not. But Josh begged.*

Leese: *Men.* (insertion of an eye-roll emoji) *See you at eight.*

I thanked her profusely, she sent back more eye rolls, and the next morning I drove to the restaurant with Eddie in his carrier. "You'll be fine," I said softly as I got out. "It's not that cold and I'll be back in half an hour."

That was all true, but I still felt guilty leaving him alone. Guilt, in spite of the fact that he was snoring when I shut the door and was likely to still be snoring when I got back.

Inside, Leese and Mia were just sitting down. I slid in next to Mia, because while Leese was many things—a top-notch lawyer specializing in elder law, a talented softball player, and a fantastic cook—small was not one of her qualities. She was a very sturdy six feet tall with brown hair almost as curly as mine. It was hard to believe she was in any way related to the thin, average-height, straight-haired

Mia. Yes, they shared half a genetic pool courtesy of their late father, but clearly the maternal genes had dominated in both cases.

"And there she is!" Leese said. "Haven't seen you in ages, seems like."

"Hi, Minnie," Mia said softly.

"Morning to you both." I looked up as Carol, the other regular waitress, came over. "No Sabrina?"

Carol shook her head. "She and Bill went on a vacation."

This pricked my interest. As far as I knew, the farthest Sabrina had ever traveled had been to Lansing, the state capital, on a fifth-grade field trip. "Where are they going?"

She shrugged. "Somewhere warm, is all I know. Now, what can I get you ladies?"

We ordered, with Leese pushing Mia to get something protein- and calorie-laden and Mia resisting, but eventually adding a side order of bacon to her plain oatmeal. When there were mugs of coffee in front of all three of us, I turned to the object of Josh's affections and said, "Mia, I have to ask you something. I'm sorry I agreed to do this, as it's really none of my business, but I made a promise and now I'm stuck, so I have to do it, though I'd really rather not."

Leese snorted. "If you keep going on like that, we're going to be here all day, and I have a nine o'clock. Get to the point, Hamilton."

I ignored her and kept my focus on Mia.

"It's okay," Mia said, staring at her coffee. "Go ahead and ask. It's about Josh, isn't it?"

"He's just . . ." I searched for the right words. Found them, realized how much he wouldn't like it, decided I didn't care, and went ahead. "He's just scared of losing you."

"He . . . what?" Mia's eyes went wide. "Losing me? Why would he think that? I love him! I love him so much it hurts sometimes."

"Then why won't you move in with him?"

A small breath escaped her. "I want to. Mostly. I mean I do, but . . ." Her voice trailed off. She looked at Leese and softly said, "It's Nana."

Leese stared at her half sister, then flopped her head against the seat back. "Good Lord in the sky. Of course it is."

"Nana?" I asked. "Is that your grandmother?"

"Not mine." Leese gave me a thumbs-up. "Nana comes from her mother's side. Lots of spare-the-rod-and-spoil-the-child parenting in that family."

"She's my grandma," Mia said. "And she loves me. But she says if I move in with Josh without being married that she'll never speak to me again."

Leese, judging from her expression, seemed to think this would be a situation to be welcomed, not avoided, but Mia's sad expression indicated she felt the opposite.

"You're good at fixing things," Mia said. "You helped my whole family after our dad was killed. Do you think you could help me this time, too? Help me and Josh?"

She gave me a long, sad look, her lower lip trembling. And there was only one answer I could give.

"I'll do what I can."

A few hours later, when Eddie, Julia, and I stopped at a lakeside park to eat our bookmobile-day lunch,

I told them both about what I'd promised that morning.

Eddie, up on the dashboard, rolled over so that his back was to us. Julia's response was a loud and long laugh. "Seriously?" she asked while wiping her eyes. "You're going to go up against that termagant? I wish you luck. You're going to need it."

Someday I'd get used to living in a small town. That day, clearly, was not the current one. "You know her?"

"Natalie and Bob Conti live across the street from the house my parents bought after all us kids moved out. Well, just Natalie now, because Bob died years ago. My dad always said she henpecked him into an early grave. My mom always said that if he couldn't stand up for himself, then he deserved what he got."

I knew Julia's parents had passed away, not too long ago, both in their early nineties, less than a year apart. They'd both had the blessing of sliding peacefully into a sleep from which they'd never woken, her mom on the back deck in the summer sunshine, her dad one night after a poker game with his friends. If I could pick, I'd take the deck. I was horrible at poker.

At some point, I realized Julia had been talking to me. "Sorry, what was that?"

She squinted at me over her baloney-and-cheese sandwich. "How, exactly, are you going to convince Natalie to do a one-eighty on her entire life's outlook?"

"I'm open to suggestions."

Julia snorted. "Not from me. I always did my best to stay away from her. Negativity just oozes out of that woman."

"Mia seems to love her."

"Only granddaughter." Julia waved her hand. "Entirely different kind of relationship. And I bet, deep down, Mia is terrified of her."

Thinking back to the morning's conversation, I wasn't sure the fear was buried very deeply. "Well, there has to be a way to bring her around."

"It's cute that you think so." Julia gave me a tolerant look. "Some people won't shift their sense of right and wrong even if they're the last metaphorical one standing. They'll just cross their arms and say the rest of the world has gone to—"

"And it's time to go." I tossed the plastic container that had formerly held my peanut butter and jelly sandwich into the depths of the console and started the motor. "Next stop, southeast Tonedagana County."

"Do you think Lawrence will be there today?" Julia asked.

It took me a blank moment to connect the name Lawrence with Mr. Zonne, the widowed octogenarian I'd never been able to call by his first name. He'd confessed last spring that he'd begun to feel a loss in range of motion and started a yoga regimen. By June he'd been able to, straight-legged, put his hands flat on the ground and in September he'd let us talk him into doing a full lotus pose, which had ended with Eddie in his lap. The man amazed me and I hoped to be more like him when I grew up.

When we pulled into the church parking lot, it was empty. Which was disappointing, but by the time we'd fired up the computers and done the rest of the regular setup, three cars had pulled into the lot, one of them being the big blue Buick driven by Mr. Zonne.

The other two cars were filled with moms and

homeschooled children who piled out excitedly as soon as the vehicles came to a stop. The door of Mr. Zonne's car had opened, but shut again as the children raced, shrieking, across the parking lot.

A busy fifteen minutes later, the children, now covered in Eddie hair, were hurtling down the bookmobile steps, the moms were thanking us, and we were all waving good-bye.

As soon as the child-filled cars left the parking lot, the door of Mr. Zonne's car opened. "Are they gone?" he called.

Laughing, I waved him over. "Don't tell me you're scared of kids."

He ambled across the gravel. "At my age, you can't be too careful. One accidental push and I'd be on the ground with a broken hip, and then where would I be?"

"In Lakeview, hanging out with Max Compton," I said promptly. "The place would never be the same."

"Max Compton," Mr. Zonne mused as he climbed the stairs as easily as the children had. "He was three years ahead of me in school, but he was such a horrible baseball player that we spent a lot of time together on the bench. I didn't realize you knew him."

"Small town," I said, smiling. Then, since this was indeed a small town, I asked if he knew Warren Jorgenson.

"Jorgenson." He rubbed his chin. "Nope, don't know any Jorgensons. Sorry."

I sighed. It had been worth a shot.

Julia looked up from the back computer desk, where she'd been entering returns. "How about Natalie Conti?"

Mr. Zonne held up his hands, palms out. "Oh, no.

I don't want that woman to hear even the faintest whisper of me saying uncomplimentary things about her. And since that would be the only kind of thing I can say about her . . ." He made the classic zipping-the-lips motion.

My plan for a cozy chat with Mia's grandmother was officially placed into the circular file. But . . . "How about our murder victims?"

"Brown Bernier." Mr. Zonne leaned against the children's nonfiction section. "He came from a different generation, and his parents were a decade older than yours truly. Can't help you there, sorry."

My expectations, which had been rising in a dramatic fashion, dropped like a rock. "Thanks, anyway, it—"

Mr. Zonne talked over me. "Emmy Sue, however, is a different matter."

Julia and I exchanged a glance. Had Mr. Zonne's razor-sharp memory started to fail? The floor under my feet suddenly seemed uneven and precarious. "Um, her name was Emily," I said gently. "Emily Acosta."

"Now, yes," Mr. Zonne said, smiling a bit smugly. "But forty-five years ago, she was Emmy Sue Worman, working as an assistant clerk for the city the Monday after she graduated from high school."

I blinked. "She . . . what?"

"Not sure how long she worked there." Mr. Zonne squinted, then shook his head. "A few years. But she moved downstate probably thirty-five years ago. Started going by Emily and got married."

"She's from Chilson?" I asked wonderingly. "Why didn't we know this?"

Mr. Zonne shrugged. "She was an only child. Her

parents moved downstate soon after she did, to be closer. Her mother and my wife were some sort of cousins and they kept up, but now they're all gone and since Emmy Sue moved back, apparently she hadn't yet reconnected with former classmates."

He rubbed his chin again. "She always was a solitary child, so I suppose that isn't much of a surprise. To be honest, the surprising part is that she came back at all."

It was a good question. But an even better question was, did Ash and Hal know that Emily Acosta was also Emmy Sue Worman?

The next morning, at seven thirty precisely, there were four people seated around the sheriff's office's scratched and scarred laminate interview room table. Detective Hal Inwood, who was intently not looking at his wife of many years. Tabitha Inwood, who was staring daggers at her husband. Deputy Ash Wolverson, who was studiously avoiding looking at anyone. And Minnie Hamilton, who was doing her best to ignore the marital undercurrents in the hopes of some actual communication and potential collaboration.

"So," I said cheerfully. "Nice to see the sun, isn't it?"

In response, I received two Inwood glares and one quick flick of what looked like a warning from Ash.

Okay, so small talk was out. I took a deep breath. It didn't matter what was going on between Tabitha and Hal. What mattered was catching a killer. "Here's what my friend here and I have found out," I said.

Hal muttered something that sounded a lot like, "I knew those two getting together would be trouble," but I chose to ignore his ridiculous statement and went ahead.

"We've found five suspects." I looked at Ash and then pointedly swiveled my gaze to stare at his notepad, which lay on the table, unopened. "Five," I repeated, but the only movement he made was to switch his attention from the tabletop to the wall behind my head.

"Ash," I said, starting to get irritated. "You do realize that I might have something of value to say, right?"

Hal stirred. "And when you do, we'll take note of it."

Next to me, I felt Tabitha stiffen. Before she could launch herself across the table at him, or even open her mouth to berate him verbally, I jumped ahead.

"We assumed you'd be looking at the spouses as potential suspects, so we've left Lindy and Emily's husband alone." I might have heard Hal's eyes roll around in his head but kept talking.

"What we wanted you to know is that Bob, Brown's brother, has been spending a lot of time with Lindy. A lot of time. And he's never been married. Not even once."

A ghost of a whisper came from across the table. "Lucky man."

"Then," I said quickly, "there's Ariella Tice. And Cody Sisk. Ariella used to work for the city. You know, with Brown? She was fired right before he retired and she got all up in his face about it. Plus, she and Emily had a big argument when Emily came into city hall, an argument that helped get Ariella fired. And Cody Sisk? He owns Paddles & Pedals, the kayak and bike shop here in town. Both Emily and Brown bought expensive bikes from him on installment, and neither one was prompt with the payments. Cody practically turns green when either one of their names is mentioned."

I waited, but neither man said a word. Fine. I'd continue without their encouragement.

"Warren Jorgenson is another suspect. He's a member of the bike club and has nothing but bad things to say about Brown and Emily. Plus, he has a history of violence. His ex-girlfriend took out a PPO against him."

I paused dramatically. Still no response from the other side of the table.

"And there are two other possibilities. Lindy said a man on a bright yellow bike had been riding past their house right before Brown was killed, and you know how they're in the middle of nowhere. It kind of creeped her out."

Ash half nodded. "The other possibility?"

"At the bike club, someone said there was a guy who'd ridden with them that Brown wasn't happy to see. Unfortunately, no one could come up with a name, other than that it maybe started with the letter A."

Even as I talked, I realized how ridiculous it sounded. I should have led with that possibility, as it was definitely the weakest. But even with that, Ash and Hal looked just the same as they had when I'd started talking. Like two blank walls.

Tabitha shoved her chair back, its feet screeching horribly on the linoleum floor. "I don't know why we bothered."

Hal sighed. "Honey, there are reasons I can't—"

"Can't what?" she snapped. "Listen to points of view different from your own? What's that you always say, that all avenues will be investigated?" She scoffed. "Seems to me you're cutting off your nose to save your 'I'm the male professional and you're the interfering female amateur' face. You know perfectly well I'm smarter than you and always have been."

"Smart isn't everything," Hal said, and though I agreed with him one hundred percent, I wasn't sure his timing for saying so was wise.

"Have I ever said it was?" Tabitha asked, yanking on her gloves. "But it seems to me that, for once in your life, you might listen to your wife sooner rather than later."

The three of us watched her go. I glanced at Ash, who looked as puzzled as I felt. Hal's face, however, was studiously blank. There was clearly something going on between wife and husband that wasn't being discussed out loud.

I stood. "Um, I'll go after her. Talk to you later?"

Ash nodded, but Hal was already on his way out of the room, headed back to his office.

Outside, I caught up with Tabitha about half a block away. "Are you okay?"

Tabitha looked over her shoulder, at what I wasn't sure, but her stare had an Eddie-like quality, one that, if focused a bit more tightly, would bring about fiery explosions. "They didn't hear a word," she said fiercely. "They weren't listening. They didn't want to hear anything we said."

It had certainly seemed that way. But there were also marital undercurrents that might have been blocking communication, and I wasn't sure how to clear the block.

Tabitha whirled around and looked at me. "Tomorrow. Tomorrow you'll find something on that bike club ride that will blow this whole thing open. Wide, wide open. Then he'll have to listen to me."

"I'm sure you're right," I said, trying to sound sincere. "Tomorrow."

Rafe and I went to Petoskey to spend Friday evening with a couple he'd known in college who were north for the fall colors. We ate dinner at Palette Bistro, walked along the waterfront of Little Traverse Bay, and ended the evening with a nightcap at the Noggin Room.

It was a wonderful night, full of laughter and stories about Rafe that I'd never heard before. I strongly suspected that I'd never heard those stories because they made him look bad. When he'd asked me if we were still going to get married, now that I knew all about him, I'd given him a long, soft kiss that had his friends whooping with delight.

"She's going to keep you, Niswander!" the male side of the couple said. "You're the luckiest man alive." His wife gave me a wide smile and I kissed Rafe again, because I knew that I was the lucky one.

Saturday morning, I rolled out of bed bleary-eyed and wholly unready for anything more than oatmeal and a cup of weak coffee.

"Mrr," Eddie said.

"Not so loud," I whispered.

"Mrr!"

I winced and shook my head. Instantly regretted doing so. It wasn't that I'd had so very many adult beverages to drink; it was more that we'd stayed out much later than my regular bedtime, and that never agreed with me.

"You're not as funny as you think you are," I said, but from the look my cat gave me, it was obvious that he disagreed with me.

I felt better after a hot shower and the food and caffeine, and by the time I got to the location posted by Terry as the bike club's starting point, my body and spirits had recovered to the point that I was happy with the world in general, and everybody I met in particular.

"Morning," my young friend Rosalind said. "You seem really wide awake."

I smiled at her as she helped me wrestle my bike out of my car's trunk. "It's early October, the fall colors are gorgeous, it's warm, and there's not a cloud to be seen. Look at that blue!"

Rosalind, who I was learning was not a morning person, gave the sky a cursory glance. "It's nice enough, I guess." She sighed. "Don't know why my grandpa needed to start this ride so early. I mean, afternoon would be just as good."

"And risk losing these conditions?" Terry, who'd approached just as Rosalind's complaint was voiced, gave his granddaughter a one-armed hug. "Buck up, buttercup. You know how changeable the weather is up here. We need to seize these great conditions and wring every last drop of biking out of them."

"Yeah, I suppose." She didn't sound convinced, though, and her grandfather heard her non-conviction.

He twisted around. "Ernie! Get over here and tell Rosalind how good it is to ride first thing in the morning."

The man Terry summoned was fiftyish, had longish hair, and looked vaguely familiar, although I was sure I hadn't seen him at either of the rides I'd been on. He ambled over, one hand pushing his bike. "Mornings are good," he said amiably. "But they'd be even better if they started later in the day."

This made both Terry and Rosalind laugh. "Both of us were right," Terry said, smiling. "Don't you love it when that happens? Say, Ernie. I don't think you've met the newest addition to the club that's not a club." He pointed at me. "Minnie Hamilton, bookmobile librarian." He pointed at Ernie. "Dr. Ernie Carpenter, family doctor extraordinaire."

At the same time, Ernie and I exclaimed, "Cade!"

Terry glanced back and forth. "You two know each other?"

"Not really," I said, "but we have a mutual acquaintance." A couple of years earlier Dr. Carpenter and I had met because of his patient and my friend Russell McCade, known to art lovers the world over as Cade. The famous painter and his wife, Barb, summered on nearby Five Mile Lake and spent their winters in Arizona.

"Haven't seen Cade or Barb in a month or so," Ernie said. "What are they up to, do you know?"

I caught him up with the McCade travel plans— exhibitions in Central and South America; twelve countries in fourteen days, which sounded exhausting to me but had thrilled Barb and Cade—and asked oh so casually, "Do you regularly ride with this group?"

By this time, Terry and Rosalind had moved off to chat with other arrivals. Ernie straddled his bike and leaned forward, putting his elbows on his han-

dlebars and resting his chin in his hands. Through a
yawn, he said, "Not so much this time of year, with
these morning rides. I make most of the weekdays,
though. At least the ones that are sunny and warm,
but not too warm. And not too windy."

"Not a die-hard rider, then?" I asked, laughing.

"And proud of it," he said. "Take this stuff too
seriously and you end up . . . well, serious, and I have
enough of that in my life already."

I nodded. "Terry told me this group wasn't intense.
Which is good, because that might have killed me . . ."
My voice trailed off. "Oh, sorry. Stupid expression.
Did you, um, did you know Brown and Emily?"

Ernie sighed. "Good people. Hard to believe
they're both dead. Murdered, no less. Makes you
wonder, doesn't it?" He looked at the people milling
about in various stages of readiness. Car doors were
slamming, wheels were being locked, helmets were
being clipped. "Is one of us next? Or . . ." He frowned.
"Could the killer be one of us? Could he be here right
now?"

"It's possible," I said. "But last time I rode, I got
this funny feeling from Warren Jorgenson—do you
know him? He practically oozed animosity toward
both Brown and Emily."

"Warren?" Ernie snorted. "The man is all bark
and no bite. He was just mad about the bike club
election. No one kills over something as stupid as
that."

I wasn't so sure, especially given the PPO his ex-
girlfriend had taken out, but I let it go. And then I
recalled Lindy's story. "Say, a friend of mine was
talking about someone who might have been riding
with this group for a while. He had a bright yellow

bike she really liked, but she can't remember what kind. Do you happen to know who that was?"

Ernie nodded. "Sure. He rode with us for a few weeks, starting in midsummer, I think it was. I don't happen to remember what make or model it was, but I remember the yellow. Don't know his number, but if you call the city, I'm sure he'd be happy to talk to you."

"The city?" I asked. "He works there? Do you have his name?"

"Sure. The new city manager, Andrew Parnell. Though I hear he goes by Drew."

Chapter 15

I t's all starting to make sense," Tabitha said that afternoon.

"Really?" I gently swatted at Eddie with my hand that wasn't holding my cell phone. "All of it?"

"Well, no, of course not. But at least we know why your bike club friend couldn't remember whether the first name of the man Brown wasn't happy to see started with an A or a D. Andrew. Drew. A common nickname, and so understandable that remembering was a problem."

I shoved Eddie a second time, resulting in a soft "Mrr," but he still didn't want to move off my backpack, which was on the houseboat's tiny dining table. This made it two wrongs, and in Eddie math, that made it a complete and total right.

"It also," Tabitha was saying, "explains why Brown wasn't happy to see Drew. What recently retired person would want to spend time with a former boss?"

"Me," I said. "Depending on the boss." Stephen, who'd been library director when I moved to Chilson, I would have crossed the street to avoid saying hello to, but Graydon and I got along well and I could easily see hanging out with him socially post-retirement.

"Point taken. Let's instead say it's possible that Brown wasn't happy to see Drew because of his recent retirement." She paused. "What we need to know is how those two men got along. Yes, it seems that Brown got along with everyone, but we need some specifics with Drew."

"And we need to know why Drew was riding his bike in front of Brown's house."

Tabitha laughed. "You make it sound like he was a six-year-old, waiting for Jimmy to come out and play."

I grinned at the visual. "Maybe it's that simple. Maybe Lindy just didn't know that Brown and Drew were riding together." It seemed reasonable. "Maybe we can—hey!"

"Excuse me?"

"Not you. Eddie." Because my cat had chosen that moment to sink his teeth deep into my hardly-ever-used checkbook and haul it across the table. "He has a thing for paper products. This time it's my checkbook."

I took it away from him, much to his disgust, and tucked it into a cabinet drawer. "Sorry about that. Next step is to plan next steps for all our suspects, right?"

"Five names," Tabitha said. "Bob, Ariella, Warren, Cody, and now Drew."

I sat back down and, since Eddie was still sprawled across my backpack, patted his head because watching his fuzzy head bob up and down always amused me. "My vote is on Warren. He just seems the type to lose his temper and lash out at whoever is nearest. Maybe . . ." I said, thinking out loud, "maybe he has something really bad going on in his life, and Brown and Emily's take on the bike club election tipped him over the edge."

"Possible," Tabitha said. "Maybe even probable. But my vote is for Ariella. She has a nasty mean streak and I can see her justifying any action she takes."

Suddenly I could see it, too. "Can I vote for two people?"

"No. And then there's Drew and Cody and Bob. Just because we happen to like young Cody, want to believe the best of our city manager, and can't think that a retired lieutenant colonel could be a double killer doesn't mean anything."

"Hang on." The names, scenarios, and relationships were getting too complicated. "Did we ever find a connection between Brown and Emily?"

"Don't remember. Let me check the spreadsheet." Tabitha tapped away on her computer keyboard. "Not outside the bike club. But that doesn't mean there isn't one, especially since she grew up here."

I did some mental math, frowning all the while because that's what math did to my face. "She was about five years younger than Brown, I think. And she was an only child. No older brothers or sisters to be friends with the Bernier boys."

"Lots of other possibilities," Tabitha said. "Cousins. Neighbors. Parents worked together. Parents were friends. Members of the same church. Fathers were in the same bowling league. Mothers on the same softball team."

"Stop already," I said, laughing, because it sounded

as if she could have kept going for hours. "Small towns, I get it. But how do we learn if any of that is true?"

"No idea. And there's something else, remember? There was bad blood between Ariella and Emily. And there's the wild card of Cody. You said he acted very strangely in front of his friends when you mentioned Brown's and Emily's deaths. We need to understand that reaction better."

She was right. We tossed around idea after idea for an hour, then started to get downright silly. When we started talking seriously about putting an advertisement in the newspaper for the killer, we knew it was time to call it quits.

"You know what?" Tabitha asked. "I think it's time for a nap. Maybe we'll wake up with some great ideas."

I couldn't think of the last time I'd taken a nap, but her yawn was contagious, and the previous late night combined with the morning's ride was catching up with me. "Sounds like a good plan," I said, and promised to text her straightaway if I thought of any ideas, good or bad. Unfortunately, when I woke up, what greeted me was a faceful of Eddie fur.

"Seriously?" I asked, then immediately regretted saying anything because when you wake up with an Eddie flopped over your neck and start talking, what you immediately get is cat hair in your mouth.

I did the *pfff! pfff!* thing a few times, setting Eddie hair to midair floating, then flung back the afghan Cousin Celeste had given me for Christmas, slid out from under Eddie, and jumped off the bed.

"Figured something out," I told Eddie. "Aren't you proud?"

My furry pal blinked at me. Didn't say anything.

"About Warren," I said. "Remember? He was on the bowling team for Gardner Insurance. Either he works there or he knows someone that does. And do you know who's been doing some work for them?"

"Mrr," Eddie said. Or sort of said, because it trailed off into a wide yawn.

"That's right. Pam Fazio."

My friend Pam, who'd not long ago sworn off doing any graphic design ever again the rest of her life because it reminded her too much of her corporate life, had recently come to the conclusion that she missed design. "Just a little, though," she'd told me last summer. We'd been on the front steps of her eclectic retail store, and both of us had been savoring our morning coffee. "A couple of clients is all I want. And I get to pick who they are."

How and why she'd chosen an insurance company, I had no idea, but in September, when Gardner had launched a complete new look, I knew who'd been behind the clean and fresh design.

So I wandered downtown and into Older Than Dirt. Pam was busy with a pair of customers, so I took advantage of the opportunity to play a little game.

After Pam had filled two big bags with purchases, topped them off with brightly colored tissue paper, and waved good-bye to her customers, she put her elbows on the glass countertop, her chin in her hands, and gave me a look. "You're doing it again, aren't you."

The game I'd taken to playing was a twist on Where's Waldo. Pam made the bulk of antique purchases for her store in the winter and supplemented those throughout the year by various mysterious means. In additional to the antiques, she also sold new items, ranging from bubble bath to teakettles to floor lamps. What I did every time I came into the store was look around to see what was new. This was harder than it sounded because Pam was a rearranger, and what looked like a new product might have just been relocated. She'd caught me last month when I'd mistakenly thought an adorable tiny dollhouse was new after she'd moved it from a shelf on one side of the room to the front window, and I was determined not to let that happen again.

I squinted and cast an eagle eye over the display on a large round table. "Of course I am. But that's not why I'm here."

"Coffee?" Without waiting for an answer, she vanished through a set of damask curtains into the back and returned with two full mugs. "What's up?"

"You're doing the graphics for Gardner Insurance, right? How well do you know the employees?"

She shrugged. "Professionally, reasonably well. Before even starting the design, I interviewed everyone. There are only six, so it didn't take long, but it was thorough. A good design matches and enhances corporate culture, and deep discussions are critical."

"Um." I'd never before heard Pam go into corporate design mode. No wonder she'd been so successful. "How about Warren Jorgenson?"

Her mug froze halfway to her mouth. "And you're asking about him why, exactly?"

I paused, wishing I'd planned this conversation all the way through before starting it. "He rides with the bike club I've gone out with a few times, and he gives off a weird vibe, if you know what I mean."

Pam sipped her coffee. Sipped again. "Here's what I know," she finally said. "One of his coworkers told me a couple of things. That he's a great insurance agent. But that his ex-girlfriend took a personal protection order out against him a few weeks ago. And last week he ran his truck into his neighbor's house."

I gaped. "An accident?"

"It happened during a shouting match with his neighbor about the appropriate time to run a power washer," she said dryly.

"So, not an accident."

"Don't see how."

I thanked Pam for the coffee and the info, said I'd say away from Warren, and left, thinking that Mr. Jorgenson's acts of violence were becoming more common. And seemed to be escalating in intensity. Could a murder be another violent act he'd committed? And what about two murders?

On the way back to the houseboat, I started to make a slight detour that would take me straight to the house. Rafe had implied during last night's dinner that he'd be hard at work all day finishing the final coats of paint in the living room and downstairs study, but I'd seen no evidence of that. Though it was possible he'd parked in the garage and pulled the curtains and shades, it wasn't likely. And if he wasn't there working, I wanted to know why he wasn't, because the calendar was inexorably ticking toward cold weather, and—

"Hey, Minnie!"

I stopped and turned to see a man about my age, but much larger and far, far taller. "Mitchell. Haven't seen you in a while. How are you and your lovely wife?"

Mitchell Koyne beamed. "Bianca is doing great. We're doing great."

One of the minor wonders of the world was that Mitchell, who up until recently had been a terminal slacker, making his way through the world through a combination of seasonal jobs and the patience of his sister, in whose attic he'd lived, was now happily married to Bianca Sims, the region's most successful real estate agent.

The love of a good woman had improved many men, but Mitchell's transformation from lawn mower and ski-lift operator to respected manager of Chilson's toy store was nothing short of miraculous.

It wasn't that Mitchell wasn't smart. It was more that until Bianca, he hadn't bothered to apply himself. Though I was almost used to the new Mitchell, there was still a teensy part of me that missed seeing him in the library's reading room, his former haunt, reading book after book because his overdue fees were too high to let him take books home.

"Haven't seen you at the library lately," I said.

"Nah, too busy at the store and with . . . well . . ." He dipped his head and scuffed his feet. "Doing projects around the house and stuff. You know."

It was a new world. The thought of Mitchell with a to-do list tacked to the refrigerator—and though I'd never been in their house, considering what I knew about Bianca, I was sure it was a shiny stainless-steel version—made my heart laugh and sing.

"With a house there are always things to do," I said. "How old is your place?"

Mitchell launched into a history of the home

where he and Bianca lived. "When Bee bought it a few years ago, she originally thought it was built right before the Great Depression. You know where it is, right, up the hill? But the foundation block work told me it was a lot older, so I started to look into it."

He talked on and on about the title documents he'd pored through, how helpful the staff at the county's Register of Deeds office and Construction Code Department had been, and how he'd put together a timeline of the property starting with its original purchase in 1871.

I started to lose interest during his description of 1893's second purchaser, and valiantly tried to feign interest through the early 1900s, but when he got to the part about scoring a copy of the 1973 building permit for a new garage, I'd had enough.

"That's great," I said. "And one of these days I'd love to hear more." Not that I was going to whip out my phone to schedule an appointment, of course. "I'll see you later, okay? Have a good—"

"Wait a minute, will you?"

I stared at him. Mitchell had sounded a little . . . panicky. Mitchell was never stressed. Ever. Whatever was making him anxious had to be serious. "Sure. What's up?" I asked, preparing myself to hear about someone's terminal diagnosis. Or maybe the toy store's owner was closing it down and Mitchell needed a new job. Or maybe, just maybe, Bianca was pregnant and Mitchell was freaking out about becoming a father.

"It's about . . . about . . ." He sighed. "You're smart, right? You have lots of college degrees and stuff."

"Don't confuse education with intelligence," I said.

"What? Oh, yeah. No, I get what you mean. Still, you know lots of stuff and I . . ." He scuffed his feet again. And again. "What are you doing for a retirement plan?"

I blinked. He couldn't possibly have said what I thought he'd said. "You're asking me for retirement advice?"

"Well, yeah. We're about the same age, and you're smart, so I figure I should probably do what you're doing."

My first instinct was to laugh hysterically. My second was to dive into a dark closet and pull a blanket over my head. But I took a deep breath and said, "Mitchell, I'm no financial wizard. That's just not my skill set." As if. I still hadn't had the financial talk with Rafe about housing costs, and though my student loans were nearly paid off, they still consumed a fair part of my income.

"Still," he said. "You must have some recommendations."

I smiled. "Other than buy low and sell high? Not really. Tell you what, though. Have you met Otto Bingham, my aunt's new husband? He's a retired accountant and spends a few hours a week at the library helping people with their finances. I'm sure he'd be able to give you some basic advice and point you in the right direction."

"Yeah? That sounds . . ." Mitchell's phone dinged. He pulled it out of his pants pocket, glanced at it, and put it back into his pocket. "Yeah, that sounds good, Minnie. Thanks!" He beamed again, gave me a wave, and strode off in the direction of the toy store.

I watched him go, squinting a little. That had been an odd conversation, even for Mitchell. I shrugged and started walking to the house. Maybe his text had been from an employee with a toy emergency. I frowned and studied the sidewalk, trying to think what an emergency at the toy store might look like. Maybe the credit card machine was broken. Or maybe a shipment of whatever the new hot toy was had been delayed and wouldn't arrive in time for the holidays. Or maybe—

A man stepped in front of me and I instinctively jumped sideways. "Sorry!"

"You should really pay more attention to where you're going," Rafe said.

I nodded, pulling in a heart-calming breath. "And you should really think more about the permanent damage you're doing to my nervous system when you do that."

He kissed the top of my head. "Nah. A good scare every once in a while is good for you."

"Oh? When was the last time you were that scared?"

"When they ran out of Pabst Blue Ribbon at the bowling alley," he said promptly. "Glad I caught you before you got to the house. I had to reprime the trim on the stairway, so you'd better stay out for a couple of days."

I made a face. Paint primer fumes gave me horrendous headaches. "Thanks for telling me before I went in."

"Nothing but the best for my fiancée." He took my hand and we started walking. "Was that Mitchell you were talking to back there?"

I nodded. "And a very strange conversation it was. We started with a detailed history of their house, including the dates of the original purchase—no, don't laugh, I am not making this up. And after we got through all that, he wanted some advice on . . ."

My voice trailed off. We'd just walked past the bike shop, and a number of puzzle pieces suddenly rearranged themselves in my head.

"Advice on what?" Rafe prompted.

"Planning for retirement," I said vaguely. "Weird, you know?"

Rafe agreed that it was weird, but my thoughts had already moved in a completely different direction.

Because what if the tie between Brown and Emily was more than biking? What if it had something to do with retirement? Both of them were recently retired from their jobs. Could that be a connection? And if so, were there other just-retired bike club members? Were they, too, about to become murder victims?

"Hello, are you in there?" Rafe squeezed my hand.

"Sorry, just thinking."

"About what?"

"Is this the time to talk about how we're going to settle on paying for the house?"

"Not even close," my beloved said cheerfully.

"Rafe . . ."

"Nope, not going there," he said. "We'll work it out, don't worry."

"But I do. Worry, I mean. Not a lot," I hastened to add, because I was doing my best to be more like Aunt Frances, who worried the least of any person I'd ever met in my life. She was also the most content person I'd ever met, and I was pretty sure the two things were linked. "We need to work this out before I move in."

"And we will." Rafe gave me a one-armed hug. "I'm just really busy right now. How about this. We'll sit down next weekend and do a spreadsheet."

"That should work," I said. "But I'd like to communicate my displeasure that you've taken so long to do this. We started talking about it right after we got engaged, and—"

"Well, hey!" Rafe called to a large man in baggy sweatpants and sweatshirt who'd just come around the corner. "How are you doing these days?"

I sighed. This was a side effect of the assistant librarian pairing up with the middle school principal. No matter where we went, one of us ran into someone we knew. This happened anywhere in Tonedagana County. It also happened throughout northwest lower Michigan, downstate, and, during a drive to Canada on the long Labor Day weekend, also managed to happen in the tiny town of Wawa.

"Mr. Niswander," said the man, shaking hands with Rafe. "And Minnie Hamilton, correct?"

"Isaac." I nodded, finally placing him in an office wearing office-type clothes. "From the city."

"For my sins." He laughed jovially, his round face managing to get even rounder in the process. "And I have a lot of them, don't I?"

Rafe smiled. "As far as I know, your sins have all been committed vicariously through your offspring."

"Ah, my wife would say the apple doesn't fall far from the tree." He laughed again.

"How are your rug rats doing these days?" Rafe asked. "Last I heard all three had actually found colleges that would take them."

"Can you believe it?" Isaac shook his head. "But turns out our middle child didn't actually want to go. She's apprenticed to an electrician and loves the work. The other two? They're costing us a fortune in tuition."

Though he grimaced, I sensed his underlying pride in his offspring. For a moment, my stomach clenched with worry. If Rafe and I had children, odds were good they'd go to college, but how would we pay for it? My parents had helped pay for my undergraduate degree, and I wanted to do the same for my own kids. And child care was so expensive; how were we going to save money for—

"Stop," I murmured to myself. I had to stop worrying and focus on the things I could control.

"What's that?" Rafe asked.

I suddenly woke up to the fact that standing right there in front of me was someone who worked with Drew Parnell, our new suspect, on a daily basis. "I've started riding with the bike club that Brown belonged to," I said. "And I hear your boss rides with them, too."

"Oh?" Isaac looked surprised. "News to me. But he's a private kind of guy. He doesn't talk about himself much. I know he came from a smaller city downstate, but other than that?" He shrugged. "Spends a lot of time in the office, that's for sure."

"Do you like working for him?"

Isaac grinned. "I'm a public servant. I work for the taxpayers of Chilson."

"All three of us do," Rafe said, and we bumped knuckles all around.

Before we shifted topics too much, I said, "When I was in with Tabitha a little bit ago, you and Cathy were talking about Ariella Tice." He nodded cautiously, and I went on. "I ran into Drew the other day and he sort of said he'd fired Ariella after something happened between her and Emily Acosta, the woman who was found in the state forest. Do you know—"

Isaac's eyes went wide. "You think Ariella killed her? And Brown?"

Nice job, Minnie, I told myself. *You've scared the daylights out of him for no real reason.* "Ariella seems like one of those people who feel life owes them a living," I said truthfully. "And, no, I don't really think she's a killer. But if there's some connection, the police should know."

"Sure, I see," Isaac said, nodding.

I was glad he did, because I wasn't sure I'd made any sense. "Do you know what Drew was talking about? Did something happen between Ariella and Emily?"

"Actually, yes," he said, sighing. "And it's my fault. Processing the event permits is one of my responsibilities, and I was out sick for a couple of days. Drew assigned the permitting to Ariella while I was out, and Emily came in for a permit to hold a bike club picnic in the waterfront park."

"Sounds easy enough," Rafe commented.

"You'd think, wouldn't you?" Isaac rolled his eyes heavenward. "But with Ariella, the simplest transaction could turn into a battle, and afterward you could never really find out why. The only thing you could count on is it wouldn't be Ariella's fault."

"So what you're saying," Rafe said, "is you don't miss Ariella?"

Isaac laughed. "Like I miss an ice pick in my eyeball." Still laughing, he waved and headed off.

And I was left with . . . nothing.

What I'd temporarily suspected, that Drew had insinuated bad blood between Ariella as a red herring, wasn't true. And my theory that retirement connected Brown's and Emily's deaths was simply a theory. I had nothing to prove it. Absolutely nothing.

Kristen and I sat across from each other at a small table that Harvey, sous-chef extraordinaire, had set up in her office. He'd just laid the table with place settings of utensils and a dessert, or what I assumed was a dessert because it was Sunday evening. At this point, however, the exact type of dessert we were about to eat was a secret, at least to me, because it was hidden by a shiny metal cover.

"Are you ready for the best dessert you've ever had in your life?" Kristen asked.

I wasn't sure how anything could be better than the crème brûlée we normally had, but I supposed it was good to try something new at least once a year. "Of course I'm ready."

She nodded at Harvey. "Will you do the honors?"

"At your command," he said, and with a flourish, he lifted the covers.

I gasped. In front of me was a towering pile of red cake layers, each so thin I wouldn't have believed their creation possible. Between each layer of cake was an even thinner layer of white frosting. On top were delicate rolls of shaved dark chocolate, and melted chocolate had artistically been drizzled over the entire thing and onto the edges of the plates.

"It's gorgeous," I said, and applauded.

"Thank you, thank you." Kristen smiled smugly. "It

was Harvey's idea, and he can go now." She flicked her fingers at him and he bowed as he departed. "Dig in."

"Can't do it," I said, shaking my head. "Too pretty."

"Food is made to be eaten." Kristen leaned forward with a fork in hand. With one firm swoosh, she sliced through my dessert from top to bottom, then made another cut to create a bite-sized wedge. "There. Now can you eat it?"

"You are the best friend ever."

"In the history of the world, yeah, yeah, I know." She snorted. "If I was really that good a friend I would have been taking better care of you. That ring finger of yours is still empty and you're still on that haven of seasickness you call a houseboat. Yet I bet you will come to Rafe's defense if I even hint at criticizing him."

"Naturally. Now you have to be quiet while I eat," I said, and took a bite of the new dessert. Taste, texture, presentation—it had it all. I chewed, swallowed, frowned. Took another bite and repeated the process. After the third sequence, I sat back and gave her a long look. "People will drive a hundred miles, one way, to eat this. Best ever."

She blew out a huge breath. "You did that on purpose. Drawing it out so I had to wait for your opinion."

"That's what happens when you criticize my fiancé without me criticizing him first."

Laughing, she said, "Fair enough. Say, have you made any progress finding out who killed Brown?"

I'd moved to the back of my brain the knowledge that Brown and Kristen's dad and been poker-playing buddies, and that I should have been keeping her up to date with what Tabitha and I had found out. Bad Minnie, for assuming Kristen had too much going on with closing the restaurant for the year to want to hear about an amateur murder investigation. "In some ways, no. In lots of ways, yes."

Kristen made wiggling motions with her fingers. "Talk to me, Hamilton. You know saying stuff out loud helps you think through things."

She was right; it did. Or at least it usually did. But when our plates were empty and our after-dessert coffee gone, I'd told her everything, and not a single spark of an idea had come to life.

Later, back at the houseboat, Eddie and I sat side by side on the dining table's bench seat. I looked at him and said, "You know, there is one thing I didn't tell her."

"Mrr?"

I rubbed him behind the ear because he was tipping his head to the side in a way that could only mean, Rub my ear, please. Although I was probably imagining the "please" part.

"When Mitchell cornered me yesterday, something he said made me wonder if the connection between the murders of Brown and Emily is more than the bike club. What if it's because both of them recently retired? What if—"

"Mrr!"

"Oh, sorry, was I doing it wrong?" I started rubbing behind his other ear. "Like I was saying, what if it's a combination of the bike club and retirement? I'm not sure how that could be a thing, but you never know, right? What if other recently retired bike club members are in danger? And how would I tell anyone that? Let's think how that conversation would go. 'Say, Terry, how long have you been retired? Only a few months? Oh, dear, you'd better start looking over your shoulder because—"

I was suddenly talking to my hand because Eddie had jumped down. "Sorry," I called after him. "I try to do it right, really I do. It's just hard when you have so much fur to scratch you in the right place and . . . what are you doing?"

Eddie, of course, didn't answer, but the noises emanating from the floor were unmistakably of the paper variety.

"Stop what you're doing, please." I started turning around. "Because I'm sure whatever it is, it's annoyingly destructive, and—Eddie!"

He whirled, ran to the end of the kitchen, leapt down the stairs in one stride, leapt up onto the bed, jumped over to the unused bunk, ran back up the stairs, circled me, and ran back to the bed.

"You are the weirdest cat ever," I muttered, leaning down to pick up the scraps of paper that had formerly been my water bill.

"Mrr!"

"Back at you," I called.

"Mrr!!"

This time I remained silent because I was staring at the water bill. Thinking.

Hard.

Then I picked up my phone. "Tabitha? How do you feel about an early morning appointment?"

The next morning, I met Tabitha in front of the sheriff's office. We huddled next to the building in a vain attempt to stay out of the biting wind. I'd started to catch her up on my new line of thinking but hadn't gone through half of it when she pulled on my coat sleeve and tugged me toward the front door.

"Let's get inside," she said. "It's cloudy, cold, windy, and it's not going to get any warmer until the end of April, and I'm too old to stand outside shivering." Though I wanted to protest that there'd be some nice days yet, in general her point was correct, so I allowed myself to get towed into the front lobby.

The office manager, Chelsea Stille, smiled at us through the thick glass. "Hi, Mrs. Inwood. And Minnie, right? Are you two looking for Detective Inwood?"

We were indeed, and in short order we were in the interview room, waiting for Hal and Ash.

"That wind," Tabitha said, shivering and huddling inside her coat. "It was zipping through me like I didn't even exist."

I frowned. She wasn't sounding like the Tabitha I'd grown so quickly to know and love. "You're not getting sick, are you?"

"Sick?" Hal asked. "Honey, what's wrong?"

"Nothing that can't be fixed with a cup of hot coffee," she said. "Which is more than I can say about you."

"What?" Ash asked. "Hal, are you getting sick?"

"This is a very odd conversation," Detective Inwood said. "And I feel sure that health issues aren't why you two ladies came in this morning."

"Thank you for making a few minutes for us." I smiled across the table at the now-seated law enforcement officials. "Sorry for contacting you so late last night, and again, thanks for making time."

Hal looked, as per usual, as if he'd never had an

emotion in his life. Ash, however, was eyeing me with a "What is she up to?" expression.

"What we didn't have time to tell you the last time we were here," I said, indicating myself and Tabitha, "is that Emily Acosta grew up in Chilson. Her maiden name was Worman, and she went by Emmy Sue back then."

Ash nodded. "We're aware."

Huh. Well, score one for the detectives. "Were you also aware that, right out of high school, she worked for the city of Chilson?"

The two men exchanged glances. They had not known.

"Before," Tabitha said, "we assumed the link between Brown and Emily was bicycling, most likely through the bike club. But no other member of the bike club has been killed, wounded, or even threatened. This would lead you to think they had something else in common, something else that connects their murders."

"That's assuming," Hal said, inspecting his fingernails, "the two murders were committed by the same party or parties."

"Any other assumption," Tabitha snapped, "is so far beyond the realm of the reasonableness standard it's preposterous to spend any time considering it as an option."

Hal started to open his mouth but paused and nodded for us to continue.

"So if bicycling wasn't the connection point," I said, "the only other commonality is that they both worked for the city." I said it triumphantly, hoping for applause and accolades, but trying to be understanding if all we got were slow nods of approval.

"Did they ever work together?" Ash asked.

I tried to simultaneously subtract in my head to calculate Emily's high school graduation date and remember if Brown had worked anywhere other than the city. "Not sure. But it would be easy enough to find out."

"Lots of people work for the city," Hal said. "Why on earth would anyone start killing off city employees? Especially one who'd worked there decades ago and had hardly set foot in the town since then?"

"But it's—"

"Let's go," Tabitha said, standing abruptly. "They're not listening, can't you hear it? They already have their minds made up that we're useless females who are wasting their precious time. Let them get back to what was so incredibly important that they don't have a moment for anything else."

She swept out of the room. This time, Hal jumped to his feet and hurried after her, but she wasn't having any of it.

"Come on, Minnie," she said, holding the lobby door open. "You and I have things to discuss."

I sent Ash a vaguely apologetic look and went with her. Outside, the wind was just as strong as it had been ten minutes earlier. "Round Table?" I asked.

She nodded, and in hardly any time at all, we were cozy in a booth with hot coffee in front of us.

"Hal and Ash," I said. "They could have just been playing devil's advocate."

Tabitha looked at me. "Do you really think so?"

"No, but I felt an obligation to offer the possibility."

She laughed, and a small tightness that had been inside me loosened. Tabitha was fine; there was just something going on between her and her husband that they needed to work out. And after umpteen years of marriage, I figured they'd get there without my help.

"Let's talk through our suspects again," Tabitha said. "We need to determine which of them has connections to the city."

And so we reviewed and considered everything we knew about all five suspects, and rejected both Bob Bernier and Cody Sisk as suspects. And, reluctantly, the increasingly violent Warren Jorgenson. That left us with two people who fit all our qualifications.

"Drew Parnell," I said.

Tabitha nodded. "And Ariella Tice."

"The man on the yellow bike was Drew."

"And it was Drew," Tabitha said, "who pointed us to suspect Ariella in the first place, as far as Emily's death went."

I frowned. "The way I remember it, Cathy and Isaac first mentioned the altercation between Ariella and Emily."

"Hmm. You could be right. Drew pushed us in that direction, though."

True enough. We sat there a moment, thinking our own thoughts.

"Right." Tabitha sighed. "Well, you have librarian duties. But there are a couple of things we need to know before we can get any further with this."

"Motive," I said.

"And proof."

"We'll find it," I said, nodding, and feeling my

face set into serious lines. "Don't worry, we'll find what we need."

Tabitha smiled faintly. "When you talk like that, I believe every word."

I nodded again and hoped she was right.

Chapter 16

I spent the first two hours of my library day doing routine tasks. Catching up with e-mails, taking care of time sheets and purchase requests, dealing with book orders, quelling the occasional small fire at the front desk; the routine work filled the morning pleasantly. Then, mid-morning, I announced to those assembled in the kitchen at break time that I was going to be incommunicado the rest of the day.

My pronouncement was greeted with a complete lack of response.

Holly, who was poking at her cell phone, didn't even look up. "Oh. Okay."

"Sounds good," Kelsey said, but since she was reading yesterday's newspaper headlines, I wasn't sure if she was referring to what I'd said or the article about a water main replacement on the other side of town.

Josh, stationed at the coffeepot in what looked like a stance to body check Kelsey if she came close, glanced at me over his shoulder with question marks in his eyes but didn't say anything.

I nodded at him, trying to communicate solidarity, calm, and a pending solution to his romantic conundrum. Not that I had one, but surely I'd come up with something soon.

"You okay?" Holly asked me. "Your face looks kind of funny."

Wrenching my face into a horrible grimace, I said, "Really? What's so funny about it?"

Holly rolled her eyes, Josh turned back to the coffee, and Kelsey flipped to the sports section.

"Right," I said cheerfully. "Well, it's been nice talking to everyone. Tomorrow's a bookmobile day, so I probably won't see you until Wednesday."

I received three vague murmurs of acknowledgment and, coffee in hand, went back to my office, thinking about the effects of heavy cloud cover in combination with what had been forecasted by Weather People Who Should Know as a long and cold winter.

"A lunch-and-learn series," I said out loud, sitting and typing into my computer. "Maybe that will perk us up in January." Without too much thought, I entered a list of possible topics ranging from personal finance to public speaking to home repair tips. This was fun, and I soon turned to the Internet for ideas. It wasn't until I took a sip of coffee and squinched my face at its tepid temperature that I realized how much time I'd spent on a task that didn't need doing. At least not today.

Sighing, I closed the list and turned my attention to the task of the day: how to staff the bookmobile for extended hours without ruining my health or destroying library morale.

Just before lunchtime, my boss stopped by my office. "How's it going?"

I leaned back in my chair. "Hey, Graydon. Do you really want to know?"

He laughed. "I'd like to say I wouldn't have asked if I didn't want to know, but that's just not true, because sometimes I do ask polite questions and keep on walking without waiting for an answer." He eased in and sat in my spare chair. "This time, however, I do actually want to know. Seems like we haven't talked in a while. So. How are things?"

I knew he meant professionally and not personally, but there are times when they blend together. "I don't suppose you know Ariella Tice? She works at the bank. No? How about Drew Parnell, the city manager . . . No, I suppose not." Graydon had moved to Chilson when he took the job, just six months ago, so none of that was a surprise, but it didn't hurt to ask.

"Why do you want to know?" He crossed his ankle over his opposite knee. "Looking to hit them up for donations?"

"No, they're just . . . people I've heard about." Which I hoped didn't sound as stupid to him as it did to me.

I looked at his cheerful expression and was almost, but not quite, tempted to tell him about inserting myself into a murder investigation with the help of the detective's wife, how we were sure there was a connection to the city, and how we were afraid there were going to be more victims.

"What have you been working on this morning?" he asked.

"Bookmobile schedule for the next six months."
I pushed at the corner of my monitor to show him.
"What do you think?"

He pulled reading glasses from his pocket and put
them on. "Let's take a look. Hmm . . . I like the evening hours, especially after the holidays when people
get bored. And full Saturdays twice a month?"

Frowning, he sat back and took off his glasses.
"This is realistic? I thought you were having problems staffing the hours we have, and this is even
more time on the road."

"Yes. But you're right about expanding the hours,
the demand is there. You're also right that the problem is staffing. And there's only one . . ."

"Only one what?" Graydon asked.

"Solution," I said vaguely. "There's only one
solution."

Because there was, in fact, only one realistic way
to cure the bookmobile's staffing woes: find more
staff. Just like there was only one solution to cure
the problem of Josh and Mia.

And maybe, just maybe, there was only one real
solution to finding Emily and Brown's killer.

Anticipate the next victim and stop the next murder before it happened.

At the end of the last bookmobile stop the next day,
Julia, in spite of the facts that she was wearing all
black and that Eddie had a propensity to shed his
white hairs in the presence of that color, plopped
him on her lap and snuggled him tight. "Oooff!" she
said, burrowing her face into his fur. "You are just
the sweetest thing ever."

Eddie looked at me over the top of Julia's arm with an expression of boredom combined with forbearance. I nodded in sympathy and sent him a telepathic promise that he'd be getting extra treats.

"You do realize," I said, "that you're calling him that simply because he slept through the visit of the Kolb triplets, which means you're calling him sweet because he spent half the night keeping me awake chasing a penny across the floor." "Half" might have been an exaggeration, but not by much.

"Sad for you," Julia said, smiling, "but it worked out, didn't it? Usually he hides from those kids and they pester the living daylights out of us trying to find the bookmobile kitty. This time they got to pet him as much as they wanted."

True enough, but that didn't mean I wasn't sleep deprived. "Silver lining." I yawned.

Julia gave Eddie one last squeeze and encouraged him into his carrier. "You know," she said, "what this bookmobile could use is a couch for napping. I'm sure some of that money you're socking away for a new vehicle could go to install one of those sliding bump-out things."

"What?" My eyes went wide in not-so-mock horror. "We'd lose shelf space!"

"Oh, right." Julia brushed a third of the Eddie hair off her lap and got up, walking the length of the vehicle with a thoughtful expression. "There's got to be a way to make this place more comfy."

I smiled. "Beanbag chairs?"

"Throw pillows?"

"Inflatable mattresses?"

We tossed out increasingly ridiculous ideas as we

battened the hatches and got ready to roll back to Chilson. The final idea was cots fastened to the ceiling that from below looked like sound-absorption devices and could be lowered by solar-powered motors.

"Excellent plan," I said. "Unfortunately, I'm too busy right now to bring it to the library board. How about you do it instead?"

Julia slid into the passenger's seat and reached for the seat-belt buckle. "If you write me a script, sure. Without words for me to say I get all knock-kneed with stage fright and can't say a thing."

"Right," I said, starting the engine. "No matter what all those Broadway reviews and Tony Awards say."

"What they say is I can act, not that I can speak in public extemporaneously."

I glanced at her, then pressed on the gas pedal. "There's a difference?"

"Please. The differences are too many to count," she said. "Acting is taking on the life and loves of a person completely different from yourself. It's not you up on that stage or in front of that camera; it's someone else, and that someone else doesn't get stage fright."

"Okay," I said slowly. "I get that."

"But speaking in public as myself?" Julia shuddered. "My own words? That would leave me open to blanket criticism. I can't believe anyone ever willingly does it."

I smiled, thinking of the many times I'd spoken in front of groups without any real fear. Small groups, sure, but still. "Most audiences are friendly. They're on your side. They want you to succeed."

"Not worth the risk," Julia said. "My second career as a bookmobile clerk and children's storyteller is the one I want, thank you very much."

I was sure she wasn't telling the exact truth about having a fear of public speaking, since she'd been teaching acting classes at the college where Aunt Frances worked when I'd lured her away, and what was teaching if not speaking in public?

Also, I hadn't thought that her job as the bookmobile clerk could rise to the level of career. But her consideration that it did made me proud and pleased.

"Say, how is that murder investigation going?" Julia asked. "Any new leads?"

I filled her in on the narrowing of suspects to Ariella and Drew. "The bike connection might be there, but we really think it's more to do with working for the city. Somehow. Brown recently retired from there and Emily worked there decades ago, so what's the common thread?"

"Hmm." Julia tapped the top of Eddie's carrier with her toes. "Both victims worked for the city and they both recently retired."

"That's the other connection," I said. "The retirements. What I'm worried about is if other people who retire will also be targets."

Julia tapped her toes again. "Hard to warn people of that. I can see the press release now. Anyone who has just retired or is about to retire, please contact Minnie Hamilton, as your life might be in danger."

I smiled. "The one good thing is I don't know anyone who's planning to—" My words caught tight in my throat.

Because I'd suddenly remembered that I did know someone about to retire.

* * *

As soon as I got back to the houseboat and returned Eddie to his current favorite place of the driver's seat, I sat at the dining table and pulled out my phone.

Minnie: *Do you know what Keith Tanaka did before he started teaching?*

Rafe:

Minnie (after thirty seconds of glaring at the phone as if that would make him respond faster): *Hey, did you see my last text?*

Rafe:

Minnie (tapping hard, after another thirty seconds, as if that would make him respond faster): *Hello? Are you there?*

Rafe:

Minnie (slapping her forehead after another thirty seconds): *Rats. You said you had a board meeting tonight, didn't you? Never mind. I'll find out some other way.*

Muttering at my stupidity, I tossed my phone onto the dining table and stared out at the lake, thinking.

If I knew Keith Tanaka better, I'd have his cell number and I'd just text him myself, but I didn't so I couldn't. So what were my options? Sure, I could wait until Rafe was done with his meeting, but his board meetings tended to run for hours. And, anyway, there was a good chance, since he was Rafe and didn't always ask people the questions any normal human being would ask, that he didn't know what Keith had done prior to becoming a teacher.

I wouldn't be able to get a decent night's sleep if I didn't track down the answer right away, so I needed to come up with another way to find out.

"What do you think?" I asked Eddie.

"Mrr," he said, but it was a soft and sighing kind of "mrr," which meant he was content with who and where he was and he wasn't going to help me.

"You're funny," I said, rubbing his cheek. "You talk half the day out on the bookmobile; then when I want some help, you curl up like a, like a crustacean."

As similes went, it was pretty horrible, but I'd heard worse. Somewhere. I was sure of it.

"Anyway," I went on, getting up from the dining bench and pacing around, "I'll just keep talking as if you're listening. How do I find out where Keith used to work? I don't even know if he's originally from Chilson. If he's from downstate, it's going to be even harder to . . . Hey, cut that out!"

When my back had been turned, Eddie had stirred himself to leap from the driver's seat to the dining table and was in the act of batting my phone off the edge of said table.

I lunged forward and caught it just before it hit the floor. "Not a toy," I scolded. Although it could be, because of game apps, but he didn't need to know that. "This is a very expensive piece of electronics and—" I stared at it. "And its connection to the marina's Wi-Fi is slow and poky. Eddie, you're a genius," I said, kissing the top of his head. "See you later, okay?"

"Mrr!"

"Yes, you're brilliant." I pulled on my coat and headed out the door, closing it on another loud "Mrr!"

"Cats," I muttered, and hurried to my car. Five minutes later, I'd parked at the library, and a minute after that I'd managed to sneak into my office without anyone noticing I was in the building.

Ten minutes after that, I was frowning at my computer. "How could he not be online?" I asked. Because the things I'd found on the Internet about Keith Tanaka were what I already knew; he was a math teacher at Chilson's middle school. Okay, it probably wasn't that unusual for a man in his sixties to not have a Facebook account—my dad was about Keith's age and he had yet to succumb to the lure of social media—but you'd think a teacher would have some online presence.

Then again, maybe that's why he didn't. Maybe he stayed away intentionally exactly because he was a teacher.

"Yeah, but that's not helpful to me right now," I said. What would be helpful was someone who knew Keith well enough to . . . "I am such an idiot."

I shut off the light in my office and headed out to the front desk. Sure enough, there was Kelsey, helping a father and his two little girls check out a stack of picture books. After she'd stuffed the two adorable little backpacks with books and waved them off, I approached.

"Hey, Minnie." She looked at me with raised eyebrows. "I thought you left half an hour ago."

"I did, then came back. And thanks again for working until eight."

"No worries." Kelsey smiled. "Every once in a while, it's nice to have my husband cook dinner, wash up afterward, make sure the kids have done their homework, make sure they have clean school clothes for the next day, and get them to bed on time all by himself."

I laughed. "Speaking of school, I have a question for you. Back in middle school, did you have Keith Tanaka for a math teacher?" I held my breath, waiting for her answer.

"Sure. It was only his second year of teaching, I think, and for us kids it was weird that he was a new teacher, but old at the same time."

My breath sighed out of me. Perfect. "About that. Do you know what he did before he became a teacher?"

She laughed. "I know everything he did. That was part of the fun with Mr. Tanaka: He had tons of stories about all his summer jobs. The worst was the summer he worked for a landscaping company and didn't know he was horribly allergic to poison ivy."

"What about professionally? Do you know what he did before he started teaching?"

"Um, let me think. I know he did electrical work, but I can't remember if he did that as a summer job or as a full-time thing."

This was not helping. "How about college? Do you know where he went? What degree he got?"

"Yes." Smiling, Kelsey snapped her fingers. "He went to Central and got an accounting degree. That's why, back then, he was able to get into teaching without too much trouble."

"So after he graduated, but before he started teaching. Do you know what he did then?"

"If I'm remembering right, and you know how memories are"—she banged the side of her head with her knuckles—"he was city's first-ever finance director. That's why they were okay hiring someone so young, because they got him cheap."

"The city," I repeated. "You mean Chilson?"

"Sure. He did that for a lot of years, but then got tired of the politics and went into teaching. Out of the frying pan and into the fire, if you ask me." She grinned. "But he was a great teacher, and—"

I'd listen to her fond memories later. "Do you know where he lives?"

Kelsey blinked. "Um, sure. We had an end-of-school party at his house and I don't think he's moved." She described a location on the outskirts of town. "Why?"

Bless small towns. "Tell you next time I see you, okay? Thanks!" I spun around and, mid-spin, realized I was about to walk smack into Mia Lacombe. "You are just the person I wanted to see," I said, swerving to keep us from colliding. "Only I don't have time right now."

"Oh, okay," she said. "Whenever is good for you."

The way she was hanging her head and curling her shoulders forward made me mentally kick myself for not talking to her and Josh earlier. "Your problem?" I called as I hurried away. "There's a solution." Well, if they had the courage. "I'll tell you about it soon, okay?"

And so Mia's brightening face was the last thing I saw before I left the building and went into the night.

The clouds were so low and oppressive that even someone as vertically compact as me felt tall enough to reach out and touch the closest one. But though the wind hadn't faded much from the morning's bluster, it wasn't raining, and the temperature was almost sixty, so there was a lot to be grateful for.

I hurried to my car and headed to Keith Tanaka's house. Ten minutes later, I wasn't sure Kelsey's directions had been very helpful. What she'd said was he and his wife lived "in that reddish house two doors down from the corner where you turn to go to that cool farmers' market place."

I knew the corner she meant, and since to me "down" meant south, that's where I was looking. But there was no house that looked reddish in the dim light, so there were three possibilities. Either south wasn't the right direction, or new houses had been built to make the "two doors down" part incorrect, or Keith had re-sided his house and it wasn't reddish any longer.

Making a rough and rude noise in the back of my throat, I banged the heel of my hand on my steering wheel and ran through my options. If the weather had been nicer, people would have been out and about doing yard work and I would have stopped, explained who I was, and asked. But in this gloom, there wasn't a soul to be seen.

I picked up my phone.

"Good evening, Chilson District Library. This is Kelsey."

"Hey," I said when she answered. "It's Minnie. I can't find—"

"Sorry," she interrupted, sounding harassed. "Do you mind calling back in a couple of minutes? There's a ton of people here all of a sudden and—"

"No, go ahead. Talk to you later." I thumbed my phone off and concluded that the option of driving down the other streets and looking for a red house was the only one that had any chance of success, at least tonight. And I had to find him tonight, because I couldn't shake the feeling that another murder was coming.

"Red . . . red . . . red . . ." I murmured as I turned

around in a dark driveway and drove in the opposite direction. But there wasn't a house to the north that looked anywhere close to red. Sighing, I turned around again and went east of the intersection. There were almost no houses that way, so I made another turn and went west.

It was then that I remembered that Kelsey lived maybe two miles farther down this road, so to Kelsey, down probably meant . . . and yes, there was a reddish house. Not one of the ranch-style houses that abounded in this part of town, but an older story and a half with a detached garage that might have once been a house for a family who, back in the early 1900s, was trying to make a living by farming.

There were lights on inside so I pulled into the driveway. Before I even got all the way out of the car, a voice called out, "Hello?"

"Is that Keith?" I peered into the direction from which the voice had come. "It's Minnie. Rafe's fiancée."

"Minnie?" Keith came around the corner of the house. He was carrying a leaf rake and wearing jeans, sweatshirt, and an old baseball cap. "What's up? No, wait, don't tell me. Rafe is having an electrical emergency and he's too embarrassed to ask me how to fix it, so he sent you."

"That could be it, but no. It's, um . . ." I shifted from one foot to the other, wishing that I'd planned this conversation better. "Do you have a few minutes? This could take a while."

"Sure, come on back. I was quitting for the night, anyway."

Keith leaned the rake against the garage and led me around to the backyard. I must have made some sort of noise, because he grinned. "Nice, isn't it? This was my summer project and now that it's done, it's almost winter and we won't get to use it for seven months."

"Life in northern Michigan," I said, looking around. "This is . . . wonderful."

And it was. A solid wood fence surrounded the entire yard. Flat limestone paths flowed into grassy areas, which flowed into flowerbeds, with low lights softly illuminating the spaces. Closer to the house was an outside kitchen with a fieldstone base next to a patio, partially covered with a wood pergola. Between the kitchen and the pergola was a brick fire pit, its small fire glowing in warm invitation.

"Just tossed in some sticks I picked up in the yard," Keith said. "Have a seat. My wife is downstate at a conference, so I'd be happy to have the company."

He slid two rattan chairs away from a glass table and arranged them on opposite sides of the fire. "Can I get you anything to drink? I know you're not big on beer, but we have lots of other possibilities." He gestured at a refrigerator tucked in next to the house, inside some clever cabinetry that undoubtedly housed everything from yard games to table linens.

I made a mental note to ask Rafe what Keith's wife did for a living, because it was hard to imagine that all this had been purchased on a teacher's salary. "Some water would be nice," I said.

"Coming right up." Keith opened the fridge. "Hope you don't mind if I partake, though. There's nothing like cold beer in front of a fire."

"I see why you and Rafe get along so well," I said,

sitting down and hopping my chair slightly closer to the fire's warmth.

"Yeah, well, if you can't get along with Rafe, there's got to be something wrong with you."

I got a goofy smile on my face and suddenly realized that getting compliments about my fiancé was better than getting compliments about myself, or even the bookmobile.

Keith handed me a bottle of water, popped his beer, and settled into the chair opposite me. "What was it you wanted to talk about?"

And, just like that, I told him everything. From finding Brown in the road, to meeting Tabitha, to learning about Emily and Emmy Sue, to our suspects and our winnowing down to Ariella and Drew, and to our growing conviction that the murders were tied by retirement and the city.

"That's what got me worried," I said. "Rafe said you're retiring soon, and an hour ago I learned that you used to work for the city. So you meet both criteria."

Keith finished off his beer. "So you think I'm about to become a murder victim because I'm retiring?"

Put like that, it sounded pretty stupid. "Yes," I said firmly. "I do."

"Lots of people retire." He tossed his empty beer can into a handy bucket. "Hardly any of them are murdered."

Clearly, he wasn't taking this seriously. Somehow I needed to communicate the danger I felt sure was all around him. "You're a math teacher. Tell me the odds of two recent retirees, who both worked at the city, being murdered within a couple weeks of each other."

He said, "I'm a math teacher, not a statistician," but I could see the wheels starting to turn inside his head.

"Though I still don't know exactly why Brown and Emily were killed," I said, "the link is there even if—"

"How long did Emily work at the city?" Keith asked. "I remember her from when I was finance director, but she was already there when I started."

"Um. Not sure."

"Think it through," he urged. "This is important."

"Well, I was told she started there right after high school, then moved downstate . . ." The water bottle was cold in my hand as I tried to do the calculations with the little information I had. "Ten years, about. Maybe a little more."

"That's it, then." Keith nodded. "There's your motive."

I had no idea what he was talking about. "What is?"

"Pension costs. Though I haven't worked for the city in years, I live here and I pay attention to what's going on at city hall. Drew Parnell, during his job interview, said multiple times that he'd get the city's budget into the black inside of two years, and if he didn't, the city could fire him." Keith looked at the fire. "I kept wondering how he'd do it, and now I know."

It still wasn't making sense. At least not to me. "Um . . ."

"Pensions," Keith said. "One of the biggest liabilities the city has is pensions. These days, most municipal pensions are just like everyone else's, defined contribution. Back when Brown and Emily started? They got defined benefit pensions, which are pushing cities, including Chilson, closer to bankruptcy than you'd want to think."

My non-math brain finally grasped what he was talking about. And it was horrified. "You mean . . ."

Keith gave me a sharp nod. "Yes. Drew is killing off retirees to help balance the city's budget."

This was the puzzle piece that locked everything together. The city's workshops on the budget. Brown's murder. The restaurant meeting with Drew and two council members. Emily's murder. Drew's second year as city manager was coming to a close. To save his job, to save his reputation, to save his career, he needed to reduce the city's budget, and fast. And now . . .

"City council has a meeting tomorrow night," I said. "Keith, I think you need to—"

My water bottle suddenly blew apart. I looked at my wet but empty hand, not understanding. What had just happened?

BANG!

The report of a rifle echoed loudly around the backyard. Just for a second, Keith and I stared at each other. Then, simultaneously, we dove for cover.

Chapter 17

I tried to quiet my panting breaths since I didn't want to transmit any feelings of cowardice and fear. But since Keith's breathing was just as loud as mine, I stopped worrying about it.

"We heard the same thing, right?" he whispered.

Before I'd moved north, I would not have been able to identify the difference between the firing of a handgun, rifle, and shotgun. In the years since, however, my horizons had expanded dramatically. "Rifle," I whispered back. "Not sure of the caliber."

"A .22 would be nice," Keith said.

It would, because while a small caliber could do a lot of damage, it was less likely to kill us. However . . .

"Yeah, but it sounded like a .30-06."

The absurdity of discussing firearms with a man I barely knew while crouching behind an outdoor kitchen to hide from a man who'd already killed twice struck me with a fierce intensity. Giggles leaked out and I put both hands over my mouth to keep the noise from escaping. The laughter was, I knew, a reaction to the life-threatening situation we had suddenly been immersed in, and I needed to stifle it if we were going to get out of this alive.

"Where do you think he is?" I asked through my fingers.

"No idea."

"At least he's a lousy shot."

Keith sort of laughed. "We were sitting ducks, sitting there by the fire. He had enough light to see us . . . well, me, I suppose. I'm the one he's really after. Sorry I doubted you at first."

I gave him a nod of acknowledgment. Noblesse oblige and all that. "Sorry I didn't anticipate him changing up his methods so much." Then I thought about angles and trajectories, which was a lot like math, so I didn't get very far. Then I remembered that I was hunkered down next to a math teacher.

"That shot hit the bottle of water," I said. "I was just lifting it to take a drink. And you were sitting directly across from me. Do you think that could have deviated the bullet?"

"In addition to not being a statistician, I'm also not a ballistics expert."

This was beginning to get exasperating. "Then what good is knowing all that math?" I asked, a bit testily. "You don't have to be a hundred percent correct here. It's not a court of law. Just give me a guess."

"No guessing," he said. "There are reasons you have to show your work on math problems. Guessing demonstrates a lack of base knowledge and a tendency to laziness."

For crying out loud. "Hypothesize."

"If we're going to hypothesize, then yes, hitting another object could have created a slight deviation of the bullet's trajectory. But, like I said, I'm not a—"

"So Drew could be a good shot. It was the happenstance of me moving the water bottle that angled it away to hit whatever it hit."

Keith turned his head and looked at me. "Do you realize what you just said? You saved my life."

Since we were still hiding, and there was still a guy out there with a high-powered rifle, the story wasn't over yet. "I don't suppose you happen to have a cell phone in your pocket."

He shook his head. "And since you're asking, I assume you don't, either?"

"In my car."

"That's too bad," Keith said. "Don't suppose you told Rafe where you were going, gave him a timeline for coming home, and when you don't show up he's going to get worried, assume the worst, call the police, and they'll come charging up here with sirens blaring?"

"No, he's in a school board meeting."

"A what?" Keith frowned. "Really? I thought they met . . . well, whatever. So that's out as a possibility."

"I've been hoping at least one of your neighbors heard the shot and called the police."

"That would be nice, but it's getting closer to hunting season and people are doing target shooting. You can't shoot inside city limits, but you can in the township, and the township starts on the other side of our back lot line."

I twisted around to look. The back fence was maybe a hundred feet away from us. "What you're saying is hearing gunshots this time of year isn't unusual, that anyone who heard it most likely didn't think twice, and it's highly unlikely that anyone called nine-one-one to send a friendly law enforcement officer our way."

"That's a good summary."

"So we're on our own," I said, just to make sure I had it right.

"Agreed."

We looked at each other, our faces about two feet apart, the fire casting a flickering light that was creepier than I would have liked.

"Maybe he left," I suggested. "Maybe that was a one-time shot and when it didn't work, he gave up. After all, he doesn't know that we've figured out who he is."

Keith didn't say anything for a moment. Then he nodded. "Possible. Let's try this." He grabbed the bill of his grimy baseball cap and slowly raised the hat.

My eyes went wide, but I could see the sense in what he was doing. If Drew was out there, waiting to pounce, he'd see the hat and take another shot. If he was gone, well, then we'd know that, too.

The hat went higher. Keith started to strain with the effort, but he kept going, sitting up and stretching . . . stretching . . .

"I think he's gone," Keith said. "There's no way—"
BANG!

The hat spun out and away, skittering across the patio and landing upside down next to the fire pit, spinning in a slow circle.

"It's a matter of geometry," Keith said tightly. "To make that shot, he has to be somewhere between the back of Watson's garage and a huge oak tree two doors down. But if there's an infrared scope on that rifle, there are too many possibilities."

His voice sounded different and I tore my gaze

away from the spinning hat to see that Keith was gripping his wrist. "You're hurt. Let me see."

"Minnie . . ."

"Don't worry, I'm trained in first aid." Not that I'd used it much on living people other than bandaging a child's skinned knee, but still. "Let me take a look . . . it's not as bad as you might think. I'd say the bullet hit one of the stones up there and you got hit by some of the chips it knocked off. You have a bunch of small holes in your skin, is all." They were deep, but now wasn't the time to tell him that. "Clean it up and you'll be fine." Along with some antibiotics and maybe some stitches.

Keith groaned. "You have got to be kidding me. Replacing one stone to match the rest is going to be impossible."

I quirked a smile, once again realizing why he and Rafe got along so well. "Looks like you already have next summer's project all lined up. Here. It's still bleeding, but I can wrap it."

Every outside coat I owned had light gloves in the pockets, and I pulled them out now. I knotted the thumbs together, wrapped the former-gloves-now-bandage around Keith's wrist, and knotted the pinky fingers together.

"That'll slow the bleeding and keep it clean," I said, patting my handiwork to make sure it would stay in place. "Soon as we get out of here, though, you should get to urgent care and have them take a look."

The nursing ministrations and associated conversation had been conducted in whispers and had only taken a couple of minutes. And now that it was all done, silence fell.

"We need to make a plan," I said. "But first off, I'd like us to assume that he does not have an infrared scope. Just seems too unlikely." Actually, it was more that I didn't want to assume the worst, but whatever.

"I'll buy that." Keith looked around as best he could while in a crouched position. "You should make a run for your car and try to get away, because he's going to come closer to see if I'm dead."

Unfortunately, there was another pertinent item that needed to be pointed out. "He also knows there were two people at the fire pit," I said. "There was enough light to see both of us, and he might have heard us talking. If he's being thorough, and all indications are that he's detail oriented, he'll want to get rid of both of us."

"Minnie—"

"And anyway, I'm not wearing the right shoes to run anywhere." I indicated the flats I'd chosen to wear that morning, a million years ago, back in a pre-sniper world. "There has to be another way."

"The best way is for you to get out of here. None of this is your fault."

"Like it's yours?" I made a scoffing sort of noise. "And I am partly to blame, because if I'd been smarter, I would have figured this out earlier, told the police, and we wouldn't be in this position in the first place."

Keith shifted his weight from one foot to the other. "That brings up a good question. Why didn't you call the police instead of coming here yourself?"

Because they wouldn't have believed me, I almost said. Instead I said, "That is a good question. When I was a kid, my parents often said I didn't think things all the way through, and it's finally occurring to me they might have been—What was that?"

We held our breaths, waiting, because the noise had sounded like a branch breaking. Was Drew sneaking up on us? Was he coming closer and closer, easing silently through the dark yards?

And we were down on the ground, cowering like sitting ducks.

"Is there a door in the fence anywhere?" I asked urgently. I hadn't seen one, but maybe it had been cleverly hidden.

Keith shook his head. "We talked about it and decided there wasn't any need, because it would just go into a neighbor's yard. We all get along, but we also all like our privacy."

Since backyard landscape projects didn't tend to have Escape Route from a Rifle-Toting Killer high on their priority lists, I didn't fault Keith and his wife for not having installed a small hatch somewhere. Still, it would have been nice.

Snap!

"He's coming closer," Keith breathed.

A man who'd killed twice was closing in on us, gun in hand, and looking to kill again. He'd already tried to kill tonight, and if it hadn't been for a little bit of luck, would already have committed another murder. Maybe two.

I pulled in a deep breath, thinking as fast and hard as I could.

There had to be a way out of this. Keith could not die tonight, and neither could I. I had to stay alive. Rafe needed me. Eddie needed me. My parents and brother and sister-in-law and nieces and nephew needed me. Kristen needed me. Aunt Frances needed me. The bookmobile needed me. Josh and Mia needed me. I needed me, and I was not going to be killed by some guy who was trying to balance a budget.

Thus fortified with righteous outrage, my bravery swelled to an astonishing size. And with it came an idea. Not a very good one, but it was an idea, and the only one I had. "If there's no door in the fence," I said quickly, "he has to come at us from the driveway side, right?"

"Yes, but—"

"So you distract him. It's pitch dark now. I'll crawl all along the fence, down behind the bushes so he doesn't see me, around the other side, sneak out, and get some help."

"Minnie—"

But I was already down on my hands and knees and gone.

Ten feet later, my stupid curly hair got caught on . . . something. I tossed my head, trying to yank it free, but that only made things worse.

I did not have time for this. Absolutely did not.

Muttering silently to myself, I leaned back on my knees, reached up to loosen my hair from whatever it was, and—

"Minnie!" Keith whispered. "Watch out for the rosebushes."

I would have made a quiet response, but I was too busy trying to stifle my cries of pain while hoping I wouldn't bleed to death from the new scratches on my hands. Rosebushes. Of course he had rosebushes in his backyard. Who didn't?

Slowly and carefully, I pulled my hair away from the thorns. And started crawling again.

This time I tried harder to see what I was heading into. By now, we'd been away from the fire long enough for my night vision to adjust. However, there had to be light for eyes to adjust to, and there wasn't much of it back here on the ground, behind the rose-bushes and next to the fence. If only I had Eddie-like eyes, I could have seen . . .

"No," I murmured, dropping down to my fore-arms to belly-crawl underneath a particularly low rosebush.

No. I couldn't think about Eddie. Couldn't think about Rafe. Couldn't think about anything except getting out of this yard and to my cell phone. I had to visualize my path. See myself reach the back cor-ner of the fence, inchworm to the other corner, and down along the other side. I needed to assume Drew wouldn't hear my car door opening and see its inte-rior lighting up. Needed to anticipate what I was going to say to 911 to get them here fast, with their lights flashing, sirens blaring, and handcuffs ready before . . . before anything bad happened.

I had my head down. Was focusing on the ground in front of me. Had it all planned out, could see it happening, could see the happy ending, down to the hugs and the backslaps. It was all going to happen, I just knew it.

SNAP!

My right elbow, with all the weight of my upper body, had broken a really loud stick. There was no chance Drew wouldn't have heard that. No chance at all. And now I was stuck, like a gopher in a bur-row, with no way forward that wasn't noisy, because now that I was paying attention, I could see that I was crawling straight into a small brush pile, and no way back that didn't result in a double homicide.

"Hey, Drew!" Keith called. "Yeah, I know it's you.

Most of us do, you know. You're not as smart as you think you are."

A small gasp escaped me. This was the distraction? Really? Keith had decided to taunt the guy with the gun? How did that make sense?

But then I realized what he was doing. He'd known I was going to run into the pile of brush; that's probably what he'd been trying to warn me about when I'd hurried off. He'd known I wouldn't be able to get around it without making some noise. And now he was trying to lure Drew toward him, sacrificing himself for the sake of my stupidity.

I sniffled once, then forced myself to stop with the emotions. Feel later. Act now.

Meanwhile, Keith was just getting warmed up.

"You know," he said loudly, "it didn't take me that long to figure out who was behind the murders. Once I realized that Emmy Sue and Emily were the same person, it was obvious."

"To you, maybe," I whispered to myself, as I slowly, carefully, and quietly pushed aside the pile of sticks and branches. Just as slowly, carefully, and quietly, I flattened myself against the fence, inched forward, and hallelujah! There was the corner! Another twenty-five feet and I'd be halfway around.

But getting this far had taken too long. How long could Keith keep talking? Drew already wanted to kill Keith for the sake of a budget; now he needed to silence him for what he knew. And there was no reason for him to wait.

Fear for Keith tasted sharp and strong. I needed to hurry, had to hurry, had to move faster . . .

Snap!

But even if I hurried, I had to be quiet. Like a cat on the hunt.

Keith coughed loudly. "But like I said, you're not as smart as you think you are. To make any substantive change to your funding level, you'd have to eliminate twenty-five percent of your retirees. And that kind of a murder spree would get noticed."

"They haven't yet."

I jumped. Drew's voice was far closer than I would have liked. Somehow I'd thought he was farther away. Somehow I'd thought I'd have time to get all the way around the yard. Somehow I'd thought this would all work out.

"How deep have you looked into the actuarial valuation?" Keith asked. "The city has six union divisions, right? You should have taken a closer look at the multipliers. What is it for the public works guys, 2.25? Hang on, it's not 2.5 percent, is it? You know, I think it is. Those are the guys you should be taking out first."

Since I had no idea what Keith was talking about, I filed it away in my mental "Look it up later" file and kept crawling.

"Most recent retirees would have the highest payout," Drew said. "Only makes sense."

Past the brush pile, the going was easier. I got up onto my hands and knees and sped to the other fence corner.

"Just on the surface," Keith said. "Actuarial calculations are based on averages; payouts are on the particulars. It's a guessing game. Family history, personal history, regular activities, they all matter. And then there are the beneficiaries."

While half my brain listened, the other half, the much bigger half, was intent on speed-crawling.

"What about the beneficiaries?" Drew asked.

There was a noise that sounded a lot like a foot-step. On the patio.

No, no, no, he can't be that close. I'm not far enough yet, I've been too slow, I need more time . . .

Keith laughed. "Don't tell me you haven't asked for a roster. Do you even know who you're paying money to? Maybe one of your retirees had a long-time spouse die, remarried someone much younger, and last week died peacefully in bed. Now you're stuck paying a pension to the beneficiary for as long as they live. Those are the people you should be tar-geting—way more bang for your buck."

My throat tightened. How could Keith keep talking like that, knowing Drew was about to come around the corner of the outside kitchen, was about to lift his gun and—

"What makes you think I haven't?" Drew asked, but his tone was truculent and defensive, like a child who'd been asked if he'd put his toys away and he'd answered yes, when what he'd actually done was shove them under his bed.

Keith gave out a scoffing laugh. Loudly and for a long time, so I took advantage of the noise to hus-tle forward. I was past the second back corner now, and wrapping back around, inching closer to Keith. And to Drew.

I crept forward. As I moved closer to the fire and the gently lit pathways, it got easier to see the ground in front of me. I pushed aside potentially noisy sticks and knee-destroying rocks and swiveled my head, stretching it high and low, trying to see Keith. Trying to see Drew.

"My research was thorough."

And there he was. A dark shape against the night, moving slowly between Keith's detached garage and house.

"I'm sure you think so," Keith said. "But your actions don't reflect a complete understanding of the valuations. The demographic tailwinds are making an impact, but the asset fluctuations ameliorate those tendencies."

If Keith was making things up, he was doing an excellent job, because it sounded real to me. But he also could have been doing some excellent spinning. I hoped I remembered enough of it to ask Otto.

"Where's your little friend?" Drew asked. He'd reached the patio and was looking down his rifle's long barrel at Keith.

Keith's mouth opened and closed a few times. Then, showing a courage that few people had, he stood and faced the man who wanted to kill him. "She ran," he said. "She's probably called nine-one-one already. I'm sure the police are on their way. You should probably leave now."

"She ran." Drew snorted. "And where is she going to go? Her car's still here. What neighbor is going to open their door to a frantic stranger babbling about gunshots?"

I almost smirked. Drew hadn't lived in Chilson very long. Odds were good that it wouldn't take me more than knocking on the door of three houses before I found someone I knew, someone who would let me use their phone and summon help.

Still, he had a point. It was possible, even if I came across an acquaintance, that minutes of explanation would be needed. And those were minutes we didn't have.

"I'd say I'm sorry about this," Drew said, "but I don't even know you, so apologizing would be a waste of my time and yours."

He squared his shoulders and began lifting the gun. With a burst of certainty, I knew what I had to do.

And I knew that I could do it.

The last months of pounding nails, sanding drywall, pounding more nails, sanding trim, and sanding even more drywall had provided an unexpected benefit of building my strength and endurance to a new level. I'd suspected this when the bike rides hadn't made me sore for a week, was pretty sure when the long-distance crawl hadn't bothered me a bit, and now that I was holding a rock in my hand while a killer was about to shoot my friend, I was absolutely certain of what I could do.

With all my strength and all my might, I hurled the rock to the far corner of the yard. It hit the fence with a sharp *thump!*

Drew stepped toward the noise, and that was all I needed. Fast and sure, I threw myself forward, head down, no need for silence any longer.

Five steps to go, three, *don't let him turn yet*, faster, faster, faster—

He heard me behind him and started to move, but it was too late. I ran straight into his midsection with all my speed and weight.

"Oooff!"

Drew, completely unprepared for the Minnie Missile, staggered sideways and dropped the rifle.

"Got it," Keith said, scooping up the gun. "Nice job, Minnie." He took a firm stance and pointed the rifle's business end at the man who'd been about to kill him. "Now, what shall we do with this guy?" His voice was low and menacing, sounding more like a truck driver who'd just had all his tires slashed than a popular math teacher. "Shoot him now and it would be self-defense, don't you think?"

"Hey," Drew said weakly. "I didn't mean it. This was all just . . . just a joke. Really."

Keith took a step closer to him, raising the rifle's sights to his eye, taking aim. "Say one more word and—"

"And how about I take this?" I laid my hands on Keith's arm. "You go inside and call nine-one-one. Okay?"

Keith's muscles tightened under my touch, then relaxed. "You're right," he said, letting out a huge breath. "Cover him, okay? I'll be right back."

He handed me the rifle and ran into the house.

Drew started to get up. "Cover me?" he asked, laughing. "You're not even five foot tall! How is a little thing like you going to keep me from walking away?"

Barely even looking at the weapon in my hands, I pointed it into the air and fired. "The next shot," I said calmly, "will go into your leg."

"You . . . you wouldn't."

I lowered the rifle and pointed the barrel at his knee. "Try me. Now, get back on the ground."

He hesitated.

Then kneeled.

I blew out a huge internal sigh of relief, because I truly hadn't been sure whether or not I'd have been able to fire a bullet into a human, no matter how despicable he was.

We were still poised like that, staring at each other, when the sirens and flashing lights arrived and the kindly officer took the gun away from me.

And took Drew away in handcuffs.

Chapter 18

A couple of hours later, on the houseboat, inside the circling comfort of my beloved's arms, and with a purring Eddie on my lap, I told Rafe the rest of what I knew.

"We were inside the city limits," I said, "so the city police took the call. But given the very awkward circumstance of having to arrest their boss, they called the sheriff's office."

The deputy who'd arrived on the scene had called Ash, who'd called Detective Hal Inwood, who'd called Sheriff Kit Richardson, and it hadn't taken long before Keith's driveway was so full of police vehicles that it became a neighborhood spectacle. The sheriff had taken one look at the gathering crowd and pointed her chin at Drew.

"Get him to the jail," she said to the deputy. "Wolverson, tape this off and be here at dawn to catalog evidence. Inwood, I need to see your notes on everything that led up to this debacle." Finally, she looked at me. "Minnie."

Her tone was just as flat and commanding as it had

been when she'd addressed her officers. Frantically, I tried to think of what I'd done wrong and came up with far too many things. "Um, yes?" I asked.

The sheriff snorted a laugh. "Have you looked at yourself?"

I had not. But now I looked down. Bits of leaves and sticks and who knew what covered my shoes. The knees of my pants were filthy with ground-in dirt and torn in more than one place. More leaf and stick pieces were stuck to my front and arms and I was suddenly aware of a stinging sensation in my elbows, which no doubt looked a lot like my knees. And my hands hurt. Slowly, I turned them over and held them to the light.

Sheriff Richardson clucked at me. "Those hands need tending to. Don't they hurt?"

"They do now," I said, amazed that I hadn't noticed the raw scrapes until now. Adrenaline could be an amazing thing. "Can I hope that my hair is still reasonably tidy and doesn't look like something an eagle might nest in?"

The sheriff reached out and plucked a whole leaf from the side of my head. "You can hope. But you should also be realistic."

We arranged for me to get dropped at the urgent care clinic, and after my wounds were cleaned up and dressed, I walked over to the sheriff's office and spent far more time than I would have liked in the interview room with Hal, Keith, and eventually Ash, going over everything that had happened. When they'd wrung every last drop of information out of us, Hal told Keith to go home, and Ash led me straight into the sheriff's private office itself, a room that until now I'd never been invited to enter.

Sheriff Richardson was already there, seated at a small conference table. The rest of the room was occupied by the largest wooden desk I'd ever seen. Most of the desk was covered with two huge computer screens and numerous precisely stacked piles of paper. The walls were hung with framed maps of the county, the city, and the various villages in the county, and painted a soft yellow, a color that almost precisely matched the flowers on the conference table.

It occurred to me that, though early one morning I'd once seen the sheriff on her front porch wearing a ratty bathrobe, I knew very little about her. I didn't know where she grew up, didn't know if she was married, didn't know if she had children, didn't know if she liked pineapple on her pizza. And on the heels of that realization, I decided I didn't need to know.

"Have a seat, Minnie." The sheriff nodded at the chair opposite her. "Did the urgent care folks take care of you?"

I held up my hands, which were bandaged and taped to the point of uselessness.

The sheriff laughed. "Well, better safe than sorry with wounds like that. I expect—ah, there he is. Hal, what can you tell us?"

Detective Inwood, with a thick file of papers in hand, sat down. "Mr. Tanaka's insistence that Mr. Parnell didn't appropriately choose his victims has, apparently, rankled Mr. Parnell. So much so that Mr. Parnell has been speaking of his accomplishments nonstop, before, during, and after his Miranda rights were read to him."

"Has he, now? How convenient." Sheriff Richardson's smile was pleasant. A sharklike version of pleasant, but still. She leaned back and put her feet on the table. "What has he said that's pertinent?"

The detective took a pair of reading glasses from his shirt pocket and slid them on one-handed. "Following a chronological timeline, Mr. Parnell first came up with the idea of killing retirees after he attended a meeting with the manager of the road commission." Hal looked up from his papers. "Not long ago, two former road commission employees passed away of natural causes. The road commission manager made a tasteless joke about the deaths helping the road commission's budget and that was how it started."

I blinked. So the deaths of Max's friends had been related to these murders. Very indirectly, but the connection was undeniable. I made a mental note to never tell him, not ever, and went back to listening to Hal.

But the rest of what he said was old information to me, and I soon found myself yawning, whereupon the sheriff glanced at the wall clock and stood. She picked up her desk phone. "Is he here? Good. Send him back."

While she'd replaced the receiver, she'd looked at me, told me Rafe was here to take me home, and now here we were in the houseboat, all comfy and cozy.

"Hey." Rafe nudged me. "Come on, you need to get to bed. You fell asleep mid-sentence."

"Did not—" But I couldn't finish the sentence because a massive yawn swallowed the rest of it.

"Up you go." Rafe tugged me to my feet, led me down the hall, supervised the brushing of my teeth, averted his eyes like a gentleman while I pulled on the long T-shirt I used as pajamas, and tucked me into bed.

"Eddie?" I called sleepily. "Where are—oh, there you are."

With my cat in the crook of my elbow and my beloved's kiss on my lips, I fell asleep and, thankfully, because for a moment or two in that backyard I'd been terribly afraid a gun would go off and someone would die, I didn't dream at all.

The next morning, after a quick shower, a rebandaging of my hands, and a hearty breakfast of oatmeal topped with blueberries (yes, Mom, I'm eating plenty of fruit), I scurried to be on time to meet Tabitha, an event we'd arranged the night before by text.

And "scurry" was the right word, because the windy bluster of the day before was hanging around and cranking itself up a notch. I zipped my coat all the way, put my head down against the wind, and told myself that having to move twice inside of two months wasn't that bad. Plus, there was undoubtedly a silver lining in there, even if I couldn't see it now.

"There you are!" Tabitha, already seated in a booth, waved at me wildly. Both the call and the waving were unnecessary, as Corner Coffee's interior was empty except for the two of us, but her enthusiasm was contagious and I found myself smiling for the first time that day.

Because though my sleep had been dreamless, the five hours I'd ended up with wasn't enough, especially on the heels of a traumatic night. What I needed was a couple of quiet days followed by a quiet weekend, all of it filled with reading coziness.

I wasn't going to get it, of course, as I needed to start packing, so I tried to absorb as much of Tabitha's boundless energy as possible.

I saw that she already had two mugs of coffee and—oh, my—a plate of scones, so I bypassed the front counter and slid into the booth.

Tabitha's bright blue eyes gave me a long look. "Drink. And eat. I want to see half that coffee gone and two, no, three, bites of pastry into your stomach before you say a single word."

"But—"

She held up a hand. "Now it's four bites."

I almost said, Yes, ma'am, but caught the words back just in time. So I ate, and I drank, and I ate a little more.

Tabitha, who'd been holding up her hand, counting on her fingers how much I'd eaten, called it. "Four. Now you can talk. I know the bare bones, Hal told me that much, but it was a dry detective's report. What I really want to know is, are you okay?"

I looked into my mug, inspecting the contents for answers. They weren't there, so I drank the rest of the coffee. "Sort of," I finally said. "Keith was the one who had the gun aimed at him for so long, not me, but . . ." And, sadly, there were no answers hiding in the bottom of the mug, either.

"Wait here." Tabitha bounced to her feet and took both our mugs to the counter for refills, adding extra cream to mine.

When she returned, I was ready to talk. "I'm not okay, but I will be. It'll take time, that's all."

Tabitha nodded. "There are going to be days you go forward two steps, and nights you go back three.

But you're going to be patient with yourself. You might talk, or not talk, be angry, or not, be sad or not sad. Everyone responds differently to traumatic events. Just don't forget that you have lots of support."

"Um, thanks." I buried my face in my mug for a moment, because I was afraid I might start crying right there in public. Tabitha would have understood, but my reluctance to make a spectacle of myself was stronger than my urge to cry, so I sipped too-hot coffee, burning my tongue and the roof of my mouth, until the feeling subsided.

And then I did talk. I told her about finding out from Kelsey that her former teacher, Keith, had worked at the city years ago, how I'd felt the need to warn him straightaway, how I'd found his house, how we'd sat in the backyard, how Keith had understood the motive for murder right off the bat, and how we'd been completely unaware of any danger until the water bottle exploded in my hand.

"After that," I said, "it was a nasty game of hide-and-seek until Keith got hold of the gun." I also had the feeling it was going to be a long time before I could sit in anyone's backyard without feeling phantom pain in my hands and knees.

"Mmm." Tabitha gave my hand bandages a pointed look. "From what Hal said Keith said, there was quite a bit more, featuring Minnie Hamilton saving the day with brilliant courage."

I shook my head. That wasn't how I saw it. If I'd been smart, I would have figured out the motive far earlier, let Keith know via a safe phone call, and notified the authorities the same way.

"We'll have to agree to disagree," Tabitha said.

"Now, let me tell you what I found out yesterday. It's old news, but I do like to have all the loose ends tied up."

"Oh?" I asked, trying to remember what ends might still be out there.

"We'd been wondering about Bob Bernier, thinking that he was spending an inordinate amount of time with his newly widowed sister-in-law."

Right. That loose end. It seemed so long ago. "What did you find out? And how?"

"Turns out that Bob plays the trumpet and has joined the local community band." Tabitha beamed. "They rehearse on Tuesday nights and their conductor doesn't mind a community member stopping by to watch."

"So handy," I said, half smiling.

"Isn't it, though? And afterward, it was easy to walk out with a particular trumpet player and encourage a certain direction of conversation."

I could just see it; the quiet Bob carrying a trumpet case across a dark parking lot, walking next to Tabitha in chatter mode. "How did you get him to tell you anything?"

"Easy. I asked him questions he wanted to answer."

My mouth opened and shut without any sounds coming out of it. So simple.

"Anyway," Tabitha went on, "Bob likes living alone and doesn't ever plan to marry. Lindy is like a sister to him, always has been and always will be. He's been spending so much time with Lindy because he's teaching her to do the things Brown always did. Opening wine bottles, starting the lawn mower, replacing the furnace filter, that kind of thing."

I made a mental note to learn about furnace filters and lawn mowers. Someday. But something Tabitha had said earlier echoed back to me. "You said Hal was talking to you about last night. But the last couple of weeks it seemed like the two of you weren't . . . well . . ." I let my sentence wander off, because I shouldn't have been asking questions that were none of my business. "Sorry," I said, "I shouldn't have said anything."

Tabitha laughed. "Don't worry, I know I've been testy lately, and it's all Hal's fault. But he finally came around this morning and I've already made the appointment."

"Um . . ."

She laughed again. "For weeks, months, I've been pestering that man to call for his annual physical. He doesn't want to do it because he knows it's time for both a stress test and a colonoscopy."

"That's why you were mad at him?"

"Mad? Not really. Exasperated, yes, frustrated, yes, but not truly angry." She smiled. "Although I can see how it might have seemed that way to outsiders."

Speaking of testy. "Can you tell me something? There's a rumor that the sheriff made Hal pass some sort of test before she hired him. Is that true?"

Tabitha looked left and right, then leaned forward and beckoned me to move close, which I did. "Yes," she whispered into my ear.

I waited, but she leaned back. "Wait, is that it?" I demanded. "You're not going to tell me anything else?"

"Not a chance. If you want to know, ask Sheriff Richardson."

I squinched my face. "You know I'm not going to

do that." The sheriff and I got along, but asking her a question out of idle curiosity was not going to get me anywhere.

Tabitha's eyes sparkled. "Then it's just going to have to remain a mystery, isn't it?"

I was still grumbling to myself in a good-humored sort of way about the stupid test when I got to the library.

"Minnie!" Holly pulled me into a big hug. "I thought for sure you'd come in late. Or not come in at all. Shouldn't you stay home today? I'm sure you should. You must have been up until all hours."

"Thanks, but I'm fine. Honest." I hugged her back, surprised but not surprised at how speedily the news of Drew's arrest had traveled. "Is Josh in? I have a—"

"Minnie!"

This time it was Donna who did the embracing. And then Kelsey. I herded them all into the kitchen and gave a one-time summary of the previous night.

"Weren't you scared?" Kelsey asked. "You talk about it so matter-of-factly."

I laughed. "Terrified. But it's all over now and—"

"What's over?" Graydon asked, walking into the room.

Everyone else in the room glanced at one another. Graydon, the Chilson newcomer, was not yet tied in to the local news connections.

"Morning," I said. "Um, would you have a few minutes to talk? Up in your office?"

He did, and it didn't take long to go over what had happened the night before. And, since it was the third time I'd told the story that morning, I was already getting tired of talking about it and started leaving out parts, some of which were apparently important, because Graydon started looking puzzled and I had to go back to clarify, which meant I should have just told the full version in the first place and it would have saved time.

At the end, Graydon sighed and shook his head. "All for the sake of a budget."

"Sort of," I said. "But if you look at it another way, it was for a man's pride and sense of self." I let the words settle a moment, then said brightly, "Speaking of budgets . . ."

Fifteen minutes later, I had Graydon's approval to hire a part-time bookmobile clerk.

"On probation," he said, scrawling notes onto a legal pad, "with the probation period lifted when he or she obtains a commercial driver's license. This is the only solution," he said, sitting back and nodding. "I'm only surprised it took you so long to come to me with this."

"Um . . ."

"Minnie." He smiled. "I knew perfectly well you couldn't expand the hours with only two people. What I wanted all along was for you to recognize and accept that."

"You did?"

"Of course. If I'd simply told you to hire someone before you were ready, you would have resisted it, possibly resented the new hire, and then we'd have an unhappy bookmobile, and no one wants that."

I turned it all over in my mind and came to an obvious conclusion. "You," I said accusingly, "are an excellent boss."

He smiled smugly. "I am, aren't I?"

"And since you are so excellent at bossing, I have a favor to ask."

I asked, he granted it, and smiling broadly, I thanked him and hurried downstairs while pulling my phone out of my pocket. At the bottom of the stairs I started texting.

Minnie: *I have a solution to your grandmother problem.*

Josh: *Yeah what*

Minnie: *No, I'm serious. Come to my office and I'll tell you.*

A panting Josh rushed into my office, and I told him. Once he'd recovered from the shock, he agreed that the answer I'd suggested would work, and he pulled out his own phone.

Late that afternoon, I posted a sign on the library's front door and a notice on the website: "The library will close at four o'clock and will reopen at five o'clock. We regret any inconvenience this may cause."

Promptly at four, Graydon locked the doors, and the entire library staff bolted to their cars, save Josh, who'd left hours earlier. We drove in a caravan to the county courthouse, me riding along with Holly. After a brief interlude while we waited for everyone to get through security, and a short period while we got lost in the vastness of a mosaic-tiled, oak-trimmed, coffered-ceilinged, hundred-year-old courthouse, we hurried into the district courtroom and literally slid into the long bench seats at the back of the room.

As we sat, a door on the far side of the courtroom opened and the black-robed district court judge walked in. Mia, in a gorgeous white calf-length dress, and Josh, surprisingly handsome in a suit I hadn't known he owned, stood. Ranged behind them were Leese, Mia's half sister, Mia's mother and brother, a white-haired woman I assumed was her grandmother, and a separate group that, judging from the prevalence of thick black hair, had to be Josh's family.

The judge, fiftyish with shoulder-length blond hair, looked up from her paperwork and smiled broadly. Five minutes later she said, "By the power invested in me by the state of Michigan, I now pronounce you husband and wife. You may kiss your bride."

And so Josh did.

Thoroughly.

After the wedding, Graydon forbade me to return to the library until the next day. "My advice," he said, "is to go home and get some sleep, but you're too young to want to do that, so instead I'll advise doing nothing."

I protested that I was fine, honest I was, that I wanted to get started on the job hunt for a new bookmobile driver and clerk, but when he asked what difference it would make if all that waited until the next day, and I couldn't come up with any real answer, I sighed and said I'd see him in the morning.

Outside the courthouse, the wind had blown all the clouds to the east—sorry about that, Canada—revealing a crisp blue sky and the most gorgeous fall colors I'd seen in . . . okay, only a year, but it seemed longer.

Smiling at the world in general and Chilson in particular, I walked the streets, enjoying the sights, smells, and sounds of autumn. The slightly musky scent of fallen leaves composting themselves. How the trees were starting to reveal things they'd been hiding for months. The crisp, light clatter of leaves skittering along the sidewalk.

"Well, look what the wind tossed my way."

Startled, I tore my mind away from the abstract and focused on my immediate surroundings. My feet had taken me on the route I'd formerly walked daily this time of year, from the library to the boardinghouse, where Celeste was on the front lawn, leaning on a rake.

"Hello there," I said. "Do you need any help?"

"Kind of you to ask, but I'm all set." She tipped her head, indicating a pickup truck with an empty trailer parked at the curb, with the name Northwest Landscaping painted on the door. "He's on the tractor, finishing up the back."

I wondered what my aunt, who had never hired anyone to do something she could do herself, would think. "Yet you're out here with a rake?"

Celeste laughed. "Just to remind myself how much I dislike raking. What are you up to?"

"Oh, this and that." Looking up at the sky, I pulled in a big breath. "It's a gorgeous day, isn't it?"

"Mmm." She eyed me. "Heard about your adventures last night. Sounded exciting."

I smiled. "I'll tell you about it someday, if you'd like."

"Sounds good," she said agreeably. "As long as it's before I leave."

"Leave? You're going on a trip?"

She laughed. "A long one. I've decided to be a snowbird and head south for the winter. The cloudy days are already getting to me and I won't be fit for man nor beast after six months of that."

It was more like seven, but I didn't correct her. "Where are you going? What are you going to do?"

"Your friend Kristen, she got me thinking. I used to tend bar, back in the day. No reason I couldn't go back to it, for a few months, down where it's warm."

I grinned, trying not to be sad about the boardinghouse being cold and dark all winter long. "No reason at all. Where are you headed? And when?"

"Soon, and not sure. I thought about southern Arizona or New Mexico, but I'm more of a water person than a desert or mountain person. I might head to Key West, just like Kristen. Maybe there will be a spot for me." She laughed, and I could have sworn she winked.

But before I could pursue that particular line of inquiry, my aunt intervened. "Minerva Hamilton!" she called from her front porch. "Get over here right now!"

"Oh, dear," Celeste said, amused. "Don't tell me you haven't talked to Frances about last night."

I'd meant to, but it had been so late when I'd left the sheriff's office and I'd been so tired that all I'd done was send a text that I'd talk to her the next day, but the flurry of wedding preparations had pushed Talk with Aunt Frances down on my list. And now it was late in the day, and she'd seen me with Celeste before I'd gone to her. The two of them had a complicated relationship, and this wouldn't help.

"Sorry," I said, crossing the street. "If it's any comfort, I didn't tell her anything about last night."

"Horrible child," my aunt said, giving me a brief, hard hug. "The important thing is you're safe and sound."

After politely declining an invitation to enjoy the

backyard's sunshine, I sat with my aunt and Otto in their almost-as-sunshiny kitchen, with coffee and cookies at hand, and I talked. They were already aware of many of the things Tabitha and I had already found out, but not everything, and it took me some time to fill in the holes and smooth out the details so it all made sense.

When I was done talking, and they were done asking questions, we sat quietly, letting the tick of the wall clock fill the space.

The whole thing was awful. It was awful that Drew had killed people for the sake of his pride, awful that Brown's and Emily's lives had been cut short, awful that Lindy and Emily's husband were now alone, and who knew what terrible things might be caused, weeks or months or years from now, by the ripple effects of one man's actions.

I sighed, wishing for anything to make sense of it all. Or if not sense, at least . . . something.

Finally, Otto stirred. "I've taken a thorough look at Cody Sisk's finances."

"Oh? Any conclusions?"

"All things considered, he's doing fine. As I mentioned before, he expanded rapidly, but he did so in order to take advantage of an unusually low price for a prime location for his type of business. What he needed was some capital."

I frowned, my ears picking up on the past tense. "'Was'? Did he come into some money?"

"In a manner of speaking." Otto smiled. "He decided to saddle himself with a minority partner who has absolutely no knowledge of bicycling or kayaking, but who does have financial experience."

"Interesting." I pushed the cookie plate in his direction, offering him the last one. "And does that partner happen to be sitting at this table?"

Otto didn't say anything, but he took the cookie, which to me was answer enough.

"Since we're speaking of life-altering events," Aunt Frances said, "I'll add to the list. I've decided to retire from teaching after the school year is over."

"About time," I murmured.

"What's that?"

"Congratulations!" I said, smiling brightly.

"Thank you." She looked from Otto to me. "I think."

I continued to smile and my face started to hurt. "Let's just say I'll believe it when I see it." To forestall any further discussion, I told them about the sudden wedding of Mia and Josh, about which they were pleased, though a bit puzzled. And then I told them the other big news.

"Graydon gave me the okay to hire another part-time bookmobile clerk. One who'll drive."

My aunt's eyebrows went up. "You're going to trust someone else to drive your bookmobile?"

"Yes," I said resolutely. "I am and I will."

She hummed a few nonsense notes and looked at the ceiling. "It's possible I know just the person."

It had taken my aunt another cup of coffee and a piece of apple pie—with ice cream—to convince me that she wasn't going to apply for the job of driving a bookmobile.

"That's not what I meant," she said on the front porch. "I'm sorry you got that impression."

She wasn't sorry, and she knew that I knew she wasn't. But I also knew, or at least suspected, that the whole thing had been a distraction so I didn't dwell on the darkness of last night, so I wasn't angry. I was, however, curious.

"You're not going to tell me who you have in mind?"

"Talk to me after you post the job," she said and, laughing, closed the door.

I gave it a scrunched-up face and started walking back to the marina, taking a roundabout route just for the fun of it. The sky was still blue, but the wind was up again. I zipped my coat high and pulled on my gloves, wondering why on earth I hadn't talked to Aunt Frances and Otto about staying with them until the house was ready for me to move in.

"Because I'm stupid," I said out loud. I stopped in the middle of the sidewalk and calculated distances. Yep, I was already more than halfway to the houseboat, too far to go back. I'd call after dinner and we could talk about moving arrangements.

I knew I should be glad to have a handy place to stay, and I was; it was just disappointing that I couldn't move straight from houseboat to house. It would have been so easy, and now . . .

I sighed. This was how construction worked. I knew that. Timelines never worked out according to plan. Materials were backordered, subcontractors had to take emergency jobs, and—and what was going on?

The house, which I could now see because I'd just come around the last corner, was lit to blazing. It looked as if every light in the house was turned on, and swags of tiny twinkling white lights were hanging from the porch ceiling and draped along the porch railings. Across the house's entire front was a huge banner, WELCOME HOME, MINIE AND EDIE!

"There you are!" Rafe pelted down the porch stairs. "Your aunt called ten minutes ago, saying you'd left. I was starting to wonder if you'd gone back to the library and I'd have to drag you out."

I gaped. "What is all this?"

"It's your house, silly." He pulled me close.

"But . . . but . . ."

"All those books you read, and you can't come up with any other words?" He kissed my forehead. "So what do you think?" he asked, spreading his arms wide.

"Um . . ."

He sighed. "Let's get this over with. Yes, the banner spelled the names wrong, but at least it was both of you and not just Eddie, because if had just been him, we would never have heard the end of it. And because it was a rush job they had to use the materials available and something had to go, so they took out the double letters. What do they really do anyway, right?"

"Right." I smiled, because he was being silly and we both knew it. "So what you're telling me is . . ." I hesitated, because I couldn't quite believe in the reality of it. "The house is done?"

"Top to bottom." He squared his shoulders and stuck his chest out proudly. "Left to right, front to back. All those night meetings I've had the last couple of months? They were secret construction meetings. I've been helping out buddies and buddies of buddies for years and it was time to call in those favors and get this done. You wouldn't believe how complicated it got to keep you out of the loop."

He kissed the tip of my nose. "It's a surprise, see? You're supposed to be happy. You're supposed to be, I don't know, squealing with delight or something. Isn't that what they do on those shows? See, once again you don't watch enough TV and—"

I looked up, and my love for him must have been shining strong and bright, because he stopped talking and took my face gently in his hands.

"I love you, Minnie Hamilton," he said softly. "This house is for you, and always has been, even when you thought you were in love with that doctor, even when you were dating Ash. And it will never be a home for me unless you're there, too."

We held each other close. It was a moment I wanted to last forever and—

"Get a room, you two!"

It sounded a lot like Chris, the marina's manager. But what would he be doing in the house?

Rafe held me a little tighter. "Ignore him. He'll go away soon."

"Niswander, get her in here. The food's getting cold and the beer's getting warm."

Definitely Chris. I pulled away, puzzled. "Rafe, what's going on?"

"Oh, you know. Not much." He took my hand. "Let's go in. I need to check on that beer."

Inside, we passed through the living room and the dining room with its now-finished wraparound bookcases and into the kitchen, which was full of fast-moving people wearing black pants and white coats, people from a different kitchen. A commercial kitchen. The Three Seasons kitchen. Only today they were here, whipping up loaded nachos and pizza and slicing sandwiches into bite-sized pieces. Harvey and his minions were chopping and cooking, and Kristen was standing to the side, observing, directing, and correcting.

"I don't understand," I said. "What is all this?"

"It's your housewarming party. Duh." Kristen tapped the side of her head and looked at Rafe. "You'd think she'd have caught on by now."

"Well, it was sudden," he said, defending me. "There's a lot to take in."

She sighed dramatically. "We all have a lot to take in. She gets a house, and I get to be as big as a house."

The world stopped spinning for a second and the only people in existence were my best friend and me. "Really?" I whispered, eyes wide.

"Really." She nodded. "I'm going to be a mother, can you believe it?"

We stared at each other for a long moment. Then I squealed with delight and flung my arms around her.

"Where do you want this?" Chris asked.

I gave Kristen a final squeeze and turned. Chris was holding a small vacuum cleaner that looked a lot like the one on my houseboat. "Um . . ."

"Downstairs," Rafe said, and once Chris was on his way, Rafe said to me, "There's something else you should know."

"You haven't told her yet?" Kristen yelled. "Do you have the sense of a soap dish?" She turned to me. "This man has lined up every person you've ever known in Chilson, and that includes everyone in town, to move your belongings from the houseboat. And out of the boardinghouse attic."

All of my . . . ? Panic seized me and I turned fast, getting ready to run. "Eddie—"

"Is upstairs," Rafe said. "I brought him over first

thing. He's upstairs in the bedroom, getting cat hair all over."

His calm tone relaxed me and I nodded, believing him. Which was when the full implication of the situation thumped me in the head. "I'm moving," I said. "I mean, you're getting me moved. I'm living here. Starting now."

Ignoring the eye rolls of my best friend and fiancé, I wandered through the house, watching the activity. Pam Fazio was carrying an armful of my hanging clothes up the stairs. Camille Pomeranz, the newspaper editor, was hauling a box of food to the kitchen, where I was pretty sure Kristen would direct it into a wastebasket. Holly and Kelsey came in the front door with bedding that went upstairs, and my aunt brought in a box of toiletries, followed by Celeste, who was carrying tote bags of my clothes.

After them came another parade, with the book boxes from the boardinghouse attic. Leese Lacombe, Chris, Mitchell, Graydon, the sheriff herself, Gareth the library's maintenance guy, and Ash, who was followed so closely by Chelsea Stille, the sheriff's new office manager, that I was suddenly happily sure they were a couple. Then came Hal, Josh in his suit, and half a dozen of Rafe's friends, the door held open by a glowing Mia, still in her wedding dress.

It was all a little weird, but more than that, far more, I was shocked that people were so willing to help. I had no idea what Rafe had said or done to convince people to drop their lives and help finish a house and move a librarian's belongings, but I would be forever grateful to him, and to them.

And then I knew what I had to do.

I rustled through my backpack for an envelope.

"Hey, everybody!" I stood on a chair and clapped my hands, wishing for the millionth time that I knew how to do the Loud Whistle thing. "It's time to announce the winner of the pool. Get out your dates."

"What's going on?" Rafe looked around as everyone gathered near, most of them opening their wallets or phones.

It was time to come clean with the love of my life. "Remember a while back there was a rumor about a betting pool for the date I moved in?"

"Yeah. You said you didn't know anything about it."

I beamed. "That was a lie. I'm the one who started the pool." Laughing at his look of complete and utter disbelief, I called out, "And the winner is . . . Mitchell Koyne! How you did it, I don't know, but you picked the exact date."

Applause erupted, and I handed over the stack of one-dollar bills to a grinning Mitchell. "Here you go. Don't spend it all in one place."

"Hang on, everybody," Rafe said, waving his arms. "There's one more thing to do publicly. Minnie agreed to marry me two months ago, and I've taken all sorts of crap because I haven't given her a ring."

"Yeah, what's up with that?" Pam called. "What kind of a slacker are you?"

Rafe nodded. "I get it. It looks bad. But let me tell you a story. In Minnie's junior year of high school, her family came north to spend Memorial Day with her aunt Frances. Kristen got the bright idea that it would be fun to go swimming in Lake Michigan, and Minnie went along with it."

"Freaking cold," Kristen said. "The water was forty degrees. We never did that again."

"No, but do you remember what else happened?"

I did. "My high school class ring. I lost it that day."

Rafe tugged a small box from his jeans pocket. "I have a buddy with a metal detector, and for months he's been working that beach. Three weeks ago—"

My face went still. "He found it?"

"Well, sort of. The metal was bashed up from the rocks, but the stone, your birthstone, is fine. And, uh, do you like how it looks as an engagement ring?"

He opened the box and held it up to me. The ring was gorgeous—the ruby had been set in white gold and was flanked by smaller diamonds—but I wouldn't have cared if it had been hideous. All I cared about was that Rafe had remembered how upset I'd been about losing that ring, so many years ago, and that he'd cared enough to try to find it for me.

I jumped off the chair and into his arms. He swung me around in a circle, hugging me tight. "I love you," I whispered into his ear.

"Get down, Niswander!" Chris shouted. "Do it right."

"Good idea." Rafe set me on my feet and dropped to one knee. "Sorry it took so long, Minnie. I know you said 'yes' a couple of months ago, but . . ." He slid the ring onto my finger. "Will you say it again, just to shut him up?"

"With pleasure," I said, laughing. "Yes, I will marry you," and kissed him. This time the applause went on for a long time.

"Okay, everybody!" Kristen shouted. "Back to work, then we can eat!"

With so many people helping, it didn't take long to get everything moved, and the party ended up where good parties always do, in the kitchen, where Rafe and I, then Mia and Josh, were toasted with cheers and beer. It was a great party, but I couldn't enjoy it fully until I did one more thing.

I quietly slipped away and went upstairs. In the master bedroom, exactly in the center of the bed, was Eddie.

"Just like Rafe said." I climbed onto the bed. "Getting cat hair all over everything. So what do you think? Are you going to like it here? Is this okay as your forever home?"

Eddie licked my face, something he rarely did.

"I'll take that as a yes," I said. "Tomorrow I'll show you around. You've been here before, but now everything is done. No smells, no tool noises. You're going to love it here, I'm sure of it."

Well, "sure" might be a strong word, but there was a lot for Eddie to like. Deep windowsills to lounge on, half walls to drape himself over, floor registers to sleep on. In many ways the place was designed for a cat.

"You know what?" I asked. "I'd say we have everything we need." I kissed the top of his furry head. "The only wrinkle is Rafe and I still haven't settled the whole 'who's paying for the house' thing. But I have great friends and coworkers, the job of my dreams, a gorgeous home, I'm engaged to a wonderful man, and I have an Eddie."

Pretty much every hope, dream, and expectation I'd ever had was fulfilled. Happiness must have been emanating from every cell in my body, spreading the joy of life out into the street, the town, the state, maybe even the universe.

"Mrr!"

"Hmm? Oh, sorry, you're right. I should have put you first on the list, because you're that important."

"Mrr!"

He still wasn't happy. "Plus you should also be at the end, that saving-the-best-for-last thing and all."

Eddie immediately settled down in my lap and closed his eyes. "Mrr."

Ready to find
your next great read?

Let us help.

Visit prh.com/nextread

Penguin
Random
House

Praise for *The 5 Love Languages Military Edition*

In our thirty-nine years in the Army and especially in the years since 9/11/01, Paula and I have witnessed firsthand the extreme stress on many military marriages and the need for couples to build "emotional love resilience." As long-time practitioners of the five love languages, we are thrilled that military couples will now have a targeted version that speaks "their own language" and will help them renew their love for each other. You can have a successful military career and a healthy marriage—*The 5 Love Languages Military Edition* will help show you the way!
—LTG (RET.) R. L. VANANTWERP, US Army

A healthy military marriage is a tall order even in peacetime. Two wars and their aftermath have exacted an immeasurable toll on millions of service members and their spouses since 9/11/01. Chapman and Green's proven insights can help emotionally wounded military couples to speak the language of love even on the chaotic journey that is post-traumatic stress.
—MARSHELE CARTER WADDELL, veteran Navy SEAL spouse and coauthor of *Wounded Warrior, Wounded Home: Hope and Healing for Families Living with PTSD and TBI*

When Barb and I learned that our two friends Jocelyn Green and Gary Chapman had teamed up to bring *The 5 Love Languages* to military marriages, we knew it was going to be a "1-2 punch"! And it is! The life message that Gary brings on the love languages through the experience and filter of Jocelyn Green, a star in the field of ministering to military families, offers the reader a powerful insight into strengthening their military home! Having ministered to military marriages ourselves, we know some of the unique needs of these heroic families. And we guarantee the reader this resource will further equip you to "crack the code" and learn how to better connect with your spouse! Read it and give it to every military family you know!
—DR. GARY AND BARB ROSBERG, America's Family Coaches, authors of *6 Secrets to a Lasting Love*, radio broadcasters, speakers, and passionate military marriage advocates

For years, our family has communicated using *The 5 Love Languages* and found the results to be incredibly successful. Now, with the military version of this book, we are able to express love in an effective, encouraging, and empathetic manner that helps our military members and their families know how much we truly care about them. As the wife of a fighter pilot and mom to sons in the Marines, Air Force, and Army, I'm delighted to recommend this critical resource to the many military groups I address on a regular basis. Buy this book for your favorite military family as a way of thanking them for their service.
—ELLIE KAY, author of the bestselling *Heroes at Home*, "America's Military Family Expert"™

ave used *The 5 Love Languages* over the past twelve years to conduct numerous marriage
ichment weekend events, in formal counseling with couples, informal counseling as I walk
ut ministering to people, and in dealing with leaders. The adaptation of the original *5 Love
guages* to a military focus will only enhance the positive effects this book produces. I firmly
eve that not only is this one of the best books for relationship improvement, but it is also
of the best leadership books on the market today. The ability to understand subordinate,
r, and senior love language needs improves every organization's relationships as leaders
t these needs. Thank you, Dr. Chapman and Jocelyn Green, for improving on a great
k so that we might reach more effectively those Soldiers, Sailors, Airmen, Marines, and
st Guardsmen to whom so many of our great ministers of faith have been called.
H (MAJ) SCOTT BROWN, US Army

As an Army wife of more than twenty-five years, I have lived the roller-coaster life of constant moves and separations. During my quest to find resources to help sustain a loving marriage I came across a lot of valuable research and advice, but it wasn't applicable for couples who face the stress of deployments and redeployments along with the fast tempo and demands of military life. FINALLY, Dr. Chapman's reputable work with *The 5 Love Languages* and Jocelyn Green's insight into military life have produced the perfect combination to help military couples see that a healthy, loving marriage and a successful military career are both possible. This is the book we have been seeking. What a treasured gift for our military families.
—HOLLY SCHERER, military life consultant and coauthor of *Military Spouse Journey: 1001 Things to Love About Military Life*; and *Help! I'm A Military Spouse—I Get a Life Too!*

This is a must-have resource in a family's "kit bag." Dr. Chapman's work has enriched our lives on so many levels, and we are overjoyed there is a special edition that speaks directly to the military community. Effective communication is instrumental in building and sustaining resilience. Knowing how to speak your partner's love language is a wonderful tool to help maintain a strong, enduring, and joyful relationship.
—NATE BROOKSHIRE, coauthor of *Hidden Wounds: A Soldier's Burden*

The 5 Love Languages Military Edition provides a valuable tool for couples trying to build a strong relationship in the midst of the enormously challenging stresses of military service. It provides practical instruction on how to identify the true needs of your spouse and gives suggestions of actions to take that will be the most meaningful to them—all within the unique context of military cross-country moves, deployments, and reintegration. For those willing to make the sacrifices and put in the hard work, this book will be a useful guide to achieving a healthy, mature, and rewarding marriage.
—RICHARD CROWLEY, Army spouse

The 5 Love Languages Military Edition is exactly what every military marriage needs. The decoding section at the back of each chapter has great tips to keep the spark going while the military member is away, but these tips can also be used when the military member is at home. Once you and your spouse learn each other's love language, life becomes much sweeter.
—MAUREEN ELIAS, Air Force spouse

As military couples, we understand what is challenging about our marriages. Rarely do we find anyone willing to supply us with practical answers for those challenges—until Dr. Gary Chapman and Jocelyn Green in *The 5 Love Languages Military Edition*. This book will give you real help for the real struggles of military marriage.
—CDR (RET.) ROBERT AND BETTINA DOWELL, US Navy

Teaching couples to discover their unique love language and learn to communicate their affection more strategically has been Dr. Chapman's mission for years. This military edition with Jocelyn Green considers the added challenges military families face, due to deployments and other geographical separations, making this book a must-have resource for chaplains, military support personnel, ministry leaders, and military couples alike. Buy more than one copy, because you will be sharing it with friends!
—JILL BOZEMAN, Army spouse and founder of Operation Faithful Support

The Secret to Love That Lasts

THE 5 *love* LANGUAGES®

MILITARY EDITION

Gary Chapman
with Jocelyn Green

NORTHFIELD PUBLISHING

CHICAGO

All Scripture quotations are taken from the *Holy Bible, New International Version*®, NIV®. Copyright © 1973, 1978, 1984, 2011 by Biblica, Inc.™ Used by permission of Zondervan. All rights reserved worldwide. www.zondervan.com. The "NIV" and "New International Version" are trademarks registered in the United States Patent and Trademark Office by Biblica, Inc.™

Edited by Elizabeth Cody Newenhuyse
Interior design: Smartt Guys design
Cover design: Faceout Studio
Cover image credits: Dog tags: Matt Smartt; Flag: Sergey Kamshylin /123RF
Authors photo credits: Gary Chapman: P.S. Photography
                          Jocelyn Green: Paul Kestel of Catchlight Imaging

Library of Congress Cataloging-in-Publication Data

 Names: Chapman, Gary D., author. | Green, Jocelyn, author.
Title: The 5 love languages military edition : the secret to love that lasts
   / Gary Chapman with Jocelyn Green.
Other titles: Five love languages military edition
Description: Chicago : Northfield Publishing, 2017 | Includes bibliographical
   references.
Identifiers: LCCN 2016045842 (print) | LCCN 2016047251 (ebook) | ISBN
   9780802414823 | ISBN 9780802494740
Subjects: LCSH: Military spouses--Psychology. | Military spouses--United
   States--Conduct of life. | Marriage. | Communication in marriage. |
   Self-help techniques. | Love.
Classification: LCC UB403 .C47 2017 (print) | LCC UB403 (ebook) | DDC
   646.7/808835500973--dc23
LC record available at https://lccn.loc.gov/2016045842

                                                              2013022819

ISBN: 978-0-8024-1482-3

We hope you enjoy this book from Northfield Publishing. Our goal is to provide high-quality, thought-provoking books and products that will help you with your real needs and challenges. For more information on other books and products that will help you with all your important relationships, go to 5lovelanguages.com or write to:

Northfield Publishing
820 N. La Salle Boulevard
Chicago, IL 60610

1 3 5 7 9 10 8 6 4 2

Printed in the United States of America

To Karolyn,
Shelley, and Derek

Contents

Acknowledgments   9

Introduction   13

1. What Happens to Love in a Military Marriage?   17

2. Keeping the Love Tank Full   25

3. Falling in Love   33

4. *Love Language #1:* Words of Affirmation   43

5. *Love Language #2:* Quality Time   63

6. *Love Language #3:* Receiving Gifts   89

7. *Love Language #4:* Acts of Service   107

8. *Love Language #5:* Physical Touch   125

9. Love Language Scramblers   141

10. Discovering Your Primary Love Language   151

11. Love Is a Choice   161

12. Loving the Unlovely   171

13. A Personal Word   187

14. Frequently Asked Questions   193

The 5 Love Languages Profile for Couples—for Him   205

The 5 Love Languages Profile for Couples—for Her   211

Notes   219

Acknowledgments

This military edition of *The 5 Love Languages* would not have been possible without the help of numerous contributors. First and foremost is Jocelyn Green. She knows the military lifestyle from personal experience. Her experience, her interviews with military couples, and her excellent writing skills have made this journey easy for me. I am deeply grateful to her.

Thanks also to my administrative assistant Anita Hall for her technical assistance, and to Betsey Newenhuyse at Northfield Publishing for her keen editorial skills.

For the past fifteen years, I have been speaking on military bases and listening to the stories of husbands and wives as they shared the stresses of daily military life. Many of them have given permission to use their stories in this edition. Of course, we have changed their names for the sake of privacy. I am sincerely grateful to each of these unnamed heroes, who have helped others by openly sharing their own experiences. Special thanks to Army wife Brenda Marlin for offering a host of ideas for our Decoding Deployments sections, to Chaplain (Lt. Col.) Tom Cox for his valuable insights into the reintegration process, and to Paula and Lt. Gen. (Ret.) R. L. "Van" VanAntwerp for sharing wisdom gleaned from nearly four decades in the Army.

The 5 Love Languages Military Edition was informed by dozens of conversations, both recent and from years past, with members and spouses from all branches and ranks of the military. Thank you for your investment in military marriages through your contributions to this volume, and thank you for your service to our country.

Thank you for purchasing *The 5 Love Languages® Military Edition*. As a military couple, you will gain more benefit from this book by reading it together. This can be challenging if you are physically separated due to deployment. If such is the case, we want to make the eBook version of this title available to your spouse at no cost. Please direct your spouse to this website for instructions on how to download the eBook: 5LoveLanguagesMilitaryOffer.com.

This limited-time offer is subject to change without notice.

Introduction

I have been a marriage counselor for many years. I have never known of a couple who got married hoping to make each other miserable. Yet hundreds of couples have sat in my office sharing the deep pain of a fractured relationship.

Their dreams had turned to nightmares, and they were ready to split. Through the process of counseling, I have seen many of those couples find renewed hope and learn the skills that create a loving, supportive marriage. One of the key elements in moving from failure to success is learning the power of love.

A number of years ago I wrote a book called *The 5 Love Languages*. It has sold more than ten million copies in English and has been translated into more than fifty languages around the world. Every week I receive emails saying, "Your book saved our marriage."

The book has been distributed widely to military couples, and the response has been extremely encouraging. One young man said, "As soon as I arrived in Afghanistan, I began reading *The 5 Love Languages*. I had never read anything so simple, yet so profound. This book enables marriages not only to survive through deployment but even thrive and deepen during the long period of separation."

I have led marriage enrichment seminars on numerous military bases, both in this country and abroad. Everywhere I go, those who seek to enrich military marriages have asked, "Why don't you write a Military Edition to *The 5 Love Languages* dealing with the unique challenges of military marriages?" This book is an attempt to answer that request.

Although exact statistics on divorce rates in the military are unavailable due to how such statistics are tracked, many chaplains have told me that numerous military marriages are under significant stress. Many couples are truly suffering. The adjustments of early marriage are often thwarted by an untimely deployment. What happens in the heart, mind, and behavior of the husband and wife during deployment often creates emotional distance. Reentry after deployment can often be traumatic. I believe the most essential ingredient in a successful military marriage is to keep emotional love alive in the relationship. What you are about to read has the potential of helping you have the marriage you've always wanted.

Author and former military wife Jocelyn Green has helped guide the shape of this edition and collected many stories you will read here about military marriages. The names have been changed to protect the privacy of the individuals. The branch of service and military rank of the individuals are usually unstated. The message of *The 5 Love Languages* applies to all military couples. If this book helps you, I hope you will share it with other military couples. I believe together we can help thousands of couples discover that a healthy marriage and a successful military career are both possible.

GARY CHAPMAN

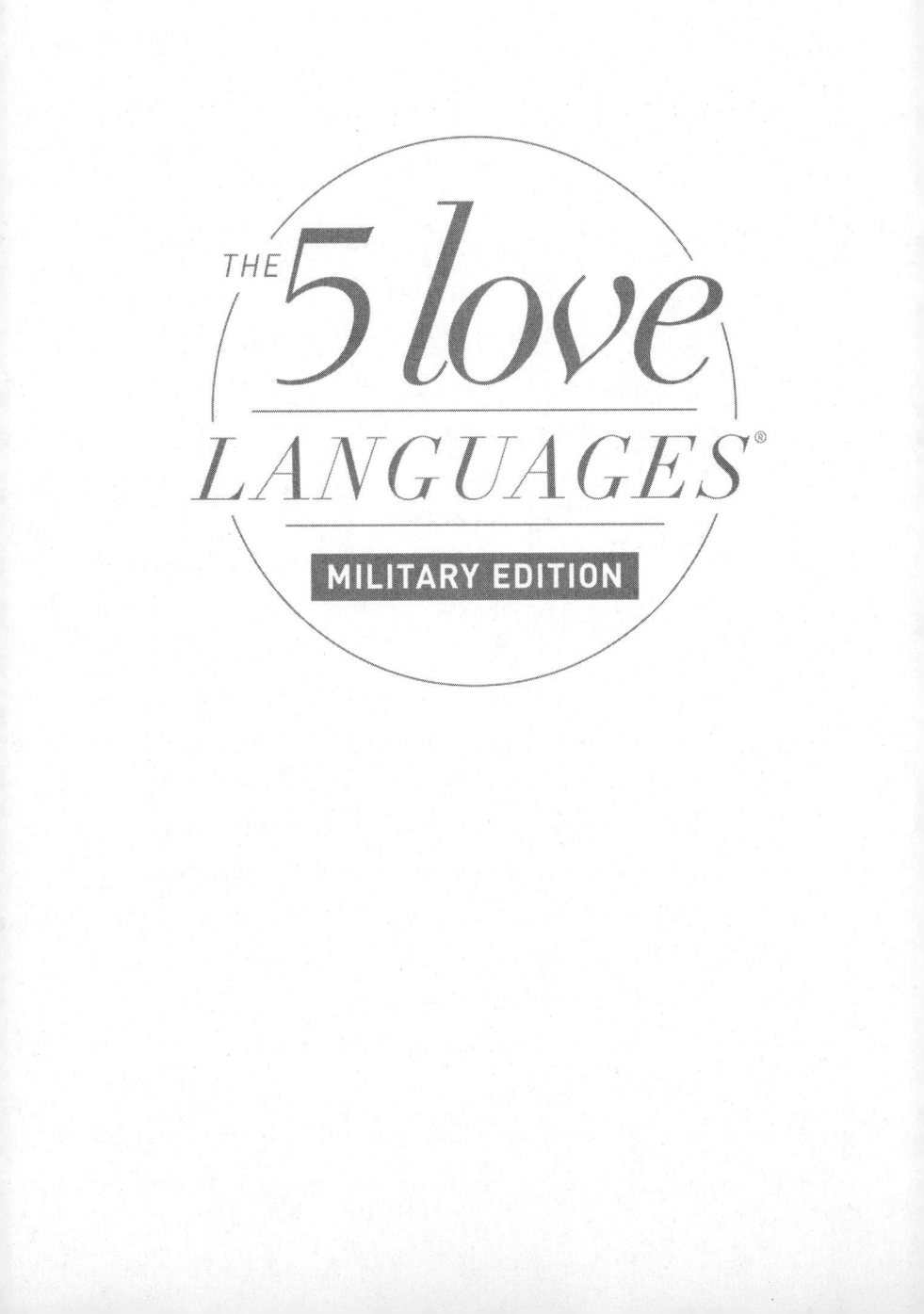

What Happens to Love in a Military Marriage?

I first met Chuck in Germany. He had a successful military career—twenty-three years under his belt. However, all was not well. In his own words: "My marriage is in shambles. I don't understand love and I'm not sure you can keep love alive in a military marriage. I was madly in love with my first wife. We were high school sweethearts. We got married right after graduation, and a month later I joined the military. The first couple of years were exciting, but eventually our love grew cold. We seemed like roommates living in the same house. On the day after our tenth anniversary, she went home to visit her mother and never returned. I didn't feel all that bad about it because by this time neither one of us loved each other."

"What about your second marriage?" I inquired.

"It was about a year after our divorce that I met Cathy. At the time, she was also in the military. It was one of those 'love at first sight deals,'" he said. "It was great. We had an awesome marriage until we got assigned to different bases. That was tough. So a year later, she left the military so we could be together. Then, the baby came along and things changed. We never rediscovered the connection we had in the first year of our marriage. It was like our love evaporated. She and our son left last Tuesday to go back to the States, and I know it's just a matter of time until she files for divorce."

"When things were going well, how did you express your love to Cathy?" I asked.

"I told her how beautiful she was. I told her I loved her. I told her how proud I was to be her husband. But after three or four years, she started complaining about petty things at first—like my not taking the garbage out, or my not hanging up my clothes. Later she went to attacking my character, telling me she didn't feel she could trust me, accusing me of being unfaithful to her. She became a totally negative person. When I met her she was one of the most positive people I had ever known. That's one of the things that attracted me to her; she never complained about anything. Everything I did was wonderful, but after a few years, I could do nothing right. I really think I tried. I honestly don't know what happened."

I could tell Chuck was experiencing internal struggle over what was going on in his marriage, so I said, "You still love Cathy, don't you?"

"I think I do," he said. "I don't have the kind of love I had when we first got married, but I certainly don't want a divorce. I think we could have made it, but I don't think Cathy wants to work on the marriage." I could tell this strong warrior had a wounded heart.

"Did things go downhill after the baby was born?" I asked.

"Yes," he said. "I felt like she gave all of her attention to the baby, and I no longer mattered. It was as if her goal in life was to have a baby, and after the baby she no longer needed me."

"Did you tell her that?" I asked.

"Yes, I told her. She said I was crazy. She said I did not understand the stress of being a twenty-four-hour nurse, and I should be more understanding and help her more. I really tried, but it didn't seem to make any difference. After that we just grew apart. After a while there was no love left, just deadness."

Chuck continued the conversation and I listened. "What happened to love after the first year of marriage?" he asked. "Is my experience common? Is that why we have so many divorces in the military? I can't believe this has happened to me twice. And those who don't divorce, do they learn to live with the emptiness, or does love really stay alive in some marriages?"

The questions Chuck asked are the questions thousands of military couples are asking. Sometimes the answers are couched in psychological research jargon that is almost incomprehensible. Sometimes they are couched in humor and folklore. Most of the jokes and pithy sayings contain some truth, but they are often like offering an aspirin to a person with cancer.

The desire for romantic love in marriage is deeply rooted in our psychological makeup. Books abound on the subject. TV, radio, podcasts, social media all deal with it. The Internet is full of advice. So are our parents and friends. Keeping love alive in our marriages is serious business.

With all the help available from media experts, why is it so few couples seem to have found the secret to keeping love alive after the wedding?

THE TRUTH WE'RE MISSING

The answer to those questions is the purpose of this book. It's not that the books and articles already published are not helpful. The problem is we have overlooked one fundamental truth: People speak different love languages.

My academic training is in the area of anthropology. Therefore, I have studied in the area of linguistics, which identifies a number of major language groups: Japanese, Chinese, Spanish, English, Portuguese, Greek, German, French, and so on. Most of us grow up learning the language of our parents and siblings, which becomes our *primary* or native tongue. Later, we may learn additional languages— but usually with much more effort. These become our *secondary* languages. We speak and understand best our native language. We feel most comfortable speaking that language. The more we use a secondary language, the more comfortable we become conversing in it. If we speak only our primary language and encounter someone else who speaks only his or her primary language, which is different from ours, our communication will be limited. We must rely on pointing, grunting, drawing pictures, or acting out our ideas. We can communicate, but it's awkward. Language differences are part and parcel of human culture. If we are to communicate effectively across cultural lines, we must learn the language of those with whom we wish to communicate.

In the area of love, it is similar. Your emotional love language and the language of your spouse may be as different as Chinese from English. No matter how hard you try to express love in English, if your spouse understands only Chinese, you will never understand how to love each other. Chuck was speaking the language of Words of Affirmation to Cathy when he told her she was beautiful, he loved her, and he was proud to be her husband. He was speaking love, and he was sincere, but she did not understand his language. Perhaps she was looking for love in his behavior and didn't see it. Being sincere is not enough. We must be willing to learn our spouse's primary love language if we are to effectively communicate love.

My conclusion after many years of marriage counseling is that there are five emotional love languages—five ways that people speak and understand emotional love. In the field of linguistics a language may have numerous dialects or variations. Similarly, within the five basic emotional love languages, there are many dialects. The number of ways to express love within a love language is limited only by one's imagination. The important thing is to speak the love language of your spouse.

Seldom do a husband and wife have the same primary emotional love language. We tend to speak our primary love language, and we become confused when our spouse does not understand what we are communicating. We are expressing our love, but the message does not come through because we are speaking what, to them, is a foreign language. Therein lies the fundamental problem, and it is the purpose of this book to offer a solution. That's why I dare to write another book on love. Once we discover the five basic love languages and understand our own primary love language, as well as the primary love language of our spouse, we will then have the needed information to apply the ideas in the books and articles.

Once you identify and learn to speak your spouse's primary love language, I believe you will have discovered the key to a long-lasting, loving marriage. These languages can be spoken even when you are separated by deployment. Love need not evaporate after the wedding, but in order to keep it alive, most of us will have to put forth the effort to learn a secondary love language. We cannot rely on our native tongue if our spouse does not understand it. If we want them to feel the love we are trying to communicate, we must express it in his or her primary love language.

YOUR TURN

Are you willing to put in the work to learn your spouse's love language?

Keeping the Love Tank Full

Love is the most important word in the English language—and the most confusing. Both secular and religious thinkers agree that love plays a central role in life. Psychologists have concluded that the need to feel loved is a primary human emotional need. For love, we will climb mountains, cross seas, traverse desert sands, and endure untold hardships. Without love, mountains become unclimbable, seas uncrossable, deserts unbearable, and hardships our lot in life.

If we can agree that the word *love* permeates human society, we must also agree it's a most confusing word. We use it in a thousand ways. We say, "I love pizza," and in the next breath, "I love my mother." We speak of loving activities: swimming, reading, running. We love objects: food, cars, houses. We love animals: dogs, cats, even pet snails. We love nature: trees, grass, flowers, and weather. We love people: mother, father, son, daughter, wives, husbands, friends. We even fall in love with love.

If all that is not confusing enough, we also use the word *love* to explain behavior. "I did it because I love her." That explanation is given for all kinds of actions. A politician is involved in an adulterous relationship, and he calls it love. However, most of his constituents call it stupidity. The preacher, on the other hand, calls it sin. The wife of an alcoholic picks up the pieces after her husband's latest episode. She calls it love, but the psychologist calls it codependency. The parent indulges all the child's wishes, calling it love. The family therapist would call it irresponsible parenting. What is "loving behavior"?

The purpose of this book is not to eliminate all confusion surrounding the word *love*, but to focus on that kind of love that is essential to our emotional health. Child psychologists affirm that every child has certain basic emotional needs that must be met if he is to be emotionally stable. Among those emotional needs, none is more basic than the need for love and affection, the need to sense that he or she belongs and is wanted. With an adequate supply of affection, the child will likely develop into a responsible adult. Without that love, he or she will be emotionally and socially challenged.

I liked the metaphor the first time I heard it: "Inside every child is an 'emotional tank' waiting to be filled with love. When a child really feels loved, he will develop normally but when the love tank is empty, the child will misbehave. Much of the misbehavior of children is motivated by the cravings of an empty 'love tank.'" I was listening to Dr. Ross Campbell, a psychiatrist who specialized in the treatment of children and adolescents.

As I listened, I thought of the hundreds of parents who had sat in my office and shared the misdeeds of their children with me. I had never visualized an empty love tank inside those children, but I had certainly seen the results of it. Their misbehavior was a misguided search for the love they did not feel. They were seeking love in all the wrong places and in all the wrong ways.

I remember Ashley, who at thirteen years of age was being treated for a sexually transmitted disease. Her military parents were crushed. They were angry with Ashley. They were upset with the school, which they blamed for teaching her about sex. "Why would she do this?" they asked.

In my conversation with Ashley, she told me of her parents' divorce when she was six years old. "I thought my father left because he didn't love me," she said. "When my mother remarried when I was ten, I felt she now had someone to love her, but I still had no one to love me. I wanted so much to be loved. I met this boy at school. He was older than me, but he liked me. I couldn't believe it. He was kind to me, and in a while I really felt he loved me. I didn't want to have sex, but I wanted to be loved."

Ashley's "love tank" had been empty for many years. Her mother and stepfather had provided for her physical needs but had not realized the deep emotional struggle raging inside her. They certainly loved Ashley, and they thought she felt their love. Not until it was almost too late did they discover they were not speaking Ashley's primary love language.

The emotional need for love, however, is not simply a childhood phenomenon. That need follows us into adulthood and into marriage. The "in love" experience temporarily meets that need, but has a limited and predictable life-span. After we come down from the high of the "in love" obsession, the emotional need for love resurfaces because it is fundamental to our nature. It's at the center of our emotional desires. We needed love before we "fell in love," and we will need it as long as we live.

The need to feel loved by one's spouse is at the heart of marital desires. A man said to me recently, "What good is all the career success, all the honors, if your wife doesn't love you?" Do you understand what he was really saying? "More than anything, I want to be loved by my wife." Status and career accomplishments are no replacement for human, emotional love. A wife says, "He's always too busy for me—until it's nighttime and he wants to jump in bed with me. I hate it." She is not a wife who hates sex; she is a wife desperately pleading for emotional love.

OUR CRY FOR LOVE

Something in our nature cries out to be loved by another. Isolation is devastating to the human psyche. That's why solitary confinement is considered the cruelest of punishments. At the heart of humankind's existence is the desire to be intimate and to be loved by another. Marriage is designed to meet that need for intimacy and love. If the need for love is not met, the intimacy we thought we had evaporates and the marriage seems empty. But if love is important, it's also elusive. I have listened to many military couples share their secret pain. Some came to me because the inner ache had become unbearable. Others came because they realized their behavior patterns or the misbehavior of their spouse was destroying the marriage. Some came simply to inform me they no longer wanted to be married. Their dreams of "living happily ever after" had been dashed against the hard walls of reality. Again and again I have heard the words "Our love is gone; our relationship is dead. We used to feel close, but not now. We no longer enjoy being with each other. We don't meet each other's needs." Their stories bear testimony that adults as well as children have "love tanks."

Could it be that deep inside hurting couples exists an invisible "emotional love tank" with its gauge on empty? Could the misbehavior, withdrawal, harsh words, and critical spirit occur because of that empty tank? If we could find a way to fill it, could the marriage be reborn? With a full tank would couples be able to create an emotional climate where it's possible to discuss differences and resolve conflicts? Could that tank be the key that makes marriage work?

I have listened to many military couples share their secret pain.

Those questions sent me on a long journey. Along the way, I discovered the simple yet powerful insights contained in this book. The journey has taken me not only through years of marriage counseling but into the hearts and minds of hundreds of military couples throughout America. From Seattle to Miami, couples have invited me into the inner chamber of their marriages, and we have talked openly. The illustrations included in this book are cut from the fabric of real life. Only names and places are changed to protect the privacy of the individuals who have spoken so freely.

Keeping the emotional love tank full is as important to a marriage as maintaining the proper oil level is to an automobile. Running your marriage on an empty "love tank" may cost you even more than trying to drive your car without oil. What you are about to read has the potential of saving thousands of marriages and can even enhance the emotional climate of a good marriage. Whatever the quality of your marriage now, it can always be better.

WARNING: Understanding the five love languages and learning to speak the primary love language of your spouse may radically affect his or her behavior. People behave differently when their emotional love tanks are full.

Before we examine the five love languages, however, we must address one other important but confusing phenomenon: the euphoric experience of "falling in love."

YOUR TURN

On a scale of 0 to 10, how full is your love tank? What do you think your spouse would say about their love tank? If their answer is anything less than 10, you might say, "What could I do to help fill it?"

Falling in Love

S he showed up at my office without an appointment and asked
my assistant if she could see me for five minutes. I had known
Rachel for years. She was thirty-six and had never married. From
time to time, she had made appointments with me to discuss a particular difficulty in one of her dating relationships. She was by nature
a conscientious, caring person, so it was completely out of character
for her to come to my office unannounced. I thought, *There must be
some terrible crisis for Rachel to come without an appointment.* I told my
assistant to show her in, and I fully expected to see her burst into tears
and tell me some tragic story as soon as the door was closed. Instead,
she burst in, beaming with excitement.

"How are you today, Rachel?" I asked.

"Great!" she said. "I've never been better in my life. I'm getting
married!"

"You *are?*" I said. "To whom and when?"

"His name is Ben," she said. "We're getting married in September. He's in the military, and I've always wanted to travel."

"That's exciting. How long have you been dating?"

"Three weeks. I know it's crazy, Dr. Chapman, after all the people I have dated and the number of times I came so close to getting married. I can't believe it myself, but I know Ben is the one for me. From the first date, we both knew it. Of course, we didn't talk about it on the first night, but one week later, he asked me to marry him. I knew he was going to ask me, and I knew I was going to say yes. I have never felt this way before. You know about the relationships that I have had through the years and the struggles I have had. In every relationship, something was not right. I never felt at peace about marrying any of them, but I know that Ben is the right one."

By this time, Rachel was rocking back and forth in her chair, saying, "I know it's crazy, but I am so happy. I have never been this happy in my life."

What has happened to Rachel? She has fallen in love. In her mind, Ben is the most wonderful man she has ever met. He is perfect in every way. He will make the ideal husband. She thinks about him day and night. The facts that Ben has been married twice before, has three children, and has been in the military for fifteen years are trivial to Rachel. She's happy, and she is convinced that she is going to be happy forever with Ben. She is in love.

Most of us enter marriage by way of the "in love" experience. We meet someone whose physical characteristics and personality traits create enough electrical shock to trigger our "love alert" system. The bells go off, and we set in motion the process of getting to know the person. The first step may be sharing a hamburger or steak, depending on our budget, but our real interest is not in the food. We are on a quest to discover love. "Could this warm, tingly feeling I have inside be the 'real' thing?"

Sometimes we lose the tingles on the first date. We find out he spends time on crackpot websites or she attended six colleges, and the tingles run right out our toes; we want no more hamburgers with them. Other times, however, the tingles are stronger after the hamburger than before. We arrange for a few more "together" experiences, and before long the level of intensity has increased to the point where we find ourselves saying, "I'm falling in love." Eventually we are convinced it's the real thing, and we tell the other person, hoping the feeling is reciprocal. If it isn't, things cool off a bit or we redouble our efforts to impress, and eventually win the love of, our beloved. When it's reciprocal, we start talking about marriage because everyone agrees being "in love" is the necessary foundation for a good marriage.

THE PLAYROOM OF HEAVEN

At its peak, the "in love" experience is euphoric. We are emotionally obsessed with each other. We go to sleep thinking of one another. When we rise, that person is the first thought on our minds. We long to be together. Spending time together is like playing in heaven's waiting room. When we hold hands, it seems as if our blood flows together. We could kiss forever if we didn't have to go to school or work. Embracing sparks dreams of marriage and ecstasy.

The person who is "in love"—we'll call her Jen—has the illusion that her beloved is perfect. Her best friend can see the flaws—it bothers her how he talks to Jen sometimes—but Jen won't listen. Her mother, noting the young man seems unable to hold a steady job, keeps her concerns to herself but asks polite questions about "Ryan's plans."

Our dreams before marriage are of marital bliss: "We are going to make each other supremely happy. Other couples may argue and fight, but not us. We love each other." Of course, we are not totally naive. We know intellectually we will eventually have differences. But we are certain we will discuss those differences openly; one of us will always be willing to make concessions, and we will reach agreement. It's hard to believe anything else when you are in love.

We have been led to believe if we are really in love, it will last forever. We will always have the wonderful feelings we have at this moment. Nothing could ever come between us. Nothing will ever overcome our love for each other. We are caught up in the beauty and charm of the other's personality. Our love is the most wonderful thing we have ever experienced. We observe that some married couples seem to have lost that feeling, but it will never happen to us. "Maybe they didn't have the real thing," we reason.

Unfortunately, the eternality of the "in love" experience is fiction, not fact. The late psychologist Dr. Dorothy Tennov conducted long-range studies on the "in love" phenomenon. After studying scores of couples, she concluded the average life-span of a romantic obsession is two years. If it's a secretive love affair, it may last a little longer. Eventually, however, we all descend from the clouds and plant our feet on earth again. Our eyes are opened, and we see the warts of the other person. Her "quirks" are now genuinely annoying. He shows a capacity for hurt and anger, perhaps even harsh words and critical judgments. Those little traits we overlooked when we were in love now become huge mountains.

REALITY INTRUDES

Welcome to the real world of marriage, where hairs are always on the sink and little white spots cover the mirror. It's a world where shoes do not walk to the closet and drawers do not close themselves, where coats do not like hangers and socks go AWOL during laundry. In this world, a look can hurt and a word can crush. Intimate lovers can become enemies, and marriage a battlefield.

What happened to the "in love" experience? Alas, it was but an illusion by which we were tricked into signing our names on the dotted line, for better or for worse. No wonder so many have come to curse marriage and the partner whom they once loved. After all, if we were deceived, we have a right to be angry. Did we really have the "real" thing? I think so. The problem was faulty information.

The bad information was the idea that the "in love" obsession would last forever. We should have known better. A casual observation should have taught us that if people remained obsessed, we would all be in serious trouble. The shock waves would rumble through business, industry, military, education, and the rest of society. Why? Because people who are "in love" lose interest in other pursuits. That is why we call it an "obsession." The college student who falls head over heels in love sees his grades tumbling. It's difficult to study when you are in love. Tomorrow you have a test on the War of 1812, but who cares about the War of 1812? When you're in love, everything else seems irrelevant. A man said to me, "Dr. Chapman, my job is disintegrating."

"What do you mean?" I asked.

"I met this girl, fell in love, and I can't get a thing done. I can't keep my mind on my job. I spend my day dreaming about her."

The euphoria of the "in love" state gives us the illusion we have an intimate relationship. We feel we belong to each other. We believe we can conquer all problems. We feel altruistic toward each other. As one young man said about his fiancée, "I can't conceive of doing anything to hurt her. My only desire is to make her happy. I would do anything to make her happy." Such obsession gives us the false sense that our egocentric attitudes have been eradicated and we have become sort of a Mother Teresa, willing to give anything for the benefit of our lover. The reason we can do that so freely is that we sincerely believe that our lover feels the same way toward us. We believe she is committed to meeting our needs; he loves us as much as we love him and would never do anything to hurt us.

That thinking is always fanciful. Not that we are insincere in what we think and feel, but we are unrealistic. We fail to reckon with the reality of human nature. By nature, we are egocentric. Our world revolves around us. None of us is totally altruistic. The euphoria of the "in love" experience only gives us that illusion.

Once the experience of falling in love has run its natural course (remember, the average "in love" experience lasts two years), we will return to the world of reality and begin to assert ourselves. He will express his desires, but his desires will be different from hers. He wants sex, but she is too tired. He dreams of buying a new car, but she flatly says, "We can't afford it." She would like to visit her parents, but he says, "I don't like spending so much time with your family." Little by little, the illusion of intimacy evaporates, and the individual desires, emotions, thoughts, and behavior patterns assert themselves. They are two individuals. Their minds have not melded together, and their emotions mingled only briefly in the ocean of love. Now the waves of reality begin to separate them. They fall out of love, and at that point either they withdraw, separate, divorce, and set off in search of a new "in love" experience, or they begin the hard work of learning to love each other without the euphoria of the "in love" obsession.

Some military couples believe the end of the "in love" experience

means they have only two options: resign themselves to a life of misery with their spouse, or
jump ship and try again. Our generation
has opted for the latter, whereas an earlier generation often chose the former.
Before we automatically conclude we
have made the better choice, perhaps
we should examine the data. The divorce
rate in second marriages is higher than in
first marriages, and the divorce rate in third
marriages is even higher.[1] Apparently the prospect of a
happier marriage the second and third time around is not substantial.

> **Once the experience of "falling in love" has run its natural course, we will return to the world of reality and begin to assert ourselves.**

Research seems to indicate there is a third and better alternative:
We can recognize the "in love" experience for what it was—a temporary emotional high—and now pursue "real love" with our spouse.
That kind of love is emotional in nature but not obsessional. It's a
love that unites reason and emotion. It involves an act of the will and
requires discipline, and it recognizes the need for personal growth.
Our most basic emotional need is not to fall in love but to be genuinely loved by another, to know a love that grows out of reason and
choice, not instinct. I need to be loved by someone who chooses to
love me, who sees in me something worth loving.

That kind of love requires effort and discipline. It is the choice to
expend energy in an effort to benefit the other person, knowing that
if his or her life is enriched by your effort, you, too, will find a sense
of satisfaction—the satisfaction of having genuinely loved another.

We cannot take credit for the kind and generous things we do
while under the influence of "the obsession." We are pushed and
carried along by an instinctual force that goes beyond our normal

behavior patterns. But if, once we return to the real world of human choice, we choose to be kind and generous, that is real love.

The emotional need for love must be met if we are to have emotional health. Married adults long to feel affection and love from their spouses. We feel secure when we are assured our mate accepts us, wants us, and is committed to our well-being. During the "in love" stage, we felt all of those emotions. It was heavenly while it lasted. Our mistake was in thinking it would last forever.

But that obsession was not meant to last forever. In the textbook of marriage, it is but the introduction. The heart of the book is rational, volitional love. That is the kind of love to which the sages have always called us. It's intentional.

That is good news to the military couple who have lost all of their "in love" feelings. If love is a choice, then they have the capacity to love after the "in love" obsession has died and they have returned to the real world. That kind of love begins with an attitude—a way of thinking. Love is the attitude that says, "I am married to you, and I choose to look out for your interests." Then the one who chooses to love will find appropriate ways to express that decision.

"But it seems so sterile," some may contend. "Love as an attitude with appropriate behavior? Where are the shooting stars, the balloons, the deep emotions? What about the spirit of anticipation, the twinkle of the eye, the electricity of a kiss, the excitement of sex? What about the emotional security of knowing I am number one in their mind?" That is what this book is all about. How do we meet each other's deep, emotional need to feel loved? If we can learn that and choose to do it, then the love we share will be exciting beyond anything we ever felt when we were infatuated.

For many years now, I have discussed the five emotional love languages in my marriage seminars and in private counseling sessions. Thousands of military couples will attest to the validity of what you are about to read. My files are filled with letters from people whom I have never met, saying, "A friend loaned me your book on love languages, and it has revolutionized our marriage. We had struggled for years trying to love each other, but our efforts had missed each other emotionally. Now that we are speaking the appropriate love languages, the emotional climate of our marriage has radically improved."

When your spouse's emotional love tank is full and he feels secure in your love, the whole world looks bright and your spouse will move out to reach his highest potential in life. But when the love tank is empty and he feels used but not loved, the whole world looks dark and he will likely never reach his potential for good in the world. In the next five chapters, I will explain the five emotional love languages and then, in chapter 10, illustrate how discovering your spouse's primary love language can make your efforts at love most productive.

YOUR TURN

Look back on that point in your marriage when "reality" set in and the initial romantic feelings faded. How did this affect your relationship, for better or worse?

WORDS OF AFFIRMATION

LOVE LANGUAGE #1

Words of Affirmation

Mark Twain once said, "I can live for two months on a good compliment." If we take Twain literally, six compliments a year would have kept his emotional love tank at the operational level. Your spouse will probably need more.

One way to express love emotionally is to use words that build up. Solomon, author of the ancient Hebrew wisdom literature, wrote, "The tongue has the power of life and death."[2] Many couples have never learned the tremendous power of verbally affirming each other. Solomon further noted, "Anxiety weighs down the heart, but a kind word cheers it up."[3]

Verbal compliments, or words of appreciation, are powerful communicators of love. They are best expressed in simple, straightforward statements of affirmation, such as:

"You look sharp in that suit."

"Do you ever look hot in that dress! Wow!"

"I really like how you always make time for our FaceTime date."

"Thanks for getting the babysitter lined up tonight. I don't take that for granted."

"I love how you always make me laugh."

What would happen to the emotional climate of a marriage if the husband and wife heard such Words of Affirmation regularly?

Several years ago, I was sitting in my office with my door open. A lady walking down the hall said, "Have you got a minute?"

"Sure, come in."

She sat down and said, "Dr. Chapman, I've got a problem. I can't get my husband to paint our bedroom. I have been after him for nine months. I have tried everything I know, and I can't get him to paint it."

I said, "Tell me about it."

She said, "Well, last Saturday was a good example. You remember how pretty it was? Do you know what my husband did all day long? He worked on updating his computer!"

"So what did you do?"

"I went in there and said, 'Dan, I don't understand you. Today would have been a perfect day to paint the bedroom, and here you are working on your computer.'"

"So did he paint the bedroom?" I inquired.

"No. It's still not painted. I don't know what to do."

"Let me ask you a question," I said. "Are you opposed to computers?"

"No, but I want the bedroom painted."

"Are you certain your husband knows that you want the bedroom painted?"

"I know he does," she said. "I've been after him for nine months."

"Let me ask you one more question. Does your husband ever do anything good?"

"Like what?"

"Oh, like taking the garbage out, or getting bugs off the windshield of the car you drive, or putting gas in the car, or hanging up his coat?"

"Yes," she said.

"Then I have two suggestions. One, don't ever mention painting the bedroom again. Two, don't ever mention it again."

"I don't see how that's going to help," she said.

"Look, you just told me he knows you want the bedroom painted. You don't have to tell him anymore. He already knows. The second suggestion I have is that the next time your husband does anything good, give him a verbal compliment. For example, if he takes the garbage out, say, 'Dan, I want you to know I really appreciate your taking the garbage out.' Don't say, 'About time you took the garbage out. The flies were going to carry it out for you.' Every time he does anything good, give him a verbal compliment."

"I don't see how that's going to get the bedroom painted."

I said, "You asked for my advice. You have it. It's free."

She wasn't very happy with me when she left. Three weeks later, however, she came back to my office and said, "It worked!" She had learned that verbal compliments are far greater motivators than nagging words.

I'm not suggesting verbal flattery in order to get your spouse to do something you want. The object of love is not getting something you want but doing something for the well-being of the one you love. It's a fact, however, that when we receive affirming words we are far more likely to be motivated to reciprocate and do something our spouse desires.

ENCOURAGING WORDS

Giving verbal compliments is only one way to express words of affirmation to your spouse. Another dialect is encouraging words. The word *encourage* means "to inspire courage." All of us have areas in which we feel insecure. We lack courage, and lack of courage often hinders us from accomplishing the positive things we would like to do. The latent potential within your spouse in his or her areas of insecurity may await your encouraging words.

Though Tricia had once been active duty herself, after she transitioned out, her identity became wrapped up in her roles as wife and mother. When an ombudsman position opened at Goodfellow Air Force Base in San Angelo, Texas, her husband, Greg, encouraged her to take it. The ombudsman is the spouse liaison for the command, answers directly to the commanding officer of a command, and is the person dependent spouses are supposed to be able to call whenever they have a question about their spouse's job.

"You can do this," Greg told Tricia. "Since you were active duty Navy yourself, you would be able to bring an interesting perspective."

Bolstered by her husband's words, Tricia volunteered. But when she learned her training would require a trip away from her family, she balked. "That trip was the first I would ever make ALONE to do something just for myself, aside from the occasional day out shopping," she remembered. "It was a week long, was taking place over Valentine's Day, and I had no idea what I would do without my children as my security blanket. Greg practically had to force me to drive away. Until I was about halfway to my destination, I kept wanting to turn around and go home. However, it turned out to be a fantastic trip. In addition to my training, I got to go to the beach and spend time alone, which was very relaxing."

Greg encouraged Tricia to enjoy her own interests, even though it sometimes meant sending her away. Tricia said, "Ever since my first duty station (as a student fresh out of boot camp) in Monterey, California, I've been in love with the beach. My husband knew this. When we were stationed in Augusta, Georgia, however, our kids were young, and we didn't know people we could ask to babysit them so we could have a weekend away. So Greg suggested I go to Myrtle Beach while he stayed home with the kids."

At first, Tricia felt like he was just trying to have time away from her. But she went, and came back feeling recharged, refreshed, and more in touch with herself. "Those trips gave me time to realize what was important to me, and to realize my husband was concerned for my well-being. Greg loved me enough to help me explore things I loved so that, in the event he did not return from one of his deployments, he could be confident I would not turn into a puddle of goo on the floor, a heaping, crying mess, unable to take care of myself, let alone my children."

> **"Greg loved me enough to help me explore things I loved."**

Greg's encouraging words gave Tricia the strength she needed to develop her own potential.

Perhaps your spouse has untapped potential in one or more areas of life. That potential may be awaiting your encouraging words. Perhaps she needs to enroll in a course to develop that potential. Maybe he needs to meet some people who have succeeded in that area, who can give him insight on the next step he needs to take. Your words may give your spouse the courage necessary to take that first step.

Please note that I am not talking about pressuring your spouse to do something *you* want. I am talking about encouraging him to develop an interest he already has. For example, a wife might pressure her husband to look for a more lucrative job. The wife thinks she's encouraging her spouse, but to him it sounds more like condemnation. But if he has the desire and motivation to seek a better position, her words will bolster his resolve. Until he has that desire, her words will come across as judgmental and guilt inducing. They express not love but rejection.

But if he says, "You know, I've been thinking about starting a handyman business on the side," then she has the opportunity to give words of encouragement. Encouraging words would sound like this: "If you decide to do that, you will be a success. When you set your mind to something, you do it. If that's what you want to do, I will certainly do everything I can to help you." Such words may give him courage to start drawing up a list of potential clients.

Encouragement requires empathy and seeing the world from your spouse's perspective. We must first learn what is important to our spouse. Only then can we give encouragement. With verbal encouragement, we are trying to communicate, "I know. I care. I am with you. How can I help?" We are trying to show we believe in him and in his abilities. We are giving credit and praise.

Most of us have more potential than we will ever develop. What holds us back is often courage. A loving spouse can supply that all-important catalyst. Of course, encouraging words may be difficult for you to speak. It may not be your primary love language. It may take great effort for you to learn this second language. That will be especially true if you have a pattern of critical and condemning words, but I can assure you it will be worth the effort.

What happens when your spouse feels his or her potential has been thwarted? Let's take a look at Jim's story for one example. Jim's wife, Sarah, always called him "The World's Greatest Fighter Pilot" even in public. "I would feel slightly embarrassed when she said it, but secretly I beamed with pride at the same time," he said. "My love language has been words of affirmation from the time I was a child. After my wife and I read *The 5 Love Languages* at a base chapel study, I realized why those positive words were so important. So did my wife. So she began to speak these words of affirmation often and freely, complimenting every act of kindness I did, every good decision I made, and every time I helped her out with the kids."

But all of that changed dramatically when he was passed over for full colonel. "It was the death of a lifelong dream for me, and I took it badly," said Jim. "I felt the Air Force was telling me I was not good enough, and it hit me hard. I've always struggled with anger, but I grew even angrier than usual after that."

Jim also began to micromanage Sarah's work at home. "I told her how to do the laundry, load the dishwasher, and season the soup," Jim recalled. "My anger got so bad the kids couldn't bring home friends for fear I would blow up. I began to hate the way I was acting, but I justified my actions by blaming the Air Force and becoming bitter toward the military."

It was a vicious circle. When Jim acted unkindly, Sarah found nothing in his behavior to praise or affirm. "It seemed as if my wife's words of affirmation dried up as much as my hope for a future Air Force career dried up," Jim said. When she didn't speak his love language, he didn't speak hers.

At the breaking point of their marriage, they sought counseling with Jim's base chaplain, who encouraged Jim to intentionally speak Sarah's love language (Receiving Gifts) by writing her cards, bringing home flowers, or picking up little souvenirs for her when Jim went

TDY. And he encouraged Sarah to grasp every small opportunity to praise Jim and speak words of affirmation. "At first, it was so hard, because I didn't feel like speaking kind words," said Sarah. "But as I asked God for specific things I could say to encourage my husband, things began to turn around. I'm so thankful for wise counsel that helped me do and say the right things to help restore our marital relationship."

Jim and Sarah's marriage began to regain the traction it once had. "We've been together ten more years since that season of sadness in our lives, and it's due to the fact that we expressed love to each other in a love language appropriate way—even during the hard times," said Jim.

Love can be restored when you speak your spouse's love language. Even difficult marriages can change rather quickly when you choose to love, rather than complain.

KIND WORDS

Love is kind. If then we are to communicate love verbally, we must use kind words. That has to do with the way we speak. The same sentence can have two different meanings, depending on how you say it. Sometimes our words say one thing, but our tone of voice says another. We are sending double messages. Our spouse will usually interpret our message based on our tone of voice, not the words we use.

"I would be delighted to wash dishes tonight," said in a snarling tone will not be received as an expression of love. On the other hand, we can share hurt, pain, and even anger in a kind manner, and that will be an expression of love. "I felt disappointed that you didn't offer to help this evening," said quietly but honestly, can be an expression of love. The person speaking wants to be *known* by her spouse. She is taking steps to build intimacy by sharing her feelings. She is asking for an opportunity to discuss a hurt in order to find healing. The same words expressed with a loud, harsh voice will be not an expression of love but an expression of condemnation and judgment.

The manner in which we speak is exceedingly important. An ancient sage once said, "A soft answer turns away anger." When your spouse is angry and upset and lashing out words of heat, if you choose to be loving you will not reciprocate with additional heat but with a soft voice. You will receive what he is saying as information about his emotional feelings. You will let him tell you of his hurt, anger, and perception of events. You will seek to put yourself in his shoes and see the event through his eyes and then express gently your understanding of why he feels that way. If you have wronged him, you will be willing to confess the wrong and ask forgiveness. If your motivation is different from what he is reading, you will be able to explain your motivation kindly. You will seek understanding and reconciliation, and not to prove your own perception as the only logical way to interpret what has happened. That is mature love—love to which we aspire if we seek a growing marriage.

Love doesn't keep a score of wrongs. Love doesn't bring up past failures. None of us is perfect. In marriage we do not always do the best or right thing. We have sometimes done and said hurtful things to our spouses. We cannot erase the past. We can only confess it and agree that it was wrong. We can ask for forgiveness and try to act differently in the future. Having confessed my failure and asked forgiveness, I can do nothing more to mitigate the hurt it may have caused my spouse. When I have been wronged by my spouse and she has painfully confessed it and requested forgiveness, I have the option of justice or forgiveness. If I choose justice and seek to pay her back or make her pay for her wrongdoing, I am making myself the judge and she the felon. Intimacy becomes impossible. If, however, I choose to forgive, intimacy can be restored. Forgiveness is the way of love.

I am amazed by how many individuals mess up every new day with yesterday. They insist on bringing into today the failures of yesterday, and in so doing, they pollute a potentially wonderful day. "I can't believe you did it. I don't think I'll ever forget it. You can't possibly know how much you hurt me. I don't know how you can sit there so smugly after you treated me that way. You ought to be crawling on your knees, begging me for forgiveness. I don't know if I can ever forgive you." Those are not the words of love but of bitterness and resentment and revenge.

The best thing we can do with the failures of the past is to let them be history. Yes, it happened. Certainly it hurt. And it may still hurt, but he has acknowledged his failure and asked your forgiveness. We cannot erase the past, but we can accept it as history. We can choose to live today free from the failures of yesterday. Forgiveness is not a feeling; it is a commitment. It's a choice to show mercy, not to hold the offense up against the offender. Forgiveness is an expression of love. "I love you. I care about you, and I choose to forgive you. Even though my feelings of hurt may linger, I will not allow what has happened to come between us. I hope we can learn from this experience. You are not a failure because you have failed. You are my spouse, and together we will go on from here." Those are the words of affirmation expressed in the dialect of kind words.

HUMBLE WORDS

Love makes requests, not demands. When I demand things from my spouse, I become a parent and she the child. It is the parent who tells the three-year-old what he ought to do and, in fact, what he must do. That is necessary because the three-year-old does not yet know how to navigate in the treacherous waters of life. In marriage, however, we are equal, adult partners. If we are to develop an intimate relationship, we need to know each other's desires. If we wish to love each other, we need to know what the other person wants.

The way we express those desires, however, is all-important. If they come across as demands, we have erased the possibility of intimacy and will drive our spouse away. If, however, we make our needs and desires known in the form of a request, we are giving guidance, not ultimatums. The husband who says, "Could you make that good pasta one of these nights?" is giving his wife guidance on how to love him and thus build intimacy. On the other hand, the husband who says, "Can't we ever have a decent meal around here?" is being adolescent, is making a demand, and his wife is likely to fire back, "Okay, you cook!" The wife who says, "Do you think it will be possible for you to clean the gutters this weekend?" is expressing love by making a request. But the wife who says, "If you don't get those gutters cleaned out soon, they are going to fall off the house. They already have trees growing out of them!" has ceased to love and has become a domineering spouse.

When you make a request of your spouse, you are affirming his or her worth and abilities. But when you make demands, you have become not a lover but a tyrant. Your spouse will feel not affirmed but belittled. A request introduces the element of choice. Your mate may choose to respond to your request or to deny it, because love is always a choice. To know my spouse loves me enough to respond to one of my requests communicates emotionally that she cares about me, respects me, admires me, and wants to do something to please me. We cannot get emotional love by way of demand. My spouse may in fact comply with my demands, but it's not an expression of love. It's an act of fear or guilt or some other emotion, but not love.

MORE WAYS TO AFFIRM

Words of affirmation are one of the five basic love languages. Within that language there are many dialects. We have discussed a few already, and there are many more. All seek to affirm the other. Psychologist William James said that possibly the deepest human need is the need to feel appreciated. Words of affirmation will meet that need in many individuals. If you are not a man or woman of words, if it is not your primary love language but you think it may be the love language of your spouse, let me suggest you keep a notebook titled "Words of Affirmation." When you read an article or book on love, record the words of affirmation you find. When you hear a lecture on love or you overhear a friend saying something positive about another person, write it down. In time, you will collect quite a list of words to use in communicating love to your spouse.

Sometimes you may not know what to say at all. When Terrence came home from war, he processed what he had been through by telling his wife, Lillian, the same stories over and over again. "At first, I wanted him to talk about something else," Lillian remembered. "But when I learned the war experiences were forever a part of who he was, I became a willing listener and a better encourager." By allowing him to share his experiences, Lillian affirmed her husband when he needed it the most. She learned to express appreciation for what he had done. She told him how proud she was of him. Her words were like medicine to his wounded emotions.

You may also want to try giving indirect words of affirmation—that is, saying positive things about your spouse when he or she is not present. Eventually, someone will tell your spouse, and you will get full credit for love. Tell your wife's mother how great your wife is. When her mother tells her what you said, it will be amplified, and you will get even more credit. Also affirm your spouse in front of others when he or she is present. When you are given public honor for an accomplishment, be sure to share the credit with your spouse. You may also try your hand at writing words of affirmation. Written words have the benefit of being read over and over again. While Luke was deployed, he learned his wife, Marlene, treasured his written words of affirmation so much that now, even when he is home, he buys her two or three cards at a time. "I love it!" said Marlene. "I have a rack up in my office where I keep all his cards. I can't tell you how many times I've reread them all."

> "When I learned the war experiences were forever a part of who he was, I became a willing listener and a better encourager."

I learned an important lesson about words of affirmation and love languages years ago in Little Rock, Arkansas, when I visited Mark and Andrea in their home off base on a beautiful spring day. The setting was idyllic—on the outside. Once inside, however, I discovered the truth. Their marriage was in shambles. Twelve years and two children after the wedding day, they wondered why they had married in the first place. They seemed to disagree on everything. The only thing they really agreed on was that they both loved the children.

As the story unfolded, my observation was that Mark was a workaholic who had little time left over for Andrea. Andrea worked part-time, mainly to get out of the house. Their method of coping was withdrawal. They tried to put distance between themselves so that their conflicts would not seem as large. But the gauge on both love tanks read "empty."

They told me that they had been going for marriage counseling but didn't seem to be making much progress. They were attending my marriage seminar, and I was leaving town the next day. This would likely be my only encounter with them, so I decided to put everything on the table.

I spent an hour with each of them separately. I listened intently to both stories. I discovered that in spite of the emptiness of their relationship and their many disagreements, they appreciated certain things about each other. Mark acknowledged Andrea was a "good mother." But, he continued, "I don't feel any affection coming from her. I work my tail off and she doesn't appreciate it." In my conversation with Andrea, she agreed that Mark was an excellent provider. "But," she complained, "he never has time for me. What's the use of having nice things if you don't ever get to enjoy them together?"

With that information, I decided to focus my advice by making only one suggestion to each of them. I told Mark and Andrea separately that each one held the key to changing the emotional climate of the marriage. "That key," I said, "is to express verbal appreciation for the things you like about the other person and, for the moment, suspending your complaints about the things you do not like." We reviewed the positive comments they had already made about each other and helped each of them write a list of those positive traits. Mark's list focused on Andrea's activities with her children, home, and church. Andrea's list focused on Mark's hard work and financial provision of the family. We made the lists as specific as possible. Andrea's list looked like this:

- He is aggressive in his work.

- He has received several promotions through the years.
- He's a good financial manager and generous.

Mark's list looked like this:

- She's a great cook.
- She helps the kids with their homework.
- She teaches first-grade Sunday school.

I suggested that they add to the lists things they noticed in the weeks ahead. I also suggested that twice a week, they select one positive trait and express verbal appreciation for it to the spouse. I gave one further guideline. I told Andrea that if Mark happened to give her a compliment, she was not to give him a compliment at the same time but rather, she should simply receive it and say, "Thank you for saying that." I told Mark the same thing. I encouraged them to do that every week for two months, and if they found it helpful, they could continue. If the experiment did not help the emotional climate of the marriage, then they could write it off as another failed attempt.

The next day, I got on the plane and returned home. I made a note to follow up with them two months later to see what had happened. When I called them in midsummer, I asked to speak to each of them individually. I was amazed to find that Mark's attitude had taken a giant step forward. He had guessed that I had given Andrea the same advice I had given him, but that was all right. He loved it. She was expressing appreciation for his hard work. "She has actually made me feel like a man again. We've got a ways to go, Dr. Chapman, but I really believe we are on the road."

When I talked to Andrea, however, I found that she had only taken a baby step forward. She said, "It has improved some, Dr. Chapman. Mark is giving me verbal compliments as you suggested, and I guess he is sincere. But he's still so busy at work that we never have time together."

As I listened to Andrea, I knew that I had made a significant discovery. The love language of one person is not necessarily the love language of another. It was obvious that Mark's primary love language was words of affirmation. He was a hard worker, and he enjoyed his work, but what he wanted most from his wife was expressions of appreciation for that work. That pattern was probably set in childhood, and the need for verbal affirmation was no less important in his adult life. Andrea, on the other hand, was emotionally crying out for something else. That brings us to love language number two.

YOUR TURN

Share instances with your spouse when words had a profound impact on your life—positively or negatively.

IF YOUR SPOUSE'S LOVE LANGUAGE IS

WORDS OF AFFIRMATION:

1. To remind yourself that "Words of Affirmation" is your spouse's primary love language, print the following on a 3 x 5 card and put it on a mirror or other place where you will see it daily:

    Words are important!

    Words are important!

    Words are important!

2. For one week, keep a written record of all the words of affirmation you give your spouse each day. You might write something like:

    On Monday, I said:

    "You did a great job on this meal."

    "You really look nice in that outfit."

    "I appreciate your picking up the dry cleaning."

    On Tuesday, I said:

    etc.

    You might be surprised how well (or how poorly) you are speaking words of affirmation.

3. Set a goal to give your spouse a different compliment each day for one month. If "an apple a day keeps the doctor away," maybe a compliment a day will keep the counselor away. (You may want to record these compliments also, so you will not duplicate the statements.)

4. As you watch TV, read, or listen to people's conversations, look for words of affirmation that people use. Write those affirming statements in a notebook or keep them electronically. Read through these periodically and select those you could use with your spouse. When you use one, note the date on which you used it. Your notebook may become your love book. Remember, words are important!

5. Write a love letter, a love paragraph, or a love sentence to your spouse and give it quietly or with fanfare! You may someday find your love letter tucked away in some special place. Words are important!

6. Compliment your spouse in the presence of his parents or friends. You will get double credit: Your spouse will feel loved and the parents will feel lucky to have such a great son-in-law or daughter-in-law.

7. Look for your spouse's strengths and tell her how much you appreciate those strengths. Chances are she will work hard to live up to her reputation.

8. Tell your children how great their mother or father is. Do this behind your spouse's back and in her presence.

DECODING DEPLOYMENTS WITH WORDS OF AFFIRMATION

Words of affirmation is one of the easiest languages to speak during separations. In fact, you may find that being intentional with this language will draw the two of you closer together than you thought possible while physically apart.

1. Before the deployment, write love notes and secretly tuck them away in various places in the service member's bags.

Likewise, the service member can write several cards and label them "For When You're Lonely," "For When You're Overwhelmed," etc., so she can open them when she needs to hear from you the most.

2. Handwrite an encouraging letter to your spouse at least weekly, more often if possible.

3. Remind your spouse of the things that attracted you to her when you first met.

4. Share what you love, admire, or respect about your spouse in a letter or during one of your phone or Internet calls.

5. Write and mail your own poem about your spouse.

6. Express appreciation. Service members, tell your spouse how much you appreciate all the things she does to keep the home front going.

7. Home-front spouse, be sure your service member still feels needed by your family, no matter how well you are managing without him.

8. If your spouse is stressed when he or she calls you, allow him the opportunity to vent. Don't try to fix the situation unless asked. Affirm him or her.

9. Write and send a tribute to your spouse.

10. Be the first to say, "I love you" in every conversation.

LOVE LANGUAGE #2

Quality Time

I should have picked up on Andrea's primary love language from the beginning. What was she saying on that spring night when I visited her and Mark in Little Rock? "Mark doesn't spend any time with me. What good are all our things if we don't ever enjoy them together?" What was her desire? Quality Time with Mark. She wanted his attention. She wanted him to focus on her, to give her time, to do things with her.

By "quality time," I mean giving someone your undivided attention. I don't mean sitting on the couch watching television together. When you spend time that way, Netflix or HBO has your attention —not your spouse. What I mean is sitting with the TV off, looking at each other and talking, devices put away, giving each other your undivided attention. It means taking a walk, just the two of you, or going out to eat and looking at each other and talking.

Time is a precious commodity. We all have multiple demands on our time, yet each of us has the exact same hours in a day. We can make the most of those hours by committing some of them to our spouse. If your mate's primary love language is quality time, she simply wants you, being with her, spending time.

When I sit with my wife and give her twenty minutes of my undivided attention and she does the same for me, we are giving each other twenty minutes of life. We will never have those twenty minutes again; we are giving our lives to each other. It is a powerful emotional communicator of love.

One medicine cannot cure all diseases. In my advice to Andrea and Mark, I made a serious mistake. I assumed that words of affirmation would mean as much to her as they would to him. I had hoped that if each of them would give adequate verbal affirmation, the emotional climate would change, and both of them would begin to feel loved. It worked for Mark. He began to feel more positive about Andrea, sensing her genuine appreciation for his hard work, but it had not worked as well for Andrea, for words of affirmation was not her primary love language. Her language was quality time.

I called Mark, who told me Andrea was still not very happy. "I think I know why," I said. "The problem is that I suggested the wrong love language."

Mark hadn't the foggiest idea what I meant. I explained that what makes one person feel loved emotionally is not always the thing that makes another person feel loved emotionally.

He agreed that his language was words of affirmation. He told me how much that had meant to him as a boy and how good he felt when his wife expressed appreciation for the things he did. I explained that Andrea's language was not words of affirmation but quality time. I explained the concept of giving someone your undivided attention, not talking to her while you watch sports or read texts but looking into her eyes, giving her your full attention, doing something with her that *she* enjoys doing and doing it wholeheartedly. "Like going to a concert with her," he said. I could tell the lights were coming on in Little Rock.

"Dr. Chapman, that's what she has always complained about. I didn't do things with her; I didn't spend any time with her. She'd always say, 'We used to go places and do things before we were married, but now, you're too busy.' That's her love language all right; no question about it. But what am I gonna do? My work is so demanding."

"Tell me about it," I said.

For the next ten minutes, he gave me the history of his climb up the ranks, of how hard he had worked, and how proud he was of the recognition he had received. He told me of his dreams for the future and that he knew that within the next five years, he would be where he wanted to be.

"Do you want to be there alone, or do you want to be there with Andrea?"

"I want her to be with me, Dr. Chapman. I want her to enjoy it with me. That's why it always hurts so much when she criticizes me for spending time on the job. I am doing it for us. I wanted her to be a part of it, but she is always so negative."

"Are you beginning to see why she was so negative, Mark?" I asked. "Her love language is quality time. You have given her so little time that her love tank is empty. She doesn't feel secure in your love. Therefore she has lashed out at what was taking your time in her mind—your job. She doesn't really hate your job. She hates the fact that she feels so little love coming from you. There's only one answer, Mark, and it's costly. You have to make time for Andrea. You have to love her in the right love language."

"I know you're right, Dr. Chapman. Where do I begin?"

I asked Mark if he had his legal pad handy—the same pad on which he had listed positive things about Andrea.

"It's right here."

"Good. We're going to make another list. What are some things that you know Andrea would like you to do with her? Things she has mentioned through the years." Here is Mark's list:

- Spend a weekend in the mountains (sometimes with the kids and sometimes just the two of us).
- Meet her for lunch (at a nice restaurant or sometimes just at Panera).
- When I come home at night, sit down and talk with her about my day and listen as she tells me about her day. (She doesn't want me to watch TV while we are trying to talk.)
- Spend time talking with the kids about their school experiences and looking at projects they've done at school.
- Go on a picnic or to a waterpark with her and the kids some Saturday.
- Take a vacation with the family at least once a year.
- Go walking with her and talk as we walk.

When Mark's list was finished I said, "You know what I am going to suggest, don't you, Mark?"

"Do them," he said.

"That's right, one a week for the next two months. Where will you find the time? You will make it. You are a wise man," I continued. "You would not be where you are if you were not a good decision maker. You have the ability to plan your life and to include Andrea in your plans."

"I know," he said. "I can do it."

"And, Mark, this does not have to diminish your vocational goals. It just means that when you get to the top, Andrea and the children will be with you."

"That's what I want more than anything," Mark said with feeling.

The years have come and gone. Andrea and Mark have had ups and downs, but the important thing is that they have done it all together. The children have left the nest, and Mark and Andrea agree that these are their best years ever. Mark has become an avid symphony fan, and Andrea has made an unending list in her legal pad of things she appreciates about Mark. He never tires of hearing them.

FOCUSED ATTENTION

It isn't enough to just be in the same room with someone. A key ingredient in giving your spouse quality time is giving them focused attention, especially in this era of many distractions. When a father is sitting on the floor, rolling a ball to his two-year-old, his attention is not focused on the ball but on his child. For that brief moment, however long it lasts, they are together. If, however, the father is texting while he rolls the ball, his attention is diluted. Some husbands and wives think they are spending time together when, in reality, they are only living in close proximity. They are in the same house at the same time, but they are not together. A wife who is cleaning out a drawer while her husband tries to talk to her is not giving him quality time, because he does not have her full attention.

Quality time does not mean we have to spend our together moments gazing into each other's eyes. It means we are doing something together and we are giving our full attention to the other person. The activity in which we are both engaged is incidental. The important thing emotionally is that we are spending focused time with each other. The activity is a vehicle that creates the sense of togetherness. The important thing about the father rolling the ball to the two-year-old is not the activity itself but the emotions that are created between the father and his child.

Similarly, a husband and wife going running together, if it's genuine quality time, will focus not on how fast or how many miles they're running but on the fact that they are spending time together. What happens on the emotional level is what matters. Our spending time together in a common pursuit communicates that we care about each other, that we enjoy being with each other, that we like to do things together.

QUALITY TIMING

For those whose primary love language is quality time, the military lifestyle presents special challenges. Demanding schedules require intentionality. Timing is key. Service members, be aware that with each PCS, the fresh absence of friends from your last station will further deplete the love tanks of those whose love language is quality time. Investing in one-on-one time with your spouse during these times will reassure him or her of your love and help ease the transition.

While the need for quality time may be felt more keenly in new environments, this is not a love language you can ever put on hold without risking harm to your relationship. Obviously, deployments are difficult (tips for coping with them are at the end of this chapter). But even while stateside, job pressures can threaten to squeeze out quality time with one's spouse. During the Gulf War in 1991, Ted was a battalion chaplain, responsible for processing soldiers headed to Iraq. "This was during a time when they projected that thirty thousand of our soldiers would be killed in the first month of the war," said Ted. "There was a lot of fear about down range, and I was trying to be a super chaplain." While Ted took calls and met with soldiers at all hours of the day and night, his wife, Penny, was earning a master's degree and raising two small children. They both worked hard, but had little time for each other.

In January, Ted began to make plans for Valentine's Day to make up for months of long hours. So he arranged for childcare, made reservations at a nice restaurant and hotel, and purchased lingerie at Victoria's Secret for Penny. Valentine's Day arrived, and the date went well—until Penny opened the gift.

As she lifted the lingerie out of the tissue paper, her face fell. "Oh. Thank you," was all she said.

"That reaction reached into my chest, pulled my heart out and threw it on the floor and stomped on it," Ted said. "I thought, 'She doesn't love me.'"

For three weeks, Ted and Penny felt cold and distant to each other, until finally, Ted decided to address what was bothering him. Her explanation shocked him. "When I opened your gift, I thought the only thing you liked about me was sex," she told him. The evening had felt like quality time to Penny until she guessed it was only a way to meet Ted's desire for physical touch.

"That was a totally foreign concept to me, but I had enough wisdom to realize it didn't matter what I thought," Ted said. "It mattered what she thought. I realized I had better figure out how to show her I love her in a way that she understands."

Since then, Ted and Penny have carved out time for regular dates, rather than waiting for the right moment and then splurging on a more expensive night out. "There's far less tension between us now," said Ted. "In fact, if Penny and I started fighting, the kids would tell us to go on a date!" Even the children knew Penny's love language was quality time. When Penny's love tank is full, she's far more willing to speak Ted's love language, as well.

"When I opened your gift, I thought the only thing you liked about me was sex."

Ted and Penny's relationship demonstrates the connection between love and sex. Without love, the sexual relationship may be extremely empty. Keeping your spouse's love tank full will also enhance your sexual relationship.

In their first year of marriage, Maria understood that her need for quality time with her husband, Jorge, took a back seat to Jorge's responsibilities to the military. For weeks, she looked forward to being together again. But when Jorge came home from sea and immediately began making plans to visit friends, she was crushed—and angry.

"I'm an extrovert," said Jorge. "And when I come home from being underway, I relax by getting together with friends. Maria is always welcome to be part of the group, but sometimes she chooses not to. If she wants to be with me so much, why would she stay home?"

Maria didn't want to be part of a group. She wanted his focused attention to reassure her of his love. "If we could have some quality time together first, just us, I'd be much happier for him to see his friends. But when he asks to do something with them right away, I wonder if he even missed me while he was gone."

Maria is clearly revealing that her love language is quality time. That is why she finds Jorge's desire to spend time with his friends as an act of rejection. If Jorge is wise, he will fill Maria's love tank before he dashes off to see his friends.

Quality time is critical and should be carefully timed—but

unfortunately, it cannot be stored up like water in a camel's hump, ready to be used on a journey through the desert. Connor was already gone from home on a TDY when he learned of an upcoming deployment with the National Guard. So he flew home every weekend to spend quality time with his wife, Stacy. Each weekend was to be spent without distractions of the Internet, email, texting, webcam, or TV.

"It was a tall order for anyone to fill, especially under such difficult circumstances, but he longed to spend quality time with me, to have my undivided attention," remembered Stacy, who contributes to an online support group for military wives. "So each weekend, we read together, prayed together, listened to the Gary and Barb Rosberg predeployment DVDs, completed a barrage of home repairs, and spent time preparing our four children, as best we could, for our next assignment. He even went out of his way to sit next to me, as I wrote blogs and devotionals, like he used to do before his TDY."

But the fact that Stacy spent any time on the blogs for military wives hurt Connor. "His heart was crushed by my inability to give him the undivided attention he needed," she said. "Through his eyes, my priorities were displaced. He no longer affirmed my writing, and he struggled to find the encouraging words I longed to hear. As a result, I struggled to express my heart, physically, verbally, and in writing. To make matters worse, there was no time to process the feelings and emotions that surfaced before he had to leave again on his yearlong deployment."

Connor is demonstrating a common source of conflict. He was making great efforts

> He was trying to "load up" on enough quality time to see him through deployment. The truth is that quality time cannot be stored up—but we can speak quality time while deployed.

to meet his own emotional need for love, probably assuming he was also meeting Stacy's need for love. When he did not get the quality time he thought he deserved, he became critical of her. Her love language was words of affirmation, so she felt deeply hurt by his negative words. So, another couple starts a long deployment with a fractured relationship.

Connor's expectations were unrealistic. He was trying to "load up" on enough quality time to see him through deployment. The truth is that quality time cannot be stored up—but we can speak quality time while deployed. (See suggestions at the end of this chapter.)

QUALITY CONVERSATION

Like words of affirmation, the language of quality time also has many dialects. One of the most common dialects is that of *quality conversation*. By quality conversation, I mean sympathetic dialogue where two individuals are sharing their experiences, thoughts, feelings, and desires in a friendly, uninterrupted context. Most individuals who complain that their spouse does not talk do not mean literally that he or she never says a word. They mean that he or she seldom takes part in sympathetic dialogue. If your spouse's primary love language is quality time, such dialogue is crucial to his or her emotional sense of being loved.

Quality conversation is quite different from the first love language. Words of affirmation focus on what we are saying, whereas quality conversation focuses on what we are hearing. If I am sharing my love for you by means of quality time and we are going to spend that time in conversation, it means I will focus on drawing you out, listening sympathetically to what you have to say. I will ask questions, not in a badgering manner but with a genuine desire to understand your thoughts, feelings, and desires.

I met Patrick when he was forty-three and had been married for seventeen years. I remember him because his first words were so dramatic. He sat in the leather chair in my office and after briefly introducing himself, leaned forward and said with great emotion, "Dr. Chapman, I've been a fool, a real fool."

"What has led you to that conclusion?" I asked.

"I've been married for seventeen years," he said, "and my wife has left me. Now I realize what a fool I've been."

I repeated my original question, "In what way have you been a fool?"

"My wife would come home from work and tell me about the problems in her office. I would listen to her and then tell her what I thought she should do. I always gave her advice. I told her she had to confront the problem. 'Problems don't go away. You have to talk with the people involved or your supervisor. You have to deal with problems.' The next day she would come home from work and tell me about the same problems. I would ask her if she did what I had suggested the day before. She would shake her head and say no.

"After three or four nights of that, I would get angry. I would tell her not to expect any sympathy from me if she wasn't willing to take the advice I was giving her. She didn't have to live under that kind of stress and pressure. She could solve the problem if she would simply do what I told her. It hurt me to see her living under such stress because I knew she didn't have to. The next time she'd bring up the problem, I would say, 'I don't want to hear about it. I've told you what you need to do. If you're not going to listen to my advice, I don't want to hear it.'

"I would withdraw and go about my business. What a fool I was!" he said. "Now I realize that she didn't want advice when she told me about her struggles at work. She wanted sympathy. She wanted me to listen, to give her attention, to let her know that I could understand the hurt, the stress, the pressure. She wanted to know that I loved her and that I was with her. She didn't want advice; she just wanted to know that I understood. But I never tried to understand. I was too busy giving advice. And now she's gone."

Patrick's wife had been pleading for quality conversation. Emotionally, she longed for him to focus attention on her by listening to her pain and frustration. Patrick was not focusing on listening but on speaking. He listened only long enough to hear the problem and formulate a solution. He didn't listen long enough or well enough to hear her cry for support and understanding.

Many of us are like Patrick. We are trained to analyze problems and create solutions. We forget that marriage is a relationship, not a project to be completed or a problem to solve. A relationship calls for sympathetic listening with a view to understanding the other person's thoughts, feelings, and desires. We must be willing to give advice but only when it's requested and never in a condescending manner. Most of us have little training in listening. We are far more efficient in thinking and speaking. Learning to listen may be as difficult as learning a foreign language, but learn we must, if we want to communicate love. That is especially true if your spouse's primary love language is quality time and his or her dialect is quality conversation. Fortunately, numerous books and articles have been written on developing the art of listening. I will not seek to repeat what is written elsewhere but suggest the following summary of practical tips.

1. Maintain eye contact when your spouse is talking. That keeps your mind from wandering and communicates that he/she has your full attention.

2. Don't listen to your spouse and do something else at the same time. Remember, quality time is giving someone your undivided attention. If you are doing something you cannot turn from immediately, tell your spouse the truth. A positive approach might be, "I know you are trying to talk to me and I'm interested, but I want to give you my full attention. I can't do that right now, but if you will give me ten minutes to finish this, I'll sit down and listen to you." Most spouses will respect such a request.

3. Listen for feelings. Ask yourself, "What emotion is my spouse experiencing?" When you think you have the answer, confirm it. For example, "It sounds to me like you are feeling disappointed because I forgot _____." That gives him the chance to clarify his feelings. It also communicates you are listening intently to what he is saying.

4. Observe body language. Clenched fists, tears, frowns, and eye movement may give you clues as to what the other is feeling. Sometimes body language speaks one message while words speak another. Ask for clarification to make sure you know what she is really thinking and feeling.

5. Do not interrupt. Recent research has indicated that the average individual listens for only seventeen seconds before interrupting and interjecting his own ideas. If I give you my undivided attention while you are talking, I will refrain from defending myself or hurling accusations at you or dogmatically stating my position. My goal is to discover your thoughts and feelings. My objective is not to defend myself or to set you straight. It is to understand you.

LEARNING TO TALK

Quality conversation requires not only sympathetic listening but also self-revelation. When a wife says, "I wish my husband would talk. I never know what he's thinking or feeling," she is pleading for intimacy. She wants to feel close to her husband, but how can she feel close to someone whom she doesn't know? In order for her to feel loved, he must learn to reveal himself. If her primary love language is quality time and her dialect is quality conversation, her emotional love tank will never be filled until he tells her his thoughts and feelings.

Self-revelation does not come easy for some of us. Many adults grew up in homes where the expression of thoughts and feelings was not encouraged but condemned or simply avoided. To request a toy was to receive a lecture on the sad state of family finances. The child went away feeling guilty for having the desire, and he quickly learned not to express his desires. When he expressed anger, the parents responded with harsh and condemning words. Thus, the child learned that expressing angry feelings is not appropriate. If the child was made to feel guilty for expressing disappointment at not being able to go to the store with his father, he learned to hold his disappointment inside. By the time we reach adulthood, many of us have learned to deny our feelings. We are no longer in touch with our emotional selves.

A wife says to her husband, "How did you feel about what Steve did?" And the husband responds, "I think he was wrong. He should have—" but he is not telling her his feelings. He is voicing his thoughts. Perhaps he has reason to feel angry, hurt, or disappointed, but he has lived so long in the world of thought that he does not acknowledge his feelings. When he decides to learn the language of quality conversation, it will be like learning a foreign language. The place to begin is by getting in touch with his feelings, becoming aware that he is an emotional creature in spite of the fact that he has denied that part of his life.

If you need to learn the language of quality conversation, begin by noting the emotions you feel away from home. Carry a small notepad and keep it with you daily. Three times each day, ask yourself, "What emotions have I felt in the last three hours? What did I feel on the way to work when the driver behind me was riding my bumper? What did I feel when I stopped at the gas station and the automatic pump did not shut off and the side of the car was covered in gas? What did I feel when I got to the office and found that the project I was working on had to be completed in three days when I thought I had another two weeks?"

Write down your feelings in the notepad and a word or two to help you remember the event corresponding to the feeling. Your list may look like this:

Event	Feelings
• tailgater	• angry
• gas station	• very upset
• work project due in three days	• frustrated and anxious

Do that exercise three times a day and you will develop an awareness of your emotional nature. Using your notepad, communicate your emotions and the events briefly with your spouse as many days as possible. In a few weeks, you will become comfortable expressing your emotions with him or her. And eventually you will feel comfortable discussing your emotions toward your spouse and the children, stimulated by events that occur within the home. Remember, emotions themselves are neither good nor bad. They are simply our psychological responses to the events of life.

Based on our thoughts and emotions, we eventually make decisions. When the tailgater was following you on the highway and you felt angry, perhaps you had these thoughts: I wish he would lay off; I wish he would pass me; if I thought I wouldn't get caught, I'd press the accelerator and leave him in the twilight; I should slam on my brakes and let his insurance company buy me a new car; maybe I'll pull off the road and let him pass.

Eventually, you made some decision or the other driver backed off, turned, or passed you, and you arrived safely at work. In each of life's events, we have emotions, thoughts, desires, and eventually actions. It is the expression of that process we call self-revelation. If you choose to learn the love dialect of quality conversation, that is the learning road you must follow.

DEAD SEAS AND BABBLING BROOKS

Not all of us are out of touch with our emotions, but when it comes to talking, all of us are affected by our personality. I have observed two basic personality types. The first I call the "Dead Sea." In the little nation of Israel, the Sea of Galilee flows south by way of the Jordan River into the Dead Sea. The Dead Sea goes nowhere. It receives but it does not give. This personality type receives many experiences, emotions, and thoughts throughout the day. They have a large reservoir where they store that information, and they are perfectly happy not to talk. If you say to a Dead Sea personality, "What's wrong? Why aren't you talking tonight?" he will probably answer, "Nothing's wrong. What makes you think something's wrong?" And that response is perfectly honest. He is content not to talk. He could drive from Chicago to Detroit and never say a word and be perfectly happy.

On the other extreme is the "Babbling Brook." For this personality, whatever enters into the eye gate or the ear gate comes out the mouth gate and there are seldom sixty seconds between the two. Whatever they see, whatever they hear, they tell. In fact if no one is at home to talk to, they will call someone else. "Do you know what I saw? Do you know what I heard?" If they can't get someone on the telephone, they may talk to themselves because they have no reservoir. Many times a Dead Sea marries a Babbling Brook. That happens because when they are dating, it's a very attractive match.

If you are a Dead Sea and you date a Babbling Brook, you will have a wonderful evening. You don't have to think, "How will I get the conversation started tonight? How will I keep the conversation flowing?" In fact, you don't have to think at all. All you have to do is nod your head and say, "Uh-huh," and she will fill up the whole evening and you will go home saying, "What a wonderful person." On the other hand, if you are a Babbling Brook and you date a Dead Sea, you will have an equally wonderful evening because Dead Seas are the world's best listeners. You will babble for three hours. He will listen intently to you, and you will go home saying, "What a wonderful person." You attract each other. But five years after marriage, the Babbling Brook wakes up one morning and says, "We've been married five years, and I don't know him." The Dead Sea is saying, "I know her too well. I wish she would stop the flow and give me a break." The good news is that Dead Seas can learn to talk and Babbling Brooks can learn to listen. We are influenced by our personality but not controlled by it.

One way to learn new patterns is to establish a daily sharing time in which each of you will talk about three things that happened to you that day and how you feel about them. I call that the "Minimum

Daily Requirement" for a healthy marriage. If you will start with the daily minimum, in a few weeks or months you may find quality conversation flowing more freely between you.

QUALITY ACTIVITIES

In addition to the basic love language of quality time, or giving your spouse your undivided attention, is another dialect called quality activities. At a recent marriage seminar, I asked couples to complete the following sentence: "I feel most loved by my husband/wife when _____." Here is the response of a twenty-nine-year-old husband who has been married for five years: "I feel most loved by my wife when we do things together, things I like to do and things she likes to do. We talk more. It sorta feels like we are dating again." That is a typical response of individuals whose primary love language is quality time. The emphasis is on being together, doing things together, giving each other undivided attention.

Quality activities may include anything in which one or both of you have an interest. The emphasis is not on what you are doing but on why you are doing it. The purpose is to experience something together, to walk away from it feeling like, "He cares about me. He was willing to do something with me that I enjoy, and he did it with a positive attitude." That is love, and for some people it is love's loudest voice.

One of Emily's favorite pastimes is browsing in used bookstores. "I love to just disappear into the stacks and see what treasures I can find," she says. Husband Jeff, less of an avid reader, has learned to share these experiences with Emily and even point out books she may enjoy. Emily, for her part, has learned to compromise and not force Jeff to spend hours in the stacks. As a result, Jeff proudly says, "I vowed early on that if there was a book Emily wanted, I would buy it for her." Jeff may never become a bookworm, but he has become proficient at loving Emily.

Quality activities may include visiting historic sites, birding, hiking, working out together, or having another couple over for barbecue. The activities are limited only by your interest and willingness to try new experiences. The essential ingredients in a quality activity are: (1) at least one of you wants to do it, (2) the other is willing to do it, (3) both of you know why you are doing it—to express love by being together.

One of the by-products of quality activities is that they provide a memory bank from which to draw in the years ahead. Fortunate is the couple who remembers a foggy early-morning stroll along the coast, the day they met their newest family member at an animal shelter, the night they attended their first major-league baseball game together, the quiet times of working side by side late at night in their home office, and oh, yes, the awe of standing beneath the waterfall after the two-mile hike. They can almost feel the mist as they remember. Those are memories of love, especially for the person whose primary love language is quality time.

And where do we find time for such activities, especially if both of us have vocations outside the home? We make time just as we make time for lunch and dinner. Why? Because it is just as essential to our marriage as meals are to our health. Is it difficult? Does it take careful planning? Yes. Does it mean we have to give up some individual activities? Perhaps. Does it mean we do some things we don't particularly enjoy? Certainly. (See Jeff and Emily.) Is it worth it? Without a doubt. What's in it for me? The pleasure of living with a spouse who feels loved and knowing that I have learned to speak his or her love language fluently.

A personal word of thanks to Mark and Andrea in Little Rock, who taught me the value of love language number one, Words of Affirmation, and love language number two, Quality Time. Now, it's on to Chicago and love language number three.

YOUR TURN

What in your marriage detracts from spending quality time?

IF YOUR SPOUSE'S LOVE LANGUAGE IS
QUALITY TIME:

1. Take a walk together through the old neighborhood where one of you grew up. Ask questions about your spouse's childhood. Ask, "What are the fun memories of your childhood?" Then, "What was most painful about your childhood?"

2. Go to the city park and rent bicycles. Ride until you are tired, then sit and watch the ducks. When you get tired of the quacks, roll on to the rose garden. Learn each other's favorite color of rose and why.

3. Ask your spouse for a list of five activities he would enjoy doing with you. Make plans to do one of them each month for the next five months. If money is a problem, space the freebies between the "we can't afford this" events.

4. Ask your spouse where she most enjoys sitting when talking with you. The next week, text her one afternoon and say, "I want to make a date with you one evening this week to sit outside and talk. Which night and what time would be best for you?"

5. Think of an activity your spouse enjoys, but which brings little pleasure to you: NASCAR, browsing in flea markets, golf. Tell your spouse you are trying to broaden your horizons and would like to join him in this activity sometime this month. Set a date and give it your best effort.

6. Plan a weekend getaway just for the two of you sometime within the next six months. Be sure it's a weekend when you won't have to call the office or have a commitment with your kids. Focus on relaxing together doing what one or both of you enjoy.

7. Read the travel section in the Sunday paper together and dream out loud about places you'd like to go. Whether you actually go to these places or not, it's fun to imagine together.

8. Make time every day to share with each other some of the events of the day. When you spend more time on Facebook than you do listening to each other, you end up more concerned about your hundreds of "friends" than about your spouse.

9. Have a "Let's review our history" evening once every three months. Set aside an hour to focus on your history. Select five questions each of you will answer, such as:

   (1) Who was your best and worst teacher in school and why?

   (2) When did you feel your parents were proud of you?

   (3) What is the worst mistake your mother ever made?

   (4) What is the worst mistake your father ever made?

   (5) What do you remember about the religious aspect of your childhood?

   Each evening, agree on your five questions before you begin your sharing. At the end of the five questions, stop and decide upon the five questions you will ask next time.

DECODING DEPLOYMENTS WITH QUALITY TIME

Those whose primary love language is quality time will naturally feel their love tanks being depleted during deployments. You may want to ramp up his or her second most dominant love language to help, but there are still several ways to experience quality time across the miles.

1. Create your own website together. Post all your news and latest photos weekly for your sweetheart. Write a daily (or as often as possible) online journal to keep your loved one up-to-date.

2. Keep a phone journal. Jot down things you want to tell your spouse when he/she calls. Rule of thumb: always say, "I love you" before anything else, just in case you lose connection.

3. Plan dates for a Skype chat when possible. When the technology won't support that, spend quality time writing intentional emails or letters to one another. Your spouse will appreciate the time you invest in any form of communication.

4. Plan a "date" with your spouse to meet at a pre-designated website and read a short article and discuss it over the phone or Internet call.

5. "Meet" at a pre designated website that describes a vacation destination you would like to go to when he returns from his deployment.

6. Read a book together; a chapter per week and discuss it the next time you talk with each other. If that is too much of a time commitment, select questions to answer from *101 Conversation Starters for Couples*.

7. Service member, remember your spouse wants to connect on a heart level despite the distance. If you can't or would rather not share what's going on at your end, at least share with her how you feel. Tired? Overwhelmed? Hopeful? Laser-focused?

8. Ask your spouse to share his or her dreams with you. Try not to minimize them in any way. Just listen and show interest.

9. Home-front spouse, become interested in a sport, hobby, or activity your service member enjoys. Share what you are learning. You might even consider taking a few lessons to help you engage with your spouse in this activity when he or she returns.

10. Make a scrapbook of things that took place while the service member was away. You'll spend quality time reliving the memories with him or her after homecoming.

11. Dream together about what you want to do after retirement from the military.

12. Tell your spouse things like, "I can't wait to spend a day _____ with you again." Fill in the blank with a favorite shared activity.

LOVE LANGUAGE #3

Receiving Gifts

Erik spent a year in Kelsey's "friend zone" before she agreed to go out with him. Since they were both big baseball fans, Erik took her to a minor-league game in Indianapolis. They were sitting in a grassy area beyond the left-field fence when suddenly a hard-hit drive came their way. Erik jumped up and made an impressive bare-handed catch—his first home run grab ever.

Two days later Kelsey found a gift-wrapped package outside her dorm room. She opened it and found a baseball in a small plastic display case (the kind collectors use). Taped to the inside of the case was a ticket stub from the game. Inscribed on the ball was the date of the game and these words:

1st home run catch

2nd best thing to happen to me that day

They were married two years after that first date. Fifteen years later that baseball, still in its display case, sits on Kelsey's dresser where she can see it every day. It is the first thing she would grab if the house were on fire.

Gifts really matter to some people. I learned a lot about gifts when I was studying anthropology, learning about different cultures all over the world. From the Aztecs to native Alaskans to aboriginal Japanese, I found that in every culture I studied, gift giving was a part of the love-marriage process.

Anthropologists are intrigued by cultural patterns that tend to pervade cultures, and so was I. Could it be that gift giving is a fundamental expression of love that transcends cultural barriers? Is the attitude of love always accompanied by the concept of giving? Those are academic and somewhat philosophical questions, but if the answer is yes, it has profound practical implications for North American couples.

"JUICE FOR YOU"

I took an anthropology field trip to the island of Dominica. Our purpose was to study the culture of the Carib Indians, and on the trip I met Fred. Fred was not a Carib but a young black man of twenty-eight years. Fred had lost a hand in a fishing-by-dynamite accident. Since the accident, he could not continue his fishing career. He had plenty of available time, and I welcomed his companionship. We spent hours together talking about his culture.

Upon my first visit to Fred's house, he said to me, "Mr. Gary, would you like to have some juice?" to which I responded enthusiastically. He turned to his younger brother and said, "Go get Mr. Gary some juice." His brother turned, walked down the dirt path, climbed a coconut tree, and returned with a green coconut. "Open it," Fred commanded. With three swift movements of the machete, his brother uncorked the coconut, leaving a triangular hole at the top. Fred handed me the coconut and said, "Juice for you." It was green, but I drank it—all of it—because I knew it was a gift of love. I was his friend, and to friends you give juice.

At the end of our weeks together as I prepared to leave that small island, Fred gave me a final token of his love. It was a crooked stick fourteen inches in length that he had taken from the ocean. It was silky smooth from pounding upon the rocks. Fred said the stick had lived on the shores of Dominica for a long time, and he wanted me to have it as a reminder of the beautiful island. Even today when I look at that stick, I can almost hear the sound of the Caribbean waves, but it's not as much a reminder of Dominica as it is a reminder of love.

A gift is something you can hold in your hand and say, "Look, he was thinking of me," or "She remembered me." You must be thinking of someone to give him a gift. The gift itself is a symbol of that thought. It doesn't matter whether it costs money. What is important is that you thought of him. And it's not the thought implanted only in the mind that counts, but the thought expressed in actually securing the gift and giving it as the expression of love.

Mothers remember the days their children bring a flower from the yard as a gift. They feel loved, even if it was a flower they didn't want picked. From early years, children are inclined to give gifts to their parents, which may be another indication that gift giving is fundamental to love.

Gifts are visual symbols of love. Most wedding ceremonies include the giving and receiving of rings. The person performing the ceremony says, "These rings are outward and visible signs of an inward and spiritual bond uniting your two hearts in love that has no end." That is not meaningless rhetoric. It is verbalizing a significant truth—symbols have emotional value. Perhaps that is even more graphically displayed near the end of a disintegrating marriage when the husband or wife stops wearing the wedding ring. It's a visual sign that the marriage is in serious trouble.

Visual symbols of love are more important to some people than to others. If Receiving Gifts is my primary love language, I will place great value on the ring you have given me and I will wear it with great pride. I will also be greatly moved emotionally by other gifts that you give through the years. I will see them as expressions of love. Without gifts as visual symbols, I may question your love.

When Davis and Anna married, they were so poor they used plain 10K gold rings Anna's parents had bought them. Within ten years, they had paid off all their debt, had money in savings, and were even able to purchase a replacement class ring for Davis, which cost several thousand dollars. "But he didn't splurge on a nice ring for me," said Anna. "This was problematic. Every time I looked at my girlfriends' left ring fingers, I saw a diamond. But when I looked at my own, I saw a plain gold band." For Anna, whose love language is receiving gifts, that visual seemed to shout that she wasn't worth a diamond.

"After five kids, ten years of marriage, and nine military moves, I felt I wanted that demonstration of love on my finger," Anna recalled. Finally, she talked to Davis about it and tried to explain her love language without sounding materialistic.

Not long after that conversation, a set of Anna's grandmother's heirloom china dishes were stolen from their household goods during a move. When the settlement check came in, it provided some discretionary funds. For their tenth anniversary, Davis gave Anna a diamond anniversary band with ten stones to replace the plain gold band. "For the last fifteen years (we are celebrating our twenty-fifth anniversary this year), every time I look down at my ring finger, I feel loved by my military man," Anna said.

Gifts come in all sizes, colors, and shapes. Some are expensive, and others are free. To the individual whose primary love language is receiving gifts, the cost of the gift will matter little, unless it is greatly out of line with what you can afford. If a millionaire gives only one-dollar gifts regularly, the spouse may question whether that is an expression of love, but when family finances are limited, a one-dollar gift may speak a million dollars worth of love.

Gifts may be purchased, found, or made. The husband who finds an interesting bird feather while out jogging and brings it home to his wife has found himself an expression of love, unless, of course, his wife is allergic to feathers. For the man who can afford it, you can purchase a beautiful card for less than five dollars. For the man who cannot, you can make one for free. Get the paper out of the wastebasket where you work, fold it in the middle, take scissors and cut out a heart, write, "I love you," and sign your name. Gifts need not be expensive.

"Every time I look down at my ring finger, I feel loved by my military man."

But what of the person who says, "I'm not a gift giver. I didn't receive many gifts growing up. I never learned how to select gifts. It doesn't come naturally for me." Congratulations, you have just made the first discovery in becoming a great lover. You and your spouse speak different love languages. Now that you have made that discovery, get on with the business of learning your second language. If your spouse's primary love language is receiving gifts, you can become a proficient gift giver. In fact, it's one of the easiest love languages to learn.

Where do you begin? Make a list of all the gifts your spouse has expressed excitement about receiving through the years. They may be gifts you have given or gifts given by other family members or friends. The list will give you an idea of the kind of gifts your spouse would enjoy receiving. If you have little or no knowledge about selecting the kinds of gifts on your list, recruit the help of family members who know your spouse. In the meantime, select gifts you feel comfortable purchasing, making, or finding, and give them to your spouse. Don't wait for a special occasion. If receiving gifts is his/her primary love language, almost anything you give will be received as an expression of love. (If she has been critical of your gifts in the past and almost nothing you have given has been acceptable, then receiving gifts is almost certainly not her primary love language.)

THE BEST INVESTMENT

If you are to become an effective gift giver, you may have to change your attitude about money. Each of us has an individualized perception of the purposes of money, and we have various emotions associated with spending it. Some of us have a spending orientation. We feel good about ourselves when we are spending money. Others have a saving and investing perspective. We feel good about ourselves when we are saving money and investing it wisely.

If you are a spender, you will have little difficulty purchasing gifts for your spouse; but if you are a saver, you will experience emotional resistance to the idea of spending money as an expression of love. You don't purchase things for yourself. Why should you purchase things for your spouse? But that attitude fails to recognize that you are purchasing things for yourself. By saving and investing money, you are purchasing self-worth and emotional security. You are caring for your own emotional needs in the way you handle money. What you are not doing is meeting the emotional needs of your spouse.

Rachel was raised in a dysfunctional home. Instead of the hoped-for son, she was the second daughter. As such, she was often overlooked and neglected. Though she didn't know it at the time, her love language was receiving gifts, which explains why it hurt so much when her parents gave her a combination birthday/Christmas gift (her birthday is December 28), and it ended up being the same gift her sister received for Christmas. When she graduated from high school, the only child of three to do so, her parents gave her a necklace. "They bragged that they bought the pearls at a garage sale for only one dollar and it turned out they were real," said Rachel. "They weren't. The cheap veneer wore off eventually to reveal the plastic beads beneath. Nothing was too cheap for me."

When Rachel married her Air Force pilot, Trent, they read *The 5 Love Languages* in a base chapel Sunday school class, and it explained why gifts were so important to her. Trent, whose love language was words of affirmation, didn't understand. "I felt that speaking a kind word was a lot easier than going out to buy a gift," he said. So he didn't speak Rachel's language on a regular basis for years.

Finally, Rachel asked him, "What if I only said 'thank you' to you once every other month? Even after you've done a lot of work around the house, or ran an errand for me, I rarely said 'thank you.' How would that make you feel?" It seemed to really penetrate his fighter-pilot brain as she continued, "Well, that's how I feel when you don't give me a simple card, or other small gift, except on holidays and my birthday. You only speak my love language about four times a year."

A couple of days later, Trent went on a TDY to Red Flag at Nellis AFB in Las Vegas, and came back with a large pair of bright pink dice for hanging on a rearview car mirror. Across the front of the dice, it said, "I'm lucky to have you. I love you."

It was a start. And though it didn't come naturally for Trent, his simple efforts helped Rachel feel loved.

If you discover your spouse's primary love language is receiving gifts, then perhaps you will understand that purchasing gifts for him or her is the best investment you can make. You are investing in your relationship and filling your spouse's emotional love tank, and with a full love tank, he or she will likely reciprocate emotional love to you in a language you will understand. When both persons' emotional needs are met, your marriage will take on a whole new dimension. Don't worry about your savings. You will always be a saver, but to invest in loving your spouse is to invest in blue-chip stocks.

THE GIFT OF SELF

There is an intangible gift that sometimes speaks more loudly than a gift that can be held in one's hand. I call it the gift of self or the gift of presence. Being there when your spouse needs you speaks loudly to the one whose primary love language is receiving gifts. Sonia once said to me, "My husband loves softball more than he loves me."

"Why do you say that?" I inquired.

"On the day our baby was born, he played softball. I was lying in the hospital all afternoon while he played softball," she said.

"Was he there when the baby was born?"

"He stayed long enough for the baby to be born, but ten minutes afterward, he left. It was awful. It was such an important moment in our lives. I wanted us to share it together. I wanted Tony to be there with me."

That "baby" was now fifteen years old, and Sonia was talking about the event with all the emotion as though it had happened yesterday. I probed further. "Have you based your conclusion that Tony loves softball more than he loves you on this one experience?"

"No," she said. "On the day of my mother's funeral, he also played softball."

"Did he go to the funeral?"

"Yes, but as soon as it was over, he left to get to his game. I couldn't believe it. My brothers and sisters came to the house with me, but my husband was playing softball."

Later, I asked Tony about those two events. He knew exactly what I was talking about. "I knew she would bring that up," he said. "I was there through all the labor and when the baby was born. I took pictures; I was so happy. I couldn't wait to tell the guys on the team, but my bubble was burst when I got back to the hospital that evening. She was furious with me. I couldn't believe what she was saying. I thought she would be proud of me for telling the team.

"And when her mother died? She probably didn't tell you that I took off work a week before she died and spent the whole week at the hospital and at her mother's house doing repairs and helping out. After she died and the funeral was over, I felt I had done all I could do. I needed a breather. I like to play softball, and I knew that would help me relax and relieve some of the stress I'd been under. I thought she would want me to take a break.

"I had done what I thought was important to her, but it wasn't enough. She has never let me forget those two days. She says that I love softball more than I love her. That's ridiculous."

He was a sincere husband who failed to understand the tremendous power of presence. His being there for his wife was more important than anything else in her mind. Physical presence in the time of crisis is the most powerful gift you can give if your spouse's primary love language is receiving gifts. Your body becomes the symbol of your love. Remove the symbol, and the sense of love evaporates. In counseling, Tony and Sonia worked through the hurts and misunderstandings of the past. Eventually, Sonia was able to forgive him, and Tony came to understand why his presence was so important to her.

> "Jake would sit in the living room by himself and not say anything, except to tell the kids to get away."

If the physical presence of your spouse is important to you, I urge you to verbalize that to your spouse. Don't expect him to read your mind. If, on the other hand, your spouse says to you, "I really want you to be there with me tonight," take his request seriously. From your perspective, it may not be important; but if you are not responsive to that request, you may be communicating a message you do not intend.

When Claire's husband came home for R&R, he was a changed man. He had survived an attack of sixty mortars. Twelve of his comrades had not. But the last thing he wanted to do was talk about it. "Jake would sit in the living room by himself and not say anything, except to tell the kids to get away," said Claire. "I didn't know what to do. I just sat beside him on the couch and didn't say a word." Sometimes she put her hand on his knee or arm. One time she sat and held his hand for an hour. Sometimes he would squeeze her hand and cry. For eighteen days, she just sat with him as often as she could, never saying anything.

When the time came to take him back to the airport, Jake gave her a big kiss and hug. "Sweetheart," he told her, "I've never felt closer to you than I have in the last few weeks." Claire was shocked. But from Jake's perspective, she had given him the gift of herself, with no strings attached. He would never forget those weeks of silent companionship.

MIRACLE IN CHICAGO

Almost everything ever written on the subject of love indicates that at the heart of love is the spirit of giving. All five love languages challenge us to give to our spouse, but for some, receiving gifts, visible symbols of love, speaks the loudest. I heard the most graphic illustration of that truth in Chicago, where I met Doug and Kate.

They attended my marriage seminar and agreed to take me to O'Hare Airport after the seminar on Saturday afternoon. We had two or three hours before my flight, and they asked if I would like to stop at a restaurant. I was famished, so I readily assented.

Kate began talking almost immediately after we sat down. She said, "Dr. Chapman, God used you to perform a miracle in our marriage. Three years ago, we attended your marriage seminar here in Chicago for the first time. I was desperate," she said. "I was thinking seriously of leaving Doug and had told him so. Our marriage had been empty for a long time. I had given up. For years, I had complained to Doug that I needed his love, but he never responded. I loved the kids, of course, and I knew they loved me, but I felt nothing coming from Doug. In fact, by that time, I hated him. He was a methodical person. He did everything by routine. He was as predictable as a clock, and no one could break into his routine.

"For years," she continued, "I tried to be a good wife. I did all the things I thought a good wife should do. I had sex with him because I knew that was important to him, but I felt no love coming from him. I felt like he stopped dating me after we got married and simply took me for granted. I felt used and unappreciated.

"When I talked to Doug about my feelings, he'd laugh at me and say we had as good a marriage as anybody else in the community. He didn't understand why I was so unhappy. He would remind me that we were doing well financially and that I should be happy instead of complaining all the time. He didn't even try to understand my feelings. I felt totally rejected.

"Well, anyway," she said as she moved her tea and leaned forward, "we came to your seminar three years ago. I did not know what to expect, and frankly I didn't expect much. I didn't think anybody could change Doug. During and after the seminar, he didn't say too much. He seemed to like it. Then that Monday afternoon, he came home from work and gave me a rose. 'Where did you get that?' I asked. 'I bought it from a street vendor,' he said. 'I thought you deserved a rose.' I started crying. 'Oh, Doug, that is so sweet of you.'

"On Tuesday he texted me from the office at about one-thirty and asked me what I thought about his picking up a pizza for dinner. That may not sound like a big deal to most people, but Doug never does anything like that. I told him it sounded great, and so he brought home a pizza and we all had a fun time together. I gave him a hug and told him how much I enjoyed it.

"When he came home on Wednesday, he brought each of the kids a box of Cracker Jacks, and he had a small potted plant for me. He said he knew the rose would die, and he thought I might like something that would be around for a while. I was beginning to think I was hallucinating! I couldn't believe what Doug was doing or why he was doing it.

"Thursday night after dinner, he handed me a card with a message about his not always being able to express his love to me but hoping that the card would communicate how much he cared. 'Why don't we get a babysitter on Saturday night and the two of us go out for dinner?' he suggested. 'I would love that,' I said. On Friday afternoon, he stopped by the cookie shop and bought each of us one of our favorite cookies. Again, he kept it as a surprise, telling us only that he had a treat for dessert.

"By Saturday night," she said, "I was in orbit. I had no idea what had come over Doug, or if it would last, but I was enjoying every minute of it. After our dinner out I said to him, 'Doug, you have to tell me what's happening. I don't understand.'"

She looked at me intently. "Dr. Chapman, this was a man who never gave me a gift, ever. He never gave me a card for any occasion. He always said, 'It's a waste of money; you look at the card and throw it away.' He never bought our kids anything and expected me to buy only the essentials. He expected me to have dinner ready every night. I mean, this was a radical change in his behavior."

I turned to Doug and asked, "What did you say to her in the restaurant when she asked you what was going on?"

"I told her that I had listened to your lecture on love languages at the seminar and that I realized that her love language was gifts. I also realized that I had not given her a gift in years, maybe not since we had been married. I remembered that when we were dating I used to bring her flowers and other small gifts, but after marriage I figured we couldn't afford that. I told her that I had decided that I was going to try to get her a gift every day for one week and see if it made any difference in her. I had to admit that I had seen a pretty big difference in her attitude during the week.

"I told her that I realized that what you said was really true and that learning the right love language was the key to helping another person feel loved. I said I was sorry that I had been so dense for all those years and had failed to meet her need for love. I told her that I really loved her and that I appreciated all the things she did for me and the kids. I told her that with God's help, I was going to be a gift giver for the rest of my life.

"She said, 'But, Doug, you can't go on buying me gifts every day for the rest of your life. We can't afford that.' 'Well, maybe not every day,' I said, 'but at least once a week. That would be fifty-two more gifts per year than what you have received in the past five years.'"

"I don't think he has missed a single week in three years," Kate said. "He is like a new man. You wouldn't believe how happy we have been. Our children call us lovebirds now. My tank is full and overflowing."

I looked at Doug. "But what about you, Doug? Do you feel loved by Kate?"

"Oh, I've always felt loved by her, Dr. Chapman. She does so much to help me and the kids. She takes care of the finances, knows where we all have to be when, stays in touch with extended family on Facebook . . . I know she loves me." He smiled and said, "Now, you know what my love language is, don't you?"

I did, and I also knew why Kate had used the word *miracle*.

Gifts need not be expensive, nor must they be given weekly. But for some individuals, their worth has nothing to do with monetary value and everything to do with love.

YOUR TURN

Reflect on ways to give gifts even if finances are tight.

IF YOUR SPOUSE'S LOVE LANGUAGE IS
RECEIVING GIFTS:

1. Try a parade of gifts: Leave a box of candy for your spouse in the morning; have flowers delivered in the afternoon; give her a gift in the evening. When your spouse asks, "What is going on?" you respond: "Just trying to fill your love tank!"

2. Let nature be your guide: The next time you take a walk through the neighborhood, keep your eyes open for a gift for your spouse. It may be a stone, a stick, or a feather. You may even attach special meaning to your natural gift. For example, a smooth stone may symbolize your marriage with many of the rough places now polished. A feather may symbolize how your spouse is the "wind beneath your wings."

3. Discover the value of "handmade originals." Make a gift for your spouse. This may require you to enroll in an art or crafts class: ceramics, silversmithing, painting, wood carving, etc. Your main purpose for enrolling is to make your spouse a gift. A handmade gift often becomes a family heirloom.

4. Give your spouse a gift every day for one week. It need not be a special week, just any week. I promise you it will become "The Week That Was!" If you are really energetic, you can make it "The Month That Was!" No—your spouse will not expect you to keep this up for a lifetime.

5. Keep a "Gift Idea Notebook." Every time you hear your spouse say, "I really like that," or "Oh, I would really like to have one of those!" write it down in your notebook. Listen carefully and you will get quite a list. This will serve as a guide when you get ready to select a gift. To prime the pump, you may look through a favorite online shopping site together.

6. Enlist a "personal shopper." If you really don't have a clue as to how to select a gift for your spouse, ask a friend or family member who knows your wife or husband well to help you. Most people enjoy making a friend happy by getting them a gift, especially if it's with your money.

7. Offer the gift of presence. Say to your spouse, "I want to offer the gift of my presence at any event or on any occasion you would like this month. You tell me when, and I will make every effort to be there." Get ready! Be positive! Who knows, you may enjoy the symphony or the hockey game.

8. Give your spouse a book and agree to read it yourself. Then offer to discuss together a chapter each week. Don't choose a book you want him or her to read. Choose a book on a topic in which you know your spouse has an interest: football, history, technology, animals, nature, current events.

9. Give a living gift. Purchase and plant a tree or flowering shrub in honor of your spouse. You may plant it in your own yard, where you can water and nurture it, or in a public park or forest where others can also enjoy it. You will get credit for this one year after year. If it's an apple tree, you may live long enough to get an apple. One warning: Don't plant a crabapple tree!

DECODING DEPLOYMENTS WITH RECEIVING GIFTS

Speaking the gifts love language is still very possible during separations. It just requires a little more planning and creativity. Here are some ideas to get you started.

1. Send your service member care packages with favorite baked items and something he enjoys having, such as a special soap, food item, etc. Be sure to check regulations on what is allowed in packages first.

2. Create a special day honoring your service member. Have family and friends send cards, emails, care packages, which communicate their support of him.

3. Service member, bring home unique gifts for your spouse. Tell her when you've purchased it just so she knows you've been thinking of her.

4. For the service member's birthday, make and send a cake-sized brownie and place hard candy letters on it that say "Happy Birthday." Be sure to send candles, plates, napkins, and plastic forks so she can share it.

5. Service member, conspire with some mutual friends or church members to have care packages delivered to your spouse's doorstep on holidays or ordinary days.

6. Home-front spouse, put together a themed care package with memories of one of your special days you shared together.

7. Create a coupon book for your spouse to redeem when you are together again.

8. During the Christmas holidays, send the service member a stocking filled with goodies. Make him his favorite Christmas cookies; send him a very small, decorated Christmas tree, or something that will have great meaning to him.

9. Celebrate Valentine's Day with special cards and gifts that are meaningful to you as a couple. Also remember birthdays, your anniversary, and Military Spouse Appreciation Day, which always falls on the Friday before Mother's Day.

10. Service member, order gifts online—books, flowers, coffee, restaurant gift cards—and have them sent directly to your spouse—no special occasion required.

LOVE LANGUAGE #4

Acts of Service

The ink was barely dry on their marriage certificate when Erin and Nathan moved to Fort Knox, Kentucky, for a nine-month assignment. Unaccustomed to military life, Erin was lonely in her new environment and not intellectually challenged the way she had been in the career she had just given up. And, she didn't know the first thing about how to be an Army wife. Nathan was busy in his new job and completely clueless as to why his bride was growing frustrated and resentful.

"He didn't realize I needed help to learn how to do the simplest things like getting an identification card so I could shop at the store, learning how to cash a check at the post bank, going to the doctor, or navigating the many offices and rules on post," said Erin. She felt thrown into a life where she knew very little, and Nathan was not speaking her love language to help her learn.

Erin's primary love language was what I call "Acts of Service." By acts of service, I mean doing things you know your spouse would like you to do. You seek to please her by serving her, to express your love for her by doing things for her. So it was with Doug, whom we met in the last chapter.

In a military marriage, "dependents" depend on the service member for help with certain tasks, such as getting an ID card, updating DEERS insurance accounts, securing passports, and finance or housing issues. All spouses need their service member to assist in these things (unless power of attorney allows otherwise), but spouses whose love language is acts of service will feel especially hurt, as Erin did, if their service members don't provide this help. Other day-to-day actions such as cooking a meal, setting a table, washing dishes, vacuuming, changing the baby's diaper, keeping the car in operating condition, and walking the dog are all acts of service. They require thought, planning, time, effort, and energy. If done with a positive spirit, they are indeed expressions of love.

Unfortunately, it never occurred to Nathan that Erin would need help with the basic aspects of adjusting to military life, and since she didn't feel loved and cared for by him, she withdrew physically from him. When he, in turn, seemed even less loving to her, she began to guess at possible reasons, ranging from regretting marrying her, to marrying her just to have a military spouse at his side in his career. "I learned and resented the old saying, 'If the Army would have wanted you to have a wife, they would have issued you one,'" Erin said.

A deployment, with its inherent communication breakdowns, only heightened tensions between them. "She seemed to hate military life," Nathan said. "I didn't know what to do, so I just worked harder to provide for us and avoided any arguments." In the meantime, on the home front, Erin volunteered at Army Community Service, where she was trained to teach new Army wives all about Army life.

Eventually, a chaplain gave Erin and Nathan tickets to attend a marriage seminar, and they discovered *The 5 Love Languages.* Finally, Erin and Nathan understood why they both felt frustrated. "We still loved each other very much, but being apart and living a demanding military life with many deployments made it far more difficult to speak the love languages of Physical Touch and Acts of Service," said Erin.

> **"I learned and resented the old saying, 'If the Army wanted you to have a wife, they would have issued you one.'"**

To ease some of the loneliness when he deployed, Nathan wrote a letter he would mail from the post the day he left. He also wrote a few letters to be opened in the days after he left. To Erin, taking the time to write letters and emails was an act of service.

Nathan's primary love language was physical touch, but acts of service was his secondary. So Erin continued to perform acts of service at home with a greater love and understanding now that she had been trained to understand Army life by Army Community Service in the Army Family Team Building program. She became so passionate about helping other women avoid the pain she and Nathan had been through she became an award-winning volunteer, training other women, receiving the Helping Hands Award, and being inducted into the Order of Saint Joan D'Arc. Both Nathan and Erin have continued to read books about marriage and family, and live out a commitment of drawing closer in their marriage each day.

CONVERSATION IN A MILL TOWN

I discovered the impact of "acts of service" in the little village of China Grove, North Carolina. China Grove sits in central North Carolina, originally nestled in chinaberry trees, not far from Andy Griffith's legendary Mayberry. At the time of this story, China Grove was a textile town with a population of 1,500. I had been away for more than ten years, studying anthropology, psychology, and theology. I was making my semiannual visit to keep in touch with my roots.

Almost everyone I knew except Dr. Shin and Dr. Smith worked in the mill. Dr. Shin was the medical doctor, and Dr. Smith was the dentist. And of course, there was Preacher Blackburn, who was pastor of the church. For most couples in China Grove, life centered on work and church. In that pristine American setting, I discovered love language number four.

I was standing under a chinaberry tree after church on Sunday when a young couple approached me. I didn't recognize either of them. I assumed they had grown up while I was away. Introducing himself, Dave said, "I hear you've been studying counseling."

I smiled and said, "Well, a little bit."

"I have a question," he said. "Can a couple make it in marriage if they disagree on everything?"

It was one of those theoretical questions that I knew had a personal root. I went right to the point. "How long have you been married?"

"Two years," he responded. "And we don't agree on anything."

"Give me some examples," I said.

"Well, for one thing, Mary doesn't like me to go hunting. I work all week in the mill, and I like to go hunting on Saturdays—not every Saturday but when hunting season is in."

Mary had been silent until this point when she interjected. "When hunting season is out, he goes fishing, and besides that, he doesn't hunt just on Saturdays. He takes off from work to go hunting."

"Once or twice a year I take off two or three days from work to go hunting in the mountains with some buddies," Dave said, irritated. "What's wrong with that?"

"What else do you disagree on?" I asked.

"Well, she wants me to go to church all the time. I don't mind going on Sunday morning, but Sunday night I like to rest. It's all right if she wants to go, but I don't think I ought to have to go."

Again Mary spoke up. "You don't really want me to go either," she said. "You fuss every time I walk out the door."

I knew that things weren't supposed to be getting this hot under a shady tree in front of a church. As a young, aspiring counselor, I feared that I was getting in over my head, but having been trained to ask questions and listen, I continued. "What other things do you disagree on?"

This time Mary answered. "He wants me to stay home all day and work in the house," she said. "He gets mad if I go see my mother or go shopping or something."

"I don't mind her going to see her mother," he said, "but when I come home, I like to see the house cleaned up. Some weeks, she doesn't make the bed up for three or four days, and half the time, she hasn't even started supper. I work hard, and I like to eat when I get home. Besides that, the house is a wreck," he continued. "The baby's things are all over the floor, the baby is dirty, and I don't like filth. We don't have very much, and we live in a small mill house, but at least it could be clean."

"What's wrong with him helping me around the house?" Mary asked. "He acts like a husband shouldn't do anything around the house. All he wants to do is work and hunt. He expects me to do everything."

Thinking that I had better start looking for solutions rather than prying for more disagreements, I looked at Dave and asked, "Dave, when you were dating, before you got married, did you go hunting or fishing every Saturday?"

"Pretty much, but I always got home in time to go see her on Saturday night. Most of the time, I'd get home in time to wash my truck before I went to see her. I didn't like to go see her with a dirty truck."

As we continued talking, I learned that Mary had gotten married right out of high school and that during her senior year Dave came to see her almost every night and stayed for supper. "He would help me do my chores around the house and then we'd sit and talk until suppertime."

"Dave, what did the two of you do after supper?" I asked.

He looked up with a sheepish smile and said, "Well, the regular dating stuff, you know."

"But if I had a school project," Mary said, "he'd help me with it. Sometimes we worked hours on school projects. I was in charge of the Christmas float for the senior class. He helped me for three weeks every afternoon. He was great."

I switched gears and focused on the third area of their disagreement. "Dave, when you were dating, did you go to church with Mary on Sunday nights?"

"Yes, I did," he said. "If I didn't go to church with her, I couldn't see her that night. Her father was strict that way."

I thought I was beginning to see some light, but I wasn't sure they were seeing it. I asked Mary, "When you were dating Dave, what convinced you that he really loved you? What made him different from other guys you had dated?"

"It was the way he helped me with everything," she said. "None of the other guys cared about all that. He even helped me wash dishes when he had supper at our house. He was the most incredible person I had ever met, but after we got married that changed."

Turning to Dave I asked, "Why do you think you did all these things for her before you were married?"

"It just seemed natural for me," he said. "It's what I would want someone to do for me if she cared about me."

"And why do you think you stopped helping her after you got married?" I asked.

"Well, I guess I expected it to be like my family. Dad worked, and Mom took care of things at the house. I never saw my dad do anything around the house. Since Mom stayed home, she did everything— cooking, cleaning, washing, and ironing. I just thought that was the way it was supposed to be."

Now we were getting somewhere. "Dave, a moment ago what did you hear Mary say when I asked her what really made her feel loved by you when you were dating?"

He responded, "Helping her with things and doing things with her."

"So, can you understand how she could feel unloved when you stopped helping her with things?" He was nodding yes. I continued. "It was a normal thing for you to follow the model of your mother and father in marriage. Almost all of us tend to do that, but your behavior toward Mary was a radical change from your courtship. The one thing that had assured her of your love disappeared."

Then I asked Mary, "What did you hear Dave say when I asked, 'Why did you do all of those things to help Mary when you were dating?'"

"He said that it came naturally to him," she replied.

"That's right," I said, "and he also said that is what he would want someone to do for him if she loved him. He was doing those things for you and with you because in his mind that's the way anyone shows love. Once you were married and living in your own house, he had expectations of what you would do if you loved him. You would keep the house clean, you would cook, and so on. In brief, you would do things for him to express your love. When he did not see you doing those things, do you understand why he would feel unloved?" Mary was nodding now too. I continued, "My guess is that the reason you are both so unhappy in your marriage is that neither of you is showing your love by doing things for each other."

Mary said, "I think you're right, and the reason I stopped doing things for him is because I didn't like how he bossed me around. It was as if he was trying to make me be like his mother."

"That's it," I said. "No one likes to be forced to do anything. In fact, love is always freely given. Love cannot be demanded. We can request things of each other, but we must never demand anything. Requests give direction to love, but demands stop the flow of love."

Dave looked thoughtful. "I did boss her around—demand, like you said. I guess I was disappointed in her as a wife. I know I said some cruel things, and I understand how she could be upset with me."

"I think things can be turned around rather easily at this juncture," I said. I pulled two note cards out of my pocket. "Let's try something. I want each of you to sit on the steps of the church and make a request list. Dave, I want you to list three or four things that if Mary chose to do them would make you feel loved when you walk into the house in the afternoon. If making the bed is important to you, then put it down. Mary, I want you to make a list of three or four things that you would really like to have Dave's help in doing, things which, if he chose to do them, would help you know that he loved you." (I'm big on lists; they force us to think concretely.)

After five to six minutes, they handed me their lists. Dave's list read:

- Make up the beds every day.
- Have the baby's face washed when I get home.
- Try to have supper at least started before I get home so that we could eat within 30–45 minutes after I get home.

I read the list out loud and said to Dave, "I'm understanding you to say that if Mary chooses to do these three things, you will view them as acts of love toward you."

"Yeah," he said, "just those things. That would really make a difference in how I feel about her."

Then I read Mary's list:

- I wish he would change the baby's diaper after he gets home in the afternoon, especially if I am working on supper.
- I wish he would vacuum the house for me once a week.
- I wish he would mow the lawn every week in the summer and not let it get so tall that I'm ashamed of our yard.

I said, "Mary, I am understanding you to say that if Dave chooses to do those three things, you would take his actions as genuine expressions of love toward you."

"I would," she said.

"Can you do what she asks, Dave?"

"Yes," he said.

"Mary, what about you? Can you do the things on Dave's list?"

"Yes, I can. In the past, it always seemed like no matter what I did, it was never enough."

I turned to Dave. "Dave, you understand that what I am suggesting is a change from the model of marriage that your mother and father had."

"Oh, my dad cut the grass and washed the car."

"But he didn't change the diapers or vacuum, right?"

"Never!" he said, grinning.

"You don't have to do these, you understand? If you do them, however, it will be an act of love to Mary."

And to Mary I said, "You understand that you don't have to do these things, but if you want to express love for Dave, here are three ways that will be meaningful to him. I want to suggest that you try these for two months and see if they help. At the end of two months, you may want to add additional requests to your lists and share them with each other. I would not add more than one request per month, however."

"This really makes sense," Mary said. "Thank you," Dave said. They took each other by the hand and walked toward their car. I said to myself out loud, "I think this is what church is all about. I think I am going to enjoy being a counselor." I have never forgotten the insight I gained under that chinaberry tree.

You may be wondering, *If Dave and Mary had the same primary love language, why were they having so much difficulty?* The answer lies in the fact that they were speaking different dialects. They were doing things for each other but not the things that were most important to the other person. When they started speaking the right dialects, their love tanks began to fill.

Before we leave Dave and Mary, I would like to make three other observations. First, they illustrate clearly that what we do for each other before marriage is no indication of what we will do after marriage. Before marriage, we are carried along by the force of the "in love" obsession. After marriage, we revert to being the people we were before we "fell in love." Our actions are influenced by the model of our parents, our own personality, our perceptions of love, our emotions, needs, and desires. Only one thing is certain about our behavior: It will not be the same behavior we exhibited when we were caught up in being "in love."

That leads me to the second truth: Love is a choice and cannot be coerced. Dave and Mary were criticizing each other's behavior and getting nowhere. Once they decided to make requests of each other rather than demands, their marriage began to turn around. Criticism and demands tend to drive wedges. With enough criticism, your spouse may do what you want, but probably it will not be an expression of love. You can give guidance to love by making requests: "I wish you would wash the car, change the baby's diaper, mow the grass," but you cannot create the will to love. Each of us must decide daily to love or not to love our spouses. If we choose to love, then expressing it in the way in which our spouse requests will make our love most effective emotionally.

There is a third truth, which only the mature lover will be able to hear. My spouse's criticisms about my behavior provide me with the clearest clue to her primary love language. People tend to criticize their spouse most loudly in the area where they themselves have the deepest emotional need. Their criticism is an ineffective way of pleading for love. If we understand that, it may help us process their criticism in a more productive manner. A wife may say to her husband after he gives her a criticism, "It sounds like that is extremely important to you. Could you explain why it is so crucial?" Criticism often needs clarification. Initiating such a conversation may eventually turn the criticism into a request rather than a demand.

FREEDOM TO SERVE

"I have served him for twenty years. I have waited on him hand and foot. I don't hate him, but I resent him, and I can't live with him anymore." That wife has performed acts of service for twenty years, but they have not been expressions of love. They were done out of fear, guilt, and resentment.

No person should ever be a doormat. We may allow ourselves to be used, but we are in fact creatures of emotion, thoughts, and desires. And we have the ability to make decisions and take action. Allowing oneself to be used or manipulated by another is not an act of love. It is, in fact, an act of treason. You are allowing him or her to develop inhumane habits—to emotionally abuse you. Love says, "I love you too much to let you treat me this way. It is not good for you or me."

Debates over "who does what" in contemporary marriages are less contentious than they used to be, but they still crop up. When Scott and Laura married, they were both on their own career paths. Busy with her own job, Laura did not make cooking a priority. When Scott joined the military, they stayed with his parents while he completed Basic Training. "I watched how his mom cooked meals every night for her family," Laura remembered. "She worked full-time, just like I did, but she really served her family with those meals, and Scott responded so much to them. You could just tell his love tank was being filled by that act of service." Laura began to understand then that it wasn't about gender but about showing love in a way her husband appreciated.

Bryant learned the same lesson while trying to express and receive love with his deployed wife, Karen. At first, he showered her with romance—emails, love letters, and care packages—but his efforts were not rewarded. "For months, my frustration grew when words of my undying love were not reciprocated," Bryant said. "My frustration grew to anger, and before long resentment filled my heart."

But when Bryant read *The 5 Love Languages*, he understood he was not filling Karen's love tank, because her language was not words of affirmation or gifts but acts of service. "She didn't want to get those care packages on a weekly basis. She didn't want a couple letters each week or an email every night," he remembered. "She wanted me to do my job of taking care of the family while she was gone and nothing else really mattered. When I told her about what our kids and I were doing, I saw her love meter rise. By being more financially responsible, I was able to afford more outings with the kids. Pictures on Facebook showing us at the park or zoo or at an activity on our installation—that filled her tank and led her to meet my need through words of affirmation."

Love says, "I love you too much to let you treat me this way. It is not good for you or me."

YOUR TURN

Many acts of service will involve household chores, but not all. What are some non chore ways of serving your mate?

IF YOUR SPOUSE'S LOVE LANGUAGE IS
ACTS OF SERVICE:

1. Make a list of all the requests your spouse has made of you over the past few weeks. Select one of these each week and do it as an expression of love.

2. Print note cards with the following:

   "Today I will show my love for you by . . ." Complete the sentence with one of the following: picking up the clutter, paying the bills, fixing something that's been broken a long time. (Bonus points if it's a chore that's been put off.)

   Give your spouse a love note accompanied by the act of service every three days for a month.

3. Ask your spouse to make a list of ten things he or she would like for you to do during the next month. Then ask your spouse to prioritize those by numbering them 1–10, with 1 being the most important and 10 being least important. Use this list to plan your strategy for a month of love. (Get ready to live with a happy spouse.)

4. While your spouse is away, get the kids to help you with some act of service for him. When he walks in the door, join the children in shouting "Surprise! We love you!" Then share your act of service.

5. What one act of service has your spouse nagged about consistently? Why not decide to see the nag as a tag? Your spouse is tagging this as really important to him or her. If you choose to do it as an expression of love, it's worth more than a thousand roses.

6. If you have more money than time, hire someone to do the acts of service you know your spouse would like for you to do, such as the yard work or a once-a-month deep cleaning of your home.

DECODING DEPLOYMENTS WITH ACTS OF SERVICE

During deployments, service members should keep in mind that spouses on the home front are doing acts of service for them daily by managing the home front solo. Spouses on the home front would do well to remember their service members are also serving them (and others) in their line of duty. However, if this is your spouse's primary love language, going the extra mile to personalize the service will reap big rewards for your marriage.

1. To avoid needless frustration on the home front, be sure spouses have the necessary powers of attorney to manage affairs in the service member's absence. (Note that there are special powers of attorney in addition to general power of attorney.)

2. Service member, make sure your property or vehicles are in good working condition before you leave in order to make life easier while you are gone.

3. Home-front spouse, connect with your in-laws and ask them to share recipes that were meaningful to them when your spouse was growing up. Make up a family recipe book and tell him about it.

4. Home-front spouse, create a special place where your service member can relax after returning home. If he is a hunter, create a lodge atmosphere with fishing and hunting items, magazines, etc. If she loves reading, create a reading corner with a comfy chair, good light, and a well-filled bookcase.

5. Set up a goal list for the house. Send before and after pictures to the service member so he or she can see your progress.

6. Service member, arrange for the lawn to be cared for, the bills to paid, etc., in your absence. Make sure the home-front spouse has a list of numbers she can call when any need arises.

7. Service member, surprise the spouse at home with some maid service, or arrange childcare through a mutual friend so the home-front spouse can get out.

8. Home-front spouse, instead of saving up a honey-do list for your service member, take care of things as they arise the best you can.

9. Service member, if your spouse is ill, email friends near your home and alert them. Ask your church to bring meals to your home or make a run to the pharmacy.

10. Service member, record yourself reading stories to your children. This will not only be a service to your spouse, who can sit back and let you "take over" during part of the bedtime routine, but it will keep you present in your children's daily lives.

PHYSICAL TOUCH

LOVE LANGUAGE #5

Physical Touch

W e have long known that Physical Touch is a way of communicating emotional love. Numerous research projects in the area of child development have made that conclusion: Babies who are held, hugged, and kissed develop a healthier emotional life than those who are left for long periods of time without physical contact.

Physical touch is also a powerful vehicle for communicating marital love. Holding hands, kissing, embracing, and sexual intercourse are all ways of communicating emotional love to one's spouse. For some individuals, physical touch is their primary love language. Without it, they feel unloved. With it, their emotional tank is filled, and they feel secure in the love of their spouse.

THE POWER OF TOUCH

Of the five senses, touching, unlike the other four, is not limited to one localized area of the body. Tiny tactile receptors are located throughout the body. When those receptors are touched or pressed, nerves carry impulses to the brain. The brain interprets these impulses and we perceive the thing that touched us is warm or cold, hard or soft. It causes pain or pleasure. We may also interpret it as loving or hostile.

Some parts of the body are more sensitive than others. The difference is due to the fact that the tiny tactile receptors are not scattered evenly over the body but arranged in clusters. Thus, the tip of the tongue is highly sensitive to touch whereas the back of the shoulders is the least sensitive. The tips of the fingers and the tip of the nose are other extremely sensitive areas. Our purpose, however, is not to understand the neurological basis of the sense of touch but rather its psychological importance.

Physical touch can make or break a relationship. It can communicate hate or love. To the person whose primary love language is physical touch, the message will be far louder than the words "I hate you" or "I love you." A slap in the face is detrimental to any child, but it's devastating to a child whose primary love language is touch. A tender hug communicates love to any child, but it shouts love to the child whose primary love language is physical touch. The same is true of adults.

In marriage, the touch of love may take many forms. Since touch receptors are located throughout the body, lovingly touching your spouse almost anywhere can be an expression of love. That does not mean that all touches are created equal. Some will bring more pleasure to your spouse than others. Your best instructor is your spouse, of course. After all, she is the one you are seeking to love. She knows best what she perceives as a loving touch. Don't insist on touching her in your way and in your time. Learn to speak her love dialect. Your spouse may find some touches uncomfortable or irritating. To insist on continuing those touches is to communicate the opposite of love. It says you are not sensitive to her needs and you care little about her perceptions of what is pleasant. Don't make the mistake of believing the touch that brings pleasure to you will also bring pleasure to her.

Love touches may be explicit and demand your full attention such as in a back rub or sexual foreplay, culminating in intercourse. On the other hand, love touches may be implicit and require only a moment, such as putting your hand on his shoulder as you pour a cup of coffee or rubbing your body against him as you pass in the kitchen. Explicit love touches obviously take more time, not only in actual touching but in developing your understanding of how to communicate love to your spouse this way. If a back massage communicates love loudly to your spouse, then the time, money, and energy you spend in learning to be a good masseur or masseuse will be well invested. If sexual intercourse is your mate's primary dialect, reading about and discussing the art of sexual lovemaking will enhance your expression of love.

Implicit love touches require little time but much thought, especially if physical touch is not your primary love language and if you did not grow up in a "touching family." Sitting close to each other as you watch your favorite television program requires no additional time but may communicate your love loudly. Touching your spouse as you walk through the room where he is sitting takes only a moment. Touching each other when you leave the house and again when you return may involve only a brief kiss or hug but will speak volumes to your spouse.

Janie is one who did not grow up in a "touching" family. "So when Ben returned from deployment, I felt like he was touching me all the time," she said. "It was a rough spot in our marriage. I was pregnant with our first child, we were in Alaska, and I just wanted him to stop touching me. It irritated me, and I thought it was piggish of him. I thought he was always wanting intimacy." She chalked it up to his self-ishness, and considered herself in a one-sided marriage. Ben's response to her resistance was anger and defensiveness.

Then she read *The 5 Love Languages*. "Suddenly, I realized he was pouring love on me when he was touching me, because physical touch is his love language!" Janie said. "So I had a decision to make. Was I going to choose to love him the way he needed to be loved, or was I going to hold on to my personality and refuse to give him that?"

> "When Ben returned from deployment, I felt like he was touching me all the time."

It still doesn't come naturally to Janie, but she deliberately speaks Ben's love language now. "If he comes into the kitchen, I will pat him first or touch his shoulder when I walk by," she said. "Immediately, when I made the change, the perceived clinginess subsided. The more I made an effort to meet his need, the less consuming it was to me."

Once you discover physical touch is the primary love language of your spouse, you are limited only by your imagination on ways to express love. Coming up with new ways and places to touch can be an exciting challenge. If you have not been an "under-the-table toucher," you might find it will add a spark to your dining out. If you are not accustomed to holding hands in public, you may find you can fill your spouse's emotional love tank as you stroll through the parking lot. If you don't normally kiss as soon as you get into the car together, you may find it will greatly enhance your travels. Hugging your spouse before she goes shopping may not only express love, it may bring her home sooner. Try new touches in new places and let your spouse give you feedback on whether he finds it pleasurable or not. Remember, he has the final word. You are learning to speak his language.

Just as important as learning physical touch is your spouse's love language may be the discovery that it is not. This was certainly the case for Vince and his wife, Audrey, who is on active duty. Vince's primary love language is physical touch, but it barely registers on Audrey's list at all. "I often find myself becoming extremely jealous of the guys around her because, of course, in the military there are so many," said Vince. "In the past my heart soured at the thought of the lack of physical touch I received, but now I understand what fills my 'love tank' doesn't fill hers. So when she does go out of her way to offer me some sort of physical touch, it means so much more. Instead of being jealous and wondering how on earth she could not want my physical touch, thinking she must want someone else's, I now get it. I get that she isn't looking toward someone else for that physical touch, she just doesn't require it."

THE BODY IS FOR TOUCHING

Whatever there is of me resides in my body. To touch my body is to touch me. To withdraw from my body is to distance yourself from me emotionally. In our society shaking hands is a way of communicating openness and social closeness to another individual. When on rare occasions one man refuses to shake hands with another, it communicates a message that things are not right in their relationship. All societies have some form of physical touching as a means of social greeting. The average American male may not feel comfortable with the European bear hug and kiss, but in Europe that serves the same function as our shaking hands.

There are appropriate and inappropriate ways to touch members of the opposite sex in every society. The recent attention to sexual harassment has highlighted the inappropriate ways. Within marriage, however, what is appropriate and inappropriate touching is determined by the couple themselves, within certain broad guidelines. Physical abuse is of course deemed inappropriate by society, and social organizations have been formed to help "the battered wife and the battered husband." Clearly our bodies are for touching, but not for abuse.

This age is characterized as the age of sexual openness and freedom. With that freedom, we have demonstrated that the open marriage where both spouses are free to have sexual intimacies with other individuals is fanciful. Those who do not object on moral grounds eventually object on emotional grounds.

Something about our need for intimacy and love does not allow us to give our spouse such freedom. The emotional pain is deep and intimacy evaporates when we are aware our spouse is involved with someone else sexually. Counselors' files are filled with records of husbands and wives who are trying to grapple with the emotional trauma of an unfaithful spouse. That trauma, however, is compounded for the individual whose primary love language is physical touch. That for which he longs so deeply—love expressed by physical touch—is now being given to another. His emotional love tank is not only empty; it has been riddled by an explosion. It will take massive repairs for those emotional needs to be met.

CRISIS AND PHYSICAL TOUCH

Almost instinctively in a time of crisis, we hug one another. Why? Because physical touch is a powerful communicator of love. In a time of crisis, more than anything, we need to feel loved. We cannot always change events, but we can survive if we feel loved.

All marriages will experience crises. The death of parents is inevitable. Automobile accidents cripple and kill thousands each year. Disease is no respecter of persons. Disappointments are a part of life. The most important thing you can do for your mate in a time of crisis is to love him or her. If your spouse's primary love language is physical touch, nothing is more important than holding her as she cries. Your words may mean little, but your physical touch will communicate you care. Crises provide a unique opportunity for expressing love. Your tender touches will be remembered long after the crisis has passed. Your failure to touch may never be forgotten.

"MARRIAGE IS NOT SUPPOSED TO BE THIS WAY"

Since my first visit to West Palm Beach, Florida, many years ago, I have always welcomed invitations to lead marriage seminars in that area. It was on one such occasion that I met Joe and Maria. They were not native to Florida (few are), but they had lived there for ten years and called West Palm Beach home. They had invited me to spend the night, and I knew from experience that such a request usually meant a late-night counseling session.

As the evening proceeded, I thoroughly enjoyed Joe and Maria's company. I found them to be a healthy, happily married couple. I learned why the next day, as they drove me to the airport.

In the early years of their marriage, they had tremendous difficulties. They had grown up in the same community, attended the same church, and graduated from the same high school. They liked the same music, the same sports, the same movies. They seemed to possess all the commonalities that are supposed to assure fewer conflicts in marriage.

They began dating in their senior year in high school. They

attended separate colleges but saw each other frequently, and were married three weeks after he received his degree in business and she a degree in nursing. Two months later, they moved to Florida where Joe had been offered a good job. The first three months were exciting— moving, finding a new apartment, enjoying life together.

They were about six months into the marriage when Maria began to feel that Joe was withdrawing from her. He was working longer hours, and when he was at home, he spent considerable time with the computer. When she finally expressed her feelings that he was avoiding her, Joe told her that he was not avoiding her but simply trying to stay on top of his job. He said that she didn't understand the pressure he was under and how important it was that he did well in his first year on the job. Maria wasn't pleased, but she decided to give him space.

She began to develop friendships with other wives who lived in the apartment complex. Often when she knew Joe was going to work late she would go shopping with one of her friends instead of coming straight home from the hospital where she worked. Sometimes she was not at home when Joe arrived. That annoyed him greatly, and he accused her of being thoughtless and irresponsible. Maria retorted, "Who's irresponsible? You don't even let me know when you'll be home. How can I be here for you when I don't even know when you'll be here? And when you are here, you spend all your time working. You don't need a wife; all you need is a computer!"

To which Joe shot back, "I do need a wife. Don't you understand? That's the whole point. I *do* need a wife."

But Maria did not understand. She was extremely confused. In her search for answers, she went to the public library and checked out several books on marriage. "Marriage is not supposed to be this way," she reasoned. "I have to find an answer to our situation." When Joe went on his laptop, Maria would pick up her book. In fact on many evenings, she read until midnight. On his way to bed, Joe would notice her and make sarcastic comments such as, "If you read that much in college, you would have made straight As." Maria would respond, "I'm not in college. I'm in marriage, and right now, I'd be satisfied with a C." Joe went to bed without so much as a second glance.

At the end of the first year, Maria was desperate. She had mentioned it before, but this time she calmly said to Joe, "I am going to find a marriage counselor. Do you want to go with me?"

But Joe answered, "I don't need a marriage counselor. I don't have time to go to a marriage counselor. We can't afford a marriage counselor."

"Then I'll go alone," said Maria.

"Fine, you're the one who needs counseling anyway."

The conversation was over. Maria felt totally alone, but the next week she made an appointment with a marriage therapist. After three sessions, the counselor called Joe and asked if he would be willing to come in to talk about his perspective on their marriage. Joe agreed, and the process of healing began. Six months later, they left the counselor's office with a new marriage.

I said to them, "What did you learn in counseling that turned your marriage around?"

"In essence, Dr. Chapman," Joe said, "we learned to speak each other's love language. The counselor did not use that term, but as you gave the lecture today, it came to me. My mind raced back to our counseling experience, and I realized that's exactly what happened to us. We finally learned to speak each other's love language."

"So what is your love language, Joe?" I asked.

"Physical touch," he said without hesitation.

"Physical touch for sure," said Maria.

"And yours, Maria?"

"Quality time, Dr. Chapman. That's what I was crying for in those days while he was spending all his time with his job and his computer."

"How did you learn that physical touch was Joe's love language?"

"It took a while," Maria said. "Little by little, it began to come out in the counseling. At first, I don't think he even realized it."

"It's true," Joe said. "I never told her that I wanted to be touched, although I was crying inside for her to reach out and touch me. Maybe with her new job responsibilities she was too tired. I don't know, but I took it personally. I felt that she didn't find me attractive. Then I decided I wouldn't even try because I didn't want to be rejected. So I waited to see how long it would be before she'd initiate a kiss or a touch or sexual intercourse. Once I waited for six weeks before she touched me at all. I couldn't stand it. My withdrawal was to stay away from the pain I felt when I was with her."

Then Maria said, "I had no idea that was what he was feeling. I knew that he was not reaching out to me. We weren't touching all the time like we did when we were dating, but I just assumed that since we were married, that was not as important to him now.

"I did go weeks without touching him. It didn't cross my mind. I was working, taking care of things at home, and trying to stay out of his way. I honestly didn't know what else I could be doing. I didn't understand why he wasn't paying attention to me. The thing is, spending time with me is what made me feel loved and appreciated."

Once Joe and Maria discovered they were not meeting each other's need for love, they began to turn things around. "It was like I had a new husband," she said.

"What amazed me at the seminar today," Joe added, "was the way your lecture on love languages carried me back all these years to that experience. You said in twenty minutes what it took us six months to learn."

"Well," I said, "it's not how fast you learn it but how well you learn it that matters. And obviously, you have learned it well."

Joe is only one of many individuals for whom physical touch is the primary love language. Emotionally, they yearn for their spouse to reach out and touch them physically. Running the hand through the hair, giving a back rub, holding hands, embracing, sexual intercourse—all of those and other "love touches" are the emotional lifeline of the person for whom physical touch is the primary love language.

YOUR TURN

Recall some nonsexual "touching times" that enhanced intimacy between the two of you. What made these times special?

IF YOUR SPOUSE'S LOVE LANGUAGE IS
PHYSICAL TOUCH:

1. As you walk from the car to go shopping, reach out and hold your spouse's hand.

2. While eating together, let your knee or foot drift over and touch your spouse.

3. Walk up to your spouse and say, "Have I told you lately that I love you?" Take her in your arms and hug her while you rub her back and continue. "You're the best!" (Resist the temptation to rush to the bedroom.) Untangle yourself and move on to the next thing.

4. While your spouse is seated, walk up behind her and give her a shoulder massage.

5. When you sit together in church, when the minister calls for prayer, reach over and hold your spouse's hand.

6. When family or friends are visiting, touch your spouse in their presence. A hug, running your hand along his or her arm, putting your arm around him as you stand talking, or simply placing your hand on her shoulder can earn double emotional points. It says, "Even with all these people in our house, I still see you."

7. When your spouse arrives at home, meet him or her one step earlier than usual and give your mate a big welcome home. The point is to vary the routine and enhance even a small "touching experience."

DECODING DEPLOYMENTS WITH PHYSICAL TOUCH

Spouses whose primary love language is physical touch have a difficult time feeling loved during deployments. As with the quality time love language, you may want to increase your efforts on your spouse's secondary love language to help compensate for the deficit he or she feels while apart. Also try the following suggestions.

1. When talking or emailing, say things like, "I wish I could give you a big hug right now," or "If I were with you, I'd give you a back massage to ease some of the tension away."

2. Send pictures of yourself to your spouse at various times while apart. Being able to hold a photo of you becomes very important when holding you in person is impossible.

3. Next time you have your hair cut, save a lock of it and send it to your spouse.

4. Spray some perfume or cologne you normally wear on a card or piece of fabric and send it to your spouse. Wives, be sure to seal your card with a kiss (wear some lipstick when you do this).

5. Trace your hand on paper and mail it to your spouse. He or she can high-five it or lay a hand on it to help feel connected to you.

6. Service members, arrange for a professional massage for your spouse at home. When you're not around, your spouse may go for weeks or months without human touch.

7. Send handwritten letters. Unlike emails, these are tangible pieces of your love that your spouse can touch.

8. Wives at home, if physical touch is your love language, try wearing a special clothing item of your husband's with his cologne placed on it. Marlene said, "I have developed

a tradition of wearing my husband's denim shirt or robe around the house while my husband is away. It feels like he is hugging me when I wear it."

9. More tips for the spouse at home with a physical touch love language: Use a heated blanket on the empty side of the bed, so the bed won't feel cold. Sleep with pillows next to you so you don't get used to having the bed all to yourself. Spray a small amount of your spouse's cologne or perfume on the pillowcase or a sachet you place inside it. Don't replace the empty spot with a child or your child will get used to sleeping there. When your spouse returns home, your child might become fearful or resent him or her for taking his or her space in your bed.

Love Language Scramblers

Some aspects of military life make it especially challenging to interpret and express love. These are love language scramblers, the experiences that can cause mixed signals and tangled lines of communication. Let's look at just a few of these together.

TACTICS TRAINING

Service members are trained to operate in a hierarchy, to take orders and give them, to complete missions. Emotions are irrelevant, and order and obedience are critical for the military to function. But in marriage, the military style of communication can drown out any love language.

"My instructions during my time overseas were simple: do your job and do it now," said Vernon. "I became good at it and enjoyed the time, because my schedule was often predictable and my training sufficient to handle most pressures I faced."

But when he came home and tried the same approach to meet his wife, Jackie's, love language, his mission failed. "At work, when given an order or task, the expectation is that it gets done with little to no delay; this laser focus is necessary in meeting mission assignments. I call this 'running sprints' in relationship building. It took me a long time to understand that relationship building at home is more of a marathon. I needed to slow down on my approach and understand that once a 'task' has been completed at home, there are many other skills that need to be developed, like becoming an empathetic listener, and speaking my wife and children's love language. This for me was a new type of training that would be a lifetime of practice, making mistakes, learning from them, and trying again."

> **In marriage, the military style of communication can drown out any love language.**

Military training, to obey orders without reference to your emotions, can be extremely helpful in speaking your spouse's love language. You don't need warm feelings to do acts of service or words of affirmation. Love begins with an attitude, moves to actions, and often stimulates positive emotions.

WHEN DUTY CALLS

Separations can mask a person's love language simply because of the limits they impose on time spent together. Vernon and Jackie spent most of their engagement on two different continents, and due to a deployment, didn't live together until six months into their marriage. During that time, neither realized their primary love languages were as far apart as their zip codes.

After redeployment, however, it became painfully clear.

"One day Vernon surprised me by coming home from work for lunch," said Jackie. "When I heard the door, I ran to hide in the closet so I could surprise and seduce him. When I jumped out, I was the one in for a surprise. He felt so unloved by the dirty dishes and clutter he saw that he was not 'in the mood.' Vernon turned around and left, confused, angry, and discouraged." Finally, it clicked for Jackie. "Vernon's love language is acts of service, and mine is quality time."

Five children later, the chaos in the household bothered Vernon much more than it bothered Jackie. Though Vernon helped with household duties as much as he could, the chaos that remained left him feeling tired, frustrated, and unwilling to give his wife the time and words she craved. "Sad to say, it was often a relief to go on multiple-day field exercises and deployments to get away from the pressures of daily trying to please my wife," Vernon said.

It's easy to see separations as time off from loving one's spouse the way they want to be loved, but the need for love does not go away. The key is learning to speak each other's language when you are together and then learning to speak it when apart.

Though it has taken years to learn to read him better, Jackie now knows how to speak Vernon's language. "Recently, I stayed up all night to clean the house to demonstrate my love for him, and it changed the entire climate of our home in minutes after he saw what had been done."

Dual military couples have the added challenge of juggling two sets of orders. When Carmen and Garrett were dating, both were active duty with overlapping deployments. Sometimes, they were literally two ships passing in the night, inbound and outbound in the Boston Harbor ship channel. "Those were tough days," said Carmen. "We weren't together long enough to get used to being together, and there was always another deployment hanging over our heads. We fought a lot. Not quite constantly, but we weren't married yet. I often wondered if we'd make it that far."

Eventually they discovered *The 5 Love Languages* and realized that in the limited time they did have together, their love was lost in translation. With short intervals together, each of them standing duty one or more days per week, and under pressure to earn qualifications, there was very little time to fill each other's "love tank." When they were together, they spoke the love language that came most naturally—their own. "But he didn't want a new shirt or something useful for his kitchen," said Carmen. "He wanted me to hold his hand and affirm him. And I would have been happy to know he was thinking of me while he was bouncing around those Caribbean islands, even if all he brought me was a shell necklace. Once we knew how the other 'heard' love, we could be more deliberate in how we spoke love to one another." Carmen and Garrett have now been married for fifteen years.

Learning to speak each other's love language can keep love alive even when we are worlds apart physically.

REINTEGRATION

If a piano player stops playing music for an extended period of time, chances are, when he finally does sit at the piano again, his music may be a bit rusty. His mind will tell his fingers what to do, but they've been out of practice and are bound to hit a few wrong notes. He may need to drill a passage a few times before it feels natural and sounds beautiful again.

In the same way, deployments interrupt a marriage's natural rhythm. When you and your spouse are together again, you may find some skills need to be relearned.

For months, Meredith and Austin looked forward to his home-coming from his first deployment. But the extended honeymoon feeling they had expected did not match reality. "Reintegration was tough," said Austin. "I remember walking in the door and being overwhelmed by all the people who wanted my one-on-one attention; three little ones at my ankles, and my beautiful wife face-to-face. Being apart for so long, and not having so much attention directed at me, I struggled to give her the attention I wanted to give her."

A given amount of time spent together after deployment may not be enough for the spouse who craves quality time, and a suffocating amount for someone else. Patience and grace are key ingredients for easing the transition. "We had to relearn how to speak our love languages in the flesh," said Meredith. "The quality time and physical touch switches we had turned off were a bit harder to just turn back on. But after lots of tears and communication, we arrived at an even better place than before."

If you've had to put your love language on hold for an extended time, you may feel anxious for your empty love tank to be filled, while at the same time, your spouse may also have a depleted love tank and their energy level may be low. The greater the need and expectation, the greater the potential for disappointments, hurts, and offense during reintegration. I encourage couples to give each other permission to ease into things and be as patient with each other as possible during this time. You may both hit a few wrong notes as you switch from playing a solo to playing a duet, but keep at it! Harmony takes practice.

Communicating love for each other during reintegration is absolutely critical. During times apart, both spouses change as individuals. Now it's time to grow as a couple again.

People whose love languages are words of affirmation and

receiving gifts tend to experience more conflict during reintegration, likely because these two languages were well-developed during separation through emails, letters, phone calls, and care packages or gifts. During reintegration, these expressions of love usually drop off—but they don't have to. If you continue to send emails and write letters to each other, or share small gifts, if that's your spouse's love language, both of you will benefit. Those who have gone to support groups during deployment will find continued encouragement from the group valuable during reintegration, as well.

If your spouse's love language is acts of service, use discernment during reintegration as to how to express this. Organizing the service member's gear may not be welcome. Taking over the family schedule may cause resentment to the spouse at home if he or she feels it's an indication of disapproval. I suggest you ask, "Would it be helpful to you if I . . . ?" Spend your energy in something that is meaningful to your spouse.

Janet, an active duty soldier herself, shared: "The hardest thing was my husband and I realizing that if I had to, I could 'do it' on my own. I can work, go to school, raise four children, and take care of a house without him. That's not how we *want* to live, but realizing that someone you love doesn't need you is a hard pill to swallow. We struggled adjusting because my husband felt he missed so much, he wanted to take over everything, which of course made me upset because he was uprooting the schedule that gave me and the children stability and a means of emotional survival. We had to sit down at the drawing board and come up with a new routine that was comfortable for all of us."

COMBAT REDEPLOYMENT

When Ted was deployed to the Middle East, he found that, while driving, his mind drifted to missing his wife and children. "Then I thought, that's going to distract me," he recalled. "I might get ambushed. It might get me killed." So he pushed the memories away and used emotional compartmentalization as a survival technique.

Nine months later, he expected a blissful reunion with his wife. "But when I looked at her, I just felt numb. I didn't feel any love. I had stuffed those emotions so deep inside myself, I did not permit myself to bring them back up. It was an unconscious process."

Three months later, Ted once again felt the love he had for his wife. For others, it may take longer for those feelings to return. The absence of romantic feelings does not mean your love has died or your marriage is doomed. Regardless of what one feels, speaking the right love language can and should still be done. (More on this in chapter 11.)

Emotional withdrawal is common for both spouses. The person who once loved quality conversation and focused attention may now have a difficult time sharing his or her heart. For the service member, part of this is an effort to protect his or her family from the experiences and memories. Bekah felt emotionally single while her husband was engulfed in his own battle with PTSD. "It's simply self-protection," she said. "Learning to live in a two-way marriage again has challenged me in so many ways, even now, seven years after he returned from Iraq. Still today I went back to what I learned about love languages when we 'missed' each other again during 'date day' (we no longer do date nights due to crowds). He still has a wounded heart that needs affirmation more than ever. We are growing, learning to communicate again, and as always, it's a process. We are imperfect in so many ways, but our heart is for the other to know they are loved."

When Hunter's post-traumatic stress was at its worst, physical touch became the most important thing to him. "It was his only connection to someone, and the only one he would connect with for physical touch was me," said his wife, Kara. Hunter experienced other bodily injuries, as well, which forced him to scale back on the acts of service he could do for Kara. With her primary love language not being spoken, Kara grew resentful and burned out. She learned to receive love from Hunter in different ways, but also looked for resources for caregivers for much-needed support.

Gail's husband, whose love language had been acts of service, needed something else upon redeployment. "After his deployment he had nightmares. We live on a large training base in Europe, so we hear a lot of loud 'booms' throughout the night and those really got to him for a while. I had to wake him up a lot. I could tell he was embarrassed about it, so I had to repeatedly tell him it didn't make him weak. I had to tell him all the time how amazing he is for going through what he did. At that time, he needed words of affirmation from me more than anything."

Rick saw three of his team killed on the same day. At the time of the event, Rick gutted through his pain and continued his job. However, two months later he started having flashbacks and nightmares. When he arrived home from deployment, his wife, Debbie, knew he was not functioning normally. She insisted he see a medical doctor. He was diagnosed with PTSD. Medication and counseling was the preferred treatment. Six months later, Rick was greatly improved.

He said, "These were the hardest months of my life. I'm sure I confused Debbie. My moods changed so quickly. One day I wanted her to hug me, but the next day I pushed her away. (My love language is physical touch.) I'm just glad she did not give up but kept speaking my love language. I love her more for putting up with my erratic behavior."

When PTSD or traumatic brain injury is present, the love languages may shift or require adaptations, such as Bekah and her husband avoiding crowds when they spend quality time together. PTSD is a topic worthy of more space than we have here in this chapter. There are many resources for veterans and spouses dealing with combat trauma. I recommend my favorites at 5lovelanguages.com/militaryedition.

Discovering Your Primary Love Language

Discovering the primary love language of your spouse is essential if you are to keep their emotional love tank full. But first, let's make sure you know your own love language. Having heard the five emotional love languages,

>Words of Affirmation
>Quality Time
>Receiving Gifts
>Acts of Service
>Physical Touch,

some individuals will know instantaneously their own primary love language and that of their spouse. For others, it will not be that easy. Some are like Marcus, whom I met at Ft. Bragg. After hearing the five emotional love languages, he said to me, "I don't know. Two of those are just about equal for me."

"Which two?" I inquired.

"'Physical touch' and 'words of affirmation,'" he responded.

"By 'physical touch,' what do you mean?"

"Well, mainly sex," Marcus replied.

I probed a little further, asking, "Do you enjoy your wife running her hands through your hair, or giving you a back rub, or holding hands, or kissing and hugging you at times when you are not having sexual intercourse?"

"Those things are fine," said Marcus. "I'm not going to turn them down, but the main thing is sexual intercourse. That's when I know that she really loves me."

Leaving the subject of physical touch for a moment, I turned to affirming words and asked, "When you say that 'words of affirmation' are also important, what kinds of statements do you find most helpful?"

"Almost anything if it's positive," Marcus replied. "When she tells me how good I look, how smart I am, what a hard worker I am, when she expresses appreciation for the things I do around the house, when she makes positive comments about my taking time with the children, when she tells me she loves me—all of those things really mean a lot to me."

"Let me ask you this. If you were having quality sexual intercourse as often as you desire, but Alicia was giving you negative words, making critical remarks, sometimes putting you down in front of others, do you think you would feel loved by her?"

"I don't think so," he replied. "I would feel betrayed. I think I would be depressed."

"Marcus," I said, "I think we have just discovered your primary love language is 'words of affirmation.' Sexual intercourse is extremely important to you and to your sense of intimacy with Alicia, but her words of affirmation are more important to you emotionally. If she were verbally critical of you all the time and put you down in front of other people, the time may come when you would no longer desire to have sexual intercourse with her because she would be a source of deep pain to you."

Marcus had made the mistake common to many men: assuming Physical Touch is their primary love language because they desire sexual intercourse so intensely. For the male, sexual desire is physically based. That is, the desire for sexual intercourse is stimulated by the buildup of sperm cells and seminal fluid in the seminal vesicles. When the seminal vesicles are full, there is a physical push for release. Thus, the male's desire for sexual intercourse has a physical root.

For the female, sexual desire is far more influenced by her emotions. If she feels loved and admired and appreciated by her husband, then she has a desire to be physically intimate with him. But without the emotional closeness, she may have little physical desire. Her biological sexual drive is closely tied to her emotional need for love.

Because the male is physically pushed to have sexual release on a somewhat regular basis, he may automatically assume that is his primary love language. But if he does not enjoy physical touch at other times and in nonsexual ways, it may not be his love language at all. Sexual desire is quite different from his emotional need to feel loved. That doesn't mean sexual intercourse is unimportant to him—it's extremely important—but sexual intercourse alone will not meet his need to feel loved. His wife must speak his primary emotional love language as well.

When, in fact, his wife speaks his primary love language and his emotional love tank is full, and he speaks her primary love language and her emotional tank is full, the sexual aspect of their relationship will take care of itself. Most sexual problems in marriage have little to do with physical technique but everything to do with meeting emotional needs.

After further conversation and reflection, Marcus said, "You know, I think you're right. 'Words of Affirmation' is definitely my primary love language. When she has been cutting and critical of me verbally, I tend to withdraw from her sexually and fantasize about other women. But when she tells me how much she appreciates me and admires me, my natural sexual desires are turned toward her." Marcus had made a significant discovery in our brief conversation.

HOW DO YOU KNOW?

What is your primary love language? What makes you feel most loved by your spouse? What do you desire above all else? If the answer to those questions does not leap to your mind immediately, perhaps it will help to look at the negative use of love languages. What does your spouse do or say or fail to do or say that hurts you deeply? If, for example, your deepest pain is the critical, judgmental words of your spouse, then perhaps your love language is "Words of Affirmation." If your primary love language is used negatively by your spouse—that is, he does the opposite—it will hurt you more deeply than it would hurt someone else because not only is he neglecting to speak your primary love language, he is actually using that language as a knife to your heart.

I remember Mary in Ohio, who said, "Dr. Chapman, what hurts me most is that Ron never lifts a hand to help me around the house. He watches television while I do all the work. I don't understand how he could do that if he really loved me." Mary's deepest hurt, mainly that Ron did not help her do things around the house, was the clue to her primary love language—"Acts of Service." If it grieves you deeply that your spouse seldom gives you a gift for any occasion, then perhaps your primary love language is "Receiving Gifts." If your deepest hurt is that your spouse seldom gives you quality time, then that is your primary love language.

Another approach to discovering your primary love language is to look back over your marriage and ask, "What have I most often requested of my spouse?" Whatever you have most requested is probably in keeping with your primary love language. Those requests have probably been interpreted by your spouse as nagging. They have been, in fact, your efforts to secure emotional love from your spouse.

You can also examine what you do or say to express love to your spouse. Chances are what you are doing for her is what you wish she would do for you. If you are constantly doing "Acts of Service" for your spouse, perhaps (although not always) that is your love language. If "Words of Affirmation" speak love to you, chances are you will use them in speaking love to your spouse. Thus, you may discover your own language by asking, "How do I consciously express my love to my spouse?"

But remember, that approach is only a possible clue to your love language; it's not an absolute indicator. For example, the husband who learned from his father to express love to his wife by giving her nice gifts expresses his love to his wife by doing what his father did, yet "Receiving Gifts" is not his primary love language. He is simply doing what he was trained to do by his father.

I have suggested three ways to discover your own primary love language:

1. What does your spouse do or fail to do that hurts you most deeply? The opposite of what hurts you most is probably your love language.

2. What have you most often requested of your spouse? The thing you have most often requested is likely the thing that would make you feel most loved.

3. In what way do you regularly express love to your spouse? Your method of expressing love may be an indication that that would also make you feel loved.

Using those three approaches will probably enable you to determine your primary love language. If two languages seem to be equal for you, that is, both speak loudly to you, then perhaps you are bilingual. If so, you make it easier on your spouse. Now he or she has two choices, either of which will strongly communicate love to you.

You may also wish to take The 5 Love Languages Profile found on pages 205–15. Discuss the results with your spouse.

Two kinds of people may have difficulty discovering their primary love language. The first is the individual whose emotional love tank has been full for a long time. Her spouse has expressed love in many ways, and she is not certain which of those ways makes her feel most loved. She simply knows she is loved. The second is the individual whose love tank has been empty for so long he doesn't remember what makes him feel loved. In either case, go back to the experience of falling in love and ask yourself, "What did I like about my spouse in those days? What did he do or say that made me desire to be with him?" If you can conjure up those memories, it will give you some idea of your primary love language. Another approach would be to ask yourself, "What would be an ideal spouse to me? If I could have the perfect mate, what would she be like?" Your picture of a perfect mate should give you some idea of your primary love language.

Having said all of that, let me suggest you spend some time writing down what you think is your primary love language. Then list the other four in order of importance. Also write down what you think is the primary love language of your spouse. You may also list the other four in order of importance if you wish. Sit down with your spouse and discuss what you guessed to be his/her primary love language. Then tell each other what you consider to be your own primary love language.

Once you have shared that information, I suggest you play the following game three times a week for three weeks. The game is called "Tank Check," and it's played like this. When you come home, one of you says to the other, "On a scale of 0 to 10, how is your love tank tonight?" Zero means empty, and 10 means "I am full of love and can't handle any more." You give a reading on your emotional love tank—10, 9, 8, 7, 6, 5, 4, 3, 2, 1, or 0, indicating how full it is. Your spouse says, "What could I do to help fill it?"

Then you make a suggestion—something you would like your spouse to do or say that evening. To the best of his ability, he will respond to your request. Then repeat the process, reversing the roles, so that you each have the opportunity to do a reading on your love tank and to make a suggestion toward filling it. If you play the game for three weeks, you will be hooked on it, and it can be a playful way of stimulating love expressions in your marriage.

One military husband said to me, "I don't like that love tank game. I played it with my wife. I came home and said to her, 'On a scale of zero to ten, how's your love tank tonight?' She said, 'About seven.' I asked, 'What could I do to help fill it?' She said, 'The greatest thing you could do for me tonight is to do the laundry.' I said, 'Love and laundry? I don't get it.'"

I said, "That's the problem. Perhaps you don't understand your wife's love language. What's your primary love language?"

Without hesitation he said, "Physical touch, and especially the sexual part of the marriage."

"Listen to me carefully," I said. "The love you feel when your wife expresses love by physical touch is the same love your wife feels when you do the laundry."

"Bring on the laundry," he shouted. "I'll wash the clothes every night if it makes her feel that good."

Incidentally, if you have still not discovered your primary love language, keep records on the tank check game. When your spouse says, "What could I do to help fill your tank?" your suggestions will likely cluster around your primary love language. You may request things from all five love languages, but you will have more requests centering on your primary love language.

Perhaps some of you are saying in your minds what one military couple said to me. "Dr. Chapman, all that sounds fine and wonderful, but what if the love language of your spouse is something that just doesn't come naturally for you?"

I'll discuss my answer in chapter 11.

YOUR TURN

Do you think by now you have a good sense of what your spouse's love language is? How about them for you? What more could you do to explore this?

If your love tank is completely empty or very full, whether you know your love language or not, play the "Tank Check" game over the next month. Ask for a reading from 0 to 10 three evenings a week, and then take the suggestions of your spouse to raise that number for him/her. If your spouse is at a "ten" consistently you can pat yourself on the back—but don't stop loving.

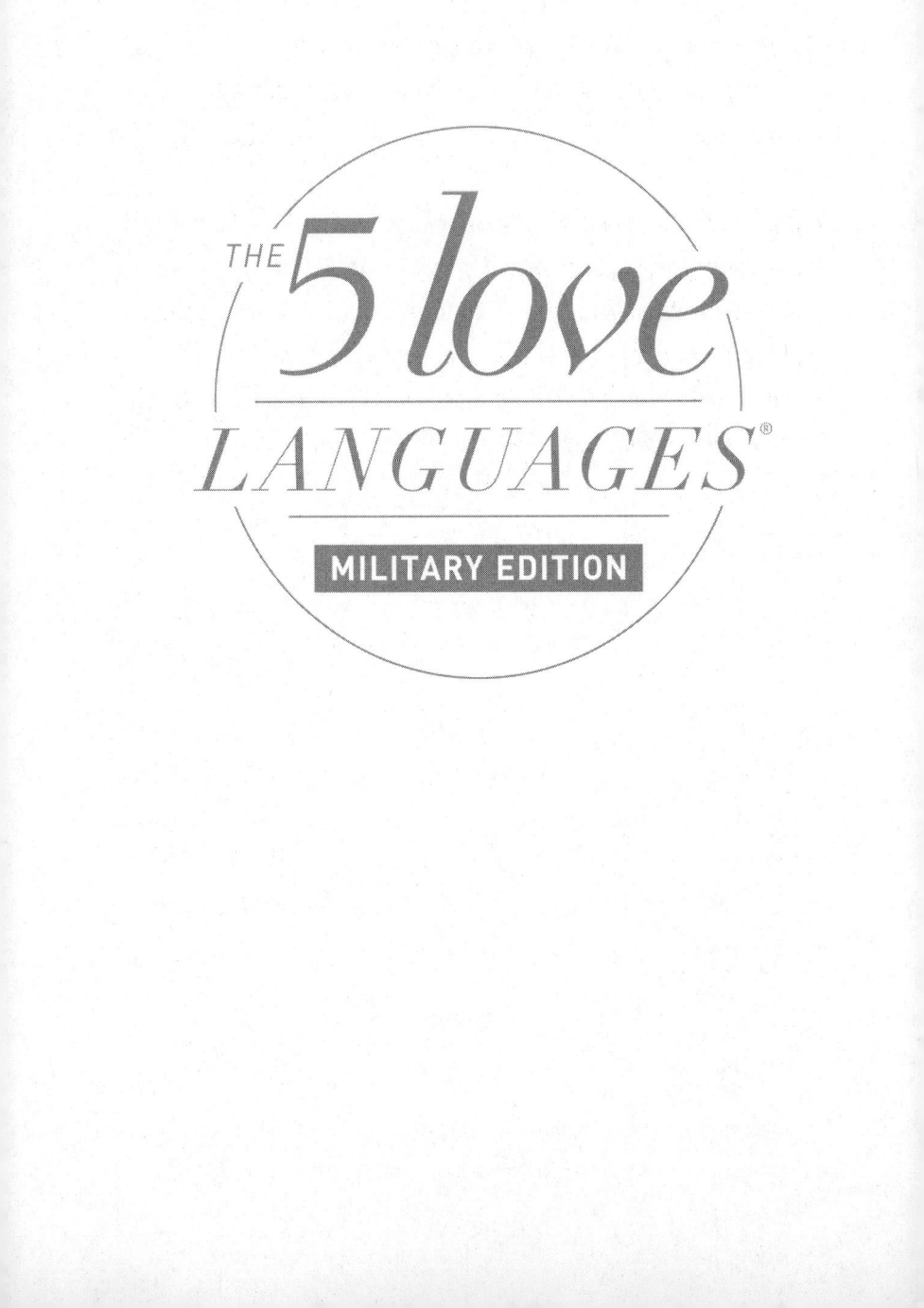

Love Is a Choice

H ow can we speak each other's love language when we are full of hurt, anger, and resentment over past failures? The answer to that question lies in the essential nature of our humanity. We are creatures of choice. That means that we have the capacity to make poor choices, which all of us have done. We have spoken critical words, and we have done hurtful things. We are not proud of those choices, although they may have seemed justified at the moment. Poor choices in the past don't mean we must make them in the future. Instead we can say, "I'm sorry. I know I have hurt you, but I would like to make the future different. I would like to love you in your language. I would like to meet your needs." I have seen marriages rescued from the brink of divorce when couples make the choice to love.

Love doesn't erase the past, but it makes the future different. When we choose active expressions of love in the primary love language of our spouse, we create an emotional climate where we can deal with our past conflicts and failures.

"I JUST DON'T LOVE HER ANYMORE"

Brent was in my office, stone-faced and seemingly unfeeling. He had come not by his own initiative but at my request. A week earlier his wife, Becky, had been sitting in the same chair, weeping uncontrollably. Between her outbursts of tears, she managed to verbalize that Brent had told her he no longer loved her and he was leaving. She was devastated.

When she regained her composure, she said, "We have both worked so hard the last two or three years. I knew we were not spending as much time together as we used to, but I thought we were working for a common goal. I cannot believe what he is saying. He has always been such a kind and caring person. He is such a good father to our children." She continued, "How could he do this to us?"

I listened as she described their twelve years of marriage. It was a story I had heard many times before. They had an exciting courtship, got married at the height of the "in love" experience, had the typical adjustments in the early days of marriage, and pursued the American dream. In due time, they came down off the emotional high of the "in love" experience but did not learn to speak each other's love language sufficiently. She had lived with a love tank only half full for the last several years, but she had received enough expressions of love to make her think everything was okay. However, his love tank was empty.

I told Becky I would see if Brent would talk with me. I told Brent on the phone, "As you know, Becky came to see me and told me about her struggle with what is happening in the marriage. I want to help her, but in order to do so, I need to know what you are thinking."

He agreed readily, and now he sat in my office. His outward appearance was in stark contrast to Becky's. She had been weeping uncontrollably, but he was stoic. I had the impression, however, his weeping had taken place weeks or perhaps months ago, and it had been an inward weeping. The story Brent told confirmed my hunch.

"I just don't love her anymore," he said. "I haven't loved her for a long time. I don't want to hurt her, but we are not close. Our relationship has become empty. I don't enjoy being with her anymore. I don't know what happened. I wish it were different, but I don't have any feelings for her."

Brent was thinking and feeling what hundreds of thousands of husbands have thought and felt through the years. It's the "I don't love her anymore" mindset that gives men the emotional freedom to seek love with someone else. The same is true for wives who use the same excuse.

I sympathized with Brent, for I have been there. Thousands of husbands and wives have been there—emotionally empty, wanting to do the right thing, not wanting to hurt anyone, but being pushed by their emotional needs to seek love outside the marriage. Fortunately, I had discovered in the earlier years of my own marriage the difference between the "in love" experience and the "emotional need" to feel loved. Most in our society have not yet learned that difference.

The "in love" experience we discussed in chapter 3 is on the level of instinct. It's not premeditated; it simply happens in the normal context of male-female relationships. It can be fostered or quenched, but it does not arise by conscious choice. It is short-lived (usually two years or less) and seems to serve for humankind the same function as the mating call of the Canada goose.

The "in love" experience temporarily meets one's emotional need for love. It gives us the feeling someone cares, someone admires us and appreciates us. Our emotions soar with the thought that another person sees us as number one, that he or she is willing to devote time and energies exclusively to our relationship. For a brief period, however long it lasts, our emotional need for love is met. Our tank is full; we can conquer the world. Nothing is impossible. For many individuals, it's the first time they have ever lived with a full emotional tank, and it's euphoric.

In time, however, we come down from that natural high back to the real world. If our spouse has learned to speak our primary love language, our need for love will continue to be satisfied. If, on the other hand, he or she does not speak our love language, our tank will slowly drain, and we will no longer feel loved. Meeting that need in one's spouse is definitely a choice. If I learn the emotional love language of my spouse and speak it frequently, she will continue to feel loved. When she comes down from the obsession of the "in love" experience, she will hardly even miss it because her emotional love tank will continue to be filled. However, if I have not learned her primary love language or have chosen not to speak it, when she descends from the emotional high, she will have the natural yearnings of unmet emotional need. After some years of living with an empty love tank, she will likely "fall in love" with someone else, and the cycle will begin again.

Meeting my wife's need for love is a choice I make each day. If I know her primary love language and choose to speak it, her deepest emotional need will be met and she will feel secure in my love. If she does the same for me, my emotional needs are met and both of us live with a full tank. In a state of emotional contentment, both of us will give our creative energies to many wholesome projects outside the marriage while we continue to keep our marriage exciting and growing.

With all of that in my mind, I looked back at the deadpan face of Brent and wondered if I could help him. I knew in my heart he was probably already involved with another "in love" experience. I wondered if it was in the beginning stages or at its height. Few men suffering from an empty emotional love tank leave their marriage until they have prospects of meeting that need somewhere else.

Brent was honest and revealed he had been in love with someone else for several months. He had hoped the feelings would go away and he could work things out with his wife. But things at home had gotten worse, and his love for the other woman had increased. He could not imagine living without his new lover.

I sympathized with Brent in his dilemma. He sincerely did not want to hurt his wife or his children, but at the same time, he felt he deserved a life of happiness. I told him the dismal statistics on second marriages. He was surprised to hear that but was certain he would beat the odds. I told him about the research on the effects of divorce on children, but he was convinced he would continue to be a good father to his children and they would get over the trauma of the divorce. I talked to Brent about the issues in this book and explained the difference between the experience of falling in love and the deep emotional need to feel loved. I explained the five love languages and challenged him to give his marriage another chance. All the while, I knew my intellectual and reasoned approach to marriage compared to the emotional high he was experiencing was like pitting a BB gun against an automatic weapon. He expressed appreciation for my concern and asked that I do everything possible to help Becky. But he assured me he saw no hope for the marriage.

One month later, I received a call from Brent. He indicated he would like to talk with me again. This time when he entered my office, he was noticeably disturbed. He was not the calm, cool man I had seen before. His lover had begun to come down off the emotional high, and she was observing things in Brent she did not like. She was withdrawing from the relationship, and he was crushed. Tears came to his eyes as he told me how much she meant to him and how unbearable it was to experience her rejection.

I listened for an hour before Brent ever asked for my advice. I told him how sympathetic I was to his pain and indicated that what he was experiencing was the natural emotional grief from a loss, and that the grief would not go away overnight. I explained, however, that the experience was inevitable. I reminded him of the temporary nature of the "in love" experience, that sooner or later, we always come down from the high to the real world. Some fall out of love before they get married; others, after they get married. He agreed it was better now than later.

After a while, I suggested that perhaps the crisis was a good time for him and his wife to get some marriage counseling. I reminded him that true, long-lasting emotional love is a choice and that emotional love could be reborn in his marriage if he and his wife learned to love each other in the right love languages. He agreed to marriage counseling, and nine months later, Brent and Becky left my office with a reborn marriage. When I saw Brent three years later, he told me what a wonderful marriage he had and thanked me for helping him at a crucial time in his life. He told me the grief over losing the other lover had been gone for more than two years. He smiled and said, "My tank has never been so full, and Becky is the happiest woman you are ever going to meet."

Fortunately Brent was the benefactor of what I call the disequilibrium of the "in love" experience. That is, almost never do two people fall in love on the same day, and almost never do they fall out of love on the same day. You don't have to be a social scientist to discover that truth. Just listen to country music. Brent's lover happened to have fallen out of love at an opportune time.

ACTIONS AND EMOTIONS

During the nine months I counseled Brent and Becky, we worked through numerous conflicts they had never resolved before. But the key to the rebirth of their marriage was discovering each other's primary love language and choosing to speak it frequently.

"What if the love language of your spouse is something that doesn't come naturally for you?" I am often asked this question at my marriage seminars, and my answer is, "So?"

My wife's love language is "Acts of Service." One of the things I do for her regularly as an act of love is to vacuum the floors. Do you think vacuuming floors comes naturally for me? My mother used to make me vacuum. All through junior high and high school, I couldn't go play ball on Saturday until I finished vacuuming the entire house. In those days, I said to myself, "When I get out of here, one thing I am not going to do: I am not going to vacuum houses. I'll get myself a wife to do that."

But I vacuum our house now, and I vacuum it regularly. And there is only one reason I vacuum our house. Love. You couldn't pay me enough to vacuum a house, but I do it for love. You see, when an action doesn't come naturally to you, it's a greater expression of love. My wife knows that when I vacuum the house, it's nothing but 100 percent pure, unadulterated love, and I get credit for the whole thing!

Someone says, "But, Dr. Chapman, that's different. I know my spouse's love language is physical touch, and I am not a toucher. I never saw my mother and father hug each other. They never hugged me. I am just not a toucher. What am I going to do?"

Do you have two hands? Can you put them together? Now, imagine you have your spouse in the middle and pull him/her toward you. I'll bet if you hug your spouse three thousand times, it will begin to feel more comfortable. But ultimately, comfort is not the issue. We are talking about love, and love is something you do for someone else, not something you do for yourself. Most of us do many things each day that do not come "naturally" for us. For some of us, that is getting out of bed in the morning. We go against our feelings and get out of bed. Why? Because we believe there is something worthwhile to do that day. And normally, before the day is over, we feel good about having gotten up. Our actions preceded our emotions.

The same is true with love. We discover the primary love language of our spouse, and we choose to speak it whether or not it is natural for us. We are not claiming to have warm, excited feelings. We are simply choosing to do it for his or her benefit. We want to meet our spouse's emotional need, and we reach out to speak his love language. In so doing, his emotional love tank is filled and chances are he will reciprocate and speak our language. When he does, our emotions return, and our love tank begins to fill.

Love is a choice. And either partner can start the process today.

YOUR TURN

A key thought here is the idea of speaking our mate's love language whether or not it is natural for us. Why is this so fundamental to a healthy marriage?

Loving the Unlovely

It was a beautiful September Saturday. My wife and I were strolling through Reynolda Gardens on the Wake Forest University campus, enjoying the flora, some of which had been imported from around the world. We had just passed the rose garden when I noticed Ann, a woman who had begun counseling two weeks earlier, approaching us. She appeared to be in deep thought. When I greeted her, she was startled but looked up and smiled. I introduced her to Karolyn, and we exchanged pleasantries. Then, without any lead-in, she asked me one of the most profound questions I have ever heard: "Dr. Chapman, is it possible to love someone whom you hate?"

I knew the question was born of deep hurt and deserved a thoughtful answer. I knew I would be seeing her the following week for another counseling appointment, so I said, "Ann, that is one of the most thought-provoking questions I have ever heard. Why don't we discuss that next week?" She agreed, and Karolyn and I continued our stroll. But Ann's question did not go away. Later, as we drove home, Karolyn and I discussed it. We reflected on the early days of our own marriage and remembered that we had often experienced feelings of hate. Our condemning words to each other had brought us hurt and, on the heels of hurt, anger. And anger held inside becomes hate.

What made the difference for us? We both knew it was the choice to love. We had realized that if we continued our pattern of demanding and condemning, we would destroy our marriage. Fortunately over a period of about a year, we had learned how to discuss our differences without condemning each other, how to make decisions without destroying our unity, how to give constructive suggestions without being demanding, and eventually how to speak each other's primary love language. Our choice to love was made in the midst of negative feelings toward each other. When we started speaking each other's primary love language, the feelings of anger and hate abated.

Our situation, however, was different from Ann's. Karolyn and I had both been open to learning and growing. I knew Ann's husband was not. She had told me the previous week she had begged him to go for counseling. She had pleaded for him to read a book or listen to a speaker on marriage, but he had refused all her efforts toward growth. According to her, his attitude was, "I don't have any problems. You are the one with the problems." In his mind he was right, she was wrong— it was as simple as that. Her feelings of love for him had been killed through the years by his constant criticism and condemnation. After ten years of marriage, her emotional energy was depleted and her self-esteem almost destroyed. Was there hope for Ann's marriage? Could she love an unlovely husband? Would he ever respond in love to her?

LOVE'S GREATEST CHALLENGE

I knew Ann was a deeply religious person and she attended church regularly. I surmised that perhaps her only hope for marital survival was in her faith. The next day, with Ann in mind, I began to read Luke's account of the life of Christ. I have always admired Luke's writing because he was a physician who gave attention to details and in the first century wrote an orderly account of the teachings and lifestyle of Jesus of Nazareth. In what many have called Jesus' greatest sermon, I read the following words, which I call love's greatest challenge.

> *"But to you who are listening I say: Love your enemies, do good to those who hate you, bless those who curse you, pray for those who mistreat you. . . . Do to others as you would have them do to you. If you love those who love you, what credit is that to you? Even sinners love those who love them."*[4]

It seemed to me that that profound challenge, written almost two thousand years ago, might be the direction that Ann was looking for, but could she do it? Could anyone do it? Is it possible to love a spouse who has become your enemy? Is it possible to love one who has cursed you, mistreated you, and expressed feelings of contempt and hate for you? And if she could, would there be any payback? Would her husband ever change and begin to express love and care for her? I was astounded by this further word from Jesus' sermon: "Give, and it will be given to you. A good measure, pressed down, shaken together and running over, will be poured into your lap. For with the measure you use, it will be measured to you."[5]

Could that principle of loving an unlovely person possibly work in a marriage as far gone as Ann's? I decided to do an experiment. I would take as my hypothesis that if Ann could learn her husband's primary love language and speak it for a period of time so that his emotional need for love was met, eventually he would reciprocate and begin to express love to her. I wondered, *Would it work?*

I met with Ann the next week and listened again as she reviewed the hurts in her marriage. At the end of her synopsis, she repeated the question she had asked in Reynolda Gardens. This time she put it in the form of a statement: "Dr. Chapman, I just don't know if I can ever love him again after all he has done to me."

"Have you talked about your situation with any of your friends?" I asked.

"With two of my closest friends," she said, "and a little bit with some other people."

"And what was their response?"

"'Get out,' she said. "They all tell me to get out, that he will never change, and that I am simply prolonging the agony. But I just can't bring myself to do that. Maybe I should, but I just can't believe that's the right thing to do."

"It seems to me that you are torn between your religious and moral beliefs that tell you it is wrong to get out of the marriage, and your emotional pain, which tells you that getting out is the only way to survive," I said.

"That's exactly right, Dr. Chapman. I don't know what to do."

"I am deeply sympathetic with your struggle," I continued. "You are in a very difficult situation. I wish I could offer you an easy answer. Unfortunately, I can't. Both of the alternatives you mentioned, getting out or staying in, will likely bring you a great deal of pain. Before you make that decision, I do have one idea. I am not sure it will work, but I'd like you to try it. I know from what you have told me your religious faith is important to you and that you have a great deal of respect for the teachings of Jesus."

She nodded affirmingly. I continued, "I want to read something Jesus once said that has some application to your marriage." I read slowly and deliberately.

> *"But to you who are listening I say: Love your enemies, do good to those who hate you, bless those who curse you, pray for those who mistreat you. . . . Do to others as you would have them do to you. If you love those who love you, what credit is that to you? Even sinners love those who love them."*[6]

"Does that sound like your husband? Has he treated you as an enemy rather than as a friend?"

She nodded.

"Has he ever cursed you?" I asked.

"Many times."

"Has he ever mistreated you?"

"Often."

"And has he told you he hates you?"

"Yes."

THE SIX-MONTH EXPERIMENT

"Ann, if you are willing, I would like to do an experiment. I would like to see what would happen if we apply this principle to your marriage. Let me explain what I mean." I went on to explain to Ann the concept of the emotional tank and the fact that when the tank is low, as hers was, we have no love feelings toward our spouse but simply experience emptiness and pain. Since love is such a deep emotional need, the lack of it is perhaps our deepest emotional pain. I told her if we could learn to speak each other's primary love language, that emotional need could be met and positive feelings could grow again.

"Does that make sense to you?" I inquired.

"Dr. Chapman, you have just described my life. I have never seen it so clearly before. We were in love before we got married, but not long after our marriage, we came down off the high and we never learned to speak each other's love language. My tank has been empty for years, and I am sure his has also. Dr. Chapman, if I had understood this concept earlier, maybe none of this would have happened."

"We can't go back, Ann," I said. "All we can do is try to make the future different. I would like to propose a six-month experiment."

"I'll try anything," Ann said.

I liked her positive spirit, but I wasn't sure whether she understood how difficult the experiment would be.

"Let's begin by stating our objective," I said. "If in six months you could have your fondest wish, what would it be?"

Ann sat in silence for some time. Then thoughtfully she said, "I would like to see Glenn loving me again and expressing it by spending time with me. I would like to see us doing things together, going places together. I would like to feel he is interested in my world. I would like to see us talking when we go out to eat. I'd like him to listen to me. I'd like to feel he values my ideas. I would like to see us taking trips together and having fun again. I would like to know he values our marriage more than anything."

Ann paused and then continued. "For my part, I would like to have warm, positive feelings toward him again. I would like to gain respect for him again. I would like to be proud of him. Right now, I don't have those feelings."

I was writing as Ann was speaking. When she finished, I read aloud what she had said. "That sounds like a pretty lofty objective," I said, "but is that really what you want, Ann?"

"Right now, that sounds like an impossible objective," Ann replied, "but more than anything, that's what I would like to see."

"Then let's agree," I said, "that this will be our objective. In six months, we want to see you and Glenn having this kind of love relationship.

"Now, let me suggest an experiment. Let's hypothesize that if you could speak Glenn's primary love language consistently for a six-month period, somewhere along the line his emotional need for love would begin to be met; and as his emotional tank filled, he would begin to reciprocate love to you. That hypothesis is built upon the idea that the emotional need for love is our deepest emotional need; and when that need is being met, we tend to respond positively to the person who is meeting it."

I continued, "You understand that this places all the initiative in your hands. Glenn is not trying to work on this marriage. You are. This hypothesis says if you can channel your energies in the right direction, there is a good possibility Glenn will eventually reciprocate." I read the other portion of Jesus' sermon recorded by Luke, the physician: "Give, and it will be given to you. A good measure, pressed down, shaken together and running over, will be poured into your lap. For with the measure you use, it will be measured to you."[7]

"As I understand that, Jesus is stating a principle, not a way to manipulate people. Generally speaking, if we are kind and loving toward people, they will tend to be kind and loving toward us. That does not mean we can make a person kind by being kind to him. We are independent agents. Thus, we can spurn love and walk away from love or even spit into the face of love. There is no guarantee Glenn will respond to your acts of love. We can only say there is a good possibility he will do so."

After we agreed on the plan, I said to Ann, "Now let's discuss your and Glenn's primary love languages. I'm assuming from what you have told me already that quality time may be your primary love language. What do you think?"

"I think so, Dr. Chapman. In the early days when we spent time together and Glenn listened to me, we spent long hours talking together, doing things together. I really felt loved. More than anything, I wish that part of our marriage could return. When we spend time together, I feel like he really cares, but when he's always doing other things, I feel like his work and other pursuits are more important than our relationship."

"And what do you think Glenn's primary love language is?" I inquired.

"I think it's physical touch and especially the sexual part of the marriage. I know that when I felt more loved by him and we were more sexually active, he had a different attitude. I think that's his primary love language."

"Does he ever complain about the way you talk to him?"

"Well, he says I nag him all the time. He also says I don't support him, that I'm always against his ideas."

"Then let's assume," I said, "that physical touch is his primary love language and words of affirmation is his secondary love language. The reason I suggest the second is that if he complains about negative words, apparently positive words would be meaningful to him.

"Now, let me suggest a plan. What if you go home and say to Glenn, 'I've been thinking about us and I've decided that I would like to be a better wife to you. So if you have any suggestions as to how I could be a better wife, I want you to know I am open to them. You can tell me now or you can think about it first, but I would really like to work on being a better wife.' Whatever his response, negative or positive, simply accept it as information. That initial statement lets him know that something different is about to happen in your relationship.

"Then based upon your guess that his primary love language is physical touch and my suggestion that his secondary love language may be words of affirmation, focus your attention on those two areas for one month.

"If Glenn comes back with a suggestion as to how you might be a better wife, accept that information and work it into your plan. Look for positive things in Glenn's life and give him verbal affirmation about those things. In the meantime, stop all verbal complaints. If you want to complain about something, write it down in your personal note-book rather than saying anything about it to Glenn this month.

"Begin taking more initiative in physical touch and sexual involve-ment. Surprise him by being aggressive, not simply responding to his advances. Set a goal to have sexual intercourse at least once a week the first two weeks and twice a week the following two weeks." Ann had told me she and Glenn had had sexual intercourse only once or twice in the past six months. I figured this plan would get things off dead center rather quickly.

"Oh, Dr. Chapman, this is going to be difficult," Ann said. "I have found it hard to be sexually responsive to him when he ignores me all the time. I have felt used rather than loved in our sexual encounters. He acts as though I am totally unimportant all the rest of the time and then wants to jump in bed and use my body. I have resented that, and

I guess that's why we have not had sex very often in the last few years."

"Your response has been natural and normal," I assured Ann. "For most wives, the desire to be sexually intimate with their husbands grows out of a sense of being loved by their husbands. If they feel loved, then they desire sexual intimacy. If they do not feel loved, they likely feel used in the sexual context. That is why loving someone who is not loving you is extremely difficult. It goes against our natural tendencies. You will probably have to rely heavily upon your faith in God in order to do this. Perhaps it will help if you read again Jesus' sermon on loving your enemies, loving those who hate you, loving those who use you. And then ask God to help you practice the teachings of Jesus."

I could tell Ann was following what I was saying. Her eyes were bright and full of questions.

"But, Dr. Chapman, isn't it being hypocritical to express love sexually when you have such negative feelings toward the person?"

"Perhaps it would be helpful for us to distinguish between love as a feeling and love as an action," I said. "If you claim to have feelings you do not have, that is hypocritical and such false communication is not the way to build intimate relationships. But if you express an act of love designed for the other person's benefit or pleasure, it's simply a choice. You are not claiming the action grows out of a deep emotional bonding. You are simply choosing to do something for his benefit. I think that must be what Jesus meant.

"Certainly we do not have warm feelings for people who hate us. That would be abnormal, but we can do loving acts for them. That is simply a choice. We hope such loving acts will have a positive effect upon their attitudes and behavior and treatment, but at least we have chosen to do something positive for them."

My answer seemed to satisfy Ann, at least for the moment. I had the feeling we would discuss that again. I also had the feeling that if the experiment was going to get off the ground, it would be because of Ann's deep faith in God.

"After the first month," I said, "I want you to ask Glenn for feedback on how you are doing. Using your own words, ask him, 'Glenn, you remember a few weeks ago when I told you I was going to try to be a better wife? I want to ask how you think I am doing.'

"Whatever Glenn says, accept it as information. He may be sarcastic, he may be flippant or hostile, or he may be positive. Whatever his response, do not argue but accept it and assure him you are serious and you really want to be a better wife, and if he has additional suggestions, you are open to them.

"Follow this pattern of asking for feedback once a month for the entire six months. Whenever Glenn gives you the first positive response, you will know your efforts are getting through to him emotionally. One week after you receive the first positive feedback, I want you to make a request of Glenn—something you would like him to do, something in keeping with your primary love language. For example, you may say to him one evening, 'Glenn, do you know something I would like to do? Do you remember how we used to go take walks in Reynolda Gardens together? I'd like to go do that with you on Thursday night. The kids are going to be staying at my mom's. Do you think that would be possible?'

"Make the request something specific, not general. Don't say, 'You know, I wish we would spend more time together.' That's too vague. How will you know when he's done it? But if you make your request specific, he will know exactly what you want and you will know that, when he does it, he is choosing to do something for your benefit.

"Do this each month. If he does it, fine; if he doesn't do it, fine. But when he does it, you will know that he is responding to your needs. In the process, you are teaching him your primary love language because the requests you make are in keeping with your love language. If he chooses to begin loving you in your primary language, your positive emotions toward him will begin to resurface. Your emotional tank will begin to fill up and in time the marriage will, in fact, be reborn."

"Dr. Chapman, I would do anything if that could happen," Ann said.

"Well," I responded, "it will take a lot of hard work, but I believe it's worth a try. I'm personally interested to see if this experiment works and if our hypothesis is true. I would like to meet with you regularly throughout this process—perhaps every two weeks—and I would like you to keep records on the positive words of affirmation you give Glenn each week. Also, I would like you to bring me your list of complaints you have written in your notebook without stating them to Glenn. Perhaps from the felt complaints, I can help you build specific requests for Glenn that will help meet some of those frustrations. Eventually, I want you to learn how to share your frustrations and irritations in a constructive way, and I want you and Glenn to learn how to work through those irritations and conflicts. But during this six-month experiment, I want you to write them down without telling Glenn."

Ann left, and I believed she had the answer to her question: "Is it possible to love someone whom you hate?"

In the next six months, Ann saw a tremendous change in Glenn's attitude and treatment of her. The first month, he treated the whole thing lightly. But after the second month, he gave her positive feedback about her efforts. In the last four months, he responded positively to almost all of her requests, and her feelings for him began to change drastically. Glenn never came for counseling, but he did listen to some of my CDs and discuss them with Ann. He encouraged Ann to continue her counseling, which she did for another three months after our experiment. To this day, Glenn swears to his friends I am a miracle worker. I know in fact that love is a miracle worker.

Perhaps you need a miracle in your own marriage. Why not try Ann's experiment? Tell your spouse you have been thinking about your marriage and have decided you would like to do a better job of meeting his/her needs. Ask for suggestions on how you could improve. His suggestions will be a clue to his primary love language. If he makes no suggestions, guess his love language based on the things he has complained about over the years. Then, for six months, focus your attention on that love language. At the end of each month, ask your spouse for feedback on how you are doing and for further suggestions.

Whenever your spouse indicates he is seeing improvement, wait one week and then make a specific request. The request should be something you really want him to do for you. If he chooses to do it, you will know that he is responding to your needs. If he does not honor your request, continue to love him. Maybe next month he will respond positively. If your spouse starts speaking your love language by responding to your requests, your positive emotions toward him will return, and in time your marriage will be reborn. I cannot guarantee the results, but scores of people whom I have counseled have experienced the miracle of love.

YOUR TURN

If your marriage is in the serious trouble discussed in this chapter, you need to begin by making a strong commitment of the will to undertake the following experiment. You risk further pain and rejection, but you also stand to regain a healthy and fulfilling marriage. Count the cost; it's worth the attempt.

1. *Ask how you can be a better spouse, and regardless of the other's attitude, act on what he or she tells you.*

2. *When you receive positive feedback, you know there is progress. Each month make one nonthreatening but specific request that is easy for your spouse. Make sure it relates to your primary love language and will help replenish your empty tank.*

3. *When your spouse responds and meets your need, you will be able to react with not only your will but your emotions as well. Without overreacting, continue positive feedback and affirmation of your spouse at these times.*

4. *As your marriage begins to truly heal and grow deeper, make sure you don't "rest on your laurels" and forget your spouse's love language and daily needs. You're on the road to your dreams, so stay there! Put appointments into your schedule to assess together how you're doing.*

A Personal Word

Well, what do you think? Having read these pages, walked in and out of the lives of several couples, visited small villages and large cities, sat with me in the counseling office, and talked with people in restaurants, what do you think? Could these concepts radically alter the emotional climate of your marriage? What would happen if you discovered the primary love language of your spouse and chose to speak it consistently?

Neither you nor I can answer that question until you have tried it. I know many military couples who have heard this concept at my marriage seminars say that choosing to love and expressing it in the primary love language of their spouse has made a drastic difference in their marriages. When the emotional need for love is met, it creates a climate where the couple can deal with the rest of life in a much more productive manner. Consider Mark and Robin. Robin figured out that Mark's primary love language was affirming words, usually involving something specific ("I like how you're protective of me; it makes me feel loved"). "Knowing his love language greatly helps me understand him," she said. "Now, that's not to imply I always say the right thing! But simply knowing how he's wired has drawn us closer." Robin says her love language is acts of service. "Mark would compliment me about something, because that's his love language, and somehow it never made me feel all that great. But when we figured out that what I really valued were acts of service, even something small like bringing me coffee in bed in the morning, our marriage took a giant step."

We each come to marriage with a different personality and history. We bring emotional baggage into our marriage relationship. We come with different expectations, different ways of approaching things, and different opinions about what matters in life. In a healthy marriage, that variety of perspectives must be processed. We need not agree on everything, but we must find a way to handle our differences so they do not become divisive. With empty love tanks, couples tend to argue and withdraw, and some may tend to be violent verbally or physically in their arguments. But when the love tank is full, we create a climate of friendliness, a climate that seeks to understand, that is willing to allow differences and to negotiate problems. No single area of marriage affects the rest of marriage as much as meeting the emotional need for love.

The ability to love, especially when your spouse is not loving you, may seem impossible for some. Such love may require us to draw on our spiritual resources. A number of years ago, as I faced my own marital struggles, I rediscovered my spiritual roots. Having been raised in the Christian tradition, I reexamined the life of Christ. When I heard Him praying for those who were killing Him, "Father, forgive them, for they do not know what they are doing,"[8] I knew that I wanted that kind of love. I committed my life to Him and have found that He provides the inner spiritual energy to love, even when love is not reciprocated.

The high divorce rate in military marriages bears witness that thousands of couples have been living with an empty emotional love tank. I believe the concepts in this book could make a significant impact upon the marriages and families of military couples.

For those of you who have children, let me encourage you to discover your child's love language and speak it regularly. You can learn their language by the time they are three or four years old by observing their behavior. If they are regularly jumping into your lap and hugging you, their language is physical touch. If they say, "Come into my room, I want to show you something," they are asking for quality time.

All parents love their children, but not all children feel loved. For further help, see *The 5 Love Languages of Children*. There I discuss how love interfaces with the child's anger, with discipline, and learning.

It is my hope that *The 5 Love Languages Military Edition* will help military couples who have experienced the "in love" euphoria, who entered marriage with lofty dreams of making each other supremely happy but in the reality of day-to-day life are in danger of losing that dream entirely. I hope thousands of those couples will not only rediscover their dream but will also see the path to making their dreams come true.

I dream of a day when the potential of the married couples in the military can be unleashed for the good of humankind, when husbands and wives can live life with full emotional love tanks and reach out to accomplish their potential as individuals and as couples.

I dream of a day when children can grow up in homes filled with love and security, where children's developing energies can be channeled toward learning and serving rather than seeking the love they did not receive at home. It is my desire that this brief volume will kindle the flame of love in your marriage and in the marriages of thousands of other military couples like you.

I wrote this for you. I hope it changes your life. And if it does, be sure to give it to someone else. I would be pleased if you would give a copy of this book to your family, to your brothers and sisters, to your married children, to your friends, and to other military couples. Who knows? Together we may see our dream come true.

For a free online study guide, please visit:

http://www.5lovelanguages.com

This group discussion guide is designed to both help couples apply the concepts from *The 5 Love Languages* and stimulate genuine dialogue among study groups.

Frequently Asked Questions

---

1. What if I cannot discover my primary love language?

"I've taken the Love Language Profile and my scores come out almost even except for Receiving Gifts. I know that's not my love language."

In the book, I discuss three approaches to discovering your love language on pages 155–156.

If, after reviewing those, you're still unsure, consider the example of one husband who told me he discovered his love language by simply following the process of elimination. He knew receiving gifts was not his language so he asked himself, "If I had to give up one of the remaining four, which one would I give up?" He concluded that apart from sexual intercourse, he could give up Physical Touch and Quality Time. This left Acts of Service and Words of Affirmation. While he appreciated the things his wife did for him, he knew her affirming words were really what gave him life. Thus, words of affirmation was his primary love language and acts of service his secondary love language.

2. What if I cannot discover my spouse's love language?

"My husband hasn't read the book, but we have discussed the love languages. He says he doesn't know what his love language is."

My first suggestion is to give him a copy of *The 5 Love Languages Men's Edition*. Since it is geared specifically to husbands, he is more likely to read it. If he reads it, he will be eager to share his love language with you. However, if he is unwilling to read the book, I would suggest you answer the three questions below:

1. How does he most often express love to others?
2. What does he complain about most often?
3. What does he request most often?

Though our spouse's complaints normally irritate us, they are actually giving us valuable information. If a spouse says, "We don't ever spend any time together," you may be tempted to say, "What do you mean? We went out to dinner Thursday night." Such a defensive statement will end the conversation. However, if you respond, "What would you like for us to do?" you will likely get an answer. The complaints of your spouse are the most powerful indicators of the primary love language.

You also might want to try a five-week experiment. The first week, you focus on one of the five love languages and seek to speak it every day and observe the response of your spouse. On Saturday and Sunday, you relax. The second week—Monday through Friday—you focus on another of the love languages and continue with a different language each of the five weeks. On the week you are speaking your spouse's primary love language, you are likely to see a difference in their countenance and the way they respond to you. It will be obvious that this is their primary love language.

3. My husband's military style of communicating hurts me. How can I help him understand this?

"Due to how the Army environment 'trains' its soldiers, my husband's tone and words are often harsh, exasperated, negative, or sarcastic. He says his comments are not aimed at me, but it is hard not to take them that way when I listen so closely for words of affirmation."

I am deeply sympathetic with your question. Because your love language is words of affirmation, harsh, critical words will hurt you more deeply than they would hurt someone who has a different love language. My first suggestion is to learn your husband's primary love language and speak it regularly for two months while making no comments about his harsh words to you. After two months, ask the question, "On a scale of 0 to 10, how full is your love tank?" or "How much love do you feel coming from me?" When he gives you an 8, 9, or 10, then you are in a position to have a positive influence on his behavior.

Now that he feels your love, you are ready to help him understand how deeply his harsh words hurt you. If his primary love language is quality time, you say to him, "I hope you know how much I love you. I want to ask you a personal question. If I withdrew from you and ignored you, and stopped spending time with you, and refused to take walks with you, how would you feel?" He may well say, "I would feel extremely unloved by you." Then you say, "That's exactly how I feel when you speak harsh, critical words to me. My love language is words of affirmation, and when you use words in a negative way, they cut me very deeply and make me feel you don't love me. I know you use harsh words every day at work, but I'm asking that you please make an effort to speak to me as a wife and not one of your men."

If his love language is physical touch, you would take the same approach and after he assures you he feels loved by you, you would say to him, "I hope you know how much I love you. I want to ask you a personal question. If I stopped reaching out and touching you, if I refused to hold hands with you and drew back when you tried to kiss me and withdrew when you wanted to have sexual intercourse, how would that make you feel?" Once he responds, then you tell him that's how deeply you hurt when he uses harsh, loud words when speaking to you. You would take the same approach whatever his primary love language is. This approach helps him understand how deeply you feel hurt by his negative, sarcastic, harsh words, and he is very likely to change his behavior.

4. How do we speak our spouse's love language when our own love tank is empty?

"I am burned out from years of intense deployment cycles. It's hard to desire to speak my spouse's love language, when mine is not being spoken. I want to desire to do that again, but I'm just so tired. How do we regain the passion to speak the love language of our husbands?"

I am certain that wives who have gone through numerous deployments can identify with your question. Physically and emotionally, we become drained with all the responsibilities upon us while they are deployed and when we are receiving very little love from our spouses. That is why I have recommended throughout this book that you learn how to speak each other's love language while you are apart, so you can keep emotional love alive in the relationship. That is the ideal.

However, I know your husband may not even be familiar with the love language concept. My first suggestion is to put a copy of this book in his hands and ask him to read the first chapter and let you know what he thinks of it. Most men who read the first chapter will end up reading the entire book and will find themselves motivated to reach out and communicate love to their wives.

It is always easier to love someone who is loving you. However, someone must start the process. Since you have read this book, and perhaps already know your husband's love language, my suggestion is that you make a conscious choice to speak his love language at least twice a week for the next three months and see what happens. My prediction is that at the end of the three months, his love tank is getting full and you can make a legitimate request of him. "Do you know what would make me happy?" or "Do you know what I would really like?" and you share with him some expression of your love language that would be meaningful to you. Because he feels loved by you, he is far more likely to respond to your request. I know to take this approach will require you to rise above your emotional, physical, sense of fatigue. But I can assure you it is worth the effort.

5. I'm married to the military. When the government calls, I have to answer. How can my wife and I deal with this issue?

"My wife's love language is quality time, and I know she hates it when I take work phone calls during our dates. But I have no choice—I took an oath to the military and have to be on call all the time as part of my current assignment."

You are reading your wife well. It is true that for those who have quality time as their love language, they are hurt and annoyed when you divert your attention from your time together to answer a phone call. I understand your commitment to the military. My suggestion would be to look at the phone when it rings, determine if it is a military call or a call from one of your friends unrelated to the military. You answer only the calls related to your military duty, and you do not answer other calls. These will be recorded in your voicemail, and you can answer them after the date is over. Many of us are much too glued to our phones. There was a day, you may remember, when we did not have cellphones and our times together at a restaurant were never interrupted by a phone. We seem to have survived rather well in those days. I applaud the convenience of cellphones, but we must make our own rules as to how they will be used so as to enhance our marital relationship, rather than detracting from it.

6. How do we find ways to communicate when we have both changed from long deployments and feel like strangers to each other?

When you first met and started dating, likely neither of you knew each other very well. How did you get to know each other and come to the place where you decided to marry? My guess is that you had many long conversations asking each other questions about your past and present. Essentially, communication is talking and listening. But questions are a key tool to open the heart and mind of the other person. Here are some suggested questions:

- When you were a child, what kind of relationship did you have with your mother? Father? Brothers or sisters? (Don't ask all of these in the same conversation.)
- What could I do to make your life easier?
- What one thing could I change that would make me a better wife? or husband?

- Did you meet any new people at work today?
- What was the biggest challenge you faced while on duty today?
- Of all the people you interact with on a regular basis, whom do you like the most and why?

Such questions tend to make it easier for your spouse to respond. Some time ago I wrote a larger collection of such questions in a little booklet entitled *101 Conversation Starters for Couples.* You can find it on Amazon or at a local retailer.

The second suggestion is for the two of you to establish a weekly date night in which the two of you go out for dinner, and agree beforehand that each of you will tell one event that was humorous while the two of you were apart, and one event that was very painful while the two of you were apart. Often, those who have been deployed are reluctant to talk about their experiences. But when you limit the conversation to one positive and one negative experience, they are less likely to be overwhelmed. Once your spouse shares the negative event, you may say, "That must have been extremely hard for you." If they respond, listen carefully and affirm their feelings. "I can see how you would have felt that way. I'm sure that was far more painful than I can imagine."

My third suggestion is that when you are together you have a daily sharing time in which each of you shares with the other— two things that happened in my life today and how I feel about them. There may be positive experiences or negative experiences. You are sharing events that happen in your life, and you are sharing your emotional response. You are building both intellectual and emotional intimacy.

Building intimacy after long deployments is a slow process. It cannot be rushed. But when you become adept at asking questions, and adept at revealing past experiences with each other, you are building a platform on which you can continue to build intimacy: intellectually, socially, physically, and spiritually.

7. Does combat trauma trump love languages?

"I have PTSD and am completely overwhelmed by the idea of speaking love languages. I have enough to deal with on my own. Can't I get a break until I feel more up to it?"

Those who have never experienced PTSD find it hard to imagine the emotional, mental effect of traumatic stress. If your spouse has not attended classes to help them understand, or read books or explored websites to gain understanding about PTSD, I would suggest you encourage her to do so. This will make them more empathetic to what you are going through.

However, we cannot postpone love while we are going through the effects of PTSD. Actually, speaking each other's love language will help you in the process of recovering from traumatic stress. Our deepest emotional need is to feel loved. When we feel loved by our spouse, we are far more likely to handle the stresses of life than if we feel our spouse has rejected us. Giving and receiving love is the heart of life; all the rest is just background music. Therefore, I am suggesting that with whatever energy you have, you invest it in the best possible way in loving your spouse. If they reciprocate your love, you are indeed a fortunate man. When each of you feels secure in the love of the other, you can walk together through the difficulties created by PTSD.

8. Do the love languages work in other cultures?

Yes. These five fundamental ways of expressing love are

universal. However, the dialects in which these languages are spoken will differ from culture to culture. For example, the kind of touches appropriate in one culture may not be appropriate in another. The acts of service spoken in one culture may not be spoken in another. But when these cultural adaptations are made, the concept of the five love languages will have a profound impact upon the couples in that culture.

9. What if I speak my spouse's love language and they don't respond?

"My husband would not read the book so I decided to speak his love language and see what would happen. Nothing happened. He didn't even acknowledge that I did anything differently. How long am I supposed to continue speaking his love language when there is no response?"

I know it can become discouraging when you feel you are investing in the marriage and receiving nothing in return. There are two possible reasons for this. First and most likely, you are speaking the wrong love language. Wives often assume their husband's love language is physical touch. In reality, his primary love language may be words of affirmation. Because she feels no love coming from him, she may be verbally critical of him. Her critical words are like daggers to his heart, so he withdraws from her. The problem is not her sincerity; the problem is she is actually speaking the wrong love language.

On the other hand, assuming you are speaking your spouse's primary love language, there is another reason why they may not be responding positively. If the spouse is already involved in another romantic relationship, either emotionally or sexually, they will often reason that your efforts have come too late. They may even perceive that your efforts are temporary and insincere and you are simply trying to manipulate them to stay in the marriage. Even if your spouse is not involved with someone else, if your relationship has been hostile for a long time, they may still perceive your efforts as being manipulative.

In this situation, the temptation is to give up, to stop speaking their love language because it is not making any difference. The worst thing you can do is to yield to this temptation. If you give up, it will confirm their conclusion that your efforts were designed to manipulate them. The best approach you can take is to continue to speak their love language on a regular basis no matter how they treat you. Set yourself a goal of six months, nine months, or a year. Your attitude is "Whatever their response, I'm going to love them in their love language over the long haul. If they walk away from me, they will walk away from someone who is loving them unconditionally." This attitude will keep you on a positive road even when you feel discouraged. There is nothing more powerful than to love your spouse even when they are not responding positively. Whatever the ultimate response of your spouse, you will have the satisfaction of knowing you have done everything you could do to restore your marriage. If your spouse eventually chooses to reciprocate your love, you will have demonstrated for yourself the power of unconditional love. And you will reap the benefits of the rebirth of mutual love.

10. Can love be reborn after sexual infidelity?

Nothing devastates marital intimacy more than sexual unfaithfulness. However, this does not mean the marriage is destined for divorce. If the offending party is willing to break off the extramarital involvement and do the hard work of rebuilding the marriage, there can be genuine restoration. In my own counseling, I have seen scores of couples who have experienced healing after sexual infidelity. It involves not only breaking off the extramarital affair but also discovering what led to the affair. Success in restoration is a two-pronged approach. First, the offending party must be willing to explore their own personality, beliefs, and lifestyle that led them to the affair. There must be a willingness to change attitudes and behavior patterns. Second, the couple must be willing to take an honest look at the dynamics of their marriage and be open to replacing destructive patterns with positive patterns of integrity and sincerity. Both of these will normally require the help of a professional counselor.

Research indicates the couples who are most likely to survive sexual infidelity are those who receive both individual and marriage counseling. Understanding the five love languages and choosing to speak each other's language can help create an emotional climate in which the hard work of restoring the marriage can be successful.

An interactive version of this Personal Profile is also available at www.5lovelanguages.com

The 5 Love Languages
Profile for Couples — for Him

The 5 Love Languages Profile will give you and your spouse or significant other a thorough analysis of your emotional communication preference. It will single out your primary love language, what it means, and how you can use it to connect with your loved one with intimacy and fulfillment. Two profiles are included so that each of you can complete the assessment.

You will now see 30 paired statements. Please select the statement that best defines what is most meaningful to you in your relationship as a couple. Both statements may or may not sound like they fit your situation, but please choose the statement that captures the essence of what is most meaningful to you the majority of the time. Allow 10 to 15 minutes to complete the profile. Take it when you are relaxed, and try not to rush through it. Then tally your results and read how to interpret your profile on page 216.

It's more meaningful to me when . . .

| 1 | I receive a loving note/text/email for no special reason from my loved one. | A |
| | she and I hug. | E |

| 2 | I can spend alone time with her—just the two of us. | B |
| | she does something practical to help me out. | D |

| 3 | she gives me a little gift as a token of our love for each other. | C |
| | I get to spend uninterrupted leisure time with her. | B |

| 4 | she unexpectedly does something for me like filling my car or doing the laundry. | D |
| | she and I touch. | E |

| 5 | she puts her arm around me when we're in public. | E |
| | she surprises me with a gift. | C |

| 6 | I'm around her, even if we're not really doing anything. | B |
| | we hold hands. | E |

| 7 | my loved one gives me a gift. | C |
| | I hear "I love you" from her. | A |

| 8 | I sit close to her. | E |
| | I am complimented by her for no apparent reason. | A |

It's more meaningful to me when . . .

9
I get the chance to just "hang out" with her. — B
I unexpectedly get small gifts from her. — C

10
I hear her tell me, "I'm proud of you." — A
she helps me with a task. — D

11
I get to do things with her. — B
I hear supportive words from her. — A

12
she does things for me instead of just talking about doing nice things. — D
I feel connected to her through a hug. — E

13
I hear praise from her. — A
she gives me something that shows she was really thinking about me. — C

14
I'm able to just be around her. — B
I get a back rub or massage from her. — E

15
she reacts positively to something I've accomplished. — A
she does something for me that I know she doesn't particularly enjoy. — D

16
she and I kiss frequently. — E
I sense she is showing interest in the things I care about. — B

It's more meaningful to me when . . .

17

my loved one works on special projects with me that I have to complete.	D
she gives me an exciting gift.	C

18

she compliments me on my appearance.	A
she takes the time to listen to me and really understand my feelings.	B

19

we share nonsexual touch in public.	E
she offers to run errands for me.	D

20

she does a bit more than her normal share of the responsibilities we share (around the house, work-related, etc).	D
I get a gift that I know she put thought into choosing.	C

21

she doesn't check her phone while we're talking.	B
she goes out of her way to do something that relieves pressure on me.	D

22

I can look forward to a holiday because of a gift I anticipate receiving.	C
I hear the words "I appreciate you" from her.	A

23

she brings me a little gift after she has been traveling without me.	C
she takes care of something I'm responsible to do but I feel too stressed to do at the time.	D

It's more meaningful to me when . . .

24
| she doesn't interrupt me while I'm talking. | B |
| gift giving is an important part of our relationship. | C |

25
| she helps me out when she knows I'm already tired. | D |
| I get to go somewhere while spending time with her. | B |

26
| she and I are physically intimate. | E |
| she gives me a little gift that she picked up in the course of her normal day. | C |

27
| she says something encouraging to me. | A |
| I get to spend time in a shared activity or hobby with her. | B |

28
| she surprises me with a small token of her appreciation. | C |
| she and I touch a lot during the normal course of the day. | E |

29
| she helps me out—especially if I know she's already busy. | D |
| I hear her specifically tell me, "I appreciate you." | A |

30
| she and I embrace after we've been apart for a while. | E |
| I hear her say how much I mean to her. | A |

An interactive version of this Personal Profile is also available at www.5lovelanguages.com

The 5 Love Languages
Profile for Couples — for Her

Here is the second profile. As previously mentioned, it will give you a thorough analysis of your emotional communication preference. It will single out your primary love language, what it means, and how you can use it to connect with your loved one with intimacy and fulfillment. Two profiles are included so that each of you can complete the assessment.

You will now see 30 paired statements. Please select the statement that best defines what is most meaningful to you in your relationship as a couple. Both statements may or may not sound like they fit your situation, but please choose the statement that captures the essence of what is most meaningful to you the majority of the time. Allow 10 to 15 minutes to complete the profile. Take it when you are relaxed, and try not to rush through it. Then tally your results and read how to interpret your profile on page 216.

It's more meaningful to me when . . .

1	I receive a loving note/text/email for no special reason from my loved one.	A
	he and I hug.	E
2	I can spend alone time with him—just the two of us.	B
	he does something practical to help me out.	D
3	he gives me a little gift as a token of our love for each other.	C
	I get to spend uninterrupted leisure time with him.	B
4	he unexpectedly does something for me like filling my car or doing the laundry.	D
	he and I touch.	E
5	he puts his arm around me when we're in public.	E
	he surprises me with a gift.	C
6	I'm around him, even if we're not really doing anything.	B
	we hold hands.	E
7	my loved one gives me a gift.	C
	I hear "I love you" from him.	A
8	I sit close to him.	E
	I am complimented by him for no apparent reason.	A

It's more meaningful to me when . . .

| 9 | I get the chance to just "hang out" with him. | B |
| | I unexpectedly get small gifts from him. | C |

| 10 | I hear him tell me, "I'm proud of you." | A |
| | he helps me with a task. | D |

| 11 | I get to do things with him. | B |
| | I hear supportive words from him. | A |

| 12 | he does things for me instead of just talking about doing nice things. | D |
| | I feel connected to him through a hug. | E |

| 13 | I hear praise from him. | A |
| | he gives me something that shows he was really thinking about me. | C |

| 14 | I'm able to just be around him. | B |
| | I get a back rub or massage from him. | E |

| 15 | he reacts positively to something I've accomplished. | A |
| | he does something for me that I know he doesn't particularly enjoy. | D |

| 16 | he and I kiss frequently. | E |
| | I sense he is showing interest in the things I care about. | B |

It's more meaningful to me when . . .

17

my loved one works on special projects with me that I have to complete.	D
he gives me an exciting gift.	C

18

he compliments me on my appearance.	A
he takes the time to listen to me and really understand my feelings.	B

19

we share nonsexual touch in public.	E
he offers to run errands for me.	D

20

he does a bit more than his normal share of the responsibilities we share (around the house, work-related, etc).	D
I get a gift that I know he put thought into choosing.	C

21

he doesn't check his phone while we're talking.	B
he goes out of his way to do something that relieves pressure on me.	D

22

I can look forward to a holiday because of a gift I anticipate receiving.	C
I hear the words "I appreciate you" from him.	A

23

he brings me a little gift after he has been traveling without me.	C
he takes care of something I'm responsible to do but I feel too stressed to do at the time.	D

It's more meaningful to me when . . .

24

he doesn't interrupt me while I'm talking.	B
gift giving is an important part of our relationship.	C

25

he helps me out when he knows I'm already tired.	D
I get to go somewhere while spending time with him.	B

26

he and I are physically intimate.	E
he gives me a little gift that he picked up in the course of his normal day.	C

27

he says something encouraging to me.	A
I get to spend time in a shared activity or hobby with him.	B

28

he surprises me with a small token of his appreciation.	C
he and I touch a lot during the normal course of the day.	E

29

he helps me out—especially if I know he's already busy.	D
I hear him specifically tell me, "I appreciate you."	A

30

he and I embrace after we've been apart for a while.	E
I hear him say how much I mean to him.	A

Look back through the letters you circled and record the number of responses in the spaces below.

A:_____   B:_____   C:_____   D:_____   E:_____

A = Words of Affirmation   **B** = Quality Time   **C** = Receiving Gifts
D = Acts of Service   **E** = Physical Touch

INTERPRETING YOUR PROFILE SCORE

The highest score indicates your primary love language (the highest score is 12). It's not uncommon to have two high scores, although one language does have a slight edge for most people. That just means two languages are important to you.

The lower scores indicate those languages you seldom use to communicate love and that probably don't affect you very much on an emotional level.

IMPORTANT TO REMEMBER

You may have scored more highly on certain love languages than others, but do not dismiss those other languages as insignificant. Your loved one may express love in those ways, and it will be helpful to you to understand this about him.

In the same way, it will benefit your spouse or significant other to know *your* primary love language in order to best express affection for you in ways that you interpret as love. Every time you or your spouse speaks each other's language, you score emotional points with each other. Of course, this isn't a game with a scorecard! The payoff of speaking each other's love language is a greater sense of connection. This translates into better communication, increased understanding, and ultimately, improved romance.

If your spouse or significant other has not already done so, encourage him or her to take *The 5 Love Languages Profile* in this book, online www.5lovelanguages.com/profile, or on The 5 Love Languages app (iOS or Android). Discuss your respective love languages, and use this insight to improve your relationship.

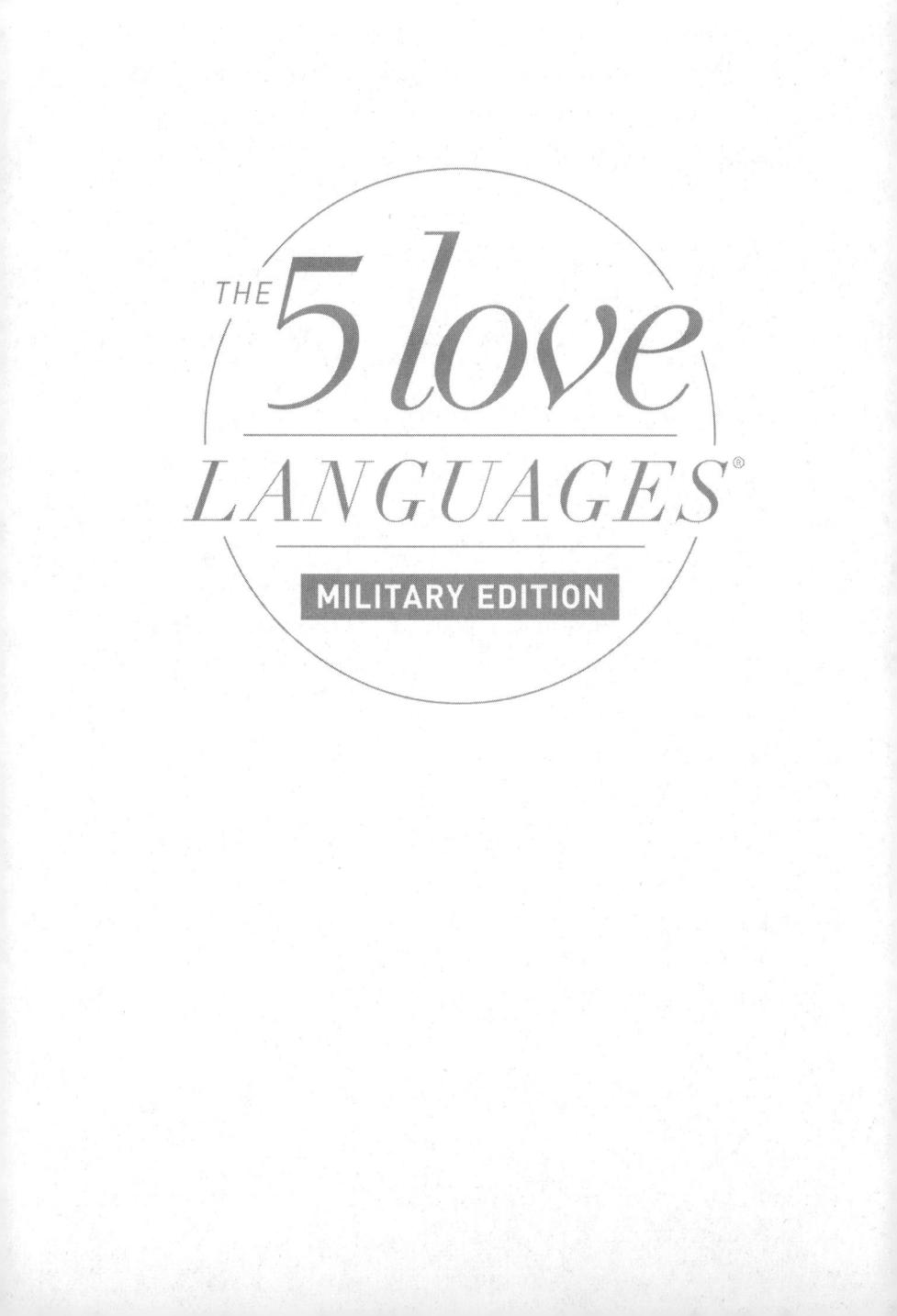

Notes

1. US Bureau of the Census, Statistical Abstract of the United States, 122nd Ed. Washington, DC: US Government Printing Office, 2006.
2 Proverbs 18:21.
3. Proverbs 12:25.
4. Luke 6:27–28, 31–32.
5. Luke 6:38.
6. Luke 6:27–28, 31–32.
7. Luke 6:38.
8. Luke 23:34.

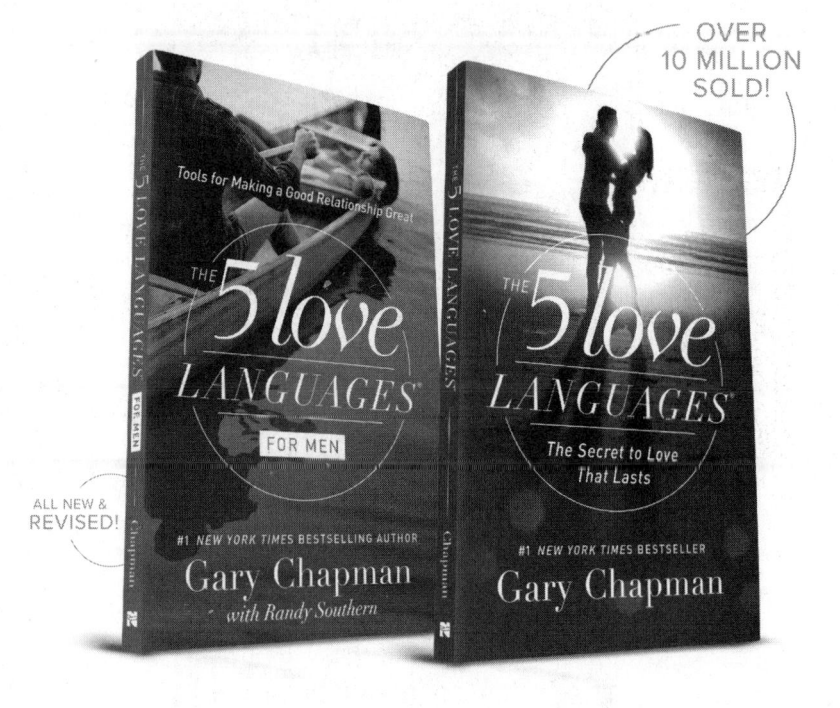

WHAT'S YOUR APOLOGY LANGUAGE?

#1 *New York Times* bestselling author Gary Chapman and Jennifer Thomas have teamed up to deliver this ground-breaking study of how we give and receive apologies. It's not just a matter of will, but it's a matter of how you say, "I'm sorry" that ultimately makes things right with those you love. This book will help you discover why certain apologies clear the path for emotional healing, reconciliation, and freedom, while others fall desperately short.

WWW.5LOVELANGUAGES.COM